EXCHANGE
OF
LOVE

BRIAN RAYFIELD

CRANTHORPE
—MILLNER—
PUBLISHERS

First published by Cranthorpe Millner Publishers (2024)

ISBN 978-1-80378-179-2 (Paperback)

www.cranthorpemillner.com

Cranthorpe Millner Publishers

Printed and bound by CPI Group (UK) Ltd, Croydon, CR0 4YY

To Maureen, Alan and Briony, who joined with me to complete the seasons, the flowers, the dragons and the four winds of heaven.

Timeless love motif by A. Rayfield

CHAPTER 1

John Townsend stood in the disused and empty living room of Peverell House. Despite the smell of dry, dusty wood and stone, it felt a strangely warm and welcoming place; eerily so. John half closed his eyes, trying to imagine how it had been when newly built back in 1620.

He felt his senses drifting, and his vision shimmered. Even as he looked, the derelict room distorted and changed. Almost lazily it was reforming back to its splendid past: two huge glazed windows, ornate tapestry hangings, carpeted floor, panelled wall and plastered ceiling. The fine carved and wide mullioned windows, which admitted the soft spring light, appeared as new. In the fireplace opposite the windows, a small fire was laid.

This could not be real. The Ransoms, who had owned the mansion for over four hundred years, had never had enough money to maintain it and John knew no restoration work had been done in that section of the house. It had been empty since Oliver Ransom took possession in 1646, after the first English Civil War. Confused, John stared around. Tall, freestanding wrought iron candlesticks materialised, complete with partly burned candles, waiting for evening use. The room was still reconstructing itself even as he gasped in surprise; imagination working too hard – whatever. *Must get out!*

Beside the nearest window, a young woman sat sewing. Adrenaline surged through him: cold fear. Despite that, he noticed small details: some unkempt red hair escaped from under her mop cap; a simple green day dress, simple but evidently made of quality fabric. She looked up suddenly.

"Cousin John!" Slate-grey eyes, thin lips, but generous smile. Her expression changed to shock and fear, colour draining from her face. "Oh, God, it can't be you, John." Her voice a mixture of sadness and fear. "You're dead, these twelve months." Her speech was highly accented, difficult to make out.

They stared at each other in total disbelief.

"I'm John Townsend, the stonemason..." his voice faded away at the banality of the words.

"Cousin John Townsend, master mason, head of the company. I know." Defiance entered her tone. "You did me no harm when you were alive, John, I'll not fear you dead!"

"I'm not dead, it's you who are—"

"You don't know you have died, do you? Oh, John, I'll show you."

Resolutely she threw down her embroidery frame, marched across the room and, without hesitation, kissed him on the cheek. Unbelievably there was full physical contact. Her face lit up in surprise and instinctively he put his arms around her in a familiar hug.

"No, John, I'm married now." She turned slightly, avoiding his attempt to kiss her lips, but then relented and returned his kiss.

Lust and passion flowed through him. There was no fear, and as they drew apart, he could see his own pleasure reflected in her. She was statuesque, almost as tall as John himself and spine-tinglingly beautiful.

"I am so pleased to see you. But these strange clothes – have you been working with your tools again, or hunting?"

He shook his head and smiled back, pulling her to him. They kissed again. She responded, then eased away from him.

"No, John, this is all very nice, but no." Her voice faltered but she shone with the excitement of their meeting. "If it were not that I am... well, married to Edward, I would be sorely tempted."

"Mr Townsend!" shouted a different woman, calling from downstairs.

John shuddered and the vision faded. The girl within his arms vanished. The room shimmered and changed again. His senses spun and reeled.

$$\infty$$

Only the basic outline of the bare deserted room remained. The same windows and fireplace, it was the same shape and size but now it was empty and dust dry. The sandwich he had been holding when he strolled in from the west wing lay discarded on the floor beside a fallen coffee cup.

"Mr Townsend?" The impatient enquiring call was from the hall below, the sound echoing in the large open space and arriving by several routes.

"Bugger!" he muttered, trying to fix in his memory the events of moments ago; the spectral woman, her face and form, and what she had said. Who was she? Who was her 'Cousin John'?

"Mr Townsend?"

Closer this time. He turned to see a small, thin figure coming up the service staircase, only head and shoulders visible. As the figure came into full view, ascending the last few steps, he was met with a girlish woman of about thirty, pale skin and dark hair, wearing a light-yellow sleeveless dress. She was almost as different as possible from the beautiful phantom of moments ago. He struggled to find his breath.

"You must be John," she said, smiling politely. "I'm Judith, Greg Ransom's daughter."

Shit, John thought. This was Judith Ransom, daughter of the owner who had commissioned his work. "Just on my lunchbreak." He gestured to the cup and the remains of the sandwich he had dropped when he had hugged the ghost woman. Awkwardly, he scooped it up. Mind racing with confusion, he added, "I just wandered in. An interesting place. Good solid workmanship—"

"It's OK, you can look around," Judith interrupted. "The old main staircase is a bit dodgy though, best not to use it."

He had noted that the central wooden staircase which led to the rooms above looked delicate and, after four hundred years, far too flimsy to use now. "Shame the room's not been restored." He turned to sweep his eyes around again: the wide fireplace and hearth now cold and yellowed; the painted panelling removed or plastered over; the tapestry hangings long gone. "Interesting room," he repeated lamely.

Judith attempted to smile, and quoted, "'Built between 1580 and 1620. Large, late Tudor-style manor house in much need of repair and renovation'. That's from English Heritage's description. They're not very impressed with our custodianship."

"It's dry, the walls are in good repair," John mused, as Judith walked towards him. His eyes kept returning to the window seat, imagining a goddess-like form, but only the seats' stone supports remained.

"My family have always had a thing about walls and roofs, at least," explained Judith. "And temporary panels were put over that window to keep the rain out – fifty years ago." She pointed to where some of the disused glazed windows had been broken and boarded over. "We Ransoms have never quite had enough money to furnish and decorate the grand parts of the house. I just wanted to discuss the electrical work with you, Mr Townsend."

God, he had just snogged a ghost without a thought; now he had to face the customer's daughter.

"One day," she was saying, "we are going to make something of Peverell. It's like we have been in temporary occupation for over three hundred years, more like camping out in the guest wing. This section has hardly been used since Lady Penelope Peverell fled from Cromwell's soldiers."

"I've read some of the history," replied John, moving to the window, no hint or scent of the vanished girl. "Needs a few pieces of stone replaced here and there." He indicated towards the masonry that had once supported the wooden planks of the cushioned window seat. "Sorry, professional interest." Still dazed, he shook his head slightly to try to clear his mind.

Judith's smile was quick, almost fleeting, before the tight pinched expression returned. "No good trying to drum up business with me, I'm afraid. My brother, Simon, controls the estate's bank account. And he is more interested in financial investments than preserving this crumbling millstone of a place."

"For a house built in local limestone, it's weathered well. Little pollution this far out in the country. No acid rain this far west." He was babbling; anything to stop him thinking. Judith Ransom had mentioned electrics, hadn't she? To keep the conversation going, he prompted with, "Must get back to work, I suppose. Check on my electrician."

She did not respond.

After a pause, he couldn't resist asking, "Is the house supposed to be haunted? Seems sort of inevitable."

"Oh, of course. 'Lady Penelope Peverell, née Jackson, walks the old private apartments looking for her husband Edward and cursing the hated Ransoms who usurped her home'. From *Weird Wiltshire Tales*. Rubbish of course. Lady Peverell knew her husband had been killed fighting for King Charles at the end of the first Civil War. Oliver Ransom, our ancestor, paid her and her twin children a pension until she died."

"Have you seen her? The ghost?"

"No, I'm afraid not. The Penny Peverell of those stories seems to have deserted the Peverell mansion this last one hundred years or so. Simon and I sneaked in here on several Midsummers' Eves and All Souls Days. Right little ghost hunters we were. But not a sign, let alone any wailing and a-cursing!" Judith paused for a moment. "There is something though – a happy presence; the feeling you get in some family homes."

John had started moving towards the service staircase as she spoke.

"Talking of the electrician, young chap, Colin?"

6

"Yes."

"Is he, well, is he trained? There are wires and cables everywhere, and he doesn't seem to have a connection diagram or a test plan."

"He's got his IET Wiring Regs Certificate Part 4, C&G qualification, and what not," said John. "It's quite a simple job." To himself he thought through the 'simple' electrical job: wiring, new fuse box, fire alarm circuits, earth leakage protection etcetera. He'd never employed Colin before. He'd best check he did have drawings and test plans. "Before we switch the power back on, I get in another contractor to do a crosscheck and full test. Quality Assurance."

"Not quite." That quick nervous smile again. "QA is getting Colin to do it right himself. An independent test is Quality Control. I'm all for it, particularly as it's our house that could burn down."

"OK, my slip. You know about these things?"

"Yes. I was a quality engineer at, well, at several places. Now I'm looking for work."

John nodded. No job was ever safe.

It was a relief for John to get his mind back on normal things. His physical contact with the spectral woman had aroused him in a way he had never experienced before. He was totally confused. Pausing at the head of the staircase, he could not resist one last fleeting glance back at the cracked and forlorn empty window seat.

"Is there something wrong?" asked Judith, catching his eye movement.

"No, it's just this room. So well-proportioned, well lit. It must have been really lovely when it was fully furnished."

"I've often thought so," she replied. "I'd love to restore the panelling, repair and repaint the plaster work, and put tapestry back along the end walls."

"Yes. You can still see some of the ironwork supports," he pointed out.

She nodded, and said wistfully, "Ah well, if I was a rich city trader, or even an accountant like Simon, who knows?"

CHAPTER 2

Penelope Peverell stood terror-struck; eyes focussed on the empty space where John Townsend had been. She was sure he had been there, real and solid. She had felt his chest against hers and his arms gripping around her. Instinctively her eyes flitted around the room, as if John had just darted away to hide like a small child.

Uncertain, she retreated back to the window seat. Outside, the sun was shining brightly, and she could see her maid marching off purposefully towards the walled kitchen garden to fetch herbs and vegetables, a basket swinging from her hand. Inside, all was as it should be; nothing had changed, altered or moved.

"It could not have been the real John." Cousin John was dead. Over a year ago. The sadness had not got any less despite the passage of time, but she was sure she had not imagined his presence. Memories flooded back.

At her home in Suffolk she and John had never been full physical lovers (neither of them could risk an unwanted child), but they had been intimate and passionate before her father had caught them in her bedroom and barred John from the house. Then Edward had arrived in the neighbourhood to visit relatives, and within a month she was a 'fallen woman'. She smiled at the memory of their first tumble together and her father's relief when Edward asked if they could marry. Poor father: a twenty-two-year-old daughter with little dowry and dubious reputation had been a grave concern to him. He had feared seeing her ruined and disgraced, not taken off to Wiltshire to be mistress of a fine mansion, Peverell House. And now, four years later, she still had no child to show for all the enjoyment she and Edward shared. Perhaps it would have been different if she had slept with John. He had been only married ten months before his wife Lily had given birth to a little girl.

"It could not have been John in this room," she declared out loud to herself. "It must have been my imagination, or his ghost." But ghosts were not supposed to catch a girl in an embrace – not that she had heard. Even the most desperate country girl had never claimed to have been seduced by a ghost! She picked up the delicate embroidery. But would anyone ever tell if they had? A woman who said 'Father, I have been ravished by a spirit' would hardly get a sympathetic reply.

She heard Edward's hard, hurried footsteps ascending the wooden staircase. Being fragile, it would never last if he pounded up and down like that with his heavy boots.

"Wench, I would—"

"Wench? This morning it was 'darling Penny', 'dearest wife', please leave me—"

"Enough!" he laughed.

A big jovial man of twenty-seven, two yards high, broad and muscular, arms like a bear, and legs... well, it was a pity men did not still wear stockings.

He was saying, "I have seen the bailiff, checked the blacksmith's work, and now—"

"You need to go to our chamber to rest?"

"No, I am recovered, but not sufficiently brave to venture back into your lair of torture."

"Well, if you will leave me for weeks on end..." Penny kissed him playfully, driving out memories of John.

"Two weeks only," he resumed. "No, I thought I would ride up over the ridge and check the flocks on the downs."

"We have shepherds enough to look to the sheep."

"But it is a bright day and an excuse for a ride, and I might discover a wanton shepherdess in need of comfort."

She flinched in memory of Cousin John as Edward caught her in his arms.

"You could ride out too and guard my virtue." His voice trailed off. For all his hearty robustness, he was very sensitive. "Of course, if you would rather not." He stepped back.

"No, not at all. I have not been on horseback for two days at least." Now it was her turn to hug him. "I had hoped you came with evil intentions to me, but I can wait until night, or perhaps the sunshine will give you some ideas. Oh, I will need to change my dress. Have the horses been saddled?" she asked.

"Will you ride post with me, or have your bay?"

"It would be cosy to ride behind you but I need a good gallop. We will be on our own so I will ride astride."

Penny changed quickly without bothering to summon her maid, choosing a simple dress of coarse cloth that would not get spoiled by hard wear. There was hardly any need for a cloak, but she bundled one up with a blanket to tie behind the saddle.

11

They rode down into Calne, forded the River Marden with its two watermills, and urged the horses up onto the sheep pasture. The grass was beginning to dry out in the hot summer, and shepherds already spoke darkly of poor grazing to come.

Edward had brought some food and watered-down wine for a mid-afternoon meal. They spread out the blanket, ate, drank and, as she had hoped, made love in the glowing sun.

That was real – very, very real – but the memory of John's appearance haunted her thoughts. She lay, still undressed, on her back gazing at the cloudless sky.

"Edward?"

"Mm," he grunted, near to sleep.

"Do you think I am out of my mind?"

"And body." His hand stroked lightly over her.

"Seriously, I am not given to imagination or madness?"

"No. You did seem a little thoughtful this morning but it passed well enough when we lay here." He stared into her slate-grey eyes with mock seriousness. "I consider too much thinking is bad for women. Men should prevent it!"

She ignored the banter and pressed on, "Have you... have you been with any other women recently?"

"I've been in women's company."

"And done what we have just done?"

"No, not since we met, and I have confessed all that happened before then. I swear on my oath. I swear on all I hold dear." He cupped one hand over her breast and the other over his groin.

"I accept that oath," she laughed. "But have you kissed anyone, passionately?"

He looked a little concerned.

"In fun," she clarified. "Not seriously, or with any expectation?"

He raised himself up on one elbow. "Has anyone been talking of me? You know I love dancing and the company in Oxford, but I vowed to you before our marriage that I would be truly faithful." He paused. "You know all of my past secrets, and I have none from you now."

"And I would have none from you. I told you of my games with my cousin."

"John? Yes, and I blamed neither you nor him. It was before you met me. I was as sad as any at his death."

"That is my trouble, Edward." She moved his hand and sat up. "Unless I am mazed or mad, I saw John, or his ghost, this very morning."

He started to make some flippant reply, but sensing her mood said, "It could be imagination. If it were John's ghost it would bear you no malice."

"He kissed me, Edward, put his arms around me and kissed me – then he vanished."

"A man after my own heart! If I come back from the dead it will be to kiss a woman, not wail in a dark churchyard or castle dungeon."

"Edward, I am not jesting. He felt as real to me as you do now."

"Then no wonder he vanished before I discovered him. I am sorry, I will be serious."

They sat silent for a while.

"I am not one to have visions or daydreams, Edward," Penny said. "I'm not some giddy mistress overcome by imagined passion. I felt it right to tell you."

"It is worth talking on it," replied Edward. "Always let the light into dark corners."

"There are no dark corners. I do not hurt over some memory of John. We were close, but now I have you. You and he were friends."

"Yes, and we visited his Lily when we could. God knows when we will be able to travel to Suffolk since that bigot Cromwell declared for parliament against the king."

A rustle of a hill rabbit disturbed these thoughts and drew their gaze out over the peaceful sunlit Peverell estate, to the prime hill grazing and farmland beyond. It was hard to realise that so many areas of England had been pillaged in the Civil War.

Penny snapped back from her reverie to the subject of John. "Do you believe me?" she asked earnestly.

"In truth, I do not know. You do not lie, and you are as hard-headed as any man. But," he shrugged, "I do not know if such things can pass."

"Neither do I. What shall I do?"

"What can you do? You did not summon him."

"No."

"We will keep close company, day as well as night. If John Townsend wishes to kiss his cousin, he can shake my hand as well. And if he wants to do more, he can kiss my fist!" He smiled in a reassuring way. "No more lone walks or rides for you, mistress. If you sew, I will read."

"And if you hie off to the tavern, I shall come too!"

"Surely—"

"And if you ride into Bath to visit the brothel—"

"You must make sure I have no need."

She lunged towards him and he recoiled in mock terror.

"No, madam! Mercy! I am quite defeated."

Penny laughed and reached out for her shift. "Then, sir, if you have no more need of me, I will cover my white body from the harsh sun. Your back is already turning red." She caressed it softly as Edward pulled his linen shirt on.

"It could be you are with child..."

"I fear not, despite all the pleasure you give me. I am a poor wife. Even the sour-faced Puritan women in the town—"

He held his finger to her lips. "Not a word. I do not complain. We have a lifetime yet for children."

They continued to dress. Penny rolled up the rug, Edward packed the bottle and remains of food into his saddlebag.

"If John does appear again and you are not there, I will call immediately," Penny stated, as Edward helped her swing up into her saddle. "We will lay the ghost or drive out my fancy – one way or the other."

CHAPTER 3

The need to talk rationally with Judith Ransom had helped John overcome the shock of his ghostly meeting with Penny Peverell. He shuddered. It was hardly a ghostly meeting; the kiss and feel of her body was only too real. Leaving Judith, John forced himself to clear his mind, get back to reality, and start doing some work. The first job was to address her concerns over the electrician.

Colin had made drawings, did have a progressive test plan, and the chaotic festoon of cable beloved of electricians everywhere was fast disappearing into very neat conduits or cable trays.

"Lady R sent you to check up on me, did she?" he asked John, not pausing from his work.

"No, I was coming anyway. Looks good."

"Quality work, mate. Now you're here, you can help with that long cable. Easier with two, and less chance of scuffing."

John moved to the end of the black steel conduit tube and began to pull gently on the leading string as Colin fed in the thick orange cable.

"No need for this level of protection," Colin commented, "but red electric string wouldn't suit in this place. Steel looks better, and can be painted a stone colour."

"I can't channel the wall for you either," commented John. "It would spoil the stonework."

Colin was young-looking, in a fleshy sort of way. He seemed to move slowly and deliberately, almost as if he paused for a brief mental check before completing any action. Despite this apparent slowness he wasted no time, and his work was as impressive as his references suggested it would be.

"What did Judith ask you then, Colin?" said John.

"Her? Asked me if I was working to BS7671, as if she would know what I was doin' anyway."

"She's a quality engineer."

"Say no more. Typical non-job invented to give women work. As if I need—"

"I'm getting Chris Doubleday in to check your work."

"No problem. Chris is a good bloke. Prices you charge, you'd be mad not to."

"I don't know how you got an idea of what I charge, but I get most of my jobs through word-of-mouth recommendation and all that. My customers expect good work."

"Sure."

"So don't go bloody upsetting the customers, or their daughter. OK?"

"No, boss. Sure, boss. I'd even help her with her bra strap if she wore one."

"They're paying over the odds; they want to see what they've asked for. If they want to see a drawing, or a test form, or to know why this is red and that's grey, you tell 'em. Talk yourself up – one of their neighbours might need his pig shit silo rewired."

"Ah," laughed Colin, "good job that. Explosive atmosphere, methane. Special cable, special fixing – high cost."

"Exactly. Worth putting in the effort for a recommendation."

John hoped his warning, and bribery, would convince Colin to do a decent job. He did not intend to work late fixing other people's mistakes. He was very pleased with his own stonework, and with the way Alf Hidson the carpenter and his apprentice, Eric, were progressing on one of the many staircases.

As John swept up the stone chippings, he became aware of Simon Ransom watching him from his office doorway.

"A word?" Simon called out.

"Yeah, just tidying up for the night. This stone dust is quite abrasive."

"Noticed the carpenter and electrician keep the place clean as well. Good. That lad Colin's quite knowledgeable. Was explaining the requirements for fire alarm circuits. Quite complicated."

"He's a bit like Alf the chippy," John lied, "ask a simple question and it's like starting a night school class."

"I never realised that woodworking was so involved," replied Simon. "Selecting old timber so it matches and won't shrink, and matching the colour."

"It's particular to restoration work," commented John, finishing his sweeping. "Quality work on a new site is much easier." He stowed his tools in the box and added conversationally, "I had a glance at the main hall at lunchtime – quite a place. Lifetime's job to get that back to scratch."

"That's what I tell my father and sister," grimaced Simon. "Our family has spent four hundred years thinking what to do with this millstone of a place, and frankly it's beyond us – always has been. We only got the house and a bit of land, not the whole Peverell Estate. Just a running sore of costs, even for basic repairs. I would like to sell up sometime, hotel chain…"

"You'd make more money if you renovated it yourself."

"Possibly, but there's risk in not selling at the end and using too much cash on one investment."

"I can see that."

Simon beckoned John into the office and gestured for him to sit. "I'm sure you can… see the big picture, that is. Nice little company you've got. Good reputation. Six men working."

"Six subcontractors, and two are women."

"Good. Self-employed or limited company?"

"Limited company." John began to feel uneasy. "This was all in my tender for the job."

"I know, just checking." Simon paused before saying, "I was wondering if you could use an injection of capital."

"I don't have any loans."

"I'm sure you don't. No, I thought perhaps a sale of forty-five percent of the company to me, subject to the usual financial checks, of course."

"I don't—"

"Think on it for a bit. You expand the business, increase profit, wider base…"

"And you take forty-five percent."

"Only of the profits, and if you sell up, of course. But you should easily improve your position if you use the capital wisely."

John tried not to overreact. 'Don't upset the customer' was his usual mantra, but he didn't want to be bought out, taken over, or anything else. "I'll think about it, but—"

"No rush. Offer's there if you change your mind. I'm always open to a good proposition."

"Well," said John, "if you ever decide to renovate the main hall and apartments, I would be willing to buy in on a partnering basis." He shrugged. "Probably only for a few percent, but I'd do that to get some of the work."

Now it was Simon Ransom's turn to be defensive. "Unlikely, but I'll remember the offer."

That night, John Townsend slept badly despite a session at the gym and a few pints in the country club. The weight training had gone well enough but he could not focus on the chat at the bar. The conversation just seemed to wash around him as he fought against the memory of blazing red hair and slate-grey eyes. Lying in bed, John's turmoil had only increased as his mind replayed the meeting with the ghost woman. She had seemed to know him. Why had he felt so easy with her? He was not in the habit of grabbing and kissing women of a moment's acquaintance – not that she had objected. Well, she had drawn a clear line by saying 'I'm married'.

Still, he could not have imagined the encounter. She had felt so real as he held her. *Had* been real, he corrected himself. If she had lived in that Jacobean-style house, she must have died over three hundred years ago. Ghosts surely would not come back for a quick snog or to finish their sewing. Perhaps she wasn't a ghost; perhaps he was. Had he gone back? Or had she come forward, bringing her room with her?

CHAPTER 4

After a night's sleep and a good breakfast, John had recovered his composure and almost forced the ghostly encounter of the previous day from his mind. It was, however, a bit of a relief discussing the renovation of a staircase with his down-to-earth carpenter, Alf Hidson, rather than working in the main hall.

"The trouble with this bloody restoration work is that you get stuck in a rut," grumbled Alf as he pared away at the base of a banister rail with a scalpel-sharp chisel.

John could barely see the join where it slotted into the original stair. "Good fit, Alf. Rub of beeswax polish and no one will spot the replacement."

"It's like living in the past." Alf straightened up. "The time I spent on this one rail..."

"What the customer wants," replied John. "First-class job, that's what he's paid for."

Despite his morning grumble, Alf viewed his work with true pride. "Last Saturday, I gave a pal of mine a hand on the new Norton St Philip estate."

"The Beazer Homes?"

"That's it. I tell you, I just couldn't keep up. In the time it's taken me for this stair, he would have done the joinery on the whole bloody house."

"Not to this standard."

"No, but bloody good work, ready for filling and painting."

"That's it, Alf: *filling and painting*. Can you imagine Simon Ransom's face if he spotted a blob of Polyfilla or mastic through the polish?" He helped Alf pick up his tools and walked with him back to the corridor, where some windows needed replacing.

"I know all that," replied Alf. "It's just that I seem to be working in museums, old houses, and cathedrals all the bloody time. Almost always on me own, living in the past. I like craft work, but I miss being on a big site. Christ, I haven't used me power router or nail gun for years!"

"Bollocks, Alf," laughed John, tracing the moulding on the narrow window frame propped up against the wall ready for fitting. "Did you do this with a plane and shave?"

"Well," shrugged Alf apologetically, "I thought it would give the real feel to the finish, sort of authentic like. Didn't take much longer, really."

"Up to you, mate. I pay for the job, not time. Just looks good."

"Bloody good," agreed Alf. "But it proves the point: it's me mindset. I'm getting locked in the past, unhealthy-like. In the pub on Saturday, I'd have rather talked about the history of this place to Eric than hear how Bristol Rovers was doin'. I've even got books on all this crap."

"Be a shame if you chuck it in," shrugged John. "Hard to get another quality chippy. Got a lot on?"

"All small jobs."

"No, I was thinking of a big restoration, several years' work, stone, plaster, wooden Tudor panels. All that sort of crap. But if you're working for Bloor or Beazers..."

"When's this?" asked Alf.

"Not for a year."

"I might have a year off – get back to real work, clear me head. What you got in mind?"

"Talk to you tomorrow lunchtime."

"Alright. See you, mate. Got to get on; stop lappin' about."

John looked back to grin at Alf, before leaving him to his careful removal of the leaded glass panels from an old frame.

∞

At lunchtime the next day, John led Alf into the living room above the main hall, with some trepidation as to what he might find. It was all as it should be: boarded-over windows, crumbled plaster, and discoloured panelling.

Alf had noted John's hesitation at the top of the service stairs. "What's up? Are we trespassing?"

John's eyes were sweeping the room like radar.

"Or are you afraid the bloody ceiling will fall in?"

"Just a feeling like I've been here before," John murmured.

"Deyja-voo." Alf nodded sagely. "Like I said yesterday, we spend too long in these crumbling old grots."

John's gaze kept returning to the window seat. Hoping for a glimpse of the beautiful woman. "You've not looked in here before?" he asked Alf.

"No, just the hall below, to see that staircase. Quite famous it is – open double helix design. Not many survived. That one needs taking down for a museum and to be used as a pattern for a replica." Alf started to walk around the room, looking initially at where huge beams had been exposed by fallen plaster, advancing suspiciously on the panelling. "Structure's probably sound. Needs a survey. This panel's bollocks – late 1900s. Old stuff could still be behind it."

"What I thought," agreed John.

A hole appeared in John's normal vision. To the left of the fireplace he could see through the protection of the old woodwork. Hidden beneath there was a large painting of a man and woman, still new and fresh. The woman had stylised ringlets of red hair, no artistically weakened chin, and looked very much like Penny. John hardly dared look at the figure beside her.

He let out a silent sigh of relief. It was not himself or cousin John, but a tall powerful man in fine clothes: elegant lace, feathered hat, velvet coat and silk breeches. Despite the slightly wavy shoulder-length hair, there was nothing fine or effete about the clean-shaven face: heavy brow, strong chin, defiant eyes...

"You OK, John?"

The picture changed. The man's face had become a burned hole, shot through and surrounded by black powder burns. A horrible jolt to the peaceful afternoon.

John felt pressure on his arm. He turned and saw Alf looking at him in concern.

"Christ, John, thought you was havin' a bloody seizure. Did you see a ghost?"

John shook his head. "No, just thinking." His vision of the panel had returned to normal – no pictures, no drama. "Just thinking about what it might have looked like."

"Watch it mate, you've got it worse than me. I thought you had gone mental."

John wrenched his gaze back from the wall, ignored Penny's seat, and focused on Alf, a forty-five-year-old with a weather-cragged face; not handsome, but reassuring.

"What's the plan, then?" Alf asked.

"Hazy," replied John. "I thought of working up an estimate for replacement and refurbishment of these rooms. As you said, the stairs are too far gone to leave for long. Sort of phased approach – some structural work and decorative stuff at each stage."

"Massive job, too big for you, me and Eric."

"Dunno," mused John. "Say we start on the hall below, remove the staircase, get the basics in order, then we look at the panelling and ceiling. Few more guys, sort of build it up?"

"Be an interestin' ideal," agreed Alf. "If Ransom could pay for it, the work here would see me time out to retirement. Not sure I want a lifetime job. How much would it all cost?"

"No idea," shrugged John. "I thought it would be worth working up a proposal, suggest getting grant money, you know."

"I could get a quick estimate together for the fancy woodwork, just to scope the price, like," said Alf.

"Was just an idea—"

"I'm not walking away from it," said Alf. "I'll give you me figure. First refusal on all the joinery, OK?"

"Need to speak to Simon Ransom before I do too much, but it could be a good project," John replied.

"You do that, John, but I need a piss. And I got a coffee and sandwiches to eat. I'm going out in the sun."

"See you later." John took a notebook from his overall pocket. "I'll just make a few notes on the stonework."

"We'll need to get into the roof space over that ceiling, take some floorboards up," said Alf as he walked away.

John studied the panelling – simple protection stuff, not more than a hundred years old. He tapped it. Could be hollow; generally was. He tried to visualise the couple he had seen, or imagined, on the hidden painting. Penny had mentioned Edward, her husband. Was he the bloke in the portrait? John wandered to the window and peered through some of the remaining leaded panes. Outside, Alf had his overalls and shirt off, and sat incongruously in safety boots and shorts eating from a plastic lunchbox; sardine sandwiches in all probability, his usual 'bait' as he put it.

John imagined how the now unkempt gardens would have looked. Very formal, he supposed, in the French or Italian style, just a step on from the medieval, before the eighteenth-century vandals Hoare and Brown had brought in the wilderness and open-park fashions. The ruined wall could have been the walled kitchen garden.

Movement caught his eye. Two people walking arm in arm strolled leisurely towards the stable block. The rusted out tractor and pile of rubble had gone. Thatch replaced corrugated asbestos. The woman was Penny, dressed in a simple brown shift dress; the man was the cavalier in the painting but in plain everyday dark breeches and white shirt. John's vision seemed to zoom in on their faces as they talked together; she half ecstatic, he attentive but proud. God, even a kid could read their emotions and know what they had been up to. Penny looked suddenly and caught John's eye. Her face registered total surprise and she turned to speak to Edward. His eyes flashed up to John blankly without recognition.

John opened the creaking window, waved and shouted, "Hi, there!"

Edward stared directly at him in utter disbelief.

John's image of them faded. The gravel walk receded to its normal distance and transformed back to a farm track. Trim hedges became brambled clumps, and an oily pool appeared in front of the garage.

"Hi," Judith Ransom called back to him from off to the left of the present-day lawn; she must have just come out of the house.

Alf looked up in surprise at John, flicked his eyes over at Judith, felt embarrassed, and continued to eat his sandwiches.

John closed the window and staggered back to regain his composure. Shock at seeing Penny and Edward, embarrassment at bawling out as if to Judith – he'd better get down there and say something sensible.

∞

On a summer afternoon in 1643, Penny Peverell stared hard into the face of Sir Edward Peverell Esq, master of Peverell House. They had hurried upstairs to their living room but found no trace of John. Edward had searched the house and now looked bemused at Penny. His face was pale, his eyes still darting around their crimson-draped room as if expecting to spot John hiding.

"You did see him, Edward?" Penny asked hesitantly.

"I have searched the house. The servants saw no one."

"But it was John."

"I know, I know. I can tell pheasant from partridge at a hundred yards and shoot either. I trust my eyes, and it was your cousin, John Jackson. At first, I just noticed a misty shape, then when he waved and called, I could see him quite clearly – it was definitely his voice."

"Then I'm not mad!"

"No, you are not mad, but he is a varlet, coming back from the dead to disturb the peace of our home. What can it mean?"

She smiled to see his mask of cavalier self-assurance had begun to slip, revealing the true Edward, much more thoughtful and questioning than many would suspect.

"I have no idea," she said as she walked to the servants' entrance at the side of the room. "I hope it is no omen. The first time he just strolled in, through this door, and then seemed shocked to see me, in my own house."

"But he recovered well enough to grasp you to him."

"Yes. Well, I may have approached him first, to lay the ghost. I did kiss his cheek."

"You said he kissed you?"

"Yes, he responded and tried to kiss my lips. Now he waves and calls as if he had arrived to visit and found us out riding."

"Thank God he didn't materialise yesterday on the Downs, he would have died again of jealousy."

The rest of the day passed easily enough with each of them often locked in their own thoughts. As light fell, they sat, backs to the window, to get the last rays of sun on the books they read. Between them one of the branched candlesticks burned yellowy. Edward put down his book on the padded window seat.

"Ah, it's time for bed and sleep."

"Book boring?"

"No, difficult. French. Written by Jean Roche, on waging war. And it's all wrong for our war."

"Oh, Edward. And it cost you so much to get it."

"No, it was worth reading. It has validity to French and German campaigns, but not to England. Here too many men fight for principle, often misplaced I agree, but they have conviction and resolve. In our battles, even untrained militia do not turn and run like paid mercenaries. That is why so many are killed on both sides. I wish Prince Rupert and some of the king's friends understood and treated all Englishmen with respect, aye, and the Scots too for that matter. The king knows his subjects better but he is unsure of himself." Edward closed the book with resignation. "I can sell this, if I can find anyone to read it."

"Edward, I've been thinking."

"Eh?"

"Seriously. Do you want to do something about Cousin John's ghost? Speak to a churchman?"

"What, a vicar with bell, book and candle? Hell's teeth, no."

Penny laughed at his shocked face. "Edward, calm down. I just thought this is your home and—"

"*Our* home," he corrected. "Would you have me cast out one of your family, even if they are but a spirit?" He paused. "I am serious. If John has returned for a purpose, then we should help him. If he needs company then I will call for an extra pipe and a can of ale."

"You are a fool."

"Good! A simple fool but one with principles. If he returns

again, we treat him as a guest. As we did in life, and as he did for us. But he must curb any indecent advances to you. A family embrace or kiss I can tolerate, even applaud. Any more and I will take drastic action."

"Edward, you are drunk!"

"I never have been drunk in all my life – one glass of wine, one tankard of beer only. I've thought long on this."

"And, my jealous husband, if my ghostly cousin o'er steps your mark, what will you do? Call for bell, book and candle after all?"

"Never. I'll use my pistols, loaded with silver ball, or take up the silver fruit knife!"

CHAPTER 5

Sir Edward Peverell believed the running of his estate should be a simple, beneficial duty but one requiring him to take some responsibility for the community. While he was away with King Charles's army in Oxford, Penny had taken on Edward's duties in his absence, including acting as justice of the peace. There was no legal authority for her to do this but most of her ruling had been accepted readily. Now, after the first halcyon days of his return, Penny had persuaded Edward to review her decisions and resolve a few outstanding issues.

There had been no raids or foraging in the area, but tensions were high in the villages and on the estate farms. There was fear of civil war coming closer; that taxes would rise even higher; men might be conscripted and dragged off to fight. In response to fear of crime and lack of law enforcement, a 'band of clubmen' had been formed to help protect the community.

"Will Tachem is a good man," Penny conceded. "Well suited to being leader of the clubmen. Anyone in the parish, village or farm can call on them at any time, day or night."

"I fully approve of all this," stated Edward. "It deters

wandering thieves and disorder."

In this climate, it seemed everyone wanted to seek their own advantage: tenant farmers argued over boundaries; villagers argued over access to common land. Often they came to Edward to settle these arguments, or to Penny when he was away. On his return from Oxford, Edward had endorsed all of his wife's decisions, but suggested that having Robert Tachem suffer a ten-lash flogging and a morning in the stocks for drunken behaviour a little harsh.

"I had to show there was no favouritism towards him. Robert is an unruly lout, picking fights with men, seeking to force his attention—"

"I agree, I agree. Robert deserved to be punished, and Will Tachem gives himself airs above his station. I'll speak to both of them. Will that suffice?"

"Better you send the son off to the wars—"

"Ah, that is enough legal business for one day. Enough for a month. I have only been gone two weeks and all our people are in dispute with each other."

Penny started to speak but Edward continued.

"Come, let us take some food and ride out along the riverbank. I know a secluded peaceful spot—"

"And I know what happens there," interrupted Penny archly. "You are insatiable!"

"You object?"

"Not in the least. But there is still more business to attend to."

"I will have both parties flogged for disturbing my peace, and our pleasure."

"All in good time," Penny continued. "What is more difficult is this boundary dispute between two of our tenants." She indicated a page of notes and other papers. "It is beyond me. They seem to dispute a boundary between the farms by about a yard."

"These two were firm friends as boys. Can't they go halfway? It's madness to fall out of friendship over this."

"They both declare no compromise is possible," Penny said. "It is a matter of principle. Each wants justice over his thieving neighbour."

"God save us from principles," said Edward bitterly. "If the king will not compromise with parliament and even the king's adviser, Culpepper, cannot compromise with Prince Rupert as to the war, how can we expect two farmers to be reasonable?" He sighed. "I suppose I must settle this. How does it lie?"

"I said I had insufficient local knowledge and would await your return," Penny said, stroking his arm.

"I have a bailiff who—"

"Who agrees with me. It's your judgement."

"And what shall I do?"

"Ride out to the spot, march up and down, huff and puff, and then say the line should be halfway."

"It's a fine day for a ride. I will take Roger, our bailiff, with me."

"He is organising the harvesting."

"Good. I will point this out to our sullen tenants and authorise Roger to charge them a harsh fee for his time, and for drawing up the new boundary in the parish record. That'll teach 'em a lesson!" He smiled fondly at Penny.

"With my husband's permission, I would ride out too."

"A detour on the way back, possibly along the riverbank?"

suggested Edward hopefully. She nodded in agreement.

"And while you find Roger I will quickly change and hasten up a bag of food and drink."

It took several hours to prise Roger from the oat field, and it was near midday by the time he and the Peverells arrived at the disputed boundary.

"This baulk marks the boundary."

"Nay, you ploughed the true one out!"

"Stop this," shouted the bailiff. "I've read the records; it's a line drawn from the church tower to the ancient oak by the pond."

"Aye," bluffed Edward sagely. "I recollect it well."

"But the oak blew down last winter," said Penny, "hence the dispute."

"God's teeth!" cried Edward. "Roger, drive a stake in the middle of the tree throw, take a sight to the centre of the church tower, and mark a line."

Suddenly there was a distant sound of two rapid gunshots.

"It's an alarm from the town," said Roger in concern. "Two shots will mean a threat to the west of St Wilfred's church tower."

"Coming away or going toward the town?" asked Edward. He stood in his stirrups looking over the hills towards Box Village. "I can see horsemen on the road riding towards us and Peverell."

"This way?" asked Penny.

"Whichever it is, the watch are sending out a warning. Fall back to the house," instructed Roger.

"Looters, I lay," shouted a farmer. "Our farmstead and granaries are here, Sir Edward. Arm yourselves, men! Stand with us, sir," he pleaded. "We only have bill hooks and staves."

"They are probably just travellers or merchants," said Penny, hopefully.

"Will Tachem wouldn't send a warning for a party of merchants," said Roger. He had pulled an ancient matchlock musket from its horse holster and was trying to strike a spark to light the match.

"Careful, man!" said Edward. "You will fire your piece by mischance."

"Not loaded yet."

"There are only five horsemen," stated Edward. "We will hold our ground here with the farm tenants."

"The house staff will be sufficient to guard Peverell well," agreed Penny. "They will have heard the warning shots. With grooms and servants, there are eight men and at least six guns."

"Henry York, our butler, is an old soldier, and will take charge," said Edward. "You have your pistol, my lady?"

Penny was already fixing the key to span and cock a small functional wheel lock pistol. "Aye, captain," she said with humour. "Do not stand to my left, this sends a jet of flame out sideways as it fires."

With the labourers concealed behind a hedge, they lined their horses up across the road, Penny, with her small lady's pistol, beside Edward.

"Can you cope with one of my horse pistols as well?" Edward asked her. "Once I fire, I'll charge with my sword."

She nodded and took the heavy handgun, feeling suddenly very much afraid.

They sat motionless on their horses, waiting as the approaching men rode through a small copse about one hundred paces away.

"Halt, in the king's name," roared Edward. "We are armed and will give fire."

The party slowed and stopped fifty yards away. Their steaming sweat-flecked horses had been ridden hard.

"Stand aside in the king's name," shouted back their leader. "Stand aside, I am Thomas Waddell, a messenger from the king, seeking Sir Edward Peverell."

"It could be a trick," whispered Roger, blowing on his carbine's match to make it glow hotter.

"I think not," replied Edward. "Roger, do not point that thing at me!" Edward moved slightly forward on his black horse, drawing himself up importantly. "I am Sir Edward Peverell," he called out. "Advance slowly, alone, and with no weapons, Master Waddell."

"If they charge, I will shoot at the two on the left," said Penny. "My horse isn't trained for gunfire and may shy, so I will shoot both pistols together."

Thomas Waddell advanced cautiously towards them, alone. "This is an outrage. An outrage for the king's messenger to be met by armed men on the road and," he sneered at Penny, "a gentlewoman."

"A gentlewoman who can shoot as well as any man," snapped Penny.

"You have a letter, sir?" asked Edward.

Waddell nodded, reaching into a pouch at his side.

"You may have noticed, sir, that we are at war. I will have no foragers or rogues plundering my tenants." He took the folded and sealed parchment and turned to Penny. "We are honoured.

The king's seal indeed, and that of Prince Rupert. The address to me has been written by His Highness Prince Rupert himself."

"I am charged," said Thomas Waddell pompously, "to bid you read the message alone and communicate it to no one. It is imperative that its contents remain an utmost secret. I am to await your answer and return."

"You will go nowhere tonight without fresh and fed horses," replied Edward. "I could supply you a fresh mount but not your escort, and you cannot travel alone with my reply." Edward stopped to praise the tenants and labourers for standing firm with him, before leading the impatient Waddell and his escort off to Peverell House.

Roger and Penny stayed behind to finish the boundary marking.

Some hours later, having dined with Master Waddell and persuaded him to stay overnight, Edward joined Penny alone in their private sitting room.

"You did well to excuse yourself from dinner. That man is insufferable!"

"So, Prince Rupert wants to capture Bristol for the king's cause?" asked Penny looking up from her book. "Is it necessary?"

"I agree it is essential," replied Edward, throwing off his jacket and taking up his pipe. "After London, it is the second most important city in England for merchants and workshops. And it is a good seaport. With the major south coast ports like Portsmouth and Dover held against us, it is our only access for large shipping; the Cornish harbours are too small and remote."

"I hear parliament is building new forts and walls at Bristol, with many cannon."

"But their commander, Nathaniel Fiennes, only has two thousand men. If we advance on it with our force of over forty thousand from Oxford and Prince Maurice brings his men and cannon, even a puritan fanatic like Fiennes will see defence is hopeless. All we need do is offer good surrender terms and hardly a shot need be fired. The men of Bristol care little enough for either their king or parliament; they will not face a siege. They want only to trade and line their pockets."

"But why does Rupert need you, Edward?"

"I know the town well and I have drawn plans of its defences. If we can convince the king that Bristol will fall to us easily, then he may let Rupert act."

"You won't be leading the assault?" she asked with concern.

"If we do this well, there need be no assault. I have tried to explain all this to Rupert, but I fear he wants to lead a heroic attack to demoralise parliament."

"More likely to add to his own glory," said Penelope.

Edward did not disagree.

They talked some more on this; laughed over the tenant farm dispute and how quickly it had been forgotten in face of a perceived threat. Edward was about to propose 'early to bed' and a passionate farewell when Penny began to tremble with fear. Thinking it was a reaction to the day or worry over him going, Edward put his arm around her shoulder.

"No, Edward, not now! Can you feel it? It is as when John appeared. But it's not John. There's someone else here – a woman this time." She buried her head against Edward's neck, still shuddering. "Oh, God, she is so distressed."

Edward looked wildly about now, aware of a chill

atmosphere. The room shimmered in the flickering light of four candles but there was no one visible to him.

Then, the indistinct shape of a woman sitting at a strange writing desk, sobbing.

"How the hell did it go wrong?" she cried out. "I tried so hard. What was wrong, Mark?"

Again more sobbing. Edward and Penny exchanged desperate looks.

"Have you seen her before?" he asked in a hoarse whisper.

"No, I have only heard her speak. Always sadly, but not like this."

Edward stepped softly towards the woman. Fearfully, Penny put out a restraining hand.

"Madam," Edward said firmly. "We see you distressed. May we be of assistance?"

"Edward, what are you doing?"

"Ghost or phantom, she is in my house and needs help."

The woman jerked in surprise and looked in startled fear around some unseen room. She stared intently towards Edward and Penny with unseeing eyes. The shock seemed to change her mood.

"Judith, you stupid fool," she said out loud. "Mark's gone. Not your fault. Pull yourself together. Imagining bloody voices." She stood up and paced the room. "Get a grip, woman, get out of this ruin. I know, I'll ring John Townsend, see how he's getting on."

"Edward, what can we do?"

"Nothing, it seems. She appears unable to see us."

The woman seemed to vanish from sight, leaving Edward and

Penny still confused and fearful.

Hesitantly, Penny asked, "Edward, have there been ghosts in Peverell before this?"

"No. My family have lived here since it was built. A happy home. We Peverells have lived and died here with no great tragedy, no apparitions, and no curses. You have not seen her before?" Edward said again.

"No, not visibly, not like this. I have heard her moving and speaking – always in this room – but nothing so vivid or close to me."

"You did not tell me of it before."

"I thought it my fancy. She was never evil or frightening. And then Cousin John appeared as if flesh and blood."

After a long thoughtful silence, Edward said, "Waddell's message has summoned me to the king at Oxford, and I must leave tomorrow. You don't need to be here on your own. We could even leave tonight and lodge at the inn in Box. You follow on slowly to Oxford and we will find lodging in the town."

A pause.

"No, Edward, this is my home, my husband's house. I will not flee from phantoms or be driven out. Besides, who will run the estate when you are off sacking Bristol?"

"There seems to be no threat to us, but we do not understand what is happening," replied Edward.

"I am sure of one thing: neither Cousin John nor this Judith bear me ill will. I shall stay. And, forgetting all this, you shall love me tonight."

Penny's alluring smile was all Edward needed to draw him over to the ornately decorated bed.

CHAPTER 6

It was a bright summer morning when John woke early from another restless night. Dreams and thoughts of the past had been interlaced with the potential of Peverell House and his discussions with Judith and Simon. It was only six a.m., but he had to get out of bed, out of the flat and into some fresh air. His eyes needed to focus on more distant horizons, his legs needed to cover some long miles. Even so, work had to come first and he meticulously checked through a bid he was putting in for a renovation and remodelling job – a stone farmhouse between Bristol and Bath.

By eight, his breakfast was eaten, the proposal sent off in an e-mail, and he was heading out of Bath city towards Mere. It was good to drive the little smooth-running Fiesta rather than his work van with its rattling tools in the back.

John's plan for the day was to leave the Fiesta in the National Trust car park at Stourhead and set off across to White Sheet Hill with its Iron Age hill fort and Stone Age camp, purposefully avoiding the stately home.

From the banked ramparts of the hill fort, John looked down

upon the town of Mere and the surrounding flat farmland. A fantastic view on such a clear day. The last time he had walked up here it had been masked with drizzle and mist. The Iron Age people who had constructed the fort had certainly known how to pick a good site.

"Hi, great morning!"

John spun around, nerves on edge. Two female horse riders stood twenty meters away, following the green lane across the Downs. The sound of horses' hooves were muffled by the grass. God, he almost expected to see Penny and Edward Peverell.

"Morning," he called back in a croak of surprise.

The women waved and rode on, leaving John to his flask of coffee and snack bar. He was miles from the Peverell estate, and any ghosts up here on the hills would be ancient Celts, not cavaliers. Had the civil war come to Mere? There was a siege at Devizes...

"For God's sake." He had come out to escape from the historical junk, not keep turning it over in his mind.

He completed a twelve-mile circular walk and returned just in time to drive into Mere and catch Yapps, the wine merchants, before they closed. He decided on two bottles of the best red burgundy he could afford.

Back in his flat, showered and with one bottle open, a steak beaten, and Bach's *Brandenburg Concerto No. 2* playing, he was utterly contented. Then his phone rang. He didn't recognise the number, so ignored it at first. He sipped at his glass of wine. Could it have been one of his mates in Bath? There was no message. He returned the call and was surprised to hear a female voice answer.

"Hi, John," the woman said haltingly. "It's Judith, Judith Ransom. It's a bit of a cheek, but if I drive into Bath, do you fancy meeting up for a burger and beer? Just to discuss the renovations."

Bugger. He was stuck for an answer on the spur of the moment.

"Nice idea, but I've had a hard day. Look, I've got a steak ready to grill..."

"So, no contest with a burger, then. Perhaps another time?" Her voice was quiet with disappointment.

"No, wait," John hesitated. Was this a good idea, hobnobbing with the client? "There are two steaks and a spare bottle of burgundy. You're welcome to come here – my place. I can cook."

There was a longish pause. It was quite a jump from casual drink to dinner in a stranger's flat.

"Wouldn't want to put you out," Judith replied eventually.

"I'd like some company." John was surprised at his own answer. Perhaps he was still lonely since his split from Helen.

An hour later, Judith arrived. He went down to meet her, accepted the bottle of supermarket 'plonk', and led her up into the flat. Nice shoes, sheer tights, short purple skirt and a contrasting yellow top – she had really made an effort to look good. Her necklace carried a large purple stone that matched the colour of the skirt. He was very impressed. In turn, Judith caught her breath when she saw the interior of John's flat. She was stunned. On the drive from Calne she had imagined some dim Victorian terrace conversion. From the outside it looked worse: a three-storey utilitarian block of basic flats. She had not been expecting the large open-plan contemporary interior with a balcony overlooking Henrietta Park. The park trees and tall shrubs shut out the other buildings, and above them she could see the Bath hills and Beechen Cliff.

"Wow, how the other half live," she exclaimed.

"What?"

"No crumbling plaster, ancient beams or dull stonework in sight. This is how I'd like to live."

"I bought it as a change from my work. You know, cathedrals, crypts, and all that."

"Or crumbling ruins like Peverell. I can understand that. View's beautiful too." She looked out from the open French windows of the balcony to the sun-filled park.

"What were you expecting?" he said, joining her. "Some grotty undercroft with water dripping down the wall and a cow in the corner?"

Judith smiled back and raised her palm. "Guilty as charged, guv."

It was the first time he had seen her smile, and it lit up her rather sad face.

"I thought at least I could bring some half decent booze – *Tesco's Finest*." She pointed to the bottle on the table and continued, "I bet that cost a lot. Must have been twenty quid, at least?"

"I wish I could have got it for that... Can I escort you to the terrace area, madam?"

They sat outside at the little table, absorbing the heady scent of the bright flowers in the park.

"Is that Beechen Cliff up there?"

"Yeah. The abbey's tower is just visible to your right. Would you like a drink?"

"I'd love a— Actually, no, better not if we are having wine. I've got to drive back later."

Too early to suggest she stay over, thought John.

Judith twisted the wine bottle to look at the label. "Do you pour this yourself, or is there a butler hiding somewhere?"

Smiling, John picked up the bottle. "It's the butler's night off. Are you sure you don't want a glass?"

"I'm fine. Let's just soak up the ambience," she remarked, enjoying the golden sunset fading behind the trees.

A while later, after they had eaten, Judith let out a rather melancholy sigh.

"I should live in a city."

"You're not fond of Peverell?" John asked tentatively.

"Oh, I'm fond of it, just don't like living there."

"Could you move out?"

"No, not now, not with Dad as he is." Judith sipped the last of her burgundy. She had finally caved on the wine front. "I could grow to love this."

"I've got another bottle."

"And I've got a car parked outside. Actually, a bloody great Land Rover Discovery."

They lingered in the easy chairs and could still see glimpses of the darkish leaves against the sky as the sun dipped low.

"I did have a house in Malmesbury until a year or so ago," Judith blurted out. "And a partner. And a good career job at Dyson. Then he walked out. Well, more or less bolted. I cracked up a bit, chucked the job and moved back home. Now Dad's too ill for me to leave."

"Simon lives elsewhere?" asked John.

"Too right. Big modern detached house, wife and two kids. And, of course, shed loads of cash." Judith finished her wine and set down the glass resolutely. "That's it for me. Thanks for a lovely meal. Any pud?"

"No. I've got some cheese in the fridge, and fruit. Why don't you raid the kitchen?"

"I will." She moved reluctantly from the table. "Anything for you, John?"

"Small piece of stilton please, and a bread roll."

"Yes, sir. You sound like Simon giving orders to his wife," she chuckled.

He relaxed back in the balcony chair and poured them one last glass of wine each, as he waited for Judith to come back with their cheese plates.

Time passed amicably as they ate, then Judith asked, "No Mrs Townsend?"

"Was. She left, and we divorced two years ago. That's when I bought this place. Doubles as my registered office and bachelor flat."

"Sorry."

"So was I. Suppose I still am. Helen left as soon as I mentioned having kids. Nothing else to say, really."

Judith took that as a hint to end the conversation, and they were silent for a while.

Eventually, John said, "Shame there's no ghost at Peverell. It would be a good selling point for a hotel." He was 'fishing' and hoped it was not too obvious.

She hesitated before saying, "I think there are ghosts. Not the grief-stricken wailing of Lady Penelope; more like a presence, as if other people are living in the place, moving about. Weird." She ate some cheese, picked up her glass and took the merest sip.

"Is that why you don't want to stay there on your own?"

"It's not frightening, more of a happy atmosphere, though that's even worse when you are a bit down. You can be sitting reading and it's as if someone has walked into the room. You can be half dozing and hear muffled voices."

"Angry? Sad?" John was astonished Judith was also aware of a slight ghostly presence at Peverell.

"No happy, very happy. At times it sounds like there's a couple 'at it' in the next room."

"Wishful thinking?" he laughed.

"No way. I've finished with all that. No one's making a fool of me again."

John ignored the remark, and to lighten the atmosphere suggested coffee. It was getting chilly outside, so they decided to move into the lounge.

John poured their coffee, placing the pot gently down on the table, then ventured rather hesitantly, "It's rather incredible, the ghost feeling. Can you hear what the voices say?"

Judith looked rather embarrassed. "I don't know. It's muffled. Very accented West Country. Hardly Radio Four." She suddenly stopped and, feeling foolish, said, "Are you stringing me along?"

John leaned forward, touching her arm gently. "No, I'm not. I was curious because... well I think I have actually seen someone." He recounted meeting Penny in the Great Hall and their embrace, then seeing Penny and Edward together through the window another time.

"So that's why you called out. You said you were calling out to the carpenter."

"I could hardly say 'pardon me, I was hailing a ghost', could I?"

"And she kissed you? Now who's imagining things..."

"It may have been a few years since Helen left but I do remember what it feels like."

"I bet you do. Are you trying to scare me?"

"No, you raised the ghost topic. Sorry, no pun intended."

Another silence. Neither knew what to say.

Finally, Judith continued. "This is gross. It's a lovely evening, and we're sitting here discussing failed relationships and spectral apparitions. Trouble is, I am too old for clubbing and too young for TV and knitting. I could really do with a wild night out."

"Me too." John realised he really meant it. He had been stuck in a rut since his divorce. "I picked up a membership for the Vespa club a few weeks back – they were just opening, and a bloke pushed a leaflet at me. We could walk around from here and give it a try for a few hours?"

"The Vespa! And you say you've been celibate for two years? Isn't it for kids?"

"Select adults-only on Saturday nights. You have to be over twenty-five to get in."

"No problems there then. Next year I'll be barred from the under thirties nights!" She grinned at John. "Usually I feel too old for clubbing, but tonight I could do with a real rave. That's if you can keep up."

"I'll see what I can do. You could crash out here rather than drive back to Peverell afterwards, if you like."

"Separate rooms?"

"Only one bedroom I'm afraid. Double bed though." Damn, why did he say that?

Judith whisked a smartphone from her small handbag. "Look, Mr Wolf, there's a Premier Inn and Travelodge in the city, for starters. One of them is bound to have a room. If I can book somewhere this late, I'm up for a few hours at Vespa's. If not, I'll drive home and listen to ghostly shagging instead."

He left her to it and began to clear up the cooking area.

"Right," she said presently, "that's fixed. Hotel says I can even get a toothbrush from their vending machine. Lucky me!"

∞

John had barely drifted back to sleep when his mobile sounded. Light streamed in at the window and mingled with his memory of flashing lights – flashing lights in the club. God, it was six thirty a.m.

"Judith?" he mumbled as he picked up the call.

"Yes, John, it's me. Fantastic night. I got a great idea for today – unless you have something on?"

"Um, sleep? We were still dancing at two. Do you know what time it is?"

"Of course. Stop spouting excuses. Weather will be good, so how about a hike up a Welsh mountain?"

"Today?"

"Yes, today. I could pick you up in an hour and we can drive to Chapel le Frith."

"I know it's Sunday, but I don't do church."

"It's a place in Wales, in the Black Mountains."

John's mind was undecided. He had nothing planned and a mountain walk sounded good, but he had walked yesterday, danced until late, and glugged down the last of the wine after leaving Vespa's.

"Sorry, I don't want to pressure. Probably got more interesting things planned," Judith continued, backing down.

"No, no. Not at all." John suppressed a yawn. "Just need to wake up. You got boots and things?"

"Always in the back of the car, with my windproof coat. Are you up for it?"

"Sure, I'm up for anything," he replied, thinking of Judith climbing the windy hills in her clubbing skirt and sheer tights.

"See you soon. Oh, John, what do you drive?"

"The van and a Fiesta. Why?"

"Would you mind driving? The roads will be narrow and there's not much parking for a Discovery."

An hour later, John lumbered downstairs to find Judith sitting, legs out of the back door of the Discovery, hauling up a pair of walking trousers.

"Spoil sport," he greeted her. "I only agreed to this thinking of you climbing the mountains in that short skirt."

"Tough. I keep these in the back, just in case I have a car problem."

The day passed easily enough – well, from a social perspective. Steep climb over a ridge west from Chapel le Frith, soggy descent, wading a stream and then walking up Waun Fach wasn't John's usual pre-Sunday lunch activity. By the time they reached the mountain's flat tabletop, his calf muscles were screaming.

"Lunchtime," he stated emphatically, throwing his rucksack onto a small boulder, though he only had several stale rolls, a tin of corned beef and coffee – nothing to be excited about.

Judith took her water bottle out. "I don't normally stop to eat when I'm on a day walk," she explained.

"I do."

After John had eaten, they walked a long flattish loop around the top of the valley, before embarking on the steep descent to the little church in Chapel le Frith. Judith had paused briefly when they looked down from the mound of Twmpa to phone and check on her dad. It seemed she did not do rest stops, and they had seen few other walkers to talk to. There was no mention of John's failed marriage or Judith being abandoned by Mark. They had chatted easily about nothing in particular as they forged along.

Back at the start and sitting in John's Fiesta, Judith said hesitantly, "John, er, is that offer of a bed at yours still, well, on offer?" Her eyes were fixed ahead on the narrow lane as he started driving.

John jolted in surprise. "Of course." Then, thinking she could just be afraid of the Peverell ghosts, he added cautiously, "Do you want the bed or settee?"

"The bed." A pause. "I was hoping you might be in it with me."

He was unsure how to reply. "Um... it would be my pleasure."

"Mine too, I hope," she said girlishly.

Should he pull over into a passing place and kiss her? Would they head straight to bed when they got back to the flat? Should he suggest a meal first? He glanced in her direction. She was still staring straight ahead, avoiding eye contact.

"I'm a bit rusty at this, John. It's been years since, well, Mark left." She swallowed hard. "Could I have a practice run as soon as we get back? Then I could treat you to that burger I mentioned."

She spoke lightly, but John could tell she was feeling embarrassed. He leaned over and stroked her arm. "We could even do a restaurant."

"I've nothing to change into. Can't do 'posh' in last night's sweaty top."

"No clothes hidden in the Discovery?"

"Dayglow vest."

"Sounds promising."

"Idiot."

John laughed, wiping the sexy image from his mind before saying, "The fridge is empty, so burgers it is."

His euphoria lasted about forty-five minutes. Just as they crossed the Severn Bridge, Judith's mobile buzzed.

"Hi, Simon."

It was her brother, he realised. John only heard snatches of conversation over the traffic noise.

"So soon? Can't you? Of course, of course. I'll be there in say— John, how long to get to Calne?"

"Straight there? An hour. But your Discovery is still outside my place."

"Bugger. Simon, I've got to come via Bath. So, between one and two hours."

There was more talk. Then she rang off.

"I'm so sorry, John. It's Dad's night carer. They've let us

down." She rambled on, "Simon's got an investors' do tonight."

John swore quietly under his breath. "On a Sunday?"

"Seems so. Semi-social dinner with investors." Her voice trailed off. "I'm so sorry. Are you angry?"

"Not angry. Bitterly disappointed." He was about to suggest 'another time' when a thought hit him. "It's a late start for the rugby, Bath playing Wasps in a friendly. There's going to be a stack of traffic as we hit Bath, more as you drive out of town back to Calne. Might be better if I take you directly home. You can collect the car tomorrow."

"Can't believe Dad and Simon have buggered up everything *again*," Judith muttered, close to tears. "First time since Mark left and..."

CHAPTER 7

Sir Edward Peverell had not managed to get to Oxford and advise Prince Rupert on how to capture Bristol. Instead, he had been diverted, and caught up in the minor but very bloody battle at Lansdown, to the north of Bath. It was now the day after the battle and Edward was leading a small party of his own men looking for any of parliament's scouts, and rounding up stragglers.

Damn, thought Edward bitterly. This had all been so unnecessary. Instead of using some discipline and their cannon to give a clear victory, General Hopton had sent the Royalist pikemen charging up a steep hill at Parliamentary musketeers, shielded by a drystone wall. Eventually it had achieved a nominal victory, in that the Parliamentary force had withdrawn, but over a third of the Royalist army were dead or seriously wounded. The king's cause couldn't afford to lose men like this, and commanders shouldn't expect them to die in such fruitless attacks.

It had left Edward in an angry and depressed mood, lost in his own reflections, until one of his men rode alongside him and pointed to a plume of smoke.

"Sir Edward, look!"

"There's no fighting upon these hills now. Probably a haystack on fire."

"More like wood smoke," said another. "A farm or steading with damp thatch."

"Looters, sir?"

"Possibly. Let's see if anyone needs help. Bristol and Bath towns declared for parliament, but most of the manor houses up on the hills towards Gloucester are still true to the king."

Edward led his dozen men across an open common, through a hedge and onto a track bordered by a thin copse. As they galloped out of the trees, they could see a large imposing manor house and surrounding farm buildings burning. Soldiers with the king's yellow colours of the day were carrying grain from a barn, loading it into carts. A pig lay with its throat cut, another squealed as it was dragged out from a sty; some sheep had escaped from a pen, pursued by whooping horsemen. Worse still, two labourers lay dead or dying beside the stable buildings. A group of men were raping a maid on the gravel path and two more struggled to rip the dress off a gentlewoman, no doubt for plunder and then rape. A young girl, eight or ten years old, ran screaming from her hiding place near the house towards the orchard. A soldier, helping to hold down the maidservant, picked up his pistol, sighted and shot the fleeing child.

Edward was too far to intervene. He saw the smoke from the pistol, the bang of a shot, sounds of laughter.

"Draw swords!" he yelled, and charged forward at the group of looters still a hundred yards away.

Unhurriedly, their leader lifted himself off the hysterical maid, fastened his breeches and shouted towards Edward. "Sir Edward! It is I, Master Thomas Waddell, foraging in the king's name."

Edward rode his horse into Waddell, knocking him over and trampling one of his men.

"Hold, sir. We are King's men. All King's men here. Why attack me?" He sprawled on the gravel, grabbing his pistol, and then realised it was discharged already.

Across the farmyard, foragers stopped and reached for weapons, but their leader was down with a pistol pointing at his head and a line of Edward's grim-faced men were poised to charge. Courage failed.

"Release that woman," shouted Edward.

"We take orders only from—"

Edward turned slightly in the saddle. "Phil, see to it!"

Phil Howells, son of Edward's bailiff, was Edward's nominal commander. He walked his horse towards the imprisoned gentlewoman, his pistol aimed directly at one of her tormentors.

"If you fire your piece, you'll hit her." The forager's voice was fearful as he looked at Phil's cocked pistol.

The horse's breath was in the woman's face but she didn't flinch. Suddenly, Phil's arm shot out. The muzzle of the gun hit the forager on the bridge of the nose and blood spurted. The woman darted away. Phil struck down, crunching the hand guard of his sabre into a second man's face.

The maid, freeing herself from the man who still held her, pulled down her skirts as she ran, stumbling to her mistress.

"Ma'am, they have ruined me."

Unbidden, another of Edward's men had dismounted and

walked to where the shot little girl's hand waved feebly. He cradled her in his arms as if she were his daughter.

"Help me," she sobbed pitifully.

"Fear not, I will stay with you." He called to Edward, a catch in his throat. "Sir..." He made a sign with his thumb down.

"Murderer," hissed Edward.

Waddell had staggered to his feet, trying to regain some dignity. "Sir, stand back from me. I have the king's warrant to forage for the army. You have no right to strike me down – me or my men. No right to impede our orders."

"To kill and to rape?" Edward asked harshly.

"They are for parliament. The cook drew a knife on me and was executed."

"Two old men, two women and a child. You have a dozen armed men. There was no need to kill and fire the manor house; to ravish one girl and murder another."

"She isn't dead."

"Not yet. I will wait until she dies before you and the coward who fired on her are hanged."

"You have no authority."

"I am Sir Edward Peverell, Justice of the Peace for Calne and its surrounding area, as vested in me by—"

"Bollocks!"

Waddell was knocked down again, this time by Phil, who said furiously, "Show respect when addressing the magistrate!"

"The girl is dead, sir, God rest her soul," called out Edward's man, as he lay the girl down on the grass.

"May she rest in peace." Edward's anger collapsed into profound sadness and he forced himself to act rationally. He ordered Waddell and the girl's killer to be pinioned. Phil and two others were sent to try and recover the cook's body from the blazing manor house.

He looked on as the mistress of the estate stood praying over the dead child's body. Finally, she stalked over to Edward.

"You, sir. Are you one of the king's felons sent to loot and murder?"

Edward patiently introduced himself and explained his office. "I will enact justice on these men, madam, and ensure your property is restored to you. The grain and other fodder have been legally requisitioned by the king. These thieves should have explained that and given you a receipt."

The woman took a deep breath. "I am Margaret Ransom, mistress of this estate. My husband is in Bath with my stepdaughter."

"Master Oliver Ransom, the clothier and farmer?" Edward asked.

She nodded.

"I know him by way of business," Edward continued. "He buys wool from my flock. A good man."

"These two burst into the kitchen where I was in discussion with Alice, my cook."

"She went for me with a knife," pleaded Waddell.

"She was chopping vegetables and had a kitchen knife in her hand. You said nothing but just slashed her with your sword." Margaret turned to Edward. "His orders to his men were 'kill them all – no witnesses'."

"They ruined me," sobbed the maid. "Three of them!"

"Tush, girl. No one falls with child on their first tumble!"

Margaret scolded. "You can see why we are for parliament," she said to Edward. "The king proclaims he has the right to rule from God and that he will rule fairly for all. Instead, he sends criminals to murder and steal. We must have rule of law. Fair and just rule – not tyranny."

"She has a point, sir," said Phil after a pause. "We cannot just hang these two without trial."

"Then we shall have one. You will be foreman of the jury; I will be the judge. I have personal judicial authority. I can imprison, flog or hang any man or woman who is not of noble birth. I am charged to seek advice of a jury only for capital offences and I do so now."

Margaret Ransom's money was found in Waddell's saddle bags and her possessions were plainly stacked onto the cart in preference to bags of grain.

Edward went through the form of a trial. Margaret Ransom and her maid gave evidence; the accused were given chance to speak, found guilty, sentenced and hanged. It was a gruesome hanging: a halter around the neck before being hauled up with a rope over a tree branch. Waddell's pinion came loose and he was able to clutch up at the rope. It took some time for his struggles and kicking to subside. The man who had shot the child also took a long time to die.

"That was shoddily done, Phil."

"Aye, sir. Not done this sort of thing before. But it will teach the other bastards a lesson. They cannot come into our county and do as they will."

It was decided that Margaret Ransom could not stay in the ruins of her home, and one of the farm carts would be used to take the family possessions into their Bath home. Edward promised that the bodies of Alice the cook and her daughter would be taken for burial in consecrated ground, not dumped into the mass graves of those killed in the battle. At the same time, Waddell's men had been allowed to continue their legitimate forage, emptying barns and storage areas of anything that was authorised by the king's order. Eventually, they led their carts away towards Melksham and Devizes.

"Party of horsemen approaching, sir. King's colour, yellow sash as a pennant."

Edward was detailing off two of his men to escort Margaret Ransom to Bath as the horsemen approached.

"Nick Stanning!" exclaimed Edward. "I thought you would be leading your musketeers off to Bath?"

"So I should be, but after the fiasco of this Lansdown battle I have to retire my force back to Devizes – what's left of them." Nick grimaced. "I lost thirty-seven men, killed just driving off the rebel dragoons from the hedges at the base of the hill. I've less than two hundred left who can fight, and no powder left. What goes here, Ed?"

"Looting, rape, murder, and arson to boot."

"And you dispensed justice?"

"It is my right, Nick. This was a bad business." He pointed to the swinging bodies. "They were sent to collect fodder – that's bad enough – but then killed one woman and child and raped another girl. You can see the people on the farm are good God-fearing folk who have friends and relations. This outrage gives more recruits for parliament, and blackens the king's name."

"Lord Hereford tries to enforce discipline but Prince Rupert gives troops leave to plunder."

"He's not fighting in the 'German States' now. We have to win the peoples' support."

"This hanging wasn't wise, Ed. Lucky for you, this man's commander is one of those killed. Chaos is everywhere. You will not be called to account."

"I do not serve 'luck' Nick. I serve justice. Has Lord Hopton not restored order?"

"He is half-blinded and quite deaf. Half a dozen Parliamentary dragoons attacked our supply wagons. One wagon carried all our remaining powder. It exploded and Hopton was close by. Several men of note were killed but Hopton recovered his senses, if not his sight. Lord Hereford is all confusion as usual, and most of the prince's horsemen have fled back to Oxford."

"The battle started well for us. What happened? What went wrong?" questioned Edward.

"Grenville led his Cornish pikemen in a bloody, stupid uphill charge at their position, against musketeers crouched behind a drystone wall and two cannon dug into the side." Nick shook his head sadly. "Hopton ordered us to follow in support. It was carnage on that slope. The idiot never tried to bring our own cannon to bear – just a mad charge."

"I saw that. Our lightweight Falconet cannon that could have blasted the wall away turned it into their death trap."

"Grenville is dead," continued Nick.

"No great loss. The man was mad."

"Sir Bevil Grenville?" butted in Margaret Ransom.

The men had nearly forgotten her and that she could overhear all they said.

"The Cornish devil! God works in His own way."

"He does indeed," said Nick. "God has rid us of a lunatic. If He would take Prince Rupert as well, we could organise an army in the west to match their general." He turned to Edward. "Who is this lady, Ed? What is going on?"

Edward explained, and Sir Nick Stanning looked pained.

"It's not possible, Ed. I cannot allow Parliamentary supporters back into Bath with news of our disarray. Waller's force is intact. I doubt he lost two hundred men in total, and he has powder."

"Mistress Ransom is not a spy. She has no knowledge."

"She knows enough now, due to my loose mouth," said Nick grimly.

"If she gave her word…"

"Never!" flared Mistress Ransom. "I cannot give my word to thieves and murderers; agents of the Man of Blood!"

"Enough. Enough of this!"

"What will you do? Kill me too?"

Both men ignored this outburst.

"I could take Mistress Ransom back to my home for a few days. Once the retreat is completed safely, she can go where she will."

"Regretfully, Edward, I had two orders. The first, to chase up stragglers and foragers, and the second to look out for one Sir Edward Peverell, personal adviser to—" Nick moved them away from Margaret Ransom. "Personal adviser to Prince Rupert."

"I cannot understand why he wants to see me. He takes no advice, even from experienced commanders," declared Edward.

"He will be at The Crown Inn – in disguise – this evening. I suggest you take rooms there for yourself and this noble lady." Nick turned and bowed to Mistress Ransom.

"I am not noble. I am a gentleman's wife."

"Either way," said Nick, "you and your maid can have a comfortable room and parlour under Sir Edward's charge. Or be confined to the barn, a prisoner under guard."

CHAPTER 8

John had tried to phone Judith on the Monday after their walk to Chapel le Frith, but she didn't pick up. It was a week later before she phoned him in a strained voice to say that her very sick father was now settled at home, and sorry she hadn't returned his calls. John had arranged to meet with Simon Ransom to discuss renovation of the central staircase that Alf had proposed. Unfortunately, Judith explained, Simon was away and could she discuss things with him instead? All very formal, nothing even mildly friendly. Eight days ago she had wanted to share his bed! At least they had arranged a meeting – he could take it from there.

Monday morning started well for John. He visited one of several work sites he had running – some restoration work on an old mill – and was pleased with progress and the quality of craftsmanship. The owner of the mill was grudgingly complimentary; he had wanted John himself to be on site but admitted that all was well.

By mid-morning, John was on his way to Peverell House and unsure how he should react to Judith. She would be there with her father, either as company for him or still arranging his nursing care and treatment. Should he feign a distant contractor role, or treat her as a prospective lover? His journey to Calne and Peverell House was, however, interrupted by a frantic call from Ted Hughes, one of his craftsmen working on an extension to The Grange, a Georgian house, built in Bath stone. It was being converted 'tastefully' into a select bijou hotel. The latest section had to blend in with the old Georgian façade, but the new work along the side elevation was to be mock-Tudor stonework.

Ted had arranged for an apprentice to arrive early and take in a delivery. Keen to impress, Kevin, aged eighteen, had demanded to see some samples of the stone. The delivery driver refused. Kevin had driven the JCB across the back of the lorry, blocking its tailgate, preventing it from unloading. By the time Ted arrived the two men were near to blows.

"I had to back Kev up," Ted explained to John. "Bit extreme but he's a good lad. Lucky I did. Opened a pallet and the stuff behind the first layer was fucking crap. I wouldn't use it for infill."

John had diverted to The Grange and found a total stalemate. The driver refused to take his load back to the quarry; Ted wouldn't allow him to unload. The client and owner of the house, Thomas Atkins, wanted his driveway cleared and was threatening to call his solicitor. By the time John had phoned the quarry owner, got the lorry moved, and placated Atkins, the morning was gone.

"I'm sorry this happened, Mr Atkins," John had said. "Neville Oolite has always been a good supplier. The lad on site was just doing a spot-check, sort of a quality audit."

"Good job he did. I got up to see for myself."

John winced.

"Bugger 'elf an' safety, I wanted to see what was going onto my property," Atkins continued. "Your lad, Kevin, explained it all to me quite clearly. Hard worker I've noticed, seems to be running the job for your foreman."

It was true, thought John. Ted was a good craftsman but he would prefer to be at his tools and leave the paperwork to Kevin.

"I won't poach your workers, but if you have to let young Kevin go at the end of his apprenticeship, I could find him a good job."

"I doubt he would take to hotel work," John smiled. Kevin had a bit of a temper and a biting tongue. "He wants to finish up as a master mason. I hope he will be working for me."

"I've other interests where he could fit in," said Atkins. "Anyway, John, I suggest you consider your choice of supplier. I know several in the Mendips, over near Shipham."

Later, John checked the load with the quarry owner, Neville Oolite, who agreed to supply a fresh batch.

"What's the problem, Nev?" John asked later over coffee. "I heard another guy had a load of crap stone a few weeks back. You trade to the top end of the craft market, mate. You lose your reputation and you're finished."

"I know, John, it's a real problem. I can't run the business and be checking details and quality. I've got to oversee machinery being refitted on site. And I'm late with the tax return. It goes on and on. Since Jeremiah retired the yard is going to pot. I got this new guy, ex-Hanson quarries, ISO 9000 qualified, the lot. F-ing useless. Trying to install some new computerised quality control system and—"

"Sack him."

"I will, he's only on six months' probation. Sort of job could suit you, John."

"No. No." John paused. "I do know a woman who's qualified though, needs a part-time job."

"A woman, in a quarry like mine? She'd need to be desperate. What's her technical background?"

"Power Electronics, I think."

"What does she know about stone?"

"Sod all, but I could fit her up with one of my guys as an inspector. She does the system work, fills in the forms, and audits your safety procedures, if you've got any. Kevin is at the workface, eyes open. He'd miss nothing."

John thought he'd rather blasted off early here. Well, Judith had said she was looking for a part-time job. It would give Kevin a few months' experience away from the basics. Good for his City and Guilds course.

"Look, Nev, you're desperate," he continued. "A few more cockups like this and you're done for. Give these two a try. Zero hours contract for three months, no liabilities either way." John was sure Kevin would be up for it if there was a bit more money. Ted would moan at losing his apprentice, but how would Judith react?

It hardly seemed worth travelling out to Peverell House, but he arrived late afternoon and tracked Judith down in the office, usually her brother Simon's domain.

"Hi," he tried as he knocked at the open door and strolled in.

Judith started and looked up. "The wandering mason! I thought you had abandoned our project."

"Well, I did text."

"Sure, I know. Bit of a relief you're late, I've been up to here." She lifted her finger to her lip in mock fashion.

"Top lip?" he interrupted. "Up to your top lip in sewage?"

"Not quite, just trying to arrange things for Dad, day care nursing... a few business things."

"Is it bad news, then?" John said, noting her tearful, stressed look.

"The worst. Bone cancer in his neck, completely inoperable. They didn't tell us at first, wanted a top guy to see him."

"I thought it was a heart problem?"

"That's just a symptom. He had a pacemaker implanted to keep his heart going, but eventually..."

"Shouldn't he be in hospital?"

"Not much they can do," she sighed hopelessly. "Chemo or radio therapy would give him a few more months of misery. He's decided to let nature—" She shuddered out a sob. "Simon doesn't even seem to care."

Instinctively, John wrapped his arm around her shoulder.

"Oh, John. I can't cope with this. A few years ago Mum and Dad were like rocks for me... when I broke up with Mark. Now Mum's gone and Dad's dying." The rest of her words got lost in sobs.

John was uncomfortable and wanted to get away, but felt she needed a sympathetic listener. He really cared for her, but what did he actually want? To get her in his bed, or in his life? He didn't know. She calmed down after a while and dried her eyes.

"Sorry, John, no one else to talk to. Have to keep cheerful for Dad. He knows what's happening."

"No problem. If I can help in any way." God, a cliché for every occasion. "I suppose all you can do is keep him involved in things."

"Settling his affairs," she said drearily.

"Anything. Planning for the future, what to do with Peverell House. He doesn't seem the type for doing puzzles or watching daytime TV. I've been working up some costings for a renovation – do you think he'd be interested?"

"Maybe. The nurses keep saying Dad should lie flat and rest. He says what's the point? He's got a neck brace and can walk around a bit." They lapsed into silence again until she said, "Sorry I broke up a bit. Let's go and look at the staircase."

"Wait. This is probably out of place now, but were you serious last Sunday about looking for a part-time job?"

"How the hell could I take on a job, John, with Dad like he is? He needs me here—"

"Not all the time. You've arranged day and night nursing. It'd do you both good if you got away for a few hours – something new to talk about."

"Christ, John, I don't know. With all this I'm such a mess. I can't get over running out on you last Sunday, after our great day and—"

"Let's slow this down, shall we. Can we sit and chat over a coffee or something?"

"OK, good idea." She moved towards the kettle and cups at the end of the desk.

John was about to offer help but then thought it best to let Judith be in charge.

"Tea or coffee?"

"Tea, please. Well brewed, no sugar."

"Builders' tea?"

"What else."

As they sipped their drinks, she listened as John explained Neville Oolite's problems and how she and Kevin could help him out.

"I know it's not much of a career move from Dyson to a clapped-out quarry, but there's nothing like being in work for helping you get the next job."

"Is that why you builder types spin jobs out?" she asked with a ghost of a smile. "I've got lots of work on, guv, but for a price I could fit you in."

"Rumbled at last, our greatest secret." John was pleased to see a spark of Judith's humour back.

"Your greatest secret is how you run a business at all when you have stupid ideas like this one."

"Have you got something else on offer?" he asked.

A hint of a nervous smile hovered around her lips. "Is last Sunday's vacancy still open?"

"Of course. Seriously, have a think about the quarry."

"I suppose it would give Dad a laugh. Simon would want to know if it's worth taking over. Did he speak to you about your firm?" Judith asked curiously.

"Polite refusal. I don't need extra investment, or a partner."

"So it was just a one-night stand you offered me after all, not a partnership. Come on, let's go and inspect stair rails."

From Simon's office they traversed several rooms, a corridor, and servants' back staircase into the first-floor main room, eventually to the living space where he had seen Penny sewing. The memory of that visitation still made him feel uneasy, a chill sensation despite the hot day and sun streaming in through open windows.

"Is it too cold?" Judith commented, noticing his hesitation on entering the room. "I've opened up the windows and shutters to let some air in."

Judith had bare legs, fitted knee-length shorts and a light-yellow t-shirt. She was the one who should be feeling the cold. Her father's diagnosis had obviously hit her hard, but she had still made an effort to dress nicely despite her eyes being red from rubbing or crying, hair hardly brushed. He felt like giving her a hug, but worried it might be misunderstood, or lead to a flood of tears she would regret later.

They discussed restoration, replacement and costs, all in a business-like way. They initially agreed that the only realistic option was to remove and conserve the original staircase and replace it with an authentic reproduction. This was what Alf the carpenter had costed out for John. Judith was amazed at the final figure.

"John, this is ridiculous. I could buy a house for less."

"Perhaps at Barrow-in-Furness. Seriously, this is a 'built as original'. Same woods, traditional working methods."

"Simon would never fund it, tight-fisted bugger. He'd suggest selling the original and putting in something basic. Could we have a concrete replica?"

John shrugged. "Nothing underneath to support the weight. That's why this is so finely made."

"I'll discuss it with Dad, something to talk about." Judith wiped a tear away, disguising it by pulling her fingers through her untidy hair.

As they were staring at the sad surroundings, juggling ideas in their heads, Judith suddenly took in a sharp breath.

"John!" She put an unsteady hand on his arm. "Do you remember me hearing ghosts? There is something here now. Like a strange presence."

John had felt it as soon as they entered the room. Judith searched his face.

"I felt something, too. A cold feeling?"

"Yes. Someone is watching us."

John was staring around wildly, fixated by the window seat where Penny had been, hands shaking slightly.

"Let's go," Judith whispered, urgency in her voice.

"No, not yet," John said, reluctant to let this moment pass. "We'll see if someone comes."

"Sod that, I'm out of—" A phone was ringing downstairs in the office and it was as if a spell had been broken. "Got to answer that, see you, John," and she ran from the room.

A shocked, and frankly disappointed, John was left standing in the room alone.

∞

"So, Cousin John. Did you bed her in my house?" said a playful female voice.

John dared not turn to look. In front of him the ancient and decrepit double helix staircase was shimmering and replenishing into its original polished glory. Colourful tapestries, painted masterpieces and ornate decorations had returned. Heart pounding, John turned to face the speaker.

"I said, Cousin John, did you bed her? And in my house too..."

"No." His voice was little more than a whisper.

"I hope my entering did not disturb your pleasure."

Penny was smiling mischievously and looked even lovelier than he remembered. Her arms were open. He couldn't lose this opportunity, and quickly seized her in a frantic hug.

"Steady, John," she giggled.

He shifted to face her and kissed her in earnest, relieved when she returned his kiss, moulding her body to his.

She moved her mouth to his ear and murmured, "John, I asked you if you have bedded her?"

"No," he protested. "Why would you think such a thing?"

She didn't move away from him, still enjoying their embrace, stroking his neck. "The way she was looking at you, the way she fled from the room in embarrassment when I entered. She was only wearing her undergarments!"

Penny was smiling at him, but it was not the simple, fond smile of cousin to cousin – he felt there was something almost hungry in her expression.

"Undergarments?"

"Aye, her under drawers and sark."

John looked blank.

"Sark, shift, camisole, underbodice. What a lady should wear under her top dress. And I see, John, that you have no breeches, shirt or jacket. Were you undressing or had you finished your tryst? I wish I had arrived early."

Penny tried to pull gently away but he held her firm. Instead of safety boots and overalls he was wearing sandals, shorts and a t-shirt. Not a bow or fancy ruffle in sight.

"I must explain that I come from a future time. Our dress has changed. This is perfectly respectable wear."

"Oh, John," Penny touched him fondly, "you are such a liar. Would a lady wander around the house wearing so little? Her servants might see her. You were about to disrobe further and—"

"No, no, not at all. Such dress is deemed perfectly acceptable, even outside in the summer."

"Do not pull away. As a respectable woman I should not look at a man so undressed." She turned her face away, feigning coyness. "How can you convince me you were not about to take advantage of that distressed woman?"

"Convince you? I could tell the truth, swear on a holy book—"

"Or a holy object?

"Anything."

Penny chuckled and stepped away from him, took one of his hands, and placed it on his groin. "Say after me: I swear by what I hold most dear that I will speak with truth, omitting nothing, and will not try to deceive."

John did so, trying to keep a straight face.

"Now, Cousin John, why could you not love that woman?"

"Because I love another, totally and utterly."

"There is no man alive so constant. Who is this woman that you love?"

He looked intently at her. "It is you. Someone I have met only twice." John made an effort to compose himself before saying, "I am not Cousin John or his ghost. I am John Townsend, master mason. My own man. We have met only twice; it is crazy, impossible, but..." He shuddered with suppressed emotion.

Penny seemed to comprehend, or at least wanted to understand. "Shh, say nothing further. Our whole meeting is impossible." She paused, as if hoping to make some sense of it, then added, "But Edward saw you at the window. He and I have seen this Judith weeping. It is all very real, and yet not real."

Their embrace had fallen away, and he stood gazing down at the rich colours of the elaborate rug covering the oak floorboards, which would last another four hundred years.

"Stop this sadness, John," she chided. "This is a happy house. Outside the world is gone mad in the revolt against our king, but in here Edward and I are happy. We leave care at the door. Edward has no objection to me exchanging a filial kiss or hug with Cousin John, so whatever you say, you will remain as my cousin."

"And if I overstep Edward's mark?"

"You would not. I will not let you," she laughed. "And if you trifle with his 'property' he has threatened to use his pistols loaded with silver ball. If he were here, I'd call him. He promised you a pipe of tobacco and a tankard of ale."

∞

Later, despite Penny's lecture about theirs being a happy house, it was a dejected John who sought out Judith. He would have just sidled off home but had to pick up some items he had left in the office.

"Did the ghost come?" she asked, looking up from her computer spreadsheet. Her expression changed to one of concern. "God, John, you look awful."

"Yes. I've just seen a ghost – a ghost of sorts. One who kisses like... like a very beautiful woman. Feels like..." he stammered to a stop. "Sod it! Whatever universe she lives in, she loves her husband and is faithful to him."

"You're smitten!"

"Totally." He slumped in a chair, near to tears. "Any encouragement and I would have tried... foolish. I've hardly met her. Too bloody stupid."

"It was like that with me when I met Mark," Judith whispered. "'A over T' as we engineers say. I don't think it was ever as intense for him. When he bunked off, I was destroyed."

They sat in silence for a while, reminiscing.

"Not much help is it," said Judith. "Saying it's worse for me."

"No."

"You must have felt the same for your wife, Helen?"

"Not really. We met at the tech where she did computer stuff. More like great mates who liked the same things – sex, walking... even seemed to get on living together for a while. Hardly romantic."

"Then she left."

"That's it. Probably best in a way. I can hardly breathe when I am with Penny. It was never like that with Helen."

"I'm not going for the *grande passione* again," stated Judith resolutely. "Your idea of best mates who enjoy the same things, even sex, is much safer. No sorrow or wretchedness to endure." She smiled, trying to shift the solemn mood. "Hey, isn't it your club's 'Select Adults Only' session tonight?"

"Saturday's the night for adults-only but it should be OK on a Friday."

"I took a flyer and booked a table in the Green Lantern – and then on to Vespa, if you're up for it?"

"Seems just the job. Your Dad be OK?"

"Simon's coming over and we have a night carer arriving at ten. You need a night out to lay the ghost."

"Is it 'Lay the Ghost' or..."

CHAPTER 9

The Crown was a large rambling inn that provided basic accommodation and stabling for travellers from the Cotswold Hill roads leading down into Bath. At the top of the three-mile descent into the city most coaches and wagons needed additional horses for the steep road. The Crown, in partnership with The White Hart at the lower level, provided such a service but little else. Margaret Ransom wasn't pleased with the bedroom and small private parlour she had been forced to hire at a 'disgraceful' rate from her restored money. She was even less happy that the main door to her room was locked. Her only access was from the parlour shared with Edward Peverell's room. Margaret Ransom was virtually a prisoner.

By the time Edward and Margret Ransom arrived at the inn, Nick Stanning had arranged a small back snug of a room for a secret meeting with Prince Rupert and his brother, Maurice. The princes slinked into The Crown with theatrical style – broad floppy hats and dark brown cloaks; their air of mystery somewhat dispelled by the landlord's deep bow and 'my lord' style of address. Rupert's infamous large dog was left to roam outside.

With food and drink ordered, Edward set out maps and explained his contact with a number of Bristol merchants. Prince Rupert was impressed with Edward's map of Bristol's fortifications, but not with ideas for an attack.

"You do not understand war, sir," said the prince dismissively. "There is no honour or gallantry in bombarding warehouses and business."

"The townsfolk care more for profit and trade than for the lives of parliament's defenders," Edward replied. "Fiennes knows he cannot defend the whole town of Bristol. There is not even a defensible wall linking the northern forts – only ditches." Edward paused and looked from prince to prince. They were not convinced, but he ploughed on. "As soon as the losses in men or materials begin to mount, Lord Fiennes, their commander, will feel his honour is satisfied and seek terms. We could avoid the carnage of a frontal assault."

Rupert did take Edward's maps and diagrams with him when he left, but still seemed fixed on the need for a frontal assault. Maurice hung back to speak with Edward.

"There is some merit in your idea, but my brother believes a sweeping victory would crush the rebels' morale. I will try to persuade him. If Lord Hopton and I had listened to you at Lansdown, we would be dining in Bath tonight."

After they had left, Edward was almost in despair and sorely tempted to bolt home to his Peverell estate; hang the consequences. He was, however, somewhat responsible for Margaret Ransom, and also wanted to know if Lord Hopton would regain his sight. Without Hopton's moderation, Prince Rupert would likely attack Bath or even Bristol, with just the remaining six hundred cavalry and two hundred dragoons against the superior forces.

Eventually, Edward roused himself from his despair and, after some personal preparations, requested Margaret Ransom join him for an evening meal in their shared parlour. The invitation was given in courtesy only and he was very surprised when she accepted. The lady explained she had already ordered a meal but they could share their food to extract something edible from the oafish landlord. Settling herself at the head of a large eight-seating table, she waited for Edward to sit at the far end.

"It is novel indeed for a Christian woman to sup alone with one who has supped with the devil," she said disdainfully.

Edward was considering her closely – tall and thin – far too bony and flat-chested for fashionable taste. Margaret Ransom's hair was austerely cut and as black as her puritan gown. He imagined her as being as capable of working with hill sheep on a foul night as she would be in polite society. He realised she was staring at him, awaiting an answer.

"If you consider me your gaoler," said Edward, "there is no impropriety in us eating together." He waved aside the wine that Margaret's maid attempted to pour. "What is this talk of the devil?" he asked. "The men I met are good Christians, and Protestants to boot."

"And one has a giant white dog, a poodle, the Devil's agent who advises and protects his master, Prince Rupert." She sipped her wine. "God, this is muck, muck turned to vinegar. Well left alone, sir."

"As our Lord Jesus blessed wine, a devil such as I spurn it. I shall have beer instead." To the maid, he said, "Girl, take this coin and ask the landlord to tap a new barrel and keep it for my use only. Bring back a full jug."

"Tell him," added Margaret, "that if the beer is as foul as the wine, this devil's high master will blast the inn with lightning!"

As the maid left, Edward asked, "Ah, pray tell me, without the aid of witchcraft, how did you know who my visitor was? He wore plain clothes."

"And allowed his devil-hound to shit in the grass outside my window. There is not such a dog outside of Hell."

"Well observed, my lady. Nick was right not to allow you back in Bath. I expect you attend on me tonight to glean more information."

"Hardly. All is so transparent. You have been plotting to sack Bristol with that foreign fiend, Rupert."

"Not at all," replied Edward, cutting himself beef pie with some trepidation. "The king will have Bristol. All the surrounding towns except Bath are ours. Rupert has fifty thousand men against a garrison of less than two thousand. The town's defences are old and crumbling."

"Not the northern forts."

"They are not complete, and no wall joins the forts. Nathaniel Fiennes should order the ships from the port, destroy his ordnance, and seek good surrender terms."

"He will not!" She did not sound convinced, and followed Edward's example by cutting a sliver of the pie and then took a slice of the cold meat.

Silence descended. The maid returned and poured Edward some beer. He tasted it and nodded approval. Margaret accepted a full mug. Not too severe a puritan, Edward thought wryly.

"My plan was to force his hand with minimum bloodshed," said Edward, chewing savagely on the beef. "Unfortunately, both Rupert and Fiennes want a bloodbath, to satisfy their honour. I do not want to see more carnage – I have friends and some family in Bristol – and the king cannot keep winning battles by sacrificing men. It is all so bloody stupid."

"I believe you are sincere," said Margaret.

"Even if I converse with demons?"

"We should try to eat a civil dinner," suggested Margaret. "The pie is not half bad, nor the cold mutton, but I fear the chicken was too long dead before cooking."

"Aye, smells worse than the wine. Not surprisingly, the beer and cider is well brewed. Draymen and carters are very particular and are oft moved to violence at the taste of bad ale."

They ate slowly and convivially, conversing little and avoiding contentious topics.

∞

Edward stripped off his soiled clothes and washed, appreciating the luxury of a real bed with nearly clean sheets. Memories of the previous day's battle and the hanging made it difficult for him to sleep. He had barely started to doze when he was woken by a thunderous banging on the door, and Sir Nicholas Stanning burst in. Edward snatched up his pistol.

"What-ho! Are we attacked?" he cried out.

"No, Ed. I just needed to check you had not been seduced by our Parliamentarian puritan."

"Not likely on several counts, Nick," he said climbing, into his britches and tucking in the two-week-old shirt. "She is in her chamber. I heard the maid going down for hot washing water."

"The one who was ravished? She looks quite recovered."

"Time will tell…"

"Look, Ed, I am sorry to bring bad news but Prince Maurice wants you and your small group to scout around the outskirts of Bath. Intercept any messengers, watch out for any sign of Waller deciding to follow us as we retreat to Devizes."

"I am not in the army, Nick. I am not to be ordered." A pause. "How long for?"

"Just a day or two. Back here each night, and then send Lady Ransom home to her husband."

Reluctantly, Edward had been forced to agree. If General Waller did break out from Bath at least Edward could give Hopton and the prince some warning. He wrote a letter to Penelope explaining the change of plan and had one of the inn boys ride with it to Peverell. In the few hours to spare before his patrolling activity started, Edward arranged for the local vicar at Cold Ashton to fit in a funeral for the cook Alice and her daughter. It was a rushed affair; the vicar was leaving to say prayers at the mass graves on the nearby hillside.

∞

Later that evening, Edward again joined Margret Ransom for dinner. Although she had been allowed to walk outside in the sunshine, close to the inn, he expected to find her ill-tempered and poor company. Instead, she seemed disposed to be friendly and had personally supervised the preparation of their evening meal in the kitchen below.

As the dinner progressed, Edward learned of Margaret's family, and that her second husband, stepdaughter, and her own daughters had moved safely down into Bath town before the Royalist advance. In turn, he spoke of Penny and Peverell, and how he had business dealings with Margaret's husband, Oliver Ransom.

"You are much alike in character and build. You could be brothers," she observed.

"We discussed it ourselves last year at the wool fair market, but as far as we can tell, our families are not related."

"No," she mused.

The evening light was fading as their conversation ran out, and the maid cleared the table before retiring to sleep. Edward was about to take his leave and turn to bed when Margaret gestured for him to stay.

"Pray, do not go yet. More beer?" She seemed uncertain, almost embarrassed and hesitant.

"No, thank you," replied Edward. "My limit is one glass of wine or a pint of ale."

"Commendable."

"Not really. In my youth I committed many indiscretions – sins even – after drinking heavily."

"God forgives sinners who repent and change their ways."

"Amen to that."

Uneasily, Edward settled back into his chair, sensing she had more to say.

"You have no child – as yet?"

"No, Penny and I hope... Perhaps once the stress of war is over."

"And no 'wild oats' from your indiscretions?" she asked.

"I was very young – seventeen; she married and only nineteen. Her husband was away. There is no excuse, the husband was much older and well..."

"He was not up to the tup," she said most seriously. "Did the girl lead you on, perhaps she needed the child very much?"

"I said I make no excuses for my actions. The husband accepted the child as his own, born full size after seven months, as it was."

"But possible."

"In my heart I knew the babe was mine. I pay an allowance to the mother towards his upkeep. He is now eleven years old." Why was he telling her all this?

"Does your wife know of this?"

"Of course, we have no secrets." He smiled to himself. "Penny is an extremely attractive woman. Before we met, she had many admirers of her own."

"My husband had three children by his first wife, but only the eldest girl survives," Margaret confided quietly.

"Not an uncommon loss, but tragic all the same," said Edward. Despite his rule, he refilled his tankard from the beer jug.

"I have had two girls," said Margaret, "Two daughters but no son to take over my farms after me. This despite Oliver paying me every attention a Christian woman could expect for near on three years."

Edward stifled a yawn. He was tired from hours in the saddle and desperately wanted his bed. He had no idea if the conversation had any meaning and had little interest, but Margaret ploughed on.

"It is not uncommon," she said. "A ram that has fathered hundreds and a ewe that has lambed before may not produce together."

"That's why we have several rams in each flock and change them around partway through the tupping season," Edward agreed, smiling.

"Aye, change the ram," said Margaret playing with her empty tankard.

She was staring intently at Edward who became suddenly alert.

"Thankfully people are not sheep, and holy scripture would consider 'changing the husband' a sin. Aye, adultery," he said.

"I think that would only be the case if the act were done in pleasure or in lust," she replied. "Oliver could die in Bath, in the next siege. I am thirty-eight, too old to take on another marriage."

Edward stood up to go but Margaret continued talking.

"I know I am asking a lot, but if you would lie with me tonight, I am sure there would be a good outcome."

"Would you tell your husband?"

"No."

"And let him raise another man's child?"

"I will be with him in two or three days. He is a lusty man – we would never be sure."

"I took you for a Godly woman, Madam."

"I am. This is not sin, it is stock breeding. Nothing to do with religion."

"Goodnight. I am going to my room."

"I am not affronted, sir, and the door to my room will remain unlocked."

As he left her, Margaret launched into a passionate tirade. "Edward, there is no love or passion in this, no betrayal of your wife's trust. It is my destiny to have a boy that Oliver cannot give me. I have buried one husband; I've run the estates while he runs the cloth business. I know my own mind and I will have what I want!" She stopped abruptly in embarrassment, realising what she was saying. Awkwardly she continued, "God... I sound like a preacher in the pulpit, but instead of speaking the Lord's word I am justifying my sin..."

∞

Later, much later, Edward awoke into the total darkness of his room. It was before the first glimmer of pre-dawn light. He got up from the low truckle bed (at least the bed ropes were tight and the sheets clean) and reached for his shirt. He decided not to wear it – it was not clean. Despite the inn laundry's effort it still smelled sweaty and soiled from days of travel and nights of sleeping outside. Fumbling in the dark, he lit a candle and made his way through the parlour to Margaret's room.

Margaret Ransom was startled at the tap on her door but relaxed as the naked figure of Edward advanced toward her bed. There was a screech from the maid who was sleeping on the floor mattress.

"Don't let 'em do it to me!"

"Lie down! This one seeks the mistress, not the maid." Margaret smiled at Edward in the flickering candlelight as he slipped under her sheet. "I am pleased you are come." She stretched out her hand and stroked down his stomach. "Well-equipped as I expected." She hitched up her nightgown to her waist in an unladylike manner and then raised her arms for him to remove it over her head. "I am still in prime condition, as you see."

What followed did give them both pleasure, but as she had suggested, there was neither love nor lust between them. Afterwards they dozed beside each other, until the maid awoke them, asking if she should go down and find breakfast.

"I must get back to my room. Sir Nicholas Stanning will be calling early."

"Not yet, sir. A man cannot prove his gallantry by standing fire just the once. I feel the pistol is reloaded."

CHAPTER 10

It was a weary and elated Edward Peverell who, with ten of his mounted dragoons, clambered down off his horse in the courtyard of Peverell House. Despite his frequent letters to Penny over the last month, he had not been able to send her advance news of his homecoming. She came running from the house.

"Edward!" she exclaimed in delight. "I am so pleased."

They embraced until the titter of Edward's men persuaded them to part.

"Wife," he whispered, "I am going to take you straight upstairs to bed."

"Not without bathing and shaving first. You stink of sweat and horse and gunpowder, and God knows what else."

"And so to bath, not bed? In that case, while water be heated, I will feast on honest food, not marching rations nor sustenance plundered from our foes."

Feasted, bathed and bedded, it was not until mid-evening that Edward and Penny settled to talk seriously. Both were in their nightclothes; she with a small glass of cider, he with his pipe and tankard of ale.

"Two tankards of ale in one day," she had chided him. "You will be a drinker yet!"

"It is but small beer, not enough to dent my reason or my manhood."

"I had noticed," she grinned. "But I fear you are not in the merriest of spirits. The war goes well for us. Most of the west is now for the king?"

"Aye. After Prince Maurice's brilliant victory at Roundway, Rupert feels he can march on Bristol, but we are buying every victory at great cost in men and horses."

Penny cuddled up to Edward. "The assault on Bristol will go badly, you believe?"

"It will be the worst yet. Rupert is determined to make a glorious frontal assault on the Northern Forts. He has enough men to eventually overrun them, but there will be carnage during the attack. Then Sir Nathaniel Fiennes will just surrender and ask for honourable terms."

"Is there no alternative, a chance to be more cautious?" she asked gently, getting up to fetch him fresh tobacco.

"I travelled into Bath with Prince Maurice and General Hopton. Now, with Waller's captured cannon, we have a battery of sixteen guns. The largest are only demi-culverin, but in a few days we could reduce the whole of Bristol's southern city wall to rubble."

"And then storm the breach?"

"Not really. We could reduce the southern wall from the river to the gate. The whole army could flood in. Outnumbered ten to one, Fiennes will ask for terms long before that."

"What will you do now?" she said quietly, hugging him close.

"Spend a few days at home with you, check on things in the estate, and then back to Bath and on to Bristol."

"Why?"

"One way or another, Bristol will fall to us – I have knowledge of trade and manufacture. We can organise the workshops and foundries to produce weapons for the king's army. There must be more guns for the musketeers. Hopefully support from France will arrive into the port."

"Have you heard of this puritan, Cromwell?"

"Aye, he comes from your part of the country. Member of parliament for Huntingdon, I believe. A godly man well regarded by the townsfolk." Edward's voice trailed off.

"He is now a commander of horse for parliament. My sister wrote some months ago and mentioned him."

"Did she say anything of a military nature?"

"Of course not," Penny said with a smile. "Rita is more interested in family than fighting. Is this Cromwell important?"

"I think he will be. He is very dangerous. Everything Prince Rupert is not: disciplined, cautious, and a master tactician. His horse and a regiment of foot held up our whole army for over a day in their fighting retreat near Lincoln. The men are well-equipped with pistol and sword, they train tirelessly, and men of ability are given command in preference to idiots with rank."

"Come, Edward, do not be so dour. Lincoln did fall to the king, didn't it?"

"It did, and Cromwell's withdrawal cost us two thousand men. He lost less than two hundred. We cannot—"

"I know, Edward, you have said. Did you also say each of his ordinary troops has a pistol?"

"Two! The best horse pistols. Like the ones I carry. They also have breast plate and helmet."

"But the cost... where does the money for all of this come from?"

"London, mainly. London craftsmen and merchants pump money into the parliament cause. They raise 'trained bands' of pike and musket to defend the city and provide paid recruits for the army. It's to match them that we must improve our musketeer numbers."

They sat huddled together in gloomy silence.

"We've had a successful year in the field," Edward murmured. "If a costly one. But if we cannot win or come to terms with parliament in the next twelve months, then we will lose the war outright. Courage and loyalty will not be enough to match the money and manpower of London and the south."

"Is money, then, the key to this war?"

"The key and the cause. The king has never had sufficient from parliament to meet his needs, his extravagances."

"He has been a spendthrift, it's true," said Penny, "but he had to support the Protestant nations of Holland and Germany against France and Spain."

"The world is mad," stated Edward. "The Protestant rulers that our King Charles helped now support parliament. And the Catholic king whom he opposed shows support for him."

Penny got up from his lap and asked softly, "When do you leave, my love?"

"In two, possibly three days," he replied.

"In that time we must finish collecting up all we can spare that is of value and transport it to Bath. As we planned, we must sell some of our surplus to raise money for the king's cause before any panic starts and values begin to fall. There will be little enough, but if all good families did this it would help to re-arm the foot regiments."

Edward nodded sadly. "But we sell only half now. The other half should be hidden for our future need or bad times."

They held each other in solemn quiet for some time.

"Wife," Edward said softly. "I have changed my plan."

Penny looked up at him in confusion.

"I'll leave early tomorrow."

"But why? Edward, don't say—"

"You will stay here until all is in order, and then I would want you to join me in Bath." He caressed her hair and swept a curl away from her eyes. He cared for her so much but the king's affairs were urgent. "I fear our time together is precious and I want you with me in Bath. At first, I shall lodge with Master Finch, my agent, and then rent a house or rooms for your arrival as soon as possible."

"At least tonight we are together."

Penny Peverell enjoyed lying peacefully in bed with Edward. She also enjoyed and joined in enthusiastically with the activities that preceded lying peacefully in bed, but this was very nice: the cool summer morning sun streaking in through the window, crimson and yellow silk bed-hangings thrown back, Edward sleeping beside her.

It was like living with a furry bearskin rug that she could snuggle into. She had often wondered if she could fashion miniature plaits on his chest and under his armpits. From the gossip shared with other ladies and female cousins, she believed that this surfeit of hair was rather exceptional. His ardour and energy in bed (and any other convenient places) also seemed to be above the norm. A friend expressed some sympathy to her situation and suggested that Edward treated her like a tavern whore. Penny had replied that she had no knowledge of tavern whores, but was most grateful for her husband's attentions.

That morning, as on many others, she reached down under the bed covering and started to gently stroke him into wakefulness. Were his feelings for her love or lust? She had no idea, but as long as his attentions were constant and intense, she didn't care. If she were recovering from her fourth pregnancy, as was Cousin Ede, it may be different, but there were many ways to enjoy love without conceiving an unwanted child. How she would like to be in that state. Yet despite all their endeavours, there were no children.

Edward was now awake, and greedily pulled her to him. How could one man give her so much pleasure?

There was a discreet but insistent rap on the door of their chamber. Carol the maid called out, "Madam, master, it is past seven o'clock."

"God's teeth. What of that?" muttered Edward as he kissed Penny and fondled her bosom.

"Madam, there is a messenger for Sir Edward in the hall. I believe the master is needed in Bath."

"Give him breakfast and some ale. My husband is fatigued and needs to sleep on."

Penny imagined Carol giggling as she tripped away. Second eldest of five children, who lived in a one-roomed cottage on the estate, she knew exactly how life was between husband and wife.

CHAPTER 11

John would not be seeing Judith until the following weekend. Simon was free for a few days, and he and Judith were supposedly spending the weekend with their father, discussing his treatments and such, though John anticipated there would be more arguing than anything else. Still, her absence left John to doze away the Saturday morning. At least, that had been his plan. Unfortunately for him – or some might say fortunately – he awoke early from the most erotic dream ever. He was with Penny in a hotel room and...

At first, he tried to get back into his dream with Penny, but it would not work. Later, fully awake, John made his decision: he had to force the issue with Penny. Sod changing the past or anything else. He was going back to Peverell to make love to her.

He had seen Penny several times and each visit had been more intimate. There had been real passion between them on their last meeting as she sat, skirt hitched up astride his knee, working herself into an ecstasy of excitement. Any red-blooded man should have rolled her over and had full sex with her. Faithfulness to Edward, loyalty to marriage vows. Yet if he had pushed the point, he was sure she would have enjoyed giving in to him. Showered, shaved and dressing carefully, he chose sandals, smart chino shorts and t-shirt – as little as possible. Judith and her father would be at the hospital, and no one else was working on site. The Great Hall would be sunlit and empty.

It was strange entering Peverell House when there were no other people present. The emptiness seemed to add to an air of decay and irrelevance to the modern world. As John walked through the abandoned spaces and climbed the servants' stairs to The Great Hall, some of his resolve and ardour evaporated, and many doubts began to enter his mind.

There was no dramatic change or the sensation of the room sliding back into the past as it had before– it was as if he had just naturally walked from his work into 1643. Instead of a forlorn dusty emptiness there was the same opulent decor and furnishing. In John's time the weather had been dingy and overcast; here in 1643 it seemed to have grown even darker. It was still mid-morning but outside summer rain lashed down, streaking across glazed windows, hammering incessantly. It was not how he wanted to experience the past, not how he wanted to meet Penny. He had the feeling that the house was being closed down; ornaments put away and dustcovers draped over some furniture.

"Oh, John!" came Penny's voice. "I am so glad you are come before I move away."

No rush towards him for a passionate embrace, no kiss with her body pressed tightly to his. What had changed? He forced a smile and advanced towards her. So excited, he could hardly breathe. He was confounded by a large tray of silver tableware that she was carrying into the room.

"I love you so much," he said, almost gasping out the words as he stood, undecided on how to act.

She turned away to place the tray carefully on a large packing hamper, "John, you know it can never be. I have been wrong to—" She was lost for words. "So wrong to lead you on, reliving my girlish dreams. Even if you were Cousin John, our romance would have ended as soon as I met Edward."

"But when we were together at our last meeting you—" John couldn't hide his disappointment or resist trying to touch her.

Penny backed slowly away. "I know. It was wrong, utterly wrong."

"But you enjoyed me kissing you, enjoyed our..." What should he say? "... embrace." John could see she was struggling with mixed emotions.

"It was no more than that, John, and we both know it. I am married to Edward and I love him. In two days' time I join him in Bath where he works for the king's cause."

"But I love you, you must know that. There has to be a way we can be together." Desperation was giving a hard edge to his voice. "I know you are in love with me."

She met his gaze, resolute and unflinching. "I am very fond of you, John. I became excited by your presence, but I have said it is Edward who I love; Edward who is my husband. Even if you were of my time and place, I would still be devoted to Edward."

"I cannot believe this. You were so—" John's voice faded.

"I enjoyed your attention, I enjoyed reliving my girlish games, but as I said before, it was ill-judged."

There was a long silence. John turned from her and walked unthinking to the window. The rain still fell on the tidy stables and the ornate Italian garden. He expected to see the ravaged present-day scene appear at any moment. Two strong, firm hands grasped him from behind.

"Please, John, let us not be unfriendly. We were both mistaken in that moment. I do not know who you are or where you are from, but you are not the ghost of my cousin, not of my time or place. We cannot be lovers, but please let us not be bitter."

He turned to face her. She was smiling. Again, he felt as if he would cry. Thirty-two years old and crying over a girl. He hadn't even cried when his wife, Helen, had left him.

"I love you so much," he whispered, wretched and near to tears. "No one else, never before—"

"Stop, John," Penny said gently. "You know this can never be."

"Can I kiss you, one last time?"

"Yes, if it is a family kiss, cousin to cousin, with no expectation on either side."

He moved towards her but she stopped him.

"One kiss, John, but consider if it is wise."

"I do not feel wise, I feel hollow and—"

"Stop, John. We will be like cousins, or nothing."

He leaned forward and pecked her on the cheek. "Halfway to paradise," he said. "I want to be your lover, but I am only your friend."

"Half is better than nothing," she replied sombrely. "I am lucky – many women I know would sell their soul to have a husband like you who is even a friend."

"And what now?" John said. "Do I leave?"

"No, John. You do not leave. You sit beside me, on this seat for two, shoulder to shoulder, but hands in your lap, not mine."

They sat in semi-easy companionship.

"And now?"

"And now you will tell me of your life. Are you a mason?"

He nodded, and in spite of the disappointment, returned her smile. He told her of his life, his work, his business, and even the failed marriage.

"You loved Helen?"

"Not really. Not when I thought about it after she left. Not when I met the real—"

"Stop." Penny put her finger to his lips. "And this Judith? I could see she ached to be your mistress. Have you lain with her yet? Come, come, tell all to Cousin Penny."

"We went dancing the other week, she came back to my flat, and..." he shrugged.

"The details!" she said with a laugh. "Do not be shy."

"We were intimate... passionate. She was very demanding."

"Did you enjoy each other?"

"Yes, very. But we slept badly together. She was restless and snored. There, Cousin Penny, are you satisfied?"

"No, of course not."

"A gentleman should never tell."

"But you are not a gentleman, John. You are a craftsman."

"It's still no," he said, and it was his turn to laugh. "Would you tell me what Edward does to you in bed, how he pleasures you?"

She met his gaze and said, "It is all rather dull. More interesting would be what I do for him: I am a very wanton wife! Ah, but we do not speak of my love life, we speak of yours. Now, this is very serious, John. Be you cousin or not. You laughed at sharing a bed with this Judith; 'Sad Judith' who still laments the loss of her lover, Mark. Do you love her, or do you trifle with her and prey on her weakness?"

Her question brought him up with a jolt. He should not have joked about Judith so trivially. "I don't love her," he said honestly. "But she knows that. She still loves Mark. At least we've both been honest with each other. We are friends who have fun and sleep together. Perhaps that will be our halfway to paradise."

"I wish you well, John. Don't throw away half a loaf in despair for the whole. A man truly starved of love and friendship would kill for a few crumbs."

"I didn't come here to discuss philosophy." He did not mean to sound so harsh.

"I know, but some things..." she shrugged sympathetically.

John was beginning to recover from his shock at her rejection. Despairingly, he tried to ease the awkward conversation away from her 'cousinly' advice.

"But now tell me – what is happening? Where are all your fine things?" He looked around the room. Most of the valuables had been removed, leaving the life-size portrait of Penny and Edward in full prominence; the same painting he had visualised in his own time when it been hidden and defaced.

"Edward is serving the king in Bath, organising munitions," Penny said proudly. "He will be there for some time and then on to Bristol, so I've packed away the house and will transfer to Bath to be with him. As the loving and dutiful wife that I am."

John choked back his jealousy. "Who are the ill-favoured couple in the picture?"

Penny chuckled, the happy sound making John catch his

breath. He couldn't help thinking of the passionate afternoon he had envisaged with her.

"That, my insolent friend, is our wedding portrait: Edward and Penelope Peverell of Peverell House, Wiltshire. Painted by Edward's friend, and one-time drinking partner, Billy Dobson. When Billy did this portrait for us, he was regarded as little more than a journeyman painter. He is now famous and the Royal Court Artist after that Van Dyke returned to Holland."

John studied the painting more carefully. As a craftsman he could appreciate the skill behind its accuracy to life.

"It is very fine; very realistic."

"Edward wanted us to be drawn as we were, with no long aquiline noses or other conventions," Penny continued. "Billy painted our faces from life, and then we left our wedding clothes with him to complete the finery of our raiment while we travelled to France for our 'wedding journey'."

John smiled teasingly at her. "I don't suppose you needed the clothes for that."

"I must confess that once we were, well, fully acquainted with each other, clothes became somewhat secondary considerations."

"I am surprised," said John, attempting to shift the talk away from Penny and Edward's sexual escapades, "that Edward does not have one of those pointy beards and bristling moustaches."

"Like the king and his courtiers? It would not suit him, and it would be scratchy to kiss him," Penny joked. " On campaign he usually allows his beard to grow naturally." Penny turned from looking at the striking portrait. "Do you know what Edward says? There is a belief that a man with a long thin nose has a long – well, you know. That is why they want to be painted with long noses.

All the fashionable portraits of men have the same nose."

"And what, my wanton cousin," John asked, "does a long nose in a woman signify?"

She punched his arm theatrically. "Pray, sir, how would I know? My nose is very short."

CHAPTER 12

Judith didn't like sleeping with John. What they did before sleeping was fantastic, but she did need to sleep. John was noisy and restless – snoring, blowing, and tossing about. It was awful. At three a.m. he was up, off to the toilet, then at six a.m. he was awake, suggesting sex, then racing around preparing for his work day. No wonder his wife had left him.

Alone at last, she snuggled back under the covers, enjoying the lingering smell of his body. She had just drifted off into a deep peaceful sleep when the mobile phone sounded like a siren. Shit, it was Mary, her father's night carer, hoping she would be back soon at Peverell House.

Shower, dress, quickly out the door without make-up or breakfast, and straight into traffic. The next time, if there was one, John would have to visit her in a hotel room and leave when the fun was over.

She arrived at Peverell House only half an hour late, to find her dad had been assisted by Mary to get up. Now showered, shaved and neatly dressed, he was in good spirits and joked, "I rather gathered from Mary that you had left somewhere in a rush, so I waited to join you for breakfast."

"Sorry, Dad. Bad night and overslept."

"Pleased to hear it," he said. "You need to get out more. Getting a bit old for wild nights at the clubs, though. Or was it a wild night in?" He seemed to think it all a joke. "Was it that John? Thought he would be a bit big for you. Might squash you flatter..."

"Don't be crude, Dad."

When Judith brought in their eggs and toast, her dad commented, "Two eggs? Exercise must be good for your appetite."

"Knock it off, Dad. I know a night out for you and Mum was two drinks and a game of crib at The Anchor but—"

"And crisps. Your mum always appreciated the finer things." He was meticulously chipping the top shell off his eggs, as she decapitated hers with a swift blow. More seriously, he continued, "The Anchor had a very good jazz evening – trad style – that we could dance to."

Her dad seemed far away with his memories for a while, and Judith looked across the table at him affectionately. This was precious time together.

∞

As Judith was eating breakfast with her father and planning to get him to the cancer clinic in Bath's Royal United Hospital, John returned back to his flat after an early morning site meeting. He knew that Judith needed to rush back to Peverell but hadn't expected his usually pristine flat to be in such disarray. A pair of skimpy pants and a wet towel were discarded on the floor, the bed unmade and a juice carton left out from the fridge in the kitchen. All trivial, but irritating when he attempted to keep everything in order. Then John remembered Judith had to get back before her dad's night carer left. She had arranged a day off from her new job at the quarry to take him to the hospital, and John felt guilty being such a grouch. It was all so irrelevant.

John thought back over the evening. Judith had offered to cook, heating two ready-meals a little and steaming some veg. A few drinks, off to Vespa's and then back to his flat for some rather wild sex. That had been the high point. She was the most restless bed-mate ever, and by three a.m. he'd got up and spent a few hours on the settee, half dozing and half listening to her flailing about. Finally, just as he had drifted off into real sleep, his alarm had gone, and whilst he'd considered asking Judith for another round, he knew he would be pushing it to get to his meeting on time.

He tidied up, ate breakfast, and tried to decide what to do. There was stone masonry waiting in the workshop and overdue paperwork there in the office, but he was just too tired. His legs ached from frantic dancing and his brain craved sleep. He headed back to bed.

Old and decrepit at thirty-two... those were his last waking thoughts that morning.

John awoke in the afternoon from the most erotic dream ever. He was with Penny in a hotel room and— No, stop! He was reliving the dream that had caused him to try to force himself on her. Embarrassment surged over him as he remembered how she had reacted: kind, understanding and even forgiving. So different from their first meeting – the kiss and embrace. Fully awake, he leapt out of bed and into the kitchen as if running away from his thoughts. Pacing the flat, he was an emotional wreck over his feelings for Penny and how he was treating Judith. He filled in the rest of the afternoon with admin work, just something to occupy his mind. Later, John resisted the urge to grab a beer or some wine and settled for strong Greek coffee on his balcony overlooking Henrietta Park. For once the splendid summer view failed to lift his mood. He had no plans for the evening and decided on a heavy gym session followed by a few beers – there might be conversation around the club bar that would break his train of thought.

He started to look for his kit, rummaging in his sports drawer for the fitness monitor and weightlifting gloves when his mobile buzzed – Judith. He didn't want to see Judith, or even talk to her. Not tonight. He let the ring time out and switched the phone to mute. No message.

Almost ready to leave, Judith rang again. It wasn't like her to try twice in ten minutes. Then the landline rang. He picked up.

"John Townsend."

"It's over, John."

"Over? What's over?"

"It's Judith. Your mobile's off. It's Dad. He... he had a stroke... died in the RUH."

John felt a surge of guilt for not answering her first call. What a rat. "I'm very sorry for your loss." The usual cliché. It made him wince.

"Probably for the best but very—" Her voice broke off.

"Where are you now? Can I help?"

"Hospital – stroke unit. Well, just outside. Simon and Nancy are away with the kids. They had no idea this would happen."

"You want me to come over?" John said gently.

"If you could. You're not busy?"

"Just gym night. Anything you want or need?"

"No, I'm OK, really. Could use... would be good to have you with me. All a bit unexpected. He was in fine form when I got home this morning. Stroke on top of everything else." Her voice trailed off, lost in tears. "I got an ambulance to bring Dad in. Could get a taxi back. Dad was in such pain, and frightened." She was descending into confused, disjointed phrases.

"Judith, I can be there in twenty minutes. I'll see you in the entrance by the hospital café. Get yourself sat down with a coffee and a sandwich or something. Don't keep standing up. And don't go outside with the smokers. I'll be there soon, OK? Promise."

John rang off. They could talk later. At least he could do something helpful for her; take her back to Peverell or bring her to the flat until she contacted Simon. He had been too young to remember his own personal bereavement, but he did not want her to feel abandoned and alone.

CHAPTER 13

Although Edward Peverell owned a small iron works and weaving shed in Bath, he was never sure of its role as a city. There was some industry there, but Bath was neither a wool town like Bradford further up the Avon nor a full industrial and trading town, as was Bristol further downriver.

Bristol had grown rich and expanded on the proceeds of trade, principally slave trade and wool export. Bath was largely confined within the ancient city walls, squatting in a bend of the River Avon. Confined by the river valley as well as the walls, it stagnated in the stench of humans and horses. Surprisingly to Edward, people travelled to Bath to drink the sulphurous water that rose from the hot springs, and that was purported to cure all manner of maladies. Cynically, Edward suspected that the town's gaming tables, whore houses, and horse racing were more of an attraction than the 'restorative water'.

Surveying a vista of the town from his agent's office in Westgate Street, Edward also speculated that the townspeople were similarly dual faceted. The town council and guilds had immediately and universally declared for parliament, but insisted that its soldiers be stationed outside the town walls. Now, with the Royalist's General Hopton and Prince Rupert in residence, the town population were all for King Charles. Even so, the small force of Hopton's men were billeted in surrounding villages while the town and guilds continued with day-to-day activities as if the war had gone unnoticed. Common soldiers were not allowed into the city but gentlemen officers with the ability to pay for entertainment were most welcome.

Edward had undertaken to arrange transport of the cannon needed for the bombardment of Bristol. He believed that this would lead to a quick surrender without the need for the frontal assaults and carnage that had lost so many men at Lansdown. For the lighter items, pack mules were the simplest and most reliable transport, but the four powerful demi-culverins, weighing over a ton each, could more easily be taken on barges. Even then, they would need unloading and portage at one point.

The arrangements were progressing well and not the greatest concern in Edward's mind. That morning the wealthy merchant, clothier and farmer Oliver Ransom, had respectfully begged a moment of Sir Edward Peverell's time to pay his respects and proffer his thanks for services to the family. All very correct and flowery, but Edward was concerned that Margaret Ransom may have had a resurgence of piety, leading to remorse and a confession to her husband. The business-like stockbreeding attitude to her coupling with Edward could well have changed and he might be obliged to fight a duel with a man he both liked and respected. He wondered whether puritans even fought duels...

Oliver Ransom was a tall upright man, similar in stature to

Edward, but older and dressed in puritan severe black. For all its lack of colourful finery, Oliver's jacket was of impeccable cut and the best quality cloth, his wide white collar trimmed with Nottingham lace. Fortunately, Edward's fears of a confrontation were totally ill-founded.

"Sir, on behalf of my wife and myself I must thank you for protecting my property and my wife's virtue."

"Please stop, Oliver. We are known to each other. There is no need for formality. My somewhat inadequate action was dictated by my duty as magistrate and my standing as a gentleman." Edward realised he was rambling on pompously but continued. "It is my regret that I arrived too late to prevent the destruction of your manor house and farm. Worse still was the death of the child, and Alice, her mother. Believe me, sir, I arrived at the scene of the outrage too late to save them."

"But you did save my wife's honour!"

Edward winced, remembering his night with Margaret Ransom.

Oliver continued, "Also, at your own expense, you arranged Christian burials for my servants who were murdered. I take much comfort that they lie in consecrated ground. I pray that with their lack of sin, they are with our Lord in Heaven."

"Amen," replied Edward hurriedly. "I did only as any Christian would do. Even the malefactor Waddell and his henchmen were given decent burials."

"You do not regret the hangings?"

"No. Their crimes were grievous and I acted within the law and my authority. God, and only God, may forgive them. I cannot."

"I agree," said Oliver. "Any person who murders deserves to burn in hell for eternity. God with infinite mercy may forgive, but like you, I cannot." Oliver paused for a moment, recovering from his outburst. "I am informed you are lodged here in Bath, giving aid to the Royalist army?"

"I do aid the king's cause to some extent but, more importantly, I seek to deflect the king's generals from violent action towards the townspeople of Bristol. I do not want to see any further loss of life, or more hardship."

"I fear, Edward, that we disagree, both in your support of King Charles and in your aim to persuade the Bristol garrison to surrender. But I consider you a friend as well as a fair man in business. And I am in your debt."

Edward was anxious to escape from any unwanted confidences and said rather dismissively, "Please, Oliver, let it pass. I only attempted to do as my conscience guides and I have strayed from virtue many times. You are not in my debt. I will hear no more of it. Let us remain friends as before."

"Agreed, although I wish it were in my power to—"

"No, enough."

Oliver Ransom rose to his feet. "I fear I must leave you to attend business in the town, but my wife Margaret desires to meet you and thank you for your gallantry. We both invite you to church on Sunday for divine service and later to join our family for Sunday dinner. If your wife, Lady Penelope, has arrived in Bath..."

Edward fell into a cold sweat, unable to contain his jumble of thoughts as Oliver was speaking. The last thing he wanted was a meeting between Margaret and Penny; possibly even more dangerous would be the exchange of gossip between their maids. He mumbled non-committal thanks and, with an effort, tried to pull himself together.

As they walked to the door Edward asked nonchalantly, "Oliver, I forget to ask – your wife's maid – has she taken any... hurt?"

"Ah, Queenie. Margaret does not think so, but it is early days. Unfortunately she revels in her notoriety, telling sordid tales to any who will listen." He shook his head sadly. "Queenie seems to take pride in the loss of her virginity. She will say anything to be the centre of attention amongst the other girls. Margaret finds her exaggerations amusing; I think it scandalous. I might decide to send her away from my house."

"There was no fault on her part, I can vouch for it," stated Edward. Then, on reflection and with a sense of desperation he remarked, "Possibly a new position would be advisable. A fresh start in another house?" The girl Queenie had been in the room while he was in Margaret's bed and was a gossip... an attention-seeking gossip.

Oliver hesitated to leave. "Edward, it is early days but," he stopped and took a deep breath, "Margaret believes she is with child. You know she has daughters by a previous marriage but she has no son. We are neither of us young and, well, we had almost lost hope of this blessing. If it had not been for your intervention, she would have been violated and I could never have been sure she was carrying my child." In a totally uncharacteristic gesture, he grasped Edward to him in a hug before he left.

CHAPTER 14

Penny had explained to John that she was closing up Peverell House and moving to Bath with Edward. John found it heartrending that she would no longer be living at Peverell – the only place they had ever been able to meet. She had firmly rejected his amorous advances, but he had hoped to see her, hoped for some contact, even just to talk and feel her near to him.

In John's own world, there was Greg Ransom's death and complex probate to finalise. Following his father's passing, Simon Ransom had become thoroughly opposed to any major expenditure at Peverell House, including renovations, though Alf Hidson had stirred up some interest from a museum regarding the staircase reconstruction, and with cash from John, that project was going ahead. Meanwhile, Judith was looking for her own place to live in Bath. She didn't want to live on her own at Peverell, even if the ghostly voices and 'other sounds' seemed to have stopped.

"In a way I sort of miss them," she confessed to John. "The house is less of a home, and without Dad the place is even more forlorn and empty."

To lighten her mood, John had changed the subject to her part-time job at the quarry. She explained that it was going well. After the first shock of seeing the pre-historic quality system and non-existent safety documentation, it was good to have something to occupy her mind.

"There was a lot of suspicion from quarrymen and masons at first, but we get on OK now," Judith explained. "Of course, having Kevin as my inspector helps a lot; he speaks their language and knows the techniques." She had decided to stay on until the procedures were up and running and then look for a full-time job elsewhere.

John and Judith saw each other once or twice a week for long hikes, nights out, and the occasional dinner. A lusty hour in bed often followed, but they rarely slept together the whole night. When they did, satisfied contentment soon ended in irritation, if not an argument. For all those niggles and spats, John knew his life was so much better for meeting Judith. He reflected on all this as he inspected stonework under the 'Oldest House in Bath', as Sally Lunn's bun shop claimed to be.

John was in the basement that had once been the original ground floor kitchen and shop, before the street outside had been raised in Georgian times. This place had already been two hundred years old in Penny's time, and there were Roman and Saxon foundations beneath that. Penny and Edward may even have eaten here. Would there be a chance of cinnamon butter at that early date? John's mind dwelled constantly on all the little things that Penny might have done. He couldn't help himself. He pulled away from these disturbing thoughts. He was meant to be costing some building repairs, not indulging in history or romantic dreams. Finished, he put away his electronic notepad with its facility for diagrams, photos and voice text. He climbed the steps up to modern-day ground level, considering what to have on a bun: cinnamon butter or lemon curd. Tea or coffee to drink? Could he ask for traditional cream and small ale?

He felt a sudden wrench at his mind, his vision fragmented into sections of ancient and modern. The disorientation and dizziness was worse than ever before. John was going back in time, but not to Peverell House. It could not be happening. His view of the room tilted then cleared, and he found himself in the first floor eating area of 1643. Now the bakery and shop were down the steps. This modest eating room with its rustic tables was empty, except for one woman in Jacobean dress with her back to the door, sobbing uncontrollably. Instinctively, he knew it was Penny. Momentarily he was too stunned to move but then rushed towards her, holding her in an embrace.

"My God, what's wrong?"

She sagged back against him. "Oh, John!"

"What has happened? Has Edward been killed?"

"No. I wish he had been. No, I do not mean that. I do not know what to think." Penny dissolved into more tears and profanities. "Edward's betrayed me. Everything I believed in..." It took some time for Penny to calm down. Turning on her stool, she clung to him. "Oh, John. I am so pleased you are come. I need a friend so badly. All I loved, all I hoped for, is gone. Forever."

John sat down on a bench beside her, a comforting arm around her shoulders. "Can you tell me what's wrong?" he said softly. "What has Edward done?"

She gulped as if unable to talk. Then a boy from downstairs arrived.

"What 'ee like, sir?"

"The same." John spoke slowly, trying to be distinct.

The reply was no more than a grunt as the boy left them, trudging sullenly down the open staircase to the ground floor bakery. If Penny had been going to confide in him, she had lost her way and dissolved into more sobs.

"I believed in him, John. I really believed in him. All Edward said – all lies."

"What? Has he—"

"He has lain with that whore Margaret Ransom. She claims herself a puritan, pure as my—"

John took her hand and shushed the outburst.

Penny lowered her voice but pressed on. "That hypocrite of a woman, all her pious preaching ways. Too old to get with child by her own husband, she tries for one with a younger man – my husband!"

"You are certain of this?" John was incredulous. "You must be mistaken."

"He confessed all to me this morning; confessed only because he feared it would become known from servants' gossip. The whore did it with him while her maid lay in the same bed chamber."

"Let us leave," he said, "get some fresh air."

"In this city of filth? An iniquity!"

She glowered at a group of people coming up to sit at another table, who were showing concern for Penny's distress. She fumbled in her belt purse and put down a small coin. John had no idea of its value. He followed her down the stairs, past the smoking bread ovens, and out into the street. The wholesome smell of baking and wood smoke was instantly submerged in the reek of animal dung and other excrement. He almost choked on the stench, made worse by the midday heat. Flies rose in swarms. No wonder plague was so common.

They were in a narrow lane that led down past Bath Abbey; an abbey made even more impressive by the shambles of wooden buildings around it. The lane opened out as it descended to the riverbank, with wharfs and makeshift jetties. In the distance a cluster of men were attempting to crane a cannon barrel onto a barge. Penny stiffened and came to a halt.

"See him there, all virtue and duty, about the king's work. I should shoot him down now, shoot him down and be burned for his murder." She pointed shakily to the imposing figure of the man directing the work.

John firmly guided her away from Edward and his men, westward along the towpath to where it opened out to water meadows and a floodplain. There was no stopping Penny now.

"I thought him scouting for the king's army before the battle on Lansdown Hill. Instead, he was lying alongside that— John, he may have bedded half the ladies in Oxford for all I know. God, he has the energy."

Her voice trailed off, leaving John desperately seeking for something reassuring to say.

"Was this... this betrayal of your love before or after the fighting?" he asked lamely.

"After. Does it matter when? It's what he did!"

"I have never fought in a war," continued John, "but I have

117

read that being part of such carnage as Lansdown, not knowing from moment to moment if you will die, seeing your friends killed—"

"That's it! Men stick together." Penny turned on John accusingly, pushing him away from her. "Make excuses for him. It did not rob him of his lust."

"No, it enhances it. Basic urges come—"

"I may have understood that if he explained. Instead, it was all about her need to have a child. I want a baby too but I do not go off with the first enemy I see, the first gentleman who passes by!"

She looked scornful and John felt her hurt and bewilderment.

"Nay, not even with a lifelong friend who loves me dearly."

He noticed the trunk of an alder tree swept over by a winter flood but now dried and bare. He steered her gently to it and persuaded her to sit down. She pulled her drab cloak around her although it was not cold, still much distressed.

"Perhaps I should—" she sobbed.

"Should what?"

"Lie with the first available man. Tell Edward the child is his. Match his perfidy with my own."

"You still have to live with yourself," he cautioned.

"I could do that. He has shown me the way." Resolutely, she stood up. "Let us walk on. The path branches away from the river within half a mile and returns to the city by way of Westgate. I do not want to walk back past Edward."

It was a pleasant sunny day for a stroll by the river, away from the stench and the clamouring. They saw parties of the king's horsemen, and boats on the river. Two men and a woman, working in a line, were hoeing a field of turnips or similar root vegetables. While they walked, Penny asked John's advice; he suggesting no hasty actions. Otherwise they spoke little. Then Penny explained that as soon as Edward had left her that morning, she had moved her things out of their lodging and taken rooms at an inn to the north of the city.

"Edward is ordered to ride to Keynsham village on the way to Bristol with Prince Maurice and Lord Hopton," she said. "Then onto Bristol by moonlight to gauge the strength of the wall. See, he has every opportunity for more fornication."

"Not with a prince in attendance." John couldn't help but to try a joke.

"Prince Maurice would applaud the 'sport' and join in! I had decided to seek Edward out this afternoon, but my nerve failed me and I hid in that wretched bakery where you found me." She had evidently stiffened that resolve, stating, "There is no benefit in speaking with Edward. My action is clear: I will hire four horsemen as escorts and leave Bath tonight."

"To Peverell?" John asked, hopefully.

"At first, to collect a few things. Then onto my father's house in Bury St Edmunds. He and my brother Benjamin are for parliament. They will protect me from Edward."

"It is a bold step to take."

"Aye, and I will make a bolder one: you shall lie with me before I leave."

"I am not sure—"

"It is what you want, what we have both wanted since we met in this ghostly way. You have often said as much."

Excitement welled up in John – more than excitement. His whole instinct was not to wait for some stuffy inn room but to take advantage of the meadow, here and now, the very moment. He wanted to be with her so much. He grasped her to him, kissed her passionately, felt her respond and then, despite his eagerness, he felt Penny's slight hesitation. Shyness? Fear? Or some residual feeling of guilt if she went on past the first embrace?

Penny would have to live with herself. If Edward were killed in the war, she would link his death with her adultery. John wanted her, desperately wanted her to love him; not be with him as an act of revenge on Edward. He moved away from her with great difficulty.

"I can't take advantage of you when you are so distraught."

"I want you now, right now, if you wish." She looked at him with a nervous smile. "I have done it under the sky with—"

"With Edward?"

"Of course with Edward, there has been no one else." Penny started to undo her buttons.

With quivering hands, John reached out. She smiled expectantly but he was not trying to assist her.

Churning inside, he said, "No, not like this." His voice was barely a whisper. "You will regret it, and I will reproach myself."

"God's grace, you reject me too. That woman, Judith—"

"No! Listen. I do not love her." He was holding Penny's shoulders, almost shaking her. "But I love you so much. I will not spoil it to spite—" He ran out of words. Breathing deeply, he continued, "Go back to Peverell. Give yourself time."

She was crying hysterically – two rejections in one day. "Give myself time? Forgive Edward?" she shouted. "To consider if I am ready to love you? Do not worry John – John Townsend – whoever you are. Your virtue will be safe from me. I will not abase myself a second time."

As Penny strode defiantly ahead, John followed – through the crumbling arch of Westgate, along the narrow filth-coated streets, to a timber inn that would be rebuilt as the current Saracen's Head.

She did not look back, far less bid him goodbye, but went directly into the building. John continued on, heading toward the brilliant ornate bulk of the abbey, back into the bakery, and back into the Sally Lunns of his own time, taking all his despair with him. In his dazed state he did not notice details, but as he moved forward in time, his dung-soiled sandals and feet became as clean as when he first entered the shop.

∞

"Mind your arse!"

A vicious shove sent Edward reeling across the barge, almost toppling into the murky water of the Avon. A mass of cannon barrel swung slowly past, still with enough momentum to crush his chest. Edward turned to face one of the boatmen, who touched the brim of his hat and apologised.

"Beg pardon, sir. The bastard swung free and—"

"Thank you, master. I should keep my mind on the work."

It was late afternoon and Edward was totally preoccupied, his mind filled with the memory of Penny's distraught face after he had confessed. His dash back at mid-morning to their lodgings, before she walked to the Ransoms' house, was not the best time. Was any time a good time? He watched, unseeing, as the two improvised cranes lowered the cannon barrel onto the prepared cradle in the barge. The safety strop had parted, but thankfully the swinging stopped and they had it secure. How in the name of Hades did Master Thomas hope to unload it? Edward realised that in his present state he was a total liability. He would try to find Penny.

"Last one loaded!" came a bellow from the riverbank.

Lord Hopton, scarred and still partially deaf from the gunpowder blast at Lansdown, had taken to shouting to compensate for his own lack of hearing. At least his sight had returned. Beside him in a wig and finery stood young Prince Maurice, Rupert's brother and the king's nephew.

"It is well past noon," he called. "We should be off for our reconnoitre. Your man Phil has horse and men ready?"

"I have business in the town," replied Edward.

"No time," was the sharp answer.

Edward damned him to Hell. There was no haste. It would take two to three days to transport the cannon. Another 'damned to Hell'. At this rate he would fill all Hell by dinnertime. He couldn't argue with the prince or General Hopton, and left the foreman of the boatmen to complete the loading of powder. That was of little account, but what would Penny do? Perhaps he would be able to go back into Bath and seek her out tomorrow morning.

∞

At her home in Peverell House, Penny Peverell had asked for a bed to be made up in one of the guest rooms – she would never sleep in their marriage bed again. Eyes red with crying, she staggered into the main living room, glass of wine in one hand, her small pistol in the other. Unsteadily, she pointed the small but lethal gun at the portrait, William Dobson's portrait, a gift to the loving couple on their wedding day. She aimed at Edward's face, wavered, and fired. A jet of flame shot out from the lock, a cloud of black smoke and powder exploding from the muzzle.

"Stupid wench," she admonished herself. "No ball in the barrel."

There was no hole, but the representation of Edward's face had been blackened out by the half-burned gunpowder, the oil paint blasted away.

"Would it were his real face," she spluttered bitterly, and stumbled off to drunken oblivion.

CHAPTER 15

Judith was on good terms with her sister-in-law Nancy, Simon's wife, so it was not a surprise to be asked out for a meal and drinks, even if this was usually followed by a request to babysit. Still, she was looking forward to chilling out over a few drinks.

Things had become a bit tense with John over the last few days. He seemed distracted, and several times she had felt he wanted to tell her something but couldn't bring himself to explain. She hoped he was not going off her. They didn't meet up every night, but had she been too intense? Or worse, were things progressing too quickly? Was he going to suggest marriage? Judith couldn't bear the thought.

Nancy and Judith had chosen to meet at Chez Gustav, the modern bijou restaurant newly opened in Argyle Street. Nancy arrived late and breezed in as though she owned the place. Judith wondered how she could go through life so free of care.

"So how's it going, then?" asked Nancy as they ordered prosecco flutes at the bar and carried menus to a table by the window.

"All good, thanks. Moved into the flat, and more or less got sorted."

"Did John help?" said Nancy with a smile as she took a gulp of her wine, almost emptying the glass.

"He did offer but I wanted to do things myself."

"No male advice."

"Exactly."

Nancy and Judith sat for a time in comfortable silence, looking out at the passers-by sauntering in the balmy sunshine towards Pulteney Weir, the menus almost unheeded.

"And the new job?"

"At Rotork? Start next week. I was lucky to get a position like that, and in Bath. I can cycle along the river path to work: no cost and good exercise."

Nancy grinned. "You look fit enough, and Simon said your walk on the Brecons with John went well."

"Except when John fell in the boggy area on top of Waun Fach. He seems to have an affinity with bogs," she laughed. "Yes, it was good. John likes walking but needs to work on his stamina, lags a bit on the hills. How are things with you?"

"Just the same daily grind: school run, checking finances for Simon, school pick up."

"Oh, I thought you had an accountant."

"We do, but you know Simon, ultra-cautious. He, well, the company, pays me four hours a day to audit the auditor, so to speak. I do find some mistakes and I'm better at spotting trends than most. BC I was fully chartered."

"BC?"

"Before children. I'm thinking of keeping on with the stay-at-home mum thing until after New Year, when Bonnie is settled at school. When I had a childminder for Charlie I was commuting to Swindon and hardly saw him so I don't want that again. But I'm getting flabby – mentally and physically!"

"You scoot to school with Charlie."

"And back, but it's not enough. I'm beginning to look like the great white whale in *Moby Dick*. It's time me and Simon took ourselves in hand before it's too late."

Their food arrived and Judith resisted the urge to comment on Nancy's shoulder of lamb on a bed of chorizo mash with spiced gravy and assorted veg, plus a bottle of red.

"I was wondering if you could suggest the best way to get fit," Nancy said between mouthfuls.

"Bath Sports Centre gym has some good fitness advisors." Judith was enjoying her healthy salad: tuna niçoise with plenty of anchovies.

"I was thinking more of a private club – Cannons or Bath Spa."

"Definitely not! There's too much temptation with the bar and restaurant being right there. I recommend spartan training, with an hour in the gym and then a swim."

"In the Bath pool? The river's cleaner."

"Not now, all refurbed. New sauna – the works."

Nancy smiled smugly. "Simon and I 'did it' in the sauna once. Nearly killed him!"

"There we are, then – gym, swim, and sex in the sauna, without vodka."

"I think I might need to get in training before we try that again," Nancy laughed.

"Let me know how it works out."

The dessert menus came and Nancy started to muse over crème caramel or tiramisu.

"So, when does the firm regime start, then?" asked Judith.

"Last binge? What will you have?"

"Black coffee, please."

"Puritan."

"Fine, a black coffee with tiramisu. I did go on a six-mile run before we came out tonight."

"Or we could share the continental cheese, with a small grappa, or a Rioja?"

There was a silence for a few minutes as they sipped drinks and then ordered dessert.

"So how is your love li—" Nancy caught her words abruptly. "Sorry, sorry, I know you don't 'do' love anymore."

"No! Not ever. No more. I enjoy myself much more with John than I ever would if I was in lurv."

"Go on... nights out, nights in, weekends away together?"

"Exactly. No expectations, no commitments."

"So, what if the Marvellous Mark Davis reappeared? You said you were madly in love with him at the time."

"He won't."

"He has. I saw him in Frome market last—"

"No!" Judith said with a stifled gasp.

"Yes, I walked straight up to him and asked how he was." Nancy paused and ate a mouthful of pudding.

"Christ, you didn't?"

"I bloody did. And, bold as you like, he introduced me to a 'work colleague' – Trudy – and asked after you."

"Oh my God," exclaimed Judith in dismay. "I don't want to see him." Her face had gone pale and she toyed with her spoon, picking at the edge of her dessert uncertainly.

"He said none of your contact details worked, and he found out you didn't live at Peverell House anymore."

"Hell. You didn't give him my address, did you?"

"Of course not!"

"Did you mention John?"

"No, nothing. You interested in what he's doing? Works in Bradford-on-Avon, has a flat there—"

"He's history – painful history," Judith blurted out. "End of subject. He promised me so much, then buggered off without even a text goodbye." Her voice had sunk to a nervous whisper. "I had assumed he was alive somewhere or other. I, well, in some perverse way hope he's moved on. I have. I certainly will not be trying to light that old fire."

Nancy put her arm around Judith in a comforting hug and topped up their wine glasses. "I get the picture, but perhaps the lady doth protest too much? I only mentioned him to warn you he's about. Less of a shock if you bump into him. Since having kids, I feel inclined to give everyone advice, even when it's not wanted—"

"Don't..." Judith started to say warily, sensing dangerous ground.

"This is too important. Don't lose John, Judith. He's been so good for you."

Judith tried to object but Nancy ploughed on.

"Shh, don't interrupt. He's good with kids, fit and healthy, good with money, and he thinks a lot of you."

"He's not bad in bed either, if we're making lists, but there isn't that zing I had with Mark. You know what I mean, you and Simon—"

"Me and Simon? Zing, love, excitement? That's not us, darling. All that just gets in the way." Nancy stole a large spoonful of Judith's uneaten tiramisu and cream before continuing with her advice. "I applied the five tests and he was OK, so I went into it, eyes open."

"What five tests?" Judith desperately wanted to leave the subject of Mark behind.

"Good friends for at least a year," Nancy started to say, "but then it's all psycho-babble like: similar interests, money and property in our case; reliable, the old 'for better for worse' bit; tolerant, up to a point. The key point was that no one else would have us."

"What about romance? Passion?"

"Best kept for books and films."

"Sex?" asked Judith in mock resignation.

"It happens. We both enjoy it, but it's not worth getting married for."

Judith pushed her plate towards Nancy, muted her mobile, and drank some coffee. "By the way, how are my delightful niece and nephew these days?"

"Worse for being on school holidays. They get so bored."

"And you've got no time on your own."

"Yesterday we went swimming, then for lunch at Pizza Extra, took the bikes around the Odd Down cycle circuit, and then they said: 'what are we going to do now?'. Bonnie demanded we go bowling and Charlie wanted to go home and play on the computer. Honestly, it's a full-time job this motherhood lark."

"It sounds like it!"

"You never see the worst of them. They are so much better when you and John are around."

"It's the baseball bat I keep handy in the Land Rover that keeps them in order," joked Judith. "And Charlie has taken quite a shine to John." She was feeling at ease now they were on to safer topics.

"I shouldn't talk about my children like that," said Nancy. "Especially when I'm going to ask a big favour."

"Any evening in mind?"

"We were wondering," Nancy hesitated before continuing, "well, it was Simon's idea, really." Another hesitation.

"Spit it out, girl," laughed Judith, smiling fondly at her sister-in-law. "We've taken them off for a whole day before now."

"What about a whole weekend? I know it's a lot to ask—"

"I am not sure I could cope with bedtime on my own if Bonnie plays up. I'd need John around to keep an eye on Charlie."

"Charlie's no problem. Reads you a chapter of his book, half an hour screen time, snuggles back down into bed and is soon asleep."

"I know. He's usually a good boy, but he does get stroppy if he's being ignored too long. John could sit—"

"Oh, he'd love that. That's what Simon hoped."

"I'll have to ask John," Judith said after a minute, thinking things through. "But he loves kids. We might, well, you know, one day." It was the first time she had hinted this to anyone and she instantly regretted it. She knew Nancy couldn't keep a secret, and if John was growing cold to her she'd feel a right idiot all over again.

"Well, don't leave it too long," Nancy was saying. "There's no problem having them in old age these days, but you need to be young to look after them!"

CHAPTER 16

Edward Peverell jerked awake, confused and disorientated. He was in the gloomy parlour of a nondescript inn to the northeast of Bristol. A single dim candle burned, showing Prince Maurice and several other King's officers dozing in chairs as they waited for the council meeting to start. A sickening dream of being shot in the face was still vivid in Edward's memory. Was it an omen that he was going to die? Die before he could be reconciled with Penny?

"Pray be upstanding for Prince Rupert of the Palatine, Duke of Cumberland."

"Bollocks! It's only me fucking brother," growled Prince Maurice.

Startled into action, Edward leapt out of the chair, pistol in hand. To his amusement he realised that His Germanic Highness had dropped his cultured foreign accent and was swearing in broad English.

Earlier that evening, after viewing the crumbling walls around Bristol, Edward had finally persuaded Hopton and Maurice that they could reduce the whole South Gate area to rubble in two days with their heavy guns. Secretly, Edward still believed bombarding the warehouses would bring about a faster surrender. Regrettably, Rupert and his party would have none of it.

"Are you afraid to scale the walls?" sneered Culpepper, one of the king's advisors who had travelled with Rupert.

"I have no fear," said Maurice, "as I showed at Roundway Down. Neither do I have wings to fly nor ladders to scale walls."

"Nor suitable trees nor tools to make the ladders!" boomed Hopton.

"I want a quick, decisive victory," said Rupert, "like yours at Roundway. We need to teach those rebels to fear us. The main army arrives tomorrow; many have not eaten since leaving Oxford. We must attack before our men disperse."

After that outburst the discussions became long and tedious, with many tired men repeating the same argument.

Much later, as dawn was breaking, Edward stood outside the inn with his friend Nick Stanning.

"Rupert is jealous of Maurice's victory at Roundway. He wants his own gallant action."

"He has a point about feeding the men, some are near to starving," remarked Nick.

"We could have brought food down river from Bath – by cart or by boat. There is never any coordination or planning." Edward felt the sense of futility creep into his voice.

By midday the first small Falconet cannon had arrived and been set up to chip away at the gatehouse. Firing only a two-pound shot, their effect was hardly dramatic, but already pieces of ancient stonework were falling down. The big guns were still coming along on the river barges. Edward, with Phil Howells the bailiff's son as second in command, watched the Cornish pikemen trussing up branches of alder and withies of willow into large faggot-like bundles down by the river. They planned to pile those high against the wall and climb over.

"Have they allowed for the ditch in front of the wall, I wonder?" asked Edward.

"Nay," said Phil pityingly. "I lay they have not even been to gauge the full height of the wall, let alone the depth of dry ditch."

"No one's planning this," agreed Edward. "Since Grenville's death they have no commander."

"God save 'em tomorrow."

"God save us all."

Thoughts of Penny and fears for the coming attack filled Edward's mind as he rode in desultory fashion along the riverbank, looking across the marshy wetland towards where Bristol's medieval walls had almost disappeared. Another month of this hot weather would dry the mud, making the area wide open to attack.

"That's why those walls were there," said Edward to himself. "The ancients understood how to protect themselves from war. Now it is all but gone."

On the far bank, two or three hundred yards back from the river edge, was an encampment of Parliamentary soldiers, no more than two dozen men. Edward observed them carefully as Phil rode up beside him.

"Good day, sir. Prince Maurice is concerned for you. Bid me check you were..." He sought for words. "Are you being cautious?"

"What else could I be? Prince Rupert does not heed my advice."

"His brother Prince Maurice now listens to you, sir. He is much impressed by the first four small guns at work. Each shot knocked away some of the crumbling stonework."

There was a pause for some time as they looked out over the waterlogged marshland, until an idea came to Edward.

"Phil, your family is from the Somersetshire levels and marshes. You know waterways?"

"Aye, my grandfather and uncle still have farms nor' of Glastonbury."

"We are slack water now – could we find a way for horses to cross as the tide ebbs?"

Phil considered the marshland before them. "It is a right treacherous river but no man from the levels dies on a mud flat. I shall investigate under the guise of seeking out fresh fish to supply our forces."

Stripped down to his shirt, Phil dragged himself through the mud and shallows, catching but a few coarse fish and three small eels, all the while facing the jeering on the opposing army. Later that evening, he reported back to Edward.

"I have found a place that is safe to cross on horseback if we have a leading rope between us. It will be dark at low tide but by first light we could be in line to charge the camp of the guards."

"Good man. We cross as you say, then move higher upriver, under that copse, and wait until Rupert and Maurice set off their first assault in the north and the south. The shock of us appearing amongst them will be totally demoralising."

"Twelve of us?"

"I will 'borrow' Nick Stanning's fifty dragoons. They are of no use against a wall, but on that open marshland they will strike fear into the defenders."

They rode lazily back to South Gate, where the master gunner now had all six Falconet cannons shooting away at the gatehouse, cast iron balls smashing out bits of masonry and killing a few men with each shot, some writhing and screaming in agony as they fell.

"This is the future of war," the gunner boasted to Edward. "City walls, castles, charging men – all will fall to the guns."

Even as he spoke to Edward, the gates of South Gate were thrown open and a troop of horsemen poured out.

"Aim and fire!" shouted the master gunner. "Load small shot, lively!"

Four of the six guns were ready and sent solid round shot carving through the knot of cavalry as they tried to get into line to charge. The delay to form up was a fatal mistake; it gave the gunners vital time to reload. The deadly spread of small shot had an even more devastating effect, scything down men and horses mercilessly. Lounging Royalist musketeers positioned to guard against such a sortie scrambled hastily to their feet, blowing on the slow matches, readying their firelocks. Edward drew sabre and pistol, galloping to urge them into action. It was not needed; a junior officer was already commanding them.

"Form line. Steady. Present. Fire!"

The threatened charge faltered in blood and confusion. The gunners were still swabbing out the cannon, but the sortie was already defeated.

A cry of, "Kurnow! Kurnow," rang out and a deadly phalanx of Cornish pikemen ripped into the survivors. It was what the

Cornish did best, no hesitation or preamble just an immediate and deadly charge before the enemy could react.

The city gates had closed. There was no retreat and few survivors.

"I've never seen such slaughter, horse and men with their guts blown out," gasped Phil, visibly shaken by the atrocities he had just witnessed. He wiped smears of blood and dirt away off his face with a trembling hand.

Sadly, Edward knew only too well that devastation and carnage. At the bloody battle of Lansdown it had been Parliamentary cannon firing into the vulnerable ranks of Cornish pikemen.

"The prince knows his business," conceded Edward. "He organised this well with pike and muskets ready to protect the guns. The demi-culverin, when they arrive, could punch holes right through these old walls. If only Rupert would wait for a few days none of this would be necessary."

"Ho there!" Lord Hopton rode up. "Well done, master gunman. Time to stop firing your pieces, the light is going."

"Why, my lord? I can see to shoot by the fire we cause. Why let the defenders sleep?"

"Not the done thing, is it?" He turned to Edward. "Peverell, what is your counsel on this?"

"If we have shot and powder—"

"Cart loads!" said Hopton.

"Then, if master gunner can perform useful practice against these rebels, why not discomfort them?"

∞

It was about two in the morning when Edward's fearful troop started to cross the river. Almost immediately they lost two men, tossed from their saddles by horses scrambling from the swampy black pits hidden under the river marshes. They disappeared without trace into the inky darkness.

"Keep your seats," hissed Phil. "Let your horses pick their own way. The bottom is treacherous."

Edward himself felt close to panic. He was meant to be in charge, in command. Instead, he was completely at the mercy of fate as the sinister darkness closed in. His only hope was the sense of his horse as it found its own footing through the malevolent shallows. If he fell, he would have no idea which way to swim. There was no sound except for the hypnotic swirling of slack tide water as it began to rise. No bats piped; no night birds called. Edward was terrified that someone would cry out in fear.

By first light they were concealed in the copse that Edward had spotted the previous day. No one from the nearby guard camp had become aware of their stealthy crossing. Throughout the night the artillery bombardment of South Gate continued and Edward hoped this would serve to convince the defenders of their vulnerability.

The attacks from both north and south Bristol were due to start by five o'clock, but as the sun crept over the horizon there was a distant roar. Far earlier than planned, the Cornish pikemen launched their attack on the southern wall. Edward could hear the shouts of the attackers; the measured fire of the defending musketeers. It had all gone wrong; there was no shock of a co-ordinated assault, and an entire hour passed before the sounds of

Rupert's attack on the northern forts drifted across to Edward.

The effect of Edward's fifty men would hardly be decisive in any real tactical sense, but he hoped their presence behind the main defences would be demoralising. His chance came when a group of a hundred or so footmen were seen hurrying from the south towards the north-west fort. Fiennes must have realised that South Gate and the wall were quite safe from Maurice's ineffectual attack and sent this group to re-enforce one of the northern forts.

"Too many, sir," said Phil, almost reading Edward's mind.

"We have surprise. Trot towards them with concealed weapons until we are alongside. They will think us Parliamentarians. At thirty yards we draw and fire, then the dragoons charge at full tilt with sabres. As soon as they break, we draw back. I want to herd them towards the main castle where their commander will be."

Edward watched apprehensively and waited as the file of Parliamentarian foot-soldiers crossed the marshlands, waiting for what he hoped would be the optimum time to start his attack.

"Your pardon, Sir Edward," came a voice beside him: one of Nick Stanning's dragoons. "Do you want me to sound command?" He indicated his bugle.

Edward looked blankly at the horseman.

"With the gunfire and screaming, no one will hear your voice," the gunman explained.

"Aye. Good man." Edward fumbled for words, quite out of his depth. "I do not want a headlong pursuit. Charge them, then hold back."

"The enemy will easily flee to the town fort," interrupted Phil.

"Exactly. Reporting us to be ten times our number. I want surrender, not a massacre. You have a simple hold back bugle call?"

"There is the 'recall', brings all the dragoons back to the colours."

Edward nodded with a sigh of relief at the suggestion – he didn't want all his efforts to be ruined.

It was time to move. Edward signalled with a wave of his hat and his column trotted forward.

"Ho! Hurry along," Edward called confidently to the Parliamentary soldiers. "We are needed in the north."

Despite his cool demeanour Edward rode with a mixture of fear and despair. He wanted so much to see Penny again; to hold her in his arms, beg her to forgive him for his infidelity. Then there was the dream of his own death: shot in the face. How many men would die?

The bugle sounded, harsh and shrill. Edward's men drew pistols, the dragoons unsheathed carbines, opening their line so each had a clear shot. A deafening ragged roar of shot, and a wall of smoke obscured the enemy.

"Wait!" roared Edward. He wanted the shock of the volley to register. "Now!"

The bugler sounded the charge and the mounted dragoons galloped forward with drawn sabres. There was no resistance, no return fire. Shocked and betrayed, Parliamentary foot-soldiers dropped unprepared weapons and fled. Edward's charge cut through their line. Unbidden, the dragoons wheeled around mercilessly, cutting down those who fled northwards, riding fugitives down, slashing at others with deadly backhand strokes, trampling bodies. As Edward pulled up his horse, a smaller group of the enemy was escaping back into the old city. Pitifully, few had survived.

"Sound the recall!"

But the bugler had joined in the slaughter, oblivious to orders.

"They're getting away," gasped Phil, pointing with his blood-stained sword.

"That's what I want," shouted Edward. "Get our lot in line to block any counterattack." *This is our problem*, he thought desperately to himself, *we have no discipline*. The dragoons were killing and stealing from the bodies without restraint. They themselves would be vulnerable to attack if there were Parliamentarian horsemen on the field.

The dragoons were intoxicated with victory and plunder; looting weapons, clothes and items of male jewellery such as rings and crosses that could be sold in the camp. Throats were cut, chests stabbed. There was no mercy. It was sickening. Those being slaughtered like animals were not regular soldiers but half-trained militia trying to protect their homes. It took Edward over half an hour to restore order and then get his force into a semblance of discipline. He hoped the routed Parliamentarians would have exaggerated his numbers to their commander at the old Bristol castle in the centre of the city. Arranging his men like an honour guard as he approached the old fort, Edward rode forward with all the appearance and confidence he could muster.

"In the name of His Highness King Charles, King of England and Scotland, lay down your arms and surrender to the king's mercy!" He sat on horseback a mere fifty yards from the castle gatehouse, within easy range of musket shot.

"And if we do not?" shouted back a voice.

"Full assault, supported by cannon. No quarter. As is the custom of war."

There was a long wait. Edward could feel sweat trickling down his backbone. The sound of bloody battle could still be heard from South Gate; a shout of Royalist triumph from the north. The situation must have looked desperate indeed to Nathaniel Fiennes, for a white sheet was raised up the castle flagpole.

"General Fiennes will only discuss terms with Prince Rupert, Duke of Cumberland. Draw back out of range. Withdraw."

"I'll try to seek out the prince and get the killing to stop," yelled Edward.

The attack on South Gate had already petered out, and gradually the Royalist forces in the north held back from their attacks. Many of Rupert's loyal commanders had been killed, along with thousands of his men. Terms were agreed, and the Parliamentarian force, who had suffered few losses, marched away with their weapons, proud and defiant. They were robbed of their possessions and baggage in contravention of the 'terms of surrender', but still an armed and viable force of soldiers.

Edward could not believe the scene at South Gate when he arrived: carts and wagons loaded with faggots of wood, and makeshift ladders rolled into the ditch in a vain attempt to scale the wall. All this in the face of murderous musket fire and a rain of burning tallow-soaked wool rolled from the wall by the town's women. Whenever a desperate man did clamber to the top, he was beaten down by pole arms, pikes or halberd. Not one Royalist attacker had succeeded in entering the city that way. A totally pointless bloodbath.

Some of the wounded had been carried into the shelter of the town, others were lying under flimsy awnings, many with terrible injuries, just waiting to die. With a sickening heart Edward found his way to an inn where his friend Nick Stanning had been taken. Nick's left leg had been shot through, shattered in two places, above and below the knee. He was pale from shock and loss of blood but trying to appear carefree.

"I have avoided bullets before, Ed," he attempted to jest. "And now I have caught two of them!"

Edward winced as he looked at the bandaged leg and realised it would have to come off if Nick had any hope of survival.

"One surgeon wants to saw the leg off, Ed, but then I could never ride again; another says I am too weak for such an amputation and puts his faith in herbs and a dead pigeon placed under my foot to draw off the noxious humours. What say you?"

Edward shook his head in despair. Gangrene was inevitable if the leg stayed on.

"Either course will give the same end," Nick said seriously. "I have seen enough wounds to know what to expect." He sighed. "And my little son is but a month old."

"There is nothing I can offer," said Edward in despair, hardly able to meet Nick's eyes.

"As a true friend, you could stay with me. I put my trust in laudanum to reduce the pain of my final hours."

"Opium and spirit? It is a deadly mixture."

"To the healthy who seek intoxication it is. But a good friend to the dying."

Edward had no wish to stay for a death vigil, but could see a fever was already beginning to build in his friend's body. Blood poisoning could be very swift. Overcome with emotion, he could not speak, but clasped the other man's hand.

"Just keep the leeches and the surgeons away from me, Ed. Let me die peacefully."

CHAPTER 17

John Townsend had a modern workshop on an industrial estate between Bath and Keynsham. Outside, he needed a yard to store stone and park his van; inside were power tools ranging from a powerful masonry saw to small handheld routers. He was working on a replica of a gargoyle-style waterspout as Judith strolled in. She liked watching him work: the concentration, attention to detail, and evident love of his craft. So different from her world of procedures, micro-electronics and software.

"Hi," John said looking up. "Didn't expect to see you until tonight."

"I have free time. Wondered if you were around. Is that finished?"

"This one, yes, but there are four more to do. Tea?"

"I'd prefer coffee, unless it's instant."

"I bought some in, and a cafetiere, just in case." He peeled off his thin safety gloves, lifted his visor and brushed chippings and sand-like residue from his overall.

"In the office?" she asked, smiling at him.

"Yes. I need to get this lot off, don't need to spread the dust."

By the time he had taken off the overalls and washed, Judith had prepared their drinks.

"You're hired, chief tea-maker!" John quipped as he came in, carefully shutting the door to keep stray dust from the computer equipment. He gave Judith a hug and a brief kiss.

"Already got a job I'm afraid, sir," she chuckled.

"How are you feeling about starting tomorrow?"

"To be honest, I'm a bit nervous," Judith confessed. "It's been a while since I had a high-tech post."

"You'll be fine. If not, the job as a tea-maker is still open," he said, sipping his brew.

"How many of those gargoyle things have you got to do?" she asked, changing the subject.

"A dozen all together for a special project – six real spouts and six dummies."

"You could set up a computer-controlled machine to do that – do one by hand and laser scan."

"I know, I know, but how much would the machine cost? And how would you keep the abrasive dust out of the sliding surfaces? It's not like metal swarf."

"I could fix that," Judith said.

"I'm sure you could. But the client expects minor variations in each one, like on the old churches. I think she's disappointed I'm using power tools at all!"

John grabbed a packet of digestives for them both and Judith helped herself to a couple.

"OK, OK. You keep to your copper chisels and wooden mallets."

"I will. Well, iron chisels, anyway," John said with a laugh.

He looked at Judith. She had cycled over, and her orange and black cycling gear showed off her slim boyish figure at its best. John couldn't help comparing her looks with the voluptuous Penny and felt a surge of guilt. Was he being fair to Judith when he spent so much time thinking of Penny?

"I've an exciting suggestion for you," said Judith, interrupting his wandering thoughts. "How would you like an exciting and lively weekend with interesting bedtime activities?"

"I smell a catch," John answered warily. "A whole weekend?"

"Well, long weekend. Friday night to Monday morning. Looking after Charlie and Bonnie while Nancy and Simon go—"

"God, Bonnie as well? I couldn't do bedtime with that little monkey!"

"I'd see to Bonnie. You just help Charlie with his bath, listen to him read a story, night-night – all that."

"It's a bit full-on, isn't it? Where would your brother be?"

"Cornwall. A luxury hotel and spa. You know, pool, gym, sauna, massages. All that decadent stuff."

As Judith described the scene, John sensed she was slightly envious.

"We could give it a try, but it's a long way back for them to come if there is a problem."

"There will be no problems that we can't cope with." Judith crossed her fingers as she said this.

"Well, once they're asleep we could get a takeaway, bottle of wine."

She shook her head. "No alcohol if we're looking after the kids."

"I'm going off this a bit. Is this how normal parents live?"

"I doubt it, at least not Simon and Nancy. Anyway, are you up for it? I can't manage on my own," Judith confessed.

"Of course." John was quite fond of little Charlie, and Judith could usually manage Bonnie. "Any ideas of what to do in the daytime?"

"I thought possibly take the bikes over to Westonbirt?"

"Well, Bonnie's only five, she can't ride far. Bowood might be better. It's got that big aerial walkway with slides all the way down to the ground, and there's bound to be a cycle track. And we could look round the house."

"No! No ghostly appearances, John. I couldn't take your Penny—"

"It hadn't been built in her time, don't worry."

"You're sure?"

"Positive." John dipped his biscuit into his tea while musing over the weekend to come. "God, I haven't been on a bike for over two years. Not sure if my one is—"

"That wreck over there against the wall?" said Judith with a laugh. "Flat tyres, covered in dust. Will it go?"

"Of course. Expensive bit of kit that was."

"Charity shop?"

"Avon Valley Cyclery. Me and—" His voice faded.

"Sorry, John. Bad memories?"

"Yeah." He forced a bright manner. "Look, I need to finish another gargoyle as a sample for tomorrow. Could you look over the bike for me?"

"Come on, now, I'm an engineer." Judith put an arm around him affectionately and kissed his cheek. "I'll fix anything if you make it worth my while."

"Pub lunch and a trial ride?"

"You're on."

He stood up and collected the cups.

"John?" she said, uncertainly.

"Yes?"

"Is something wrong? If you don't want to look after—"

"No. No. It's just that—" He faltered, not sure of how to continue. "Is it OK with you, the way we are with each other? The 'no commitments', and all that?"

Judith was taken aback, fearful of what was coming next. "It's what we agreed, isn't it?" she said in a small voice. "If you don't want to see me anymore..."

"No, no, not at all. It's me." He sat back down, staring at the table. "Last week I had one of my flits back in time."

"But you haven't been to Peverell House..."

"It was in Bath. Sally Lunn's. It was all a bit of a shock, seeing Penny again."

"Why? You've met her before."

"This was for four hours, in the Bath of 1643."

"Oh. Did anything... happen?"

"If you mean sex, no. I've admitted I tried it on with Penny before. This time it was her idea, but it wouldn't have been right."

Judith gasped, sitting bolt upright, white-faced and intense. "Because of me?"

"Partly. Partly because she was in a state over her husband and I'd be taking advantage."

"Oh great, thanks." Judith could not hide her feelings of jealousy and bitterness.

"No, look." John was suffering too. "I'm in a mess over this," he spluttered. "I just want to be honest about things."

There was a long silence and John looked imploringly at Judith.

"Fine. If we're being honest, I'll be honest too. My ex, Mark, is back in the area, and I'm told he wants to make contact with me."

"But I thought it was all over between you two?"

"I thought it was, too. Now I'm in a pickle. Do I borrow one of your hammers and rearrange his face? ... But then I had a surge of excitement that he wanted to see me again. It's all too bloody complicated."

"Do you want to go back to him?" asked John.

"I don't know. I don't bloody know. That's what I said."

They sat in a stressful silence for some time.

"So that's it, is it?" Judith said hesitantly. "When we're intimate, you're thinking of Penny, and you think I'm—"

"No. No and bloody no. When I'm with you, I'm with you. Hell, you know it's you I want."

"And afterwards, you're thinking of Penny?" Judith couldn't stop herself from asking.

"You're saying," John flung at her angrily, "when we're doing it, you're thinking of Mark and I'm thinking of Penny?" He kicked furiously at some wood with his hefty work boots and sent it spinning across the floor.

"No, that's what you're saying!"

"Bollocks. If I'm with you, I'm with you. That's all there is to it – no one else."

"And Penny Peverell? What about her? You can't tell me it's

'me and no one else' when you don't shut up about her," Judith retorted quietly, though she felt like screaming at him.

"Like I said, I get excited when I see her. I don't know how it would be if it were real. But she isn't. Not now. She's not coming to our time and I'm not going back to her time." John's thoughts were in a jumble as he hesitated for a fraction. What if he had to choose which woman to be with, no matter where?

"I suppose it's nice to know I am not being dumped for a ghost. Wish Mark had stayed in the past. He's not spoiling anything again, believe me." To clear her mind, Judith moved away to look out of the dusty workshop window and into the large yard beyond. Hating the unpleasant tension between them, she turned back to John with a wan smile. "Look, can we leave this? It's going nowhere. It's not changing anything, well, not on my side, anyway. Let's just... move on, OK?"

"OK," agreed John, "but there is one thing I need to say."

"No stop, John..." Judith began to shake slightly, trying to control her pent-up feelings. It seemed everything was slipping away.

"One thing. Since I've been with you, I've never been happier, and I mean that Judith."

John's confession took Judith a moment to adjust to. She had been convinced he was going to say something else; that their relationship was too much for him, or that he was ready to move to the next stage. Knowing she had made him happy was a relief to say the least.

She blushed, smiling sheepishly at him. "Oh knock it off, John, don't go all soppy on me."

Although she spoke in jest, John noticed that her fingers

trembled as she smoothed back a stray piece of hair.

"You go and break some stone," she told him. "I've got a bike to fix for the weekend!"

∞

Saturday morning it rained, so they took Charlie and Bonnie swimming and bowling at the sports centre instead. Fortunately, the weather was better in the afternoon, so they tried a trail bike ride around Victoria Park. There was some yelling from Bonnie because Judith wouldn't let her go over the ramps on her bike, but apart from that it was a much more pleasant experience than the sports centre. Bedtime was surprisingly easy, and both children were fast asleep in no time after their busy day.

Sunday was a fine, if overcast, day, so they decided to follow John's plan of going to Bowood House. The adventure park boasted some awesomely high aerial walkways between the trees, with a terrifying long, fast slide back down to ground level.

John hated himself for acting like an overprotective parent, but he couldn't stop crying out, "Don't climb on the side netting! Don't rock the rope bridge! Keep your arms in on the drop slide!"

"God, John. You sound like an old granny," Judith said with a laugh.

"Like that one?" He pointed to a small, elderly lady racing her grandchildren across the rope bridge to shouts of 'go, Granny, go!' from a group of young adults beneath.

"That's where you should be!"

"I have been up there four times already but Bonnie wanted to do it 'all on her own', so I'm grounded."

Throughout the weekend Judith and John had tried their best to put their painful midweek row behind them, and Sunday was so far turning out to be enjoyable and relaxing for them both. John had almost forgotten all the angst that had been building up.

Sensing Charlie was growing bored with the adventure park, John ruffled the boy's hair fondly and said with a grin, "Right, you up for a bike ride?"

"If you can keep up, Uncle John."

"It's about three miles," warned John, not sure Charlie would appreciate the distance, but the boy seemed quite happy with the idea. He started off well, but riding up a gradient and on the grassy path was harder going than Charlie expected. After a mile he suggested a stop for a drink and a snack.

Halfway through his salt and vinegar Monster Munch, Charlie asked seriously, "Are you going to marry Aunty Judith?"

John froze in shock for a moment, recovering quickly. "I don't know. If I do, it won't be for a while." John fished around in the rucksack and brought out some apples, offering one to the boy, hoping that food would distract him.

"Do you like her?" Charlie pressed on.

"Yes, very much."

"If you do bad things to her, my daddy will put a contract on you," Charlie said in a menacing voice, as he ignored the apple and produced a chocolate bar from his own bag.

"Well I shall have to make sure I don't do that then."

Charlie nodded. "That's what Daddy did with Mark. Mark was horrible. Never did fun things like today. So Daddy had him contracted."

May as well play along, thought John. "Well it sounds like your daddy did the right thing if he wasn't any fun."

"Daddy told Mummy that he didn't think Mark was right for Aunty Judith, and that he would pay him off. That's what contract him means. Mark went away after that. No one knows where, except me and Daddy's men."

"Oh, sounds like a big secret."

"It's not a joke," Charlie insisted. "Daddy is a very dangerous man."

John conjured up a picture of placid, amiable Simon. John didn't think he'd say boo to a goose, but he was known as a ruthless businessman, a different character altogether when building up his 'empire' and wealth over the years. Still, hardly a Mafioso!

"His hitmen killed Mark and disposed of his body."

"A secret grave?"

"No, too dangerous." Charlie was warming to his story. "They took him to Mendip Quarry and fed him through the stone crusher!"

"Gosh!"

"I think they would have killed him first but he might have been fed in alive." Charlie shuddered in delight. "Daddy took me to the quarry to meet the men who work there." Charlie leaned close to John. "They were quite friendly but hadn't cleaned it up very well. There was dried blood all over the crushed bed."

John gulped; the boy really was convinced. "It's hematite in the limestone. Soluble iron oxide like rust, makes it a ruddy colour."

"That's what they said, but then they would, wouldn't they? I know the difference between rust and blood. Have you got any

Haribos? I'm still starving—"

"Hey, can I have a word?" said a voice from behind them. Unnoticed, a groundsman had come towards them, looking rather annoyed.

"Hi," responded John, carefully putting Charlie's crumpled crisp bag back into the rucksack.

"Did you pay to come in?" the man asked.

"Sure," replied John. "The ticket's in the motor on display and—"

"Then you would have seen the notice about—"

"Yeah, no dogs, fires – nothing about food."

"It also said no bikes, scooters, skates or any other wheeled vehicles other than prams or invalid wheelchairs.

"I'm very sorry," said John. "I stopped reading at dogs and horses. The kids were so excited about the aerial adventure walk."

The groundsman explained the problems of bike tyres cutting up wet paths and kids on scooters playing havoc in the grounds. "I don't want to spoil your fun though, so if you wheel the bikes through that glade and then take our service road to the car park, you can ride on that without being seen."

∞

It was only when Bonnie and Charlie were safe in bed that John remembered Charlie's story and raised it with Judith.

"Oh no! He's not off on that again?" she said, with amusement.

"He warned me to be nice to you. Or else!"

"Good lad! Seriously, it's a bit of a problem. Perhaps if he were to see Mark..."

"He'd think it was a ghost or a zombie!" joked John.

"I'll mention it to Simon," Judith chuckled.

CHAPTER 18

Penny realised that it would be far from easy to travel from the Royalist southwest to her father and sister, Rita, in Parliamentarian East Anglia. Her first impulse was to flee Peverell House on horseback, but she would need several remounts to complete the journey and places to stay overnight. A single woman travelling alone would be very vulnerable.

It was therefore several days after Edward's devastating confession that Penny rode out of Peverell House courtyard for the last time in a hired carriage with a driver, guard and two mounted outriders as escorts. The Civil War had created a huge demand for riding and draught animals, and the two horses pulling the semi-closed carriage were ill-matched and unimpressive. The carriage itself was rather dilapidated but quite comfortable with a good roof and side screens that shielded off most of the drizzle. She took nothing of Edward's and nothing Edward had given her. Ornaments and jewellery such as necklaces and rings were left behind. She had some money of her own and of course her clothes, but nothing more. She had left a curt note for him if he did return to Peverell. Inside the carriage, her maid

Carol was sobbing in distress, but refused to explain why.

Summer rain fell steadily, sufficient to water crops but not flatten corn. It was so unlike the time when she and Edward had first arrived. From their wedding in Suffolk they had waited in Devizes for a bright spring day to arrive at Peverell; an omen for their life of sunshine and love together. Tears filled Penny's eyes, but there was no going back; no possibility of forgiveness; no children to consider – despite their efforts. Just that ancient puritan hag carrying Edward's child. Carol handed Penny a small handkerchief and she dried her eyes. Seeking composure in detail, she opened her lap bag and took out Edward's letter. It was in two parts. One was a factual note saying that Nick Stanning, one of their closest friends, was badly shot and dying. There was little hope of recovery and he was too ill to move. Edward had promised to stay with Nick until the end came. The letter hardly mentioned the attack on Bristol and said nothing of Edward's part in it.

The second parchment was an impassioned plea for Penny to forgive him. The letter was immaculately written, unlike Edward's usually strained, barely legible penmanship. Its phrases were carefully correct, written in Edward's style but probably copied again and again until near perfect. It had almost persuaded her to stay. Edward hardly ever apologised and never grovelled. In the letter he did both, but she would not weaken.

Her reverie was broken by the sound of two horsemen galloping off.

"The outriders, ma'am," called her coachman in alarm, "they have fled!"

It was hard to follow events from the confusion, and with the coach shutters drawn against the drizzling rain, she could see little.

From up ahead a new voice bellowed, "Stop your horses, driver. Leave your weapons, or we shoot!"

"Don't fight!" shouted Penny, "I want no blood spilled."

The carriage rocked to a halt and there was a thud as the guard's musket was thrown to the ground.

"A sensible action, my brave sir."

From the now half-raised blind, Penny cringed as the mounted hooded figure approached.

He threw open the door and boomed, "Lady Peverell and mistress Carol."

He knew their names. This was planned; their escort in collusion with the robbers.

"Come over here, Robin," the man called. "We have two pretty skirts to lift!"

Suddenly, the carriage was filled with the flash, bang and smoke of Penny's pistol. Small but deadly accurate, it hit the masked robber in the throat. Blood spurted, and the near decapitated head lolled back as his horse shied. The carriage surged forward against the brake as the horses took fright. A shot sounded from above; the coach guard had a second, hidden gun. Penny grabbed for the large military-style pistol hanging in the corner of her carriage. Outside, more shooting. Her guard screamed in agony and fell from the box.

Penny was hanging perilously in the carriage doorway as the driver whipped up his team to flee. Partially off balance, she fired the massive pistol. Its recoil knocked her headlong onto the grass verge. She was aware the carriage had stopped its short dash and saw her second target loll sideways and fall from his horse.

"Don't move," she cried. "I have a second pistol. Move and I kill you." It was a lie – both her pistols were fired. The small wheel lock with its rifled barrel took an age to reload; the big flintlock gun was gone God knows where. She remembered: the guard had thrown down his musket. Desperately she sprinted back down the road and snatched up the weapon. It was not discharged, not even cocked. Now re-armed she advanced on the injured would-be robber.

The driver showed no such caution. He had jumped down from the driver's box and lumbered across to the injured man who was now squirming in pain, trying to rise. An expertly aimed cudgel blow sent him sprawling and, almost in the same arc, came around to strike the back of his head.

"Bastard! Bastard's done for Jem! I'll kill 'ee!"

"Stop!" shouted Penny. "Don't kill him. We take him alive – he must face the full force of the law." The musket was now pointed towards the driver, who realised that this trembling gentlewoman had already shot two men and might easily kill him if he did not obey her.

"Full force of the law," he said with a growl. "Full force of the law. Aye. A trial and a long, slow hangin's much better. I know's the 'angman."

The wounded man was now quite still, either from the blows or loss of blood. When they turned him over and removed the hood, he was a boy of about sixteen. As she had tumbled from the carriage, Penny's shot had hit him sideways in the left shoulder, crushing bones and muscle, forcing a patch of clothing deep inside the wound where the ball was lodged.

"Better get 'ee to the magistrate quick, he'll not last long."

The boy began to scream and writhe as Carol staunched the blood flow with a hand towel and made a makeshift bandage. Penny held the gun's muzzle low down against the boy's gut to deter any sudden bid for escape, unlikely as it was in his condition. The coachman was right: no one would survive for long with such a wound.

∞

Curled up in a guest bed at the mayor's townhouse, Penny alternately sobbed and replayed the events of the day over and over. Somehow the driver had packed the two dead men and the dying boy into the carriage while Penny rode back into Calne on one of the robber's horses. This alone was an embarrassment; she had to cut her long skirt from hem to thigh before she could get into the man's saddle. Her maid, Carol, sat beside the driver in total shock, not speaking or moving for the whole journey.

The mayor, one of the town's biggest producers of broadcloth, was also magistrate and chief justice. He and his wife knew the Peverells well; he had sat in justice with Edward and had often entertained them at his home. Even as Penny sat with the justice's wife during the evening, she could hear piteous screams from a distant part of the house. The boy was being interrogated violently, tortured until he gave the names of the accomplices and the innkeeper who had set up the robbery. The justice was enraged that a woman of quality, a friend, could be betrayed by a dishonest innkeeper and attacked on the road so close to 'his' town. Justice had to be swift and severe in these troubled times;

the boy would hang tomorrow along with the innkeeper and his son.

Tossing and turning, restless and unhappy in her bed, Penny could still see the distraught mother of the boy as she pleaded for his life. No one bothered to listen; the law was the law and he was a murderer, whatever his age. The wife of the guard who had been killed defending the carriage was trying to claim his body for burial. Another woman cursed Penny for killing her man; ran at her screaming with hands outstretched, only to be knocked down by a town watchmen. It had become a wretched, ugly scene; a scene that Penny couldn't get out of her mind, haunting her, no matter how hard she tried to sleep. If only she had given up her possessions, the men would be alive and the boy not sentenced to hang.

All she wanted was Edward; Edward to hold her and love her and make her feel at peace with herself.

CHAPTER 19

Penny didn't go to the hanging, but the house gossip ensured she could not ignore the grisly details of how the barely conscious boy was carried out in a chair for his long slow death. The festival-like atmosphere, so usual at these events, was totally sickening to her.

The innkeeper, who had seemed so helpful to Penny in arranging the carriage, had been first to be seized on the basis of the hanged boy's confession. In a desperate attempt to 'save his own neck' the innkeeper had in turn given up the names of the others involved, including his own son.

"It will be of no avail," the mayor had told Penny with a laugh. "I must still show the law applies to all. After a new trial we will have a multiple hanging in the town square, after all!"

She had tried to shut all this out of her mind but the shock of the attack on her carriage had almost overwhelmed her. She had fired on the first highway robber in self-preservation, but now she could not erase the picture of his shattered neck and lolling head. The sight of the injuries to the second robber, the now hanged boy, was even worse. She and Carol had tried to bandage him as he wrestled in agony, sobbing incoherent words and cloaked in the mud of the roadside. He had been a mere boy, and dying, but they had hanged him, anyway.

Penny was required to give evidence at the travesty of a hastily set up second trial. The jury were a dozen men, handpicked by the magistrate, many of whom stood to benefit from the innkeeper's death – either by taking the trade or buying the property. Four guilty verdicts in half an hour, and already bets were being taken on who would struggle the longest at the ropes' end. As she left the guildhall after the trial, a woman again screamed that it was Penny who was a murderer, who had shot 'her man'. More refined, wealthy ladies applauded Penny's defence of virtue and property, enquiring if she would visit their homes.

Death was common and often visible in this violent and brutal age, but Penny was still horrified by the attack on her carriage and the savagery of the summary justice. As she hastened back through the town, she realised that Edward had seen worse, much worse than this, at the battles of Lansdown and Bristol. He had seen friends killed and had faced the risk of death or maiming many times. Even now, he was with their dying friend Nick Stanning – Nick whose wife, Gertie, had a month-old son. Against this backdrop of tragedy, what importance was a night of lust in a squalid inn bedroom with that hypocritical, middle-aged puritan Margaret Ransom? She remembered Edward's pleading letter again and felt a twinge of remorse.

∞

As Penny was wrestling with her emotions and trauma in Calne, Edward was finally leaving Bristol. He had stayed with Nick until the end; several days of pain and delirium that even the opium could not quench until the apothecary was bribed to administer a near-lethal dose and end the suffering. In a world of vicious execution, murder and sudden death in battle, the priests still insisted that a dying man's agony could not be ended. To Hell with them.

Between the hours he sat at Nick's bedside, Edward had worked tirelessly to set up the production of muskets and guns in the Bristol workshops, promising payment that he knew King Charles could not make; anything to keep his mind from the trauma of war. There was still no letter from Penny; no word or sight of her since that terrible morning in Bath when he had confessed his adultery with Margaret.

Now with the words of Nick's funeral service still clogging his mind, he prepared to ride away from Bristol for Bath and Peverell. Where should he look for Penny? Would she stay in Bath or return to the estate? He hoped above all that she would not attempt the journey back to Suffolk and her family. That was what she had threatened as she slapped his face and threw her wedding ring to the floor. She had the courage and resolve to do anything, however hazardous.

As he led his horse from the stables to join Phil and the waiting troops, a rough hand seized his shoulder.

"Hold, sir! I order you do not leave your post!"

It was Prince Rupert.

A sudden rage flared in Edward. "Take your hand from me, sir!" Edward bellowed with no respect for rank or protocol. "Touch me again and I will strike you down."

"I will have you hanged."

"Out of jealousy! Out of jealousy that I forced my way into Bristol with fifty men while you, sir, wasted half the king's army."

"Insolence! It is not true."

"It is what men believe. They know I was there first, sir. I am not of the army. I am a private gentleman. Call me out, if you dare."

The two men stared at each other with naked aggression. Unseen by either of them, Edward's men cocked their pistols, following Phil's example. The prince's small retinue had hands to their swords.

"I would teach you manners but I am a prince. I cannot brawl with a common oaf."

"And, sire, you are too important for the king's cause," said a courtier as he tried to stand between Edward and the prince.

"Too important for parliament's cause," said Edward with cold sarcasm. "Another heroic victory like this and our king will have scarce a man to fight for him."

Prince Rupert angrily grabbed for his sword but the courtier restrained him. Now several men had forced their way between the two antagonists.

"That's right, boy," said Edward coldly, addressing the courtier. "Protect your master." All the despair at the wasted lives; the senseless separation from Penny... his bitterness was all building within him. But would killing Rupert ease that ache?

The sound of a pistol shot resounded around the stable yard. Edward and Rupert leapt apart.

"Sorry, sir," shouted Phil. "Me pistol discharged his-self." Then, to his men, "Hold your weapons. No attack."

It has taken a farm boy from the marshes to bring some sense to his betters, thought Edward. "Good day, my prince," he said with a bow. "I look forward to continuing our discussion when this war is won."

Rupert shrugged off the restraining hands. "I will call you to account for this, Peverell," came his bitter retort.

"And I look forward to it with pleasure," Edward replied, pleased to see that Prince Maurice and Lord Hopton had now arrived.

"God speed, Peverell," roared Hopton, oblivious to the anger between Edward and Rupert. "Get that foundry of yours working on the muskets – we need every one."

Poor Hopton, thought Edward as he urged his mount forward. Since his hearing loss, Hopton missed most of what was happening. Edward could only hope Prince Maurice would be able to calm his brother down. Two hundred guns from Edward's foundry would buy a lot of tolerance – forgiveness, even.

"I thank you, Phil," he said as they rode out onto the open road. "It's good you keep a cool head."

"I was more afraid you would have a stretched neck," replied Phil grimly. "He is an evil man, given to act in haste."

"And would you have shot down a royal prince?" asked Edward, smiling.

"Any time, sir. He had but five popinjays to protect him while we had twelve trained men. I have no allegiance to foreign princes!"

"That is a problem for our whole army," mused Edward. "The men do not like Prince Rupert in command, far less the way he throws lives away on his madcap attacks."

As they rode towards Bath, Edward rehearsed in his mind

what he would say to Penny. How far should he try to explain? How far to grovel and plead? He could be lying in Nick Stanning's cold grave with no chance for... For what? Forgiveness? Would things ever be the same between them? Despair sank into him. Perhaps he and Penny had been too carefree, too absorbed in their passion to see the true meaning of—

"I need to speak to you, sir," said Phil quietly, as the horses ambled easily along the bridleway.

Edward was half aware that the rest of the troops had fallen back a furlong behind, no doubt at Phil's bidding. "Sorry, Phil, I was lost in a black reverie," replied Edward. "Is this a serious matter?"

"Very serious," replied Phil. There was a long pause and then, abandoning all attempts at subtlety, he blurted out, "I wish to leave your service. And I want to take Lady Peverell's maid, Carol, with me."

Edward turned in the saddle to stare at Phil. "Why? Are you treated badly? ... I did not know that you and Carol were—"

"We are very careful." He suppressed a smile. "Very careful in all things. We have had an understanding for nearly two years."

"My congratulations, Phil. She is a good maid – sorry – a good woman, I mean." Edward was saying the right things but felt many questions were unanswered. "Why ask my permission? You should ask her father!"

"I have. He is delighted."

A daughter off his hands, thought Edward.

"But Carol's father says times are difficult for you with this futile war," continued Phil. "And my own father says I should not leave when you are in need. You have been good to us all."

"Then why do you want to leave, Phil?"

"It's all this fighting and killing. It's not right. And the war's already lost, is it not? So many killed at Bristol, and now Prince Rupert wants to attack Gloucester and Lyme. We'll have no men left. I do not want to die for a wasted cause."

"But King Charles is our rightful ruler."

"I know nowt of Kings or of Parliamentarians. They are all just rich men taxing the poor."

Edward was shocked; he had assumed Phil Howells was loyal to the king. He sat stunned in the saddle, allowing the horse to walk on as Phil continued.

"I've fought in two battles out of loyalty to you, but it's enough. If the mistress takes Carol to Suffolk, I may never see her again."

As I may never see Penny, thought Edward.

"So married or not, I will take Carol up to the Fen country in Norfolk. It's similar to the Somerset Levels I believe, and we can hide away from the war."

"It's all held by parliament there, Phil."

"I know. But behind their lines it is said to be safe for honest, God-fearing folk. I've killed four men in battle and hanged two others. I don't blame you for the hangings, but I've finished with all the killing."

In silence Edward mulled Phil's words over. The sentiments were not far from his own, but he was a gentleman sworn to the king – he would not run off to France or Italy, or even Norfolk. Penny might have already gone.

"I am sorry I questioned your intent, Phil. You are not some bondsman who I can place under orders. If Carol goes with you freely—"

"No fear of that. The mistress has been kind to her but—"

"She needs her own life – with you," Edward cut in. "We will both miss you and Carol, but we wish you well."

"Thank you, sir."

"Just one request: if possible, do not fight for parliament. I should hate us to meet on the field of battle." Edward wiped his face to hide his confusion at the swift turn of events in his personal life. God, the whole world was crumbling around him.

"I should hate to meet you in battle, sir," said Phil. "You ride and shoot better than I."

Edward hardly noticed how they reached Bath, traversed its reeking dung-covered streets, and sought out the house they had rented. Uncharacteristically, he dithered outside, hesitating to ride into the courtyard and seek out Penny. But Penny was not in the rented house, nor at the inn to which she had fled after Edward's confession. Edward dispersed his men and set out to Peverell House with Phil. He had no news of Penny and she had left no message.

A fast ride to Peverell House and his worst fears were confirmed. Richard York, the butler, explained that the mistress had arranged for her belongings to be taken in a cart to Calne where she would hire a carriage and escort for Oxford. From there, she would seek a royal pass to allow her to go on to her father's house in Bury St Edmunds.

"And you let her go?" shouted Edward, as he read Penny's short note.

"How would I stop her, sir? Bundle her up in a sheet and

imprison her in your rooms? I had no word from you."

"I know, I know. Pardon, Richard. I am concerned for her safety. Did she travel alone?"

"Carol the maid is with her, and Roger the bailiff went with her to Calne to help with arrangements. She would not have him leave the estate for longer."

"Phil, back to the saddle. We are for Calne, and then Oxford."

"The mistress and Carol will return?" Phil questioned, disturbed at the news.

"I do not know." Edward felt near to tears. All the hopes and plans they had together, all their love killed off by one transgression. "The world is turned upside down, Phil. I have fallen off it. I don't know when—" His voice petered out in despair.

"To Calne, sir?"

"Yes, then Oxford, if needs be. If they want to go on to Suffolk you can escort them to Bury and then take Carol off to the Fens."

Halfway or more to Calne they spotted a single rider coming towards them at a reckless gallop that would soon exhaust the horse. Seeing them, the rider slowed for a moment, then continued on.

"Drawing a pistol, I lay," said Phil.

"But we are two to one. Pull over to the right, I go left, and he can pass between us. My God, it's Penny. Wait here, Phil." Gathering his reins, Edward set off towards her. "Penny!" he shouted, spurring his horse into a gallop. "It's Edward!" She rode bolt upright as usual, reins loose in her right hand, pistol in the left . "Don't shoot. It's me, Edward!"

Trying to passionately embrace while on separate horses was

171

never going to succeed and ended with them both on the ground clutching each other in a babble of questions.

"Are you all right, darling? What has happened? How do you come here?"

Phil rushed up to them. "Where's Carol?" he shouted hoarsely. "What has happened?"

"Phil?" asked Penny, surprised. "Why so forward?"

"Phil is Carol's lover. He is afraid—"

"She has come to no harm, Phil. She is in Calne with our bags while I ride back to Peverell for assistance. She is safe enough. But do go on to the Raven's Nest." She smiled at Edward and then said to Phil, "She is much shocked. Comfort her until tomorrow. I have no need of her tonight." And to Edward coyly, "Do I?"

"I sincerely hope not!"

CHAPTER 20

After their hectic time looking after Charlie and Bonnie for the weekend, John and Judith had arranged a midweek walking break in Dartmoor. The holiday didn't start well, and John believed it had every potential to get worse. An accident on the M5 delayed their arrival at the Plume of Feathers campsite on Dartmoor, and by the time their tents were pitched the pub was overflowing with other campers, meaning they would be waiting a while to order, let alone eat. The overcrowding and potential long delay seemed to have resurrected Judith's Girl Guiding memories, and she gleefully offered to rustle up an evening meal on a disposable barbecue.

This, thought John, surveying his plate grimly, *is survival cooking at its worst*. Curried beans and boil-in-the-bag rice.

As he tried to dilute the ferociously spiced beans with half-cooked rice, his concern shifted to the conflicting weather forecasts. The BBC said heavy rain as the day progressed, but a local, specialist site indicated overcast cloud with sporadic drizzle. He hadn't walked Dartmoor in any serious way and was concerned they might face the mists, mires and moving paths so often shown in old films.

Judith professed to be an expert, having completed the Ten Tors expedition and her Duke of Edinburgh Award. She had planned a series of walks, printing out ordnance survey maps for her waterproof map carrier. This seemed a bit primitive to John, so he took the precaution of programming the route finder app on his smartphone with a number of key way points. The names sounded evocative: Nun's Cross, Fox Tor, Haytor. The distances were less encouraging: about nineteen kilometres for the following day, much of it over rough ground. This was not going to be a trivial walk.

He awoke the next morning cold, stiff and disorientated, struggling against his sleeping bag.

"Christ, five thirty!" he swore under his breath.

"You OK?" came Judith's voice. She was up and out of her own tent and looked in on him, grinning. "What's up?" she asked. "Sounded as if you were having a nightmare."

He forced himself awake. "I was. Cold and in agony from this stupid sleeping bag, shut in a coffin-sized tent!"

"Baby, I thought you liked walking holidays?"

"I do, somewhere warm with a hotel and hot meal at the end of the day." He paused. He didn't want to moan and he had agreed to camp when the other options were full. "Just joking. This will be a good day, ideal weather."

"Liar! Tea's brewed. Get dressed and join me?"

"I quite like tea in bed."

"I know," she said, "and it usually gets cold."

"Only because you distract me."

"Not this morning!"

John had persuaded her to wait until the bunkhouse café opened for cooked breakfasts at seven a.m., and the day took on a decidedly better turn after a massive fry-up. Although the cloud hung low, it was quite warm, and they enjoyed the walking. The track was easy to follow due-south to Nun's Cross, but when they arrived John did take the opportunity to check his GPS app. Judith seemed amused.

"You don't rely on that, do you?" she asked. "Not out in the wilds."

"Why not? It's accurate to a few metres and gives actual position."

"Provided you get a phone signal. It's not a true GPS that takes data from satellites."

"Don't think that's a problem," he replied, pointing back to the massive communication mast that soared up from North Hessary Tor and overshadowed the whole area.

"I prefer a simple compass – it can't go wrong. Well, unless there are anomalies, like ferrous ore deposits over at Ryder's Hill."

"I remember seeing that effect near a hill fort on the Cotswold Way," agreed John. "Our outdoor pursuits master used it to demonstrate that you should never totally rely on one device."

"So, you rely on one app?"

"No, I've got a Judith, who has a map and compass."

They soon passed Nun's Cross and the ford, and began heading down the path towards Fox Tor.

"Could veer across to Craven Hill since we're making good time?" Judith suggested, gesturing towards the slowly ascending dark hill to their left. "It's just a bit higher than most points around here and would give us a good view of South Moor."

"Worth the climb?"

"Always is. We should see Sheep's Tor, possibly down to Plymouth."

The half-mile ascent was surprisingly hard work with no defined path; an indication of the walking to come. Still, as Judith had predicted, the climb was well worth the effort, despite the partly obscured sun casting the hills and tors in a dingy light. John couldn't really discern the landmark Judith was pointing out. At her suggestion they continued further south to view the prehistoric rows of stones, before returning to Craven Hill.

"When it's like this, I feel you get more of the spirit of Dartmoor than when it's bright sunshine," Judith remarked.

"Do you prefer full-on rain or mist?" John joked, hugging her playfully.

They had only been walking for a few hours but agreed to rest for a bit and take in the view. John had a small shockproof water-resistant camera, ideal to snap a picture of Judith against the backdrop of Dartmoor.

"Do you ever look at your pictures once you get back?" she asked, squinting to make out the picture of herself on the view-screen.

"Oh yeah, when I download them to the computer."

"A thousand and one miscellaneous pics."

"All filed and catalogued for each year. This one will be in both the 'walking' file and the 'lovely Judith' file, along with the ones from the hidden webcam in my bedroom," John winked, looking over at Judith and hoping for a reaction.

She blushed and swatted at him with the back of her hand. "You sod! Is that true?"

"No, no, just a joke. So far I have about three pics of you, all fully clothed and decent."

"Thank God for that. You had me for a minute there."

They were amazed how relaxed and happy they were, as if they had been together for years, settling into an easy, fond silence as they sat beside one another. Was it the openness of the sky with bright purple heather below? It truly was a breathtaking place.

Judith pointed out their route and the contrast between the purple heather and the yellow flowered gorse. John tried several photographs, but the light was too difficult for his simple camera. When he stood up to take a shot to the south, he was shocked to see all the lower land to the edge of the moor was white with mist. Miles away, but still alarming.

"It's low-lying stuff," said Judith, confidently.

"All the same, I think we should get back on a defined path," John suggested.

"I don't think it will be too bad," she pondered. "We can head towards Fox Tor by sight and I can measure the bearing, then we can follow a route back to the minor road if the mist comes down."

The route to Fox Tor was not easy, but at least it was clear-cut. John cast frequent glances behind and was reassured that the way back to the dark dome of Craven Hill was still clear. They crossed the path that Judith pointed out and came to the clump of rocks that was labelled Fox Tor on the map.

When the mist did come down on them it was hideously quick. It seemed to boil off the hill and sweep along remorselessly to envelop them, cutting visibility to less than twenty-five metres. It was cold and damp and shut out sound until the quiet became a sound of its own.

"So much for the forecast," Judith muttered. "I think it's time for plan B."

"Agreed," said John. "We lost some time and direction with the deviation, but the GPS has reset and shows a direction almost due north."

"I'm not sure about pushing on that way," said Judith. "There's no path – well, not much of one. I'd prefer to go back up the slope until we cross the Whiteworks path and then follow on to the road."

After a brief discussion, Judith conceded that going back would be an even greater waste of time.

"Are you *sure* this is the path we need, John? It's not on the map."

"Quite a lot of them aren't," he replied. "Let's give it a go for five minutes and then come back here if there's a problem."

There was a problem – the 'path' gradually faded away and the ground got boggier.

"No go, John. Just a sheep track. Let's turn back."

He consulted the phone's screen. "I'm sure this is right," he said.

"I'm not... this looks like Fox Tor Mire."

John could tell Judith was becoming increasingly anxious. "We just turn left, go west and find your path," he suggested.

"Not good, John. We're getting more and more lost."

John felt annoyed with himself, and Judith, for getting in this situation. They should have been more cautious once the weather became terrible. Deciding that following the GPS was their safest option, he strode off, without realising he had left Judith still staring at her map and compass.

The first few steps were on firm ground and his confidence started to grow. Then, his right boot squelched down into a pit of bog water between two tussocks of marsh grass. Desperately, he threw himself to the left, arm flailing in a futile attempt for balance. He was on his left side in stinking bog water, scrambling to get up, both boots overtopped. John had lost his grip on the phone and it disappeared into the murky water between tufts of marsh grass. Standing now up to his ankles, he turned slowly to face the way he had come. No sign of Judith; no footprints; the phone lost in the mire. He doubted he could see twenty metres.

Cold fear and panic gripped him. He was stupidly alone, boot-deep in the largest mire on Dartmoor, and with no navigation. The urge to run back and find Judith was strong, but enough common sense prevailed. The first rule of hiking in the mountains was to remain calm, and during bad weather, the key was to find shelter, hole up, and wait for conditions to improve. Or, if shelter was unavailable, stay where you were and make the best of it. There was no shelter, but at least he wasn't sinking.

He suddenly remembered that there was a miniature, almost ornamental, compass on his rucksack strap: a joke present from his ex-wife. If he could walk northwards back uphill and to the west, he should find solid ground. Judith would probably do the same – it was what she had wanted to do all along. With trembling fingers and some difficulty, he detached the compass and groped in the rucksack's side pocket for his whistle. Even before he released it, he heard a shrill blast from Judith's whistle, muffled in the mist, off to one side. Six short blasts – an internationally recognised distress signal. He replied and took several careful steps. He looped the string of the whistle and the compass around his wrist and waited for Judith to signal again. Then he saw her, barely fifteen metres away.

They linked up, Judith swearing, "You bloody bastard. If you run off on me again, I'll leave you to it!"

"Sorry, I thought you were following."

"What, down into the bog? You'll smell of sheep shit for days." Despite her harsh words, she looked at him with fierce concern. "John, you could have drowned." She gave him a hug, squeezing bog water from his clothes. "I would kiss you, but I don't want to catch anything!"

They stood silently for a moment, listening to the water running through the peat channels beneath their feet.

"I'm so sorry," he said.

"It alright. You're safe, that's all that matters. Though I suggest we follow my lead from now on."

"My mobile's in the mire anyway, though I do have a compass."

She grinned at the tiny compass and John gently nudged her side.

"Oi, it's a perfectly good compass. You just need a magnifier to read it, that's all."

Judith laughed and hugged him fondly.

Once they had decided on a bearing, they walked for thirty metres then turned north, only to hit the mire again. It was hardly dangerous walking, but they were both wet and chilly, and in desperate need of somewhere warm and dry. Eventually, almost in despair and miles off the planned route, they came across the Nun's Cross path again and headed back to Princetown and the

Plume of Feathers. Suddenly, as the track became visible and distinct, the mist cleared. Or, more accurately, it was washed away by sheeting rain.

The deluge continued without ceasing as they squelched the last few miles back to a waterlogged Plume of Feathers campsite, where pools of water lay suspended in the grass. Several smaller tents had collapsed under the impact of the downpour, including John's. Inside there was about an inch of water. The sleeping mat was floating and the sleeping bag saturated. He shuddered at the mere thought of it.

"Mine's not too bad," commented Judith. "Perhaps we could make do with one tent?"

"I'm wet through and bloody cold," replied John. "Much as I'd like to be in there with you, I think I'll decline and sleep in the car."

"Come off it, John. You're six foot two and the seats in your Fiesta don't even recline properly! Perhaps there's room in the bunkhouse. Let's ask—"

Judith was interrupted by an excited squeal. The larger, more substantial family tents all seemed intact, and out of one – an enormous canvas bell tent – a small naked boy appeared, rapidly pursued by a man in Speedos and flip-flops. They were followed more slowly by a woman in a bikini with a pregnancy support belt worn around a well-developed baby bump. She carried a rucksack with a bright orange waterproof covering.

"Bath time," she commented to Judith with a smile. "Must keep the routine!"

"He'll need it," Judith laughed.

The boy and his father had been jumping up and down on a

patch of waterlogged grass, and now 'accidentally' slipped over and lay full length on their backs, driving their heels into the mud, shouting with laughter.

"Jumping up and down in muddy puddles," said the woman with a chuckle. "I knew this would happen."

"Too much *Peppa Pig*," Judith quipped.

"Peppa Pig?" asked John, as the pregnant mother herded the boys towards the toilet block.

"Children's cartoon on TV," Judith replied. "I've seen it with Simon's kids. Often ends with splashing in muddy puddles like that."

"Whatever turns you on," said John.

"Strangely, it does," replied Judith. "Seeing them having fun together – not the cartoon." She turned John to face her. "Now I understand. That's why you dived into the bog, isn't it? Practising for fatherhood."

"Let's try for a hot meal and a room in the Plume," John suggested, putting his arm around Judith, "and I'll show you exactly how I practise for fatherhood."

Any tension between them had already been washed away by the deluge, and seeing the happiness of the other family had lifted their spirits.

With so many ruined barbecues and swamped trek tents, the pub was full to overflowing. There were no rooms in the bunkhouse or the pub itself.

"Sorry, mate," explained the harassed landlord, "but we're already topped up with orders for food, and every bed's taken..."

"We could manage on the kitchen floor of the bunkhouse," suggested Judith.

"Four are booked into that already. I'm well over the fire certificate limit for the building."

"Fire being very likely on a night like this," John said sarcastically under his breath.

"It is," countered Judith. "Too many people crowding in, trying to cook and dry clothes."

"Perhaps we could get a quick meal and head back to Bath," John suggested.

"Sorry, mate, hate to be a moan but food's booked solid until ten, then I quit. I'm trying to help out as much—"

"I'm sure," apologised John. "Sorry to grouch. Is there any other place we could try, after I've had a pint of Jail Ale." He looked to Judith. "Do you want a drink?"

"Only if I'm not driving. A large glass of red – Merlot, thanks."

"A lady with taste!"

As he turned to get the wine, the landlord added, "We've friends in Tavi who run a B&B-style guesthouse. I know they had a room vacant – a cancellation due to the weather – when we spoke at five, but they are expensive, over a hundred pounds a night, no evening meal—"

"How far?" asked John

"He'll take it," said Judith. "It's his tent that fell in."

"Sorry, ma'am, thought you was a couple."

"With him? Not a chance!"

∞

"The tower was built in the thirteen hundreds to adorn the prior's

183

residence," the owner of the guesthouse was explaining to John. "This section is much later."

"I can see by the style of the stonework—" John started to say, but Judith cut in.

"I know this is riveting stuff but it's getting late and it's raining. I need a shower and food."

The owner had been giving a running commentary to John as he led them through the hall and into the 'Queen Room', supposedly decorated in Elizabethan style, but with a totally modern *en suite* shower room.

Even after using the facilities and changing into drier clothes, neither John nor Judith felt like searching for a restaurant or pub. They ordered an Indian set meal for two, a side order each, and two large bottles of Cobra. By now the weather had improved considerably, so they delayed the food and took a stroll along the River Tavy to take advantage of the weak evening sun. Judith suspected they could have reinstated the tents, but John had emphatically refused to 'rough it' in a soggy sleeping bag, despite Judith's assurance that he would warm up as the night progressed.

"Was there any ulterior motive in arranging this trip?" John asked warily with a smile, as they sat down cosily together at the small oak table in their bedroom. "Was it an endurance test? Or an assassination by exposure, with a phoney will already written, leaving you all my worldly wealth?"

"Hardly," Judith chuckled. "With what Mum and Dad left me, I've far more than your business is worth. Even without Peverell."

"Immoral purposes, then?" he asked with a grin. He sipped his beer with appreciation.

"I hope so, but no need for a holiday to get that started. Just a minute, need to rinse this curry sauce off my hands." She retreated into the bathroom and came back, almost at once flicking water at John. "The plan – my plan – was for several days of relaxed walking together; no interruptions or serious navigating." She paused for a moment and took a peach they had bought at a corner shop from her bag. "Wanted to discuss a few things without it getting too heavy or intense."

"Or Simon screaming for a babysitter."

"Exactly."

They finished most of the meal and John settled back into his chair with some trepidation.

"OK, have you got a list?"

"In here, John, in here." She tapped her forehead and took a deep breath. "I wondered how you think we get on together. Are we a long-term item? Do you think of us as being in a relationship?"

John shivered inwardly. This was a lot more direct than he had expected. His beer seemed a long time gone and he wished he'd bought them two bottles each.

"I'm not sure about the future, but I don't want to wreck anything," he said hesitantly.

"How do you mean?"

"Well, changing things, either big decisions or—"

Judith got up for a moment to wash her sticky fingers after the peach. She sat down again and slowly continued. "You want to drift on as we are?"

"No, that's not what I was going to say. I don't want things drifting on and fading out." He got up and sat beside her, gave her a big hug, and confessed, "I'm happier than I can ever remember, but there are some issues. It's difficult."

"I know. There's your snoring, for one..."

"What? You are the one—" He stopped – this was not about 'issues' in bed, or snoring. He made himself speak calmly. "I was thinking that we've both been mangled emotionally. Probably my fault in my case. And you—"

She interrupted him curtly, "There's an elephant in the room to discuss, John – the *baby* elephant. You'll never be happy without children, will you? When you saw that dad with his little boy at the Plume campsite you were green with envy."

"It's not jealousy; I just felt happy for them. I can't explain it, but that's how I wanted to be with my ex-wife. I just—"

"I know, I know. That's why I feel we need to discuss the future. We could never live together, John – one of us would commit murder within the first six months."

He knew it would be difficult, but they could get a big place – separate bedrooms. What about the family bit? Was she afraid of having children?

They sat in silence for a while until John whispered, "So, are you suggesting we split up? Is this a gentle let-down?"

"No! Christ, no. Being with you is great. I don't want to give it up."

"And Mark?"

"Yeah, well. I've realised what a controlling, dominating rat he was. Me getting promoted ahead of him was probably just too much for him."

"So what's your solution?" John asked warily, afraid and tense.

"That's what I wanted to talk about." A brief hesitation and then, "What would you think of co-parenting?" Her last words came out in a rush, almost like she was embarrassed.

John was taken aback. "What, living like divorced parents but not bothering with the marriage and break-up first?

"Not how I would have put it, but I suppose so..." Her voice trailed off.

Lost for words, John stared at Judith. She was trying to look nonchalant but John knew she must be trembling inside, awaiting his reaction. There had been a growing affection between them, sure, but never a hint of discussing a family. He needed time to get his head around this... or did he? This was what he had always wanted, after all. What he had always missed in his previous relationship. Yes, it wouldn't be the same as living together full time, but he would still be a dad. John felt a surge of warmth inside.

Judith, desperate to fill the silence, blurted out, "More like when one parent is weekending for work – separate houses but sharing the parenting evenly."

John took both her hands in his and smiled reassuringly. "I can't believe you want to do this with me," he said stupidly.

Smiling, she pushed him gently away. "John, this is serious! We've got to discuss this rationally."

"I don't feel rational!" His voice was all choked up. "I'm just so happy."

They sat looking at each other, until John hugged Judith tightly to him.

"Do I get to stay over some nights?" he asked.

"Not a chance! I'm not putting up with your snoring any

more than I have to."

John laughed. At least he wouldn't have to put up with Judith's snoring either. Then he sobered. "Surely that would be very disruptive for a child?"

"It needn't be. It's a much better situation than most military families, or when one parent works away. There's even an agency for mature-ish professionals who want to do this; people who cannot find romance, don't want marriage, but do want a family. Haven't you heard of Cupid's Bow?" She couldn't believe she was bringing up that ridiculous website.

"You're kidding, really?" John shook his head, baffled by the idea. "Seriously though, our own natural children, not adopted or anything?"

"I hope not. It's a bit of a step and would need planning, but it's better than hoping for a condom failure. That's why I wanted to lead you into the idea gently."

John pulled Judith into his lap and kissed her softly. "Had you any timeframe in mind?"

"In a few years, I suppose? Just to give me time to get my career on track, build up some maternity leave."

"Well, I suppose we can have fun practising!"

CHAPTER 21

In the plush four-poster bed at The Priory Guest House, Judith slept like a tormented soul in the grip of hideous nightmares. However often John turned her over in bed, her thrashing and rolling soon brought her to sleeping flat on her back in the snoring position. It was amazing to John that such a small chest could produce such prodigious volumes of sound.

Eventually, driven by the fatigue of the day and helped by the beer, he did fall asleep, only to be woken by Judith roughly shaking him.

"John! Can't you lie still and quiet? I can't sleep through that din!"

He retreated to one of the square upholstered chairs for the rest of the night, pulling a spare coverlet over himself. The high back of the chair was supportive and absorbed much of the sound from the bed. The heavy tapestry bed curtains also muffled the noise, and John finally slept well.

Suddenly, it felt as though the room tilted and shook. Startled, he roused. Judith was now more or less quiet; just producing the occasional snuffle. Weak with dizziness, he looked around him.

Sitting in an identical chair to his own, dressed in a white lacy nightgown, was Penny Peverell, her mass of red hair trapped under a white lace cap. What was she doing in Devon? How long had she been there? How much had she seen of him and Judith together?

"So, this is how men keep their vows of love."

John gasped. "You rejected me."

"And when I did offer myself to you, you rejected me 'out of honour'. Now I see why: you were saving your strength to debauch poor broken-hearted Judith."

Momentarily confused, he almost reacted angrily, before he realised that Penny was teasing. Beside her chair a tall candlestick shed a flickering, eerie light, picking out the smile and features that left him breathless. He had spent several hours discussing parenthood with Judith and the first part of the night practising how to create the children they would share. Now, all his pent-up passion for Penny was returning. Did she still want him to make love to her?

"Step into my space, John," Penny said, almost coyly. "My space or my time. We don't want to awaken your... *mistress*."

John stood, as though lifted by an invisible force, and took a few paces towards Penny. Turning back to the bed for a moment, he realised he was no longer in The Priory Guest House, but in Penny's own time. His mind was whirling in complete confusion – he felt dizzy and delighted. Was it the flight back through time, or the overwhelming emotion of being with Penny once again? The *en suite* bathroom of his era was now a sizeable dressing room to the side of Penny's bedroom, dimly lit by a single candle. In another time, Judith must be thrashing and snoring, closed off by an ornate painted door that John had passed through.

"Edward is sound asleep," Penny said. "He sleeps like the dead after he has been with me."

"So, you are back together? Reconciled?" John asked.

"And very happy." She smiled fondly. "Although there have been grievous times for both of us; more for him than for me. We have both sinned. We now forgive and start again."

John hoped she would explain, but instead, silence seemed to stretch into an age.

"How is it that we can meet like this?" John eventually asked. "I thought it was only possible at Peverell."

"And the baking house in Bath. We can meet in any place that exists in both our worlds."

John was finding it difficult to concentrate on Penny's words; her beauty and allure had always been a distraction to him, even though he knew any relationship was impossible. There was a passion for Penny that clawed at his heart; so different from the warm, almost familial love he felt for Judith.

Oblivious to John's agitation, she continued. "The Stanning family bought this ruin years ago and Nick's father converted it into a house. Since her husband's death, Gertie moved in here with her family. She cannot bear to be in the manor house with all its memories."

Penny explained about the grievous wounds Nick Stanning had received at Bristol, his lingering death witnessed by Edward, and their decision to travel to Cornwall to sustain Gertie with her young child.

"It's no worse for her than hundreds of other women, but at least she has money and property."

"And good friends," added John. "And you have forgiven Edward?"

"How could I not? I would have done the same with you if you had taken advantage of my misery. I was more than tempted, John."

"I still am." John realised that his hands were trembling now, and turned himself slightly so that she wouldn't see. His yearning for her was like an illness, an obsession.

"You would lie with me even with Judith asleep in your bed?" she asked.

"Yes," he continued earnestly. "We both love elsewhere; her love as hopeless as mine. We are good friends, we enjoy sex together. We may even have children, but will not marry or live together." The concepts of civil partnership and the co-parenting they had discussed were too complicated to explain to Penny.

"Do not dismiss what you have with Judith," Penny said, stroking his arm softly in sympathy. "I have said to you before, I have friends in desperate, loveless marriages who would sell their very souls for the happiness you have, however unconventional it may be." Penny shook her head sadly. "I have all the love a woman could expect and I have realised that everything is so fragile, particularly with this senseless rebellion by parliament. Edward could easily have been killed or maimed at Bristol, along with his friends. So many men we knew died there."

Penny then went on to tell John of the attack on her carriage; how she had shot a man dead and wounded another; how she had shot a mere boy and handed him over for execution. John tried to picture the carnage as Penny talked matter-of-factly of war. It was so different from modern war, but the utter shattering of lives was the same.

A loud voice boomed from Penny's bedroom, breaking the spell between them.

"Wife! Where are thee? Skulking in the privy? I need you here!"

Softly, Penny whispered, "I will leave you, John. I hope we can speak again!" She leapt from the chair, kissed him full on the lips, and bounded away to Edward.

"Remove that ridiculous garment, woman, it is not winter!"

John heard struggles and giggling and backed away in embarrassment.

∞

"Christ, John, what's happening?" Judith ran across the room to grab him, dragging him over to the bed. "I've been looking for you."

He blinked in the glare of the main bedroom light, struggling with the transformation across centuries.

"You came through the bloody bathroom wall!"

"You must've been dreaming."

"I wasn't bloody dreaming. I've been looking for you for ages, even searched downstairs, and when I checked the bathroom you weren't there, so how the hell did you just walk through the wall?"

What could he say? He slipped down onto the bed, pulling her into a sitting position beside him.

"John, please tell me."

"You know this place is old, right? Very old."

Judith nodded.

"Well... I went back into the past."

"To The Priory?" she asked, incredulity in her voice.

"Yes, but to the 1600s. Penelope Peverell once stayed here."

"That bloody woman again. You've been with her?"

"Not like that." John felt hopelessly entangled with his mixed emotions and the need to calm Judith.

"Did she offer you sex again?" Judith was surprised at how jealous she felt. They were still supposed to be unattached free agents, despite her co-parenting plans. Judith had been so hurt by Mark; she couldn't take it again.

"No, no, she's made up with her husband."

"Then she's a fool – once men go off the rails, it never stops." She paused. "Tell me John, if you had screwed her; had knocked her up, would you have stayed in the past? What about your commitment to our happy family?"

"I didn't, and I won't. Please let me explain." John did explain, and as he did so, he could feel Judith moving away from him, physically and emotionally.

Judith's chest felt tight. Had she been betrayed just when she thought trust and a true solid relationship was building between them? "I can't live with this, John, this constant uncertainty." She supressed a sob. "If it was just going off for a 'quickie' that's one thing, but what if you get her pregnant?"

"It won't happen," John said soothingly. "I can't change the past, can I?"

"We don't know that – any time, any place where Penny has been..." Tears were beginning to fall now. Although she knew John was trying to reassure her, she was getting more and more distressed as possibilities occurred to her. "What if you just disappear from my life one day, like Mark? Utterly gone; back four or five hundred years. I'd never know. I thought we really had something..."

John put his arm around her shoulders and said quietly, "We still have something, Judith. Nothing's changed. It was me who brought up the need for commitment. Anyway, I don't think anything I take to the past would stay there. I know I can't bring anything back to our time." He smiled at the memory.

"Oh, did you try to steal a gold doubloon?"

"No," John grinned, "it was horse shit from the streets of Bath."

"Whatever turns you on – bog water from Dartmoor or horse shit from Bath. Seriously, though, what about diseases, plague, smallpox?"

Suddenly, Judith leapt up from the bed and began to pace the room with nervous energy. This was getting them nowhere.

"Tea?" she asked desperately.

John nodded and a silence descended as the hotel kettle boiled. She opened their pack of biscuits; anything to keep her hands busy.

Sitting back alongside John, she blurted out, "And there's the jealous husband!"

"He's no cause—"

"So what? He wakes up in the middle of the night, finds his wife snogging or making love to another man – try explaining that! You may not bring a bullet back with you, but there will still be a bloody great hole if he shoots you."

They looked uncertainly at each other and realised everything was getting out of hand.

"Sorry, John, I don't mean to go on, but once deserted, always suspicious."

"Tell you what," smiled John, "if I see Penny again, I'll tell her to bite my ear to see if it's still bleeding!"

"I'll bite something more important than your ear if you don't stop talking about her!"

They continued sitting side by side on the bed in an oppressive silence, faces fraught.

Finally, Judith said, "There is nothing more to say, is there? Things are as they are and I've just got to accept it."

"No. Look, nothing's going to happen."

"Too right. I'm not leaving you alone where that woman can get to you." Inwardly, she grimaced. Being in the same room with John tonight hadn't stopped anything. She continued, "Right now, we need some sleep if we're doing a long walk tomorrow."

"Back to the chair?" John suggested, wrung out by emotion.

"Not, it's too far away. I want you here with me so I can keep hold of you."

CHAPTER 22

The trauma of the night and Judith's distress at Penny's ghostly visit had faded away with the dawn. John and Judith seemed to have recovered their composure and their comfortable relationship. The day started well with a cooked-to-order breakfast and a good weather forecast: overcast but warm, a breeze but no wind or mist; ideal walking weather. Dave, the owner of The Priory, took John on an interesting tour of the building, with details on dates and building styles. Meanwhile Mary, his wife, had suggestions for the day's walk.

"One of Dave's routes," Mary said as she pointed it out on the map as if visualising each tor and stream. "You should be fine up there today. It would have been difficult in yesterday's mist. You OK with a map and compass?"

Not sure how she should describe John, Judith said, "I thought I was, until my pal out there marched off into Fox Tor Mire."

Big smirk from Mary. "You're not the first to get that wrong. The marked path is fine, but if you detour up on the tor rocks and short-cut northwest," she indicated on the map, "then you can easily catch the west edge of the mire."

"We did. John trashed his phone with its GPS app."

"They're good for positioning, but not routes," said Mary with a sad shake of the head. "Don't take into account rough ground or bogs."

"Well, John's one doesn't even do that now. He dropped it in half a metre of filthy bog water."

"Best place for it!"

"Out of interest," asked Judith, warming to their friendly landlady, "I think John's tent is broken and his kit waterlogged. Would you have any rooms so we can stay another night?"

"Your one's free until Friday, so you could have it tonight and tomorrow night. It was a last-minute cancellation."

"Do you have a second room free?"

"No. We are fully booked, busy season." She looked confused. "Sorry I thought you were a couple, but now I remember Dave said you asked for separate rooms."

"We are half and half, I suppose," Judith explained, slightly embarrassed at how strange it would seem "It was OK for one night. John spent most of the evening sleeping in that antique chair." She paused. "I thought a few days away together might sort us out, one way or another."

"Take it from me, single tents and separate beds isn't going to sort out anything!" laughed the landlady.

"You should try sleeping with him. He—"

"A few years ago, and I might well have. Fine man like that, I don't think I'd kick him out of bed."

"It's the snoring and thrashing about... it's like sharing a bed with a donkey."

"Sounds good to me!"

"Oh, the excitement's OK – but trying to sleep afterwards... and he's so picky – everything so neat and tidy. Leave the lid off the milk or your pants on the bathroom floor and there's a major crisis."

"If he's worried about the milk when you're all passionate..."

"Exactly."

"So, it's not just the snoring?"

"No. We just live our lives in different ways," explained Judith.

"Because, if it's snoring, you don't do so badly yourself. The pair of you sounded like a two-tone siren last night!"

"*I* don't! Well, not that bad..." Judith admitted sheepishly.

John and Dave returned from their excursion.

"I've booked you in for another night here," Judith said. "Only one room. My tent's fine."

John grimaced but didn't respond.

The rest of the day went much as Judith had hoped. They avoided mentioning Penny's 'visit' and instead discussed parenting – how it might work – along with Judith's new job after the quarry, and how her career might develop over the next few years.

"I'd want you to be a hands-on dad," she suddenly blurted out.

"Of course! That's what I want too." He sounded confused. "I didn't know we'd formally agreed to be co-parents yet?"

"We haven't," she said with a laugh. "I've just taken out a five-year option."

"Five! I'll be thirty-six by then. Getting a bit late for me if you back out. I'd have to start looking—"

"Easy, just put an ad on the internet: tall, good-looking, virile male, own business, good income etc., seeks woman to be the mother of his future kids."

"That's daft." As realisation dawned, he laughed, "Is this a wind-up?"

"Of course, I'm just teasing. But seriously, I don't think you'd have much trouble finding someone. As I said last night, there's even a specialist website for singles who want to co-parent."

"I'd rather imagined a family life with someone I like, not a commercial arrangement."

"Typical man. Never pay if you can get it for free! Cuts both ways – you might fall in love with someone. Helen might come back, or you might leg it back to the seventeenth century and Penelope Peverell!" She realised immediately as she saw pain in his face that her banter had gone too far. "Sorry, John, that was below the belt."

They walked on in silence towards a pile of rocks that were one of Dave's waymarks.

"No, it's a fair point to consider. What would you do if Mark came back?"

"It won't happen."

"How do you know?

"My sister-in-law has seen him out with a new woman. He's moved on from me."

They abandoned the discussion and concentrated on the beauty of the moor landscape. Judith realised how little she knew about John. He was an orphan brought up by an aunt and uncle; he had a sister and a cousin about whom she knew little. She didn't think his childhood had been particularly happy, and he rarely spoke of it.

"I thought Mark and I both wanted children, a proper family," she said softly. "Now I don't know. Oh, I don't know, John. I feel we're more like mates who have sex together – not lovers. But that's better than what half my friends have ended up with: divorced, broken homes." She touched his hand, hoping for some response, and got a hug in return.

"The point is," he pressed on, speaking over her confused words, "if we do have children, we will need commitment; commitment to be parents, not a quick fling and a poor lonely little sod brought up by Simon or my sister Ann while we bugger off with new lovers. Being an orphan was bad enough, being abandoned..."

Judith could think of nothing to say.

They walked on, almost as if avoiding each other, until Judith grasped John's arm earnestly and said, "I'm sorry, I got that out in the wrong way, John. Blurting things out as if I don't rate you much as a dad."

"I got a bit overheated, too," he agreed and, grabbing her shoulders, kissed her cheek gently. "I suppose it's because it's so important for us."

"Let's think it over for a few months; not get caught up in the details."

"Eight happy kids!" he joked, but she still looked very tense.

"Be serious. First, we decide what we want, then we define details."

"Three happy..."

Judith gave him a shove, beginning to relax a little. "When we are really sure we want to go ahead, we'll think about everything else."

"You sound just like a manager briefing a project. People don't plan families like that."

"Then I'm an alien who just happens to be a bloody good screw. I like to plan ahead, John."

"Talking of planning ahead," he said after a while, "in fifteen minutes we stop for a snack and a drink."

"OK."

"And you're not really sleeping in your tent tonight, are you?" John asked slowly as he slipped the rucksack off his shoulders. His back was aching from sleeping in the chair and he needed to stretch out.

"No one's made me a better offer yet, but I could grow to like sleeping in four-poster beds!"

$$\infty$$

"So you're both stayin' on," said their host knowingly when they arrived back at the guest house.

"I couldn't resist dry bedding and that thick mattress," replied Judith with a grin.

"Could be a bit more peaceful, too. Todd at the Plume said he's got several school groups camping out tonight and over the weekend. A lot of furtive footsteps after dark as kids swap tents!"

They chatted with Mary for a while, explaining the route they had taken and how much more enjoyable Dartmoor was when the sun shone. Their room looked even more inviting tonight with warm late afternoon sunshine filtering in through the bay window. On each bedside table lay a packet with a handwritten label that read: *Present from Dartmoor.*

"Bit bloody presumptuous!" exclaimed John, expecting condoms.

"It's earplugs," laughed Judith. "Disposable earplugs. I haven't seen these since Mark left me. Cheeky woman!"

John laughed along with her. Their hosts were evidently prone to humour.

"Right, I'm first for the shower!" exclaimed Judith, peeling off her t-shirt and diving for the bathroom.

"We could share?"

"No, for once I need my privacy."

"Bugger!" John murmured a few moments later as she turned on the shower, the sound of running water having its usual effect. He'd have to go back downstairs.

∞

It was the last night of their holiday on Dartmoor and John was delighted with how good it had all been. They had taken one day off from the moors to walk a coastal path, but the other two had given them time to absorb Dartmoor's unique atmosphere. They had just walked and talked together, or walked in companionable silence, drinking in the open views with splashes of yellow gorse against the dull colours of grass and bracken. John had been half afraid they would get bored, run out of conversation or, worst of all, have one of their blazing rows, but it had been a near-perfect holiday.

Now, after gentle and loving sex, John was slumped in his

usual Elizabethan-style chair, thinking that every night didn't need to be like a tempest.

Despite his promise to sleep with Judith, he had compromised by moving the chair closer to the bed. An almost continual thrashing and snoring quite defeated the earplugs. She suddenly started a furious running motion – one hundred-metre sprint speed – kicking off the sheet they had used as a bedcover. There was a whimper of fear, a half sob, and the gyrations stopped. He wondered what had chased her through that nightmare. If he was a cruel bugger, he would make a video on her phone and show her in the morning. Instead, he prised himself from the chair to give her a cuddle. In his happy, contented state, John had not once thought of Penny Peverell.

CHAPTER 23

Penny and Edward should have enjoyed their autumn ride across a sunlit Dartmoor, the first part of their return journey from Tavistock back to Peverell. Instead they were sombre, remembering the desperate plight of Nick Stanning's widow, Gertie. She and Nick had readily sold off everything that they could to finance his support for the king, buying weapons, paying and feeding men. It had cost them so much, and little had come back from the king's impoverished exchequer.

Penny realised that from being a proud, prosperous and loved wife before the war, Gertie was reduced to being a figure of pity and poverty. The only option for her and the children had been to return to her father's converted priory.

"At least she will be housed with her family, and her children clothed and fed," Edward said, comfortingly. He knew Penny was deeply upset by their friend's circumstance. "So many of the widows from both sides will be starving and in rags, dependent on their family or their parish to keep them alive."

"The king cannot pay wages to the living, far less care for the dependants of the dead," agreed Penny, as they rode slowly along the trackway that was termed The Moor Road.

"It is evil, pitiless and wasteful," continued Edward in despair. "Would that some higher power could force the lords and gentry on both sides to fight their differences out on their own, and leave the common people to plough the land or make their cloth."

In silence once more, Penny thought again on her surprise nocturnal meeting with John in the Stanning family house at Tavistock. Seeing him with his mistress, Judith, had almost driven Penny wild with jealousy. After all his ardent advances he had turned her down when she needed consolation: had it been consolation or revenge on Edward? Now she was reconciled with Edward, she should be grateful for John's chivalry, not begrudging of his happiness. Edward had strayed; hurt her deeply in the worst possible way. He had cuckolded Oliver Ransom. Or was it that Margaret Ransom had betrayed her husband? If it was not Edward, then it would have been some other lusty fellow. If she still felt angry at Edward for his infidelity, how could she justify her feeling for John?

For all that, she was so glad she had not bedded with John. It seemed so much worse for a wife to stray. Or was it? Several of her married friends boasted of their conquests like the worst of men. Jacinda Bragg was little more than a married harlot.

Now she was back in harmony with Edward – lustful harmony at that – why had she felt so angry that John had been with that woman, Judith? Was it because Judith was a *Ransom*? Both the men she loved had rutted with Ransom whores. *Lord forgive me*, Penny thought to herself. She was still excited by John's attention and thoughts of forbidden pleasures. All this despite her very true love for Edward. She dwelled on those worrying thoughts, slowly trotting beside her husband, hardly noticing the beautiful moorland landscape.

"You are very pensive, my love."

Edward's words cut through her thoughts. "Aye, dark thoughts for such a bright day, and such a vista." Desperately she sought to rid her mind of the memories of John and Judith. Should she tell Edward? But what was there to tell? "It is midday," she stated. "Let us stop beside that rocky outcrop."

"Tor," Edward said kindly, "the locals call them tors – devil's tombstones for fallen angels."

"I fear I am too melancholic to enjoy this journey," she mused, as they slid down from their mounts and rummaged in saddlebags for the bread, cheese and apples that had been given by Gertie.

Both seemed to fall into a state of reverie and it was over an hour later that they clambered to their feet to proceed on their journey. Since leaving Tavistock, they had only passed one old decrepit inn, surrounded by tin workings and miners' huts, so they pressed on to Moretonhampstead. Edward had hoped they could reach Exeter but Penny was feeling strangely fatigued, and after five hours riding wanted to stop well before dark and any risk of missing their way.

The New House Inn had no suite of rooms for gentlefolk travellers, but there was a private room available for the exhausted couple. Warm, cosy and free from fleas, it provided a haven for Penny. They ate 'in chamber' and Penny immediately retired to bed, not wanting company. Edward left her and carried a candle into a public room downstairs that had a good fire and a smattering of other travellers eating, drinking and conversing in small groups of three or four men. Edward placed his candle on a vacant table, opened his book and began to read.

"Ale, sir?" asked a tap man civilly.

"Aye, a good pint tankard," he replied.

"Rather foul and cloudy today," mumbled the man. "Cider'd be better."

"Because that's meant to be foul and cloudy?" Edward felt relaxed, enjoying the conversation.

"Nay, 'tis prime – from my brother's orchard. The best!"

"Aye, it always is," Edward grinned. "Then bring me a pint of that, a slice of cheese and a hunk of bread. The mutton at dinner was slightly greasy." The drink was in fact excellent; the cheese rancid but spreadable on the hard surface of the coarse stale bread. Strangely it melded well with the cider, but he knew from experience the dangers of the seemingly gentle-tasting drink and sipped it slowly.

In the centre of the room, close by the smouldering peat fire, a large group of carters were discussing the progress of the war. They openly boasted of smuggling supplies through the Royalist blockade to parliament's General Blake in Taunton. The carters obviously believed that parliament would win with a decisive battle in the north or east.

"And what then?" asked one. "What happens to King Charles, the Man of Blood'?"

"Aye," asked another. "Is it exile or death? And do we set up General Fairfax or Cromwell as a new king?"

"No new king!" said another. "Parliament will govern by consent of the people. King Charles and his papist French queen must die, and liberty—"

Edward did not wait to hear more. Quietly he closed his book, blew out his light, and started back towards their bedchamber. He was shocked by the venomous hatred these carters expressed towards King Charles; equally dismayed by the trust they showed for the upstart, self-seekers who sat in parliament. As he was closing the door, he could make out some more remarks.

"We need a king, we've always had a king!"

"No! When Adam did hoe and Eve did spin, tell me, who was the king then?"

"That be levellers' talk!"

"And what's wrong o' that?"

∞

Over the next few days, Edward and Penny travelled in easy stages towards the Royalist headquarters at Bridgewater. They skirted Taunton, where the Parliamentarians under Blake still stubbornly resisted, keeping to the western, seaward side. Outside the intermittent Royalist siege lines there seemed to be few patrols, and it was easy to see how supplies or reinforcements could infiltrate the barricades to help the defenders.

Past Taunton, almost back to Bridgewater, Penny and Edward had passed several picket outposts of bored and uninterested royal soldiers. These men had received little food and no pay for months despite the money delivered to Lord Goring. It seemed no patrols had been conducted for weeks, and the captain's main concern was to avoid conflict with the nearby villagers who resented their presence.

"What a sad group," Penny commented as they rode off. "I would have expected them to be training on a fine day like this."

"Aye. They could at least be practising drills, but they have lost all heart. They have barely enough powder for one skirmish so cannot do any live shooting of their weapons. A sad lot indeed."

"I believe they have food and drink a-plenty," said Penny. "And coin to gamble, from what I notice?" Penny glanced sideways at Edward and felt a thrill of desire. He was very dynamic and she hoped the boredom of the day would be replaced by an intimate evening.

The pair rode on and were about to turn inland for Bridgewater when Penny noticed a small flash of reflected sunlight out to the west.

"Look!" she pointed to Edward.

Roused from his reverie, he too noticed it. "A glint on a glass?" he considered. "More likely polished metal."

"No country folk have polished steel, far less a mirror. Soldiers?"

"Parliamentary helmets or breastplates, more like."

"A signal?"

"Hardly. It would need a precise direction and someone looking out for them. More likely careless field craft."

Carefully, they turned diagonally towards the sighting and rode up a low hill for a better view. There were no trees or scrub for cover so the last bit they travelled on foot, bending low.

"If we noticed them, they may have already seen us," whispered Penny.

"I doubt it considering the sun's direction. If they did, we would look like simple travellers, and we have now ridden on out of their sight." Edward smiled reassuringly.

From the slight vantage point they could see a convoy of riders over half a mile away.

"In open sight!" hissed Penny. "They have no fear."

"Not of the patrols. There are none," agreed Edward. "But still they take care. See how the mounted escorts are spaced out from the carts, safe from explosion and wide enough to detect ambush?"

"It's too far to shoot and no cover to get closer. Possibly from that copse?"

Penny pointed to a small belt of trees, but even as Edward considered it two troopers were dispatched in that direction to scout for sharp shooters.

"Damnation, their commander is vigilant. But see – only he and a companion have helmets and breastplates. Cromwell's Ironsides."

"This far south, but only two?"

"Probably arrived with a supply ship, sent into the area to command and train the local Parliamentary militia. We can do nothing."

"We ride back to the patrol camp and rouse them to action. Do not let us succumb to being defeatist, Edward."

CHAPTER 24

It was with very mixed feelings that Judith had agreed to meet Mark Davis, so that in his words he could 'explain a few things'. She had a real fear of an explosive scene; even worse of being conned into falling under his spell again. She did hope it would clear her mind of any residual feelings and answer some of the questions that had haunted her for the last two years. Questions like why had he gone; what did he want now, and the not so obvious 'who the bloody hell do you think you are coming back into my life!'?

Judith had chosen to meet Mark in Pizza Express after work; the restaurant was an open, public venue in the middle of Bath. There would be a few other people there at six p.m., which should act as a civilizing influence, and plenty of space between herself and Mark, to avoid any suggestion of intimacy. Carefully, Judith tethered up her bike to a sturdy lamppost, the cable through front and back wheels as well as the frame. All the fittings were secured with star-hex screws.

"For God's sake, stop this prevarication!" she told herself severely. Mark wouldn't arrive until six thirty.

Inside, Judith accosted the manager and asked for a side table in view of the pizza area and cash desk. He showed a healthy interest in her Lycra-clad legs and seemed very attentive. She explained in a whisper that it was a delicate meeting with her ex, and could he not seat anyone else too close unless it got very busy. The manager smiled briefly and led her to a far table, moving discreetly away to a distant corner where he pretended to be setting up glasses and crockery along the counter, furtively admiring her.

Judith waited with an untasted coffee, nervous and edgy, until Mark strolled in on time – a first. He was wearing a suit and tie for Christ's sake! Mark's eyes flicked around the room until he noticed Judith and marched towards her with supreme confidence and a broad smile.

"Hi, Jude, you look great. Sorry about the kit, I'm straight from work."

A software engineer wearing a suit at work? No chance, not even if he was meeting the CEO. He did look good, she had to admit to herself; not as tall as John, but fit, tanned and bursting with self-assurance. Over Mark's shoulder she could see the manager hovering. Did his earpiece link to a directional microphone? There must be hundreds of 'interesting' conversations to listen in on. A waitress appeared with some menus for them that Judith took politely, but with no intention of ordering a meal. Instead, she asked for two fresh coffees.

"You still drink Americano?" she butted into Mark's spiel about how stupid he had been to leave her.

"Same as always, babe. I haven't changed a bit." He took his jacket off and draped it over the back of his chair, seemingly without a care in the world.

"Shame. I have."

Judith noticed her hand was shaking slightly as she held the unwanted menu. Mark didn't notice, but ploughed on with his tale: of how he'd been diagnosed with an untreatable prostate cancer – it had already spread throughout his body – one year, tops. He had decided to leave and spare her the agony of seeing him die a lingering death. Now there was a new treatment.

Judith just couldn't keep her voice low and blurted out, "For God's sake, Mark. Knock it off! All this had nothing to do with Simon paying you to sod off."

"Shit! He told you?"

"No, I found out. Charlie had heard a bit of it and got it all wrong, but once I started digging—" She shrugged dismissively. "So why all this crap about cancer and no doubt a miracle cure?"

His smile barely faltered. "Looks bad I know, but when Simon offered me the cash I took it and headed off, a year of high living before the end. It was peanuts to Simon."

"And our joint bank account, the investment bond – you took it all!" She couldn't help raising her voice. Did Mark really think he could get away with the lie? He was such a prat.

"That... that was very wrong, but I thought I was dying. I'd had some problems. The GP sent me for tests, ultrasound and—"

It sounded genuine enough, a plausible story. But she didn't buy any of it. Mark was such a toerag, she couldn't believe anything he said.

Judith kept as calm as she could before saying, "You left me broke. You almost destroyed me. I had to sell up and crawl back home to Mum and Dad."

"Sorry to hear about your parents. I had hoped one day we would get on; I would be part of the family."

She yelled at this, too. "You hated them!" Then she buried her nose in the pizza menu hoping to avoid the inquisitive looks from customers across the room.

Mark smirked sheepishly as she drained her cup of cold coffee. "Surely Simon could have helped?"

"He was fully committed financially from paying you off. He never told me, or even Mum and Dad, that he had done that."

Why had she agreed to meet Mark? Perhaps for a truthful explanation as to why he had taken Simon's money and just walked out of her life, like the bastard he was. More importantly, she wanted to seize the initiative for once and shut Mark out of her mind for good.

"So, what happened? You run out of money?"

"It's not like you think. In America there was a new experimental therapy. I paid to go on the trial."

"A wonder drug?" Judith was brought up sharp. Was he entirely innocent and really had been terribly ill? She started to feel a touch of remorse, and guilt; even pity for him.

"No, a radioactive dye that attaches to the cancer cells," Mark was saying. "It was very aggressive but I'm clear now, almost the three years. It's all true. They're even using it on kids in the UK now."

Forcefully, Judith pressed on. "I'm sure you've done your homework, but why meet up now? You've been home in the UK for months, working back at Dyson and then that software security unit."

"Like I said, the three years is almost up and then it's 'all clear'. I thought we might give it another—"

"Nothing to do with me inheriting Peverell House, then?" It came out so smoothly, she was pleased with herself for keeping her nerve.

"Have you? I didn't know."

Mark hailed a waiter and ordered a beer; offered Judith a wine, which she declined. She needed to keep a clear head, and her temper.

"Give it a rest, you bastard. You're still living with a girl called Trudy who's got a good job and a wealthy family. Did you think I'd be a better bet after all?"

"Of course not." Mark swallowed some of the pale liquid. "Me and Trudy are just mates..." He tailed off, losing his impetus for the first time.

"Not according to sweet Trudy when we met up yesterday for lunch."

"She told me she'd gone back to Birmingham for a few days," he croaked, "to see her parents."

"She has now, after our chat. After I showed her the foreclose notice on our house when you did a runner; after I showed her a copy of your agreement with brother Simon to loan half a mil to set up a new company before you did a runner; the withdrawal on our joint account." Judith felt triumphant. Just for a moment, she was ahead in this sordid discussion.

"Stop, wait. He never gave me that much," Mark protested violently. "There was no written agreement with your brother."

"There is now. Verifiable signature, fingerprints on the paper, even some DNA and a stray hair."

Mark looked like he had run into a wall. There *was* a forged document, not as elaborate as she'd suggested, but a bit of exaggeration was always useful. Initially, Judith had persuaded Simon not to use it if Mark stayed away.

"It's a forgery!" he blustered.

"Of course it is. Cost thousands, no doubt. But getting between my Big Bad Bro and his money is very dangerous. Simon's solicitor is a real villain too, got all the background papers in place."

Mark slammed his fist on the table, seething with rage. "It's stupid. I can't pay anything like that back."

"Simon knows that. You'll be bankrupt. Word will get around to your employer. A security firm needs to trust its people. You'll never work again; never con some other rich girl. You know, Mark, that girl Trudy really loved you. She's almost as gullible as I was; believed you would marry, have kids, for Christ's sake." Judith suddenly felt drained and exhausted. It had all been such a strain, an ordeal to stand up to Mark after the hurt and damage he'd caused her by his abrupt disappearance, even if it was two years ago.

There was a silence for some time until Mark said, slowly, in the most sincere tone, "I know I behaved badly, but I want to make a fresh start. The cancer bit is true, and then Simon's offer..."

"A fresh start. Marriage and kids?"

"Yes, I mean it."

Judith shook her head, wearily. "It's all bullshit, Mark. If you'd had that radiation therapy your wedding tackle would be shrivelled to nothing. You'd be both impotent and infertile."

"No, not always."

"Always. Uncle Ron is dying of prostate cancer. We all follow the developments, we know the facts." She stopped and looked aghast as realisation hit her. "You bastard, you rotten scheming... You knew Uncle Ron had it; one more turn of the sympathy key. You just wait, by the time we've finished with you, you'll be sleeping on the streets, busking for coppers in Bath."

"In your dreams," Mark scoffed, leaping up, sending his chair flying. "I'll get even with you, you bitch. And Simon, and that bit of rough you're shagging."

"The one with his own company, no debts and no deficiencies?"

They yelled more insults until the manager and the short burly pizza chef arrived at the table.

"Sir, it would be better if you left now. And stop shouting." His voice was low and calm from experience with late-night drunks – men and women.

"Why me?" cried Mark, raising his voice even more. "Chuck *her* out. Give me one good reason—"

"I don't have to, sir. These are licensed premises. I can order anyone to leave."

"Order?"

"Yes." The manager was still keeping his cool, detached manner.

"And if I don't go?"

"I'll call the police. It's fixed procedure. I report an affray on licensed premises and they have to respond."

Mark waivered.

"Sivlana," the manager called to a waitress who was hovering beside a wall-mounted keypad, phone in hand. "Pre-set nine. When the police answer, read out the message on the card."

"Stop. Wait. I'm going." Mark grabbed his coat from the chair. Then he turned furiously and poked a finger towards Judith. "I'll get even with your family, you'll see." He turned to the manager. "I'll see you around, pal."

"I'll make it easy for you, *pal*." The same calm voice, but all hint of the civil manager replaced by flat hardness. "I drink at The Vic opposite Victoria Park. Thursday nights. I'll look forward to seeing you."

Mark left.

The manager turned to Judith again. "I'm sorry your evening ended so badly."

"It's not ended," Judith answered, trying to appear unflustered by the events.

"Do you want a taxi?"

"No, I've my bike outside and I need food, please." She realised how hungry she felt. "Olives and garlic bread to start, I think." Then added, "Devilito pizza, extra peppers and artichokes. Oh, and an egg in the middle, like on a Florentino."

"It's not standard," apologised the manager.

"I'm sure you can add it to the bill."

"Another coffee? That one's gone cold."

"No, a bottle of Valpolicella."

Judith sat back and relaxed, feeling rather drained, but she had laid her own personal ghost to rest. She was fully rid of Mark; brain swept clean. If she could bullshit like that about the 'agreement', she could go into politics. Judith wondered if she should have admitted to Simon about forging the documents.

Ah, what the heck, she thought. No-one would listen to Mark, anyway.

The manager kept watch on Judith as she gulped down her first glass of wine and then as she pulled out her phone to make a call.

"Hi, it's me. I need a favour."

He could not hear the reply, but it was a man's voice.

"Never say 'anything'! Joking aside, in about an hour I'm going to be too drunk to ride my bike home. Could you give me a lift?"

Again the manager couldn't hear the answer.

"Home, of course." A chuckle. "Well, maybe. I'm celebrating – you could join me."

It was a longer reply from the other end of the phone this time.

"No, you're kidding? Did you say a Bach recital at Bath Abbey? I despair. You turned down an evening with your mates for that?"

The phone conversation continued and the manager considered possibilities. It was a quiet evening. He could leave early, Carlo would close up. He could easily fit her bike in his SUV. One thing could lead to another... Damn it, she'd talked someone into joining her and was still speaking to them on her phone.

"OK, you push my bike back to yours and I'll stagger."

More chat and giggling, but he'd lost interest.

Judith called over to the waitress. "Hi, Sivlana, a friend's joining me soon. Could you bring another glass? Oh, and a bottle of fizzy water for him."

Judith settled back on the bench seat, contented and happy, with an air of expectation as she waited for John.

CHAPTER 25

Penny was hot and tired from a very hard ride and the arduous task of washing down and brushing her new mare, Connie. Together, they had shown clear hooves to a picket of dragoons exercising on Clifton Down who had given good-natured chase as Penny galloped by in her pale blue riding coat and matching hat, hair streaming behind her. They even gave her a gallant cheer when their poor cavalry mounts had been easily outdistanced. Of course, Penny knew it was not a fair race – they carried more weight in men and equipment and were fatigued. Even so, it was gratifying to leave the mock pursuit behind and keep up the pace for so long. It was exhilarating to be riding out on the Downs alone.

Since her return from Tavistock, Penny had bought a fresh horse from Lady Cavendish who had decided to desert England for France after her husband had died storming Bristol. Penny had spent a lot of time training Connie to improve the horse's stamina, which had been lost due to inactivity. In truth, there was little else for Penny to do – even the most social of the officers' wives had grown tired of each other's company. It was a small dedicated group who stayed on in Bristol with husbands or lovers. Meanwhile, Edward busied himself with organising the production of muskets and uniforms, but this had slowed due to the shortage of supplies and lack of funds to pay workers or factory owners. As with the dismal attacks on Taunton, it was lack of finance that crippled their attempts to equip the army.

Bounding up the stairs of the rented house towards their bedroom, she paused only to order hot water for washing. Penny was surprised to find Edward sitting dejectedly in the small withdrawing room, staring blankly at the bags and boxes that held most of their smaller valuables.

"Edward! I'm so pleased. I did not expect you back from Gloucester for several hours."

He rose to greet her; a big all-embracing hug somehow lacking his usual ardour.

"A good ride, I see," he was saying. "You smell of horses and fresh air. No doubt I will suffer the usual reproach for letting my madcap wife out riding on her own."

She followed his lead. "I pray, sir, what will your excuse be?" She removed her felt hat, and red hair tumbled down around her shoulders.

To Edward, she looked even more desirable. "I give no man or woman excuse for my wife. If they had horses and skill to keep up with you—"

"I out-ran four cavalry officers on the Downs today. Not one of them could match me for speed." She pushed him gently away. "Enough of my chatter." She glanced at Edward's glum face and asked him quietly, "I see your day at Gloucester was disappointing. The Birmingham merchant did not make you an offer?" She pointed to the boxes on the table.

He shrugged unhappily. "Oh yes, he made offers. Offers of less than half the true values." Edward handed her a sheet of cheap paper – an inventory of the items he had attempted to sell.

"Edward, you included your mother's clock?"

"The movement is primitive and needs adjustment every day, but the case is gold with pearls. I thought it could go, but not for such a low price."

Penny read the figures in astonishment. "Are these sums his valuation? He is a rogue, he should be whipped!" she said furiously. "Wait, my wedding bracelet—"

"He did not want it, not even for the metal." Edward sat forlornly. "He only agreed to meet me in Gloucester as a favour to our mutual friend, Richard Boscombe."

"A good man, but he deals with this... this thief?"

"The jeweller did explain his problem," said Edward. "Every second Royalist supporter is trying to sell jewellery, plate, pictures – anything to raise money for King Charles's cause. No one has the money to buy. Trade is slack due to the rebels' war."

Again Edward looked beaten, but Penny decided to try another idea.

"In England and Scotland, I agree, but France and Spain?" she questioned.

"French and Spanish merchants know our prices and will not give good value even if they could."

"So they can make a fortune from our despair when they get back to Paris or Madrid, or Vienna or Prague further on."

"There are some severe risks trading in gems."

"Rubbish, Edward! There are two French ships in Bristol

dock as we speak, one loading your broadcloth heading for the Loire." Penny gripped him by the shoulders. "We leave in two days and hawk our wares in Paris."

Unexpectedly, Edward said, "That is what I was going to propose, but not *we*, my love. It will be I alone. It is late in the year for safe passage, and parliament's ships patrol the Channel."

"And I will not trust my handsome, virile husband to a gang of Parisian ladies." She touched his arm affectionately and caressed his face. "If you go alone, I will follow on the next ship."

He made as if to argue but kissed her instead, only stopping when Penny's new maid arrived with 'water for madam's toilet'. Knowing they were alone, Carol would have discreetly knocked and waited, but alas. He hoped the new maid would learn quickly.

∞

It was late in the sailing season and the small cargo ship *Marianne* suffered the full force of a sudden, unexpected Channel gale. It seemed to Edward the vessel attempted to stand on its bows, roll on its side, and sit upright on its stern. With each roll or pitch he feared they would never regain equilibrium. He had crossed the Channel to France many times before, often continuing onto Spain, but never felt so afraid. He didn't vomit, but could not eat and feared to drink except in sips. Penny revelled in the thrill and excitement of the foul weather and spent as much of her time as possible on the open quarterdeck secured by a safety line.

Often, while Edward was indisposed, she traded banter with the merchant who owned and captained the vessel. She practiced her French and asked about trading conditions and politics in Paris. Surprised at her commercial knowledge, the captain joked that if Penny did not have such a formidable husband they would make a good partnership. What was marriage, anyway? Adam and Eve were not married unless the serpent performed the ceremony!

All in jest, of course, thought Edward angrily through his seasickness. *Just nonsense until some woman responded.* The captain might value Edward as a trading partner but he would not hesitate to seduce Penny given a chance. If the ship's captain knew how much potential wealth they had in their threadbare bags, would he banter and jest so much?

As they rounded Brittany, past Brest, and headed towards Lorient and the mouth of the Loire, they were sheltered from the northern gale, and the sea became calmer. For the first time in several days Edward felt safe to eat a full dinner, even if it was only cold meat and bread.

Sitting in relaxed fashion with Penny while the captain was on deck waiting for the first sight of the river estuary, Edward asked, "You enjoy conversing with the gallant captain?"

"Only to stir your jealousy." She wiped her fingers fastidiously and added, "He is an incredible bombast and no doubt a lecherous man, if given a chance!"

"Aye," said Edward agreeing with her. "You'd think he owns half of Nantes to hear him boasting. Still, he is quite successful and has many contacts."

"Not with goldsmiths or jewellers," commented Penny. "But I have learned a lot of the situation in France."

"I need to get on deck – fresh air," gulped Edward as the effect of the ripe French cheese hit home.

They walked forward to the bow of the ship, away from the captain's place near the helmsman. The ship glided along effortlessly on a few sails as the lookouts scanned the distant coastline, calling out as they sighted landmarks in turn.

"France. Mouth of the River Vilaine, Penestin, and La Roche-Bernard."

Marianne turned smoothly to the south and picked up a little more speed as additional sail was hoisted to catch the wind from the northwest. They watched the sailing evolutions with interest for a while.

"Did you know that the king, Louis XIII, died suddenly and that his son LouisX1Vis only five years old?" Penny asked.

"I had heard. That is why our King Charles has little support from France. The queen regent has no sympathy for him."

"Our captain suggests that the first minister, Mazarin, is pleased to see the English squandering its strength by fighting a civil war."

"Possibly," agreed Edward, "but if the rebel Protestants win in Britain, they will oppose a Catholic France at any turn." He shook his head, worrying about the future and a possible war with France.

Edward glanced over the ship's rails to see the low undulating landscape covered in dense trees along the Loire estuary and thought how peaceful it seemed, even in these troubled times.

"What is more important," said Penny, "is that there is a growing enmity between the queen regent and the French nobles. She banishes or imprisons any who oppose her."

"Does this affect our plans, do you think?" he asked.

"I think so," Penny observed warily. "The nobility is hoarding its wealth from The Crown, and Paris itself is in turmoil – riots occur almost every month due to higher taxes. Not a good place to be hawking valuables."

"No, definitely not.

"Better to stay at Nantes or Angers," Penny continued. "They are said to be stable trading towns with rich merchants and secure nobility who have little interest in the power struggle."

Edward looked at Penny in pure admiration. "My, my, what a wealth of information you have obtained. I can almost forgive your familiarity with our lascivious captain."

"It required very little guile," Penny replied. "He is a simple soul who would not stop talking. But, my husband, if you wish me to play the spy again, please choose someone with more wit and less garlic on his breath!"

∞

It had taken another two days to enter the Loire estuary and longer still to beat up the river to Nantes, arriving in the late evening. It was too late in the day to search for suitable lodgings long-term, and their ship's cabin was swapped for a room in one of the many dubious harbour-side inns. At least the bed did not roll with the constant sea motion that Edward hated so much. Suspecting fleas or bedbugs, Penny slept on an un-upholstered bench, using some spare clothes for a mattress. Hardly Edward's idea of a romantic first night in France.

The next day, after a spartan breakfast, they sought out an austere but clean suite of rooms as would befit a travelling merchant and his lady companion. This fitted their claim to be seeking new opportunities for trade, away from the disruption and chaos of rebellion-ravaging commerce in England. They refused to comment on any allegiance to the king or parliament, and similarly to either Protestant or Catholic faith.

"We are just simple merchants who wish to live and trade in peace," Penny had replied to the landlord's prying questions. "We pray and serve God as best we may, giving offence to no one."

CHAPTER 26

With the shadow of Mark lifted from her life and becoming settled in her new job, Judith felt she had enough energy to consider Peverell House. The offices previously used by Simon and her father, Greg Ransom, were easily rented out to a marketing company that needed more space. John had contacts with a former technical college that wanted to reinstate some craft training courses they had abandoned. Such courses were now becoming attractive to create skilled apprentices, and John believed some of Peverell's rooms and outbuildings could have facilities improved for this purpose.

Judith realised that planning for a future at Peverell was exciting in a way she couldn't have ever imagined. It had been a barren, unhappy time for her after Mark had walked out. Now it was almost as though she was beginning to wake up to life and love again. It was really fulfilling to be setting up a company to achieve some dynamic joint projects with John.

While those ventures would bring in some income, there remained the problem of what to do with the large central block. Simon had pushed his idea of creating a set of luxury function rooms with some exclusive high-class accommodation. Judith wasn't keen on this and still longed to achieve an authentic restoration, particularly of the hall and main living room. Partly to stall Simon, and partly to satisfy her own curiosity, she enlisted John and Alf Hidson's help to start removing the false panels which in places blocked off whole walls.

John and Judith were now waiting with nervous apprehension as Alf carefully levered off one of the panels covering the end of the large dayroom; the room where John had first seen and been enchanted by Penny. It had been an agonising wait as they cleared back layers of paper, paint, and finally antique varnishing. This had revealed nothing of interest, but after carefully cutting along the line of the support battens, Alf was levering away the boards.

"Can't you just rip it off?" Judith exclaimed in frustration.

"No," replied Alf, pausing. "I'll not risk damaging what's underneath, or these boards." He turned. "Whoever put these up was a real craftsman. He couldn't just nip to the builders' merchants, buy the stuff he had to—"

"Please! No lectures, Alf. Just get on." Judith had difficulty containing her impatience, and excitement.

"I would if people would let me."

The first panel sprang away with a sudden *pop*. John helped Alf lift it clear to reveal a vertical row of three pictures on gilt frames – two in oil and an ink etching.

"Bloody hell!" exclaimed Alf. "See why I was careful?"

John and Judith were speechless, and held hands without thinking. The pictures had been hidden centuries ago and never seen the light of day since.

"Think these are valuable?"

"No idea," said Judith, "but their frames are beautifully done."

"I noticed that one before," whispered John, pointing to a painting. "Hanging over the door." Overcome with emotion, he realised that the same picture had been displayed in the ornate tapestried room when he first glimpsed Penny sewing. Then, he shakily remarked, "They've all been moved to this wall and covered over."

Judith glanced sideways towards him, understanding his unease. She felt suddenly jealous; she just couldn't help it.

Alf turned round for a moment, considering the find. "I think you should get in an art conservation expert before we—"

"No, do the central panel." John was hoarse with expectation. "Let's see what Judith's got here."

"I'll fetch my proper camera and tripod," said Judith, recovering quickly. "Don't uncover anything else until I get back!"

"I'll take a while to cut down to the next batten line," Alf continued. "See here, John, the back of this panel is rough cut with an adze. The front was planed, and..."

John wasn't listening. He was transfixed by the small signature on the drawing of *Tors on Dartmoor*.

P Peverell '43.

It was her work!

The sight of Penny's signature sent a wave of emotion surging through John, and he realised how hard it must have been for her to leave Peverell House. To conceal his feelings, John started to help Alf cut the next panel free.

"Are you OK, John?" Judith asked, once she had returned.

"Yeah, I'm fine. It's just the dust."

This time, the larger panel fell in pieces as they removed it, clattering to the hard, oak plank floor like a drum roll.

"Is that her?" gasped Judith as she stared at the life-size portrait of Penny and Edward; Penny in radiant glory, Edward with his forehead shot through, most of his face obscured by gunpowder residue. "You poor sod," whispered Judith to John, moving close to him. "You poor, poor sod."

"An allegorical figure," stated Alf, peering to look at the detail of the painting.

"She was all too real," muttered John, breathing deeply, trying to stop his sudden dizziness.

"Painted by William Dobson, about 1638 or so, I would think," commented Alf. "An early work but quite finely done."

"I didn't know you'd studied art," said Judith, unable to take her eyes away from the painting of her rival.

"I bloody didn't," Alf laughed, turning to speak to her. "I'm having you on. I'm standing in front of the signature and date in this corner. And anyone can see it's a good work." He noticed John's distressed look. "Christ, John, mate, you all right? I've seen you like this before, like you've seen a ghost."

"He just has," said Judith softly. "Bit of a shock."

"Wonder what happened to the bloke's face."

"She shot it in a jealous rage when she found Edward had been unfaithful," explained John.

"Bloody good job for him it wasn't for real," said Alf, insensitive as usual. "She'd a-blasted his brains out the back of his head. Not a woman I'd like to cross!" Alf looked at John and

Judith, and suddenly became aware of a noticeable tension between them. Not understanding, he shrugged before saying, "Come on, you two, stop gawping and let's get the last bit down. Then you can snap some photos and take 'em to an expert. I lay there's a good few thousand quid's-worth hanging on that wall!"

∞

It was late afternoon before they had removed the last panel and revealed another set of smaller paintings. It had taken time to tidy away the debris and for Alf to salvage as much of the ancient panelling as possible to use in restoration work.

Now alone, Judith and John perched on empty crates, cups in hand, staring at the array of pictures that had been hidden for so long.

"They sold off all their portable valuables in France to raise money for the king's cause, but these were too big to transport, or of sentimental value. Penny must have moved all the pictures to this one wall and boarded it over for safekeeping when she realised the war was lost. Looting would have been—" John paused abruptly, trying to steady his nerves. He found it hard to hide his memory of sharing an embrace with Penny. The portrait was vivid, so alive.

"Was she really like that?" asked Judith quietly. She just had to know, even though the truth would hurt her badly. "She's like a goddess... must be nearly six feet tall..."

"That's her, warts and all as they said then!" John smiled lamely.

Judith wasn't fooled, and could tell how much effort it took for him to be flippant. "I can see all the warts... I can see why anyone would be infatuated. I haven't a chance, have I?"

"It's not like that, it's really not..."

His words petered out and she did not reply.

"Let's give it a rest for today," Judith said, after a considerable time. "Tomorrow I'll research this Dobson painter and find out who I should speak to about restoration and valuation."

"I'll put Alf off, then," said John. "He wants to have a go at that door we found panelled over. I'm sorry about my reaction. Hell of a shock."

"No big deal. Like you said on Dartmoor, we've both got to live with being second best. I just didn't know how far second I was."

He started to try and placate her, but she stopped him speaking.

"No more talk on this. If we were sensible, we would both go home and reflect."

"If we were sensible," John smiled wanly.

"Yeah, well, we're not, are we? Let's meet up tonight as planned – no guilt or tension."

"At Noya's Kitchen, that Vietnamese place?"

"Then on to Vespa's."

"Not one word of exes or ghosts!"

"The only decision tonight will be your place or mine."

"My bed is bigger," joked John. "And afterwards the chair's more comfortable!"

CHAPTER 27

Edward and Penny soon learned that these were indeed unsettled times in France. The Crown and nobility were in an increasingly hostile power struggle; taxes were rising; and the queen regent had vowed to suppress the remaining French Protestants. Against this backdrop, portable, easy to conceal valuables such as gems and works of art were in high demand.

It was under the guise of a gentleman merchant seeking to raise money for a trading venture that Edward sought out one of the town's most respected jewellers. The premises did not look auspicious – a dilapidated 'shop' set in the middle of a row of similarly dour-fronted mercantile trading warehouses. For all its initial appearance, Edward noted that the walls and doors were sound, the window well barred, and the locks and hinges on the door recently oiled.

Inside there was more light than expected, and the furnishings, although austere, were of good quality. The merchant they had come to see had opened the outer door himself, after scanning them and the street from a small bowed window and checking their names before the door was fully opened. Rather than the ancient miser that they had expected, he was a tall and well-dressed young man in velvet trousers and fine lined shirt of oriental cut and tasteful embroidery. As a clothier, Edward was well aware of their quality.

Monsieur Alceste (surely not his real name) first expressed his surprise that Edward would be accompanied by his wife; most unusual, unconventional. He then began to politely explain how the market was very weak. Penny interrupted him; her spoken French was much more fluent than Edward's. She explained that she and Mr Peverell worked as partners, and that as merchants and manufacturers of goods they had spent some time sounding out the market and approximate value of what they had to sell.

"So," Edward said more directly, "it's best if we get down to serious business without preamble."

"Madame wants to sell?" asked the jewel merchant, switching to clear English.

"Here are samples of our goods. We want to hear your offer," Penny said in a no-nonsense tone.

"If I make one," was the smooth reply.

"Your evaluation?" suggested Edward. "Then we will decide if we will sell."

There was a silence as Monsieur Alceste carefully examined their items, making brief notes in some script unknown to Edward and Penny. After some time, he called in a woman of foreign appearance, her face partially veiled. She took his eyeglass and conversed in a non-European language as she looked at selected stones. Watching her closely, Penny found it difficult to gauge her age, but she seemed both young and confident. The jeweller certainly appeared to defer to her opinion on the gemstones. Eventually they concluded and sat back in their chairs.

"Can you supply more merchandise of this quality?" the man asked.

"Easily," lied Edward smoothly. "I will be travelling regularly from England to France. You are well aware of the difficult situation for men of commerce in England due to the rebellion. We intend to establish a factory in Nantes, hence our need for capital."

"I have an agent in London, but your civil war cuts me off from Bristol and York." The jeweller seemed to consider his words carefully and spoke briefly to the woman, who just nodded. "I will be frank."

"Please do," said Penny, wary of deception.

"The gold is of no interest to me. Europe is awash with gold. Every year the Spanish treasure fleet arrives with tons of gold. Yearly the value of gold falls."

"How can gold fall in value? Everything is priced in gold."

"It does," Monsieur Alceste asserted. "As more gold comes into Europe from the Spanish Americas, the original gold coin loses value – it can buy less. The price of everything else rises, including gemstones, works of art, such as this filigree and ruby necklace." He fingered one of Penny's favourite necklaces lightly. "These are the things I need to buy."

Edward looked aghast while Penny asked, "Is that why the Dutch concentrate on diamonds?"

"Also spices and other rare commodities such as ivory, lapis, incense from the East."

"Walrus tusk and narwhal horn is coming into Bristol,"

suggested Edward.

"I can take all you can supply and have it carved here to mimic oriental treasure." The jewel merchant began to reckon up what he could offer.

"Do you speak Greek?" asked Edward suddenly in that language.

A look of surprise.

"Pardon, sir, I do not comprehend."

"Do you speak Ancient Greek?"

"No," he smiled. "Only English, Dutch, Spanish, and of course Hebrew and Arabic." He continued writing and handed his tally to Penny. "As a token of goodwill and future cooperation, I could remove the emeralds in the bracelet," he pointed to their value on his list, "and replace them with good copies in tourmaline. Few people would note the difference."

"Do we take this offer?" Edward asked Penny, speaking covertly in Ancient Greek.

She nodded. "Twenty times more than we could get at home. Do you intend to trade with him?" Penny was still rather concerned that the jeweller might be untrustworthy.

"We do it only for the king's profit." Edward smiled at her reassuringly, though he was nervous of the situation.

They discussed the offer, and then nodded their agreement.

"You will appreciate," said the jewel merchant, "that I do not keep such a sum in gold coins in any one place. I suggest giving you one fifth today in payment for these pieces." He slid a small selection to one side. "You may return in, say three days. Then we complete the transaction."

"Agreed," said Penny before Edward could answer.

Edward stood up and extended his hand to seal the bargain.

Monsieur Alceste looked surprised and, as they shook hands, said, "You do not mind taking the hand of a Jew?"

"It is the hand of the man, not his faith," replied Edward. "Besides, after what I have seen in the wars, I have no religion at all. So it is I who am damned if there is a God."

"Γεια σου ο κυριοσ," said the veiled woman, before continuing in perfect Ancient Greek to add, "and may your god seek you out and be with you."

$$\infty$$

While their money was collected, Edward and Penny had several days to spend in the town. They hired saddle horses to ride out into the surrounding countryside for a day, and on Sunday visited local churches – Penny went to the Huguenot Protestant church; Edward joined a Catholic mass to see what it was like.

Later that evening, relaxing during their meal together at the Auberge, Edward took a taste of his French wine, enjoying the full-bodied Bordeaux.

"The spectacle in church was better than any London play," he remarked to Penny, "although some of the Latin readings were in error!"

"You should not mock other people's true beliefs," scolded Penny.

"I did not. I behaved with all due deference and joined in the chanting and hymn singing."

"That could be cause for war!" laughed Penny. She too sampled a small glass of wine and was enjoying the rich beef casserole. Then she added slyly, "Did you confess?"

"Aye, I did – to an excess of carnal lust."

"Edward! Did you shock the poor priest?"

"Not a jot. He just asked who my passion was for. When I said my wife, he stated it was no sin. He is a good man." Edward smiled fondly, suddenly longing for bed.

"An understanding one at least. Was there more?"

"Aye." Edward paused. "I felt guilty at my deceit. It started as a joke, no mockery intended. I explained this to him and admitted I had no faith in any god, a view strengthened by the horrors of war."

"That is honest; you have often said so."

"In a quiet understanding voice the priest said that it was not uncommon, but not to confuse the evil of man with the word and love of God."

"And will you go back and read the word of God in the gospels?"

"No, but it has given me cause to doubt my views of churchmen." Edward took the last gulp of his wine and wiped his chin with his cuff. "Come, wife, enough of this deep discussion. Now, with the approval of the church, it is time for more 'excess of carnal lust'!"

∞

On the day before they were to make the final sale, Edward and Penny decided to take an afternoon stroll around the Isle de Nantes, a small island in the middle of the Loire that had been the original safe berthing place for boats travelling up river. It was a disappointingly drab landscape with warehouses and quays falling into disrepair; their function being taken over by newer buildings on the town waterfront. It was getting late and their main concern was where to go for their evening meal.

"I am rather taken with this town," Edward was saying, as they reached the landing point where they had sculled across from Nantes earlier in the afternoon. "It seems free from politics and strife; a place where an honest man could set up in business and make a good living."

"I just hope the religious tolerance will continue," replied Penny. "The rumours are that the queen regent plans to renew persecution of the French Protestants."

"Ho! Edward Peverell!" called out a man's voice.

They turned to see two men dressed in austere puritan fashion, hurrying towards them from another path.

"We have been seeking you," shouted one.

"We need to speak on your conduct," shouted the other aggressively.

"You could call on us at our lodging," yelled back Edward. "Should I know you?"

"You shall soon!" The more aggressive stranger had drawn his sword.

"Stand back!" roared Edward, drawing his own sword. "We are armed and will defend ourselves."

Penny rested her hand on Edward's arm, attempting to dissuade any confrontation. "There is no need for weapons," she said pleasantly. "We can speak civilly, I am sure. Why these raised voices?"

"We have searched the island for you," said the first stranger.

"Better to have waited by the boat, or at the inn," replied Edward.

For a few moments, the argument continued, while the tension seemed to increase between them.

"Thomas Pierce of Norfolk, my name. I saw you at Peterhouse, the Cambridge college. I took you for a good Protestant."

"Aye. Your point?" Edward answered warily.

"Yesterday, you were seen attending a Church of Rome. Also we suspect you are raising money for Charles Stuart, the Man of Blood."

"My business is my own, sir." Edward was sharp in his reply. "I answer to no man. As to the church, I conversed with an enlightened man, but did not consider joining his church, or any other."

"It is common knowledge that we come to Nantes to seek opportunity for trade," said Penny, attempting to calm the situation.

"Enough of this banter, Tom," said the second stranger. "Let us cut them down, then to their inn and see what they have."

"I am not given to murder, or robbery," replied Thomas Pierce, addressing Edward again. "All we need is your assurance, sworn on this copy of Holy Stricture, that you do not aid Charles."

"I am loyal to my lawful king," replied Edward with menace. "Put away your book of fairy tales and go your way."

"Blasphemy!" Thomas drew his sword and lunged at Edward, only to be beaten back by clubbing blows from Edward's heavy blade.

"Go home, boy. Go home and calm down. If you are a gentleman, we shall fight like gentlemen tomorrow."

The answer was a renewed attack by both assailants, the second man attempting to encircle Edward.

The crack of Penny's pistol fire startled Thomas Pierce. His guard faltered as he saw the savage spurt of flame and his companion falling in an untidy heap. Edward lunged, an automatic reaction, his blade striking deep.

"Gods, I did not mean to kill him," Edward gasped.

"Nor I," whispered Penny, looking down in dismay at the writhing man she had shot in the hip. "He came on so fast to stab you in the back."

"Wench, your shot has burned my arse," Edward said with a relieved laugh, as he brushed burned gunpowder from his britches. "Better your gun flash than that varlet's sword."

"It is not for jesting, Edward." Penny was close to tears and trembling. "He is near to dying."

"Aye," he said soberly, hugging her to him. "They left us no option but to defend ourselves."

"You goaded him, Edward!"

"It was my intent once I saw fight was inevitable. I didn't expect a stab in the back."

Thomas Pierce was already dead from Edward's sword thrust. The other attacker whimpered piteously, clasping his hip to staunch the bleeding, his leg skewed backwards at an unnatural angle from the shattered hip joint.

"Help me, I beg," he mumbled through clenched teeth.

Edward crouched down, made a quick examination, and looked into the man's frightened eyes. "The joint is shattered. The shot smashed out shards of bone that have punctured your gut. You are dying as surely as you meant to murder me and my wife. You expect sympathy?" He stood up and moved to comfort Penny.

"Should we do anything?" she whispered. "I don't want him hanged."

"I've no idea how French justice would view a fight between English louts. They may hold us all guilty."

She nodded, remembering again the sham trail and executions in Calne.

Edward continued, "Doubt he will live long, but he could suffer for days if the bleeding is stopped."

"What do we do? Just leave them here to—"

"As they would have done to us," he cut in. "We wait awhile to see if anyone is attracted by your shot. If not, we cast their boat adrift and return to the inn. We see our jewel merchant in the morning. The ship leaves at noon."

No one disturbed their vigil over the dead and dying as Penny and Edward kept in the shadows of the quayside huts.

After some time Edward said emphatically, "I will not leave a dying man to suffer."

"The crows watch already." Penny pointed to the trees.

"One clean thrust and he will know nothing," Edward said hesitantly. "Will you walk away while I—"

"No! I am responsible," said Penny. "I must not shirk from the effects of my hasty action."

Penny walked over to the body of Thomas Pierce and, taking the small bible from his sash, carried it over to the dying man. "Will this give you comfort?" she asked.

He pushed her hand away. "Papist bitch!"

Edward's dagger smashed through the side of his skull, ending life instantly.

Penny staggered away, appalled by her husband's sudden violence.

"God, Edward! How could you do that?"

"Better than a lingering death," he replied gravely.

They did what was needed in a strained, shocked silence that lasted until their boat began to cross to the shore.

"You have seen such things before?" Penny asked.

"Too often, but I have never had the courage to end a man in a mercy killing." There was a pause as he worked the oars. "I do not enjoy it, Penny. It leaves a mark."

"I know. That mark is on me, too – from Calne and now afresh from today."

When Edward and Penny rowed back to the boatyard, the owner asked if they had seen two Englishmen who had also hired a boat from him. They replied in a non-committal negative and sauntered away is if to a relaxed dinner. For fear of another assault, they spent a watchful night in the inn before completing their sale with Monsieur Alceste, the jeweller, the next morning. As Edward had hoped, they were safely on a vessel back to Bristol by noon, with a trunk of French and Spanish gold for the king's cause.

CHAPTER 28

Judith awoke from a frantic dream. In a total state of panic, dressed only in a t-shirt with no underwear, she was being chased through Vespa's nightclub by Mark. She was awake but dazed, not her flat – big double bed. Stretching out, she found a naked male body; vague memories of the nightclub, dancing, and shots of vodka. Furtively she used the light on her watch – 4.39 a.m. More importantly, it was not a stranger or Mark who was in bed with her. Reassuringly, it was John. Why had she allowed herself to get so worked up over that bloody portrait of Penny? There had been no need to be so spiteful to John; no need to get pissed at Vespa's. She went to the toilet, and in the kitchen forced herself to drink a pint of water before returning to bed and snuggling up to John's inert sleeping body. If this was 'second best', it was still very nice.

∞

Judith surfaced from a contented, seemingly dream-free sleep to the smell of toast and coffee. The bedroom was flooded with light despite the thick curtains.

"Christ! Eleven thirty." She was meant to be at work three hours ago. Then she remembered it was Saturday. Judith rolled out of bed carefully but was pleased to find she was quite steady. In one of John's drawers she found a voluminous shirt and in another a collection of underwear she had left for emergencies.

"Heard you moving about," said John, as she staggered into the kitchen where coffee, toast and apricot jam had been laid out on a breakfast tray. A second tray held chopped fresh fruit and yoghurt.

"What's all this?" Judith asked, looking at the tray and the glass vase that held a splendid solitary red rose.

"Breakfast, m'lady. I was about to bring it to you and welcome the new day."

She laughed, "M'lady!" She had thought to make some quip but realised how much trouble he had taken. "John, this is so nice. Let's eat out here together." She indicated the small balcony overlooking Henrietta Park. "M'lady! Don't you try that soppy stuff on me."

"Point taken."

"I'm kidding, it's lovely. If I wasn't afraid of being hurt again, I could almost believe I was falling in love with you."

John leaned across the table and kissed her forehead lightly. There was little conversation as they ate breakfast until Judith realised how little she remembered from the previous night.

"Did we do it – last night?" she asked.

"What, after all my efforts, you can't remember?" he replied.

"Well, I suppose I do a bit," she giggled "I was hardly in a state to give informed consent!"

"Consent? God, woman, it was you who woke me up!"

"I seem to remember that," she smiled. Another long but comfortable silence settled between them. "John, I'm going back to bed for a while. I don't think the wonton soup agreed with me."

"Nothing to do with the vodka shots?"

"No, I've had vodka before – didn't have this effect. You coming?"

"OK, but no sex. You shagged me out."

Later, John awoke to being caressed.

"John?"

"Yeah?"

"You know you said no sex?"

"OK, OK, I recant."

She rolled on top of him. "I'll do the work."

At one thirty p.m. they were both awoken by the doorbell ringing. John groaned and slid out of bed, scrabbling to pull on boxers and a t-shirt as he staggered to the intercom.

"Hi, John, it's me, Alf – Alf Hidson. Can I come up?"

"Look, Alf, I've someone with me – it's not really convenient."

"It's important, John. I can't contact that Ransom girl."

"Judith?"

"That's the one. Her mobile's off, or something."

"Probably. We were out late last night. You had better come up. Door's opening." John hurriedly pulled on some trousers in time to meet Alf. "What's the rush?" he asked.

"I've got that bloody door open," Alf said excitedly. "The oil spray worked on the hinges and—"

"I told you to leave it!" shouted Judith, erupting out of the bedroom wearing not very much. "Don't gawp. Why did you open—"

"I didn't bloody open it," snarled Alf. "I said I'd got the bloody thing open – just enough to move it. I thought you'd be pleased." He smirked at John. "Didn't know I'd be interrupting, like."

"You're not," said John defensively. "We just left Vespa's a bit late. I know it looks as if—"

"And it is," cut in Judith smugly. "So what?"

"Nothing." Alf shrugged – he took most things in his stride.

There was an embarrassing pause until John said, "Look, Alf. Thanks for coming round. We're a bit fragile, and it's Saturday. Let's leave it till Monday. We've got to contact the art historian, then."

"She works at The Roman Baths," said Judith. "I know her well enough to call her at home over the weekend."

"Nothing Roman in that house," muttered Alf.

"I know," agreed Judith, "but... look, have a cup of coffee with us, Alf. We'll see if we can decide what to do next."

∞

It was mid-morning on the following Monday before John and Judith met Alf and the art historian, Stella Rigby, at Peverell House.

"I wish you hadn't told me that you'd uncovered a William Dobson," said Stella to Judith as she lugged her kit up the stairs to the Peverell House dayroom.

"Why not?"

"Well, you should have asked me to come and view some 'hidden' painting that might be worth putting up for auction."

"And?"

"I could then say, 'The Brilliant Stella Rigby immediately recognised it as a Dobson'!"

"That was me," muttered Alf. "I read his blooming signature."

"The signature was obscured by dirt or spider webs, but the brilliant Stella immediately recognised it. I'm famous overnight and no one can claim you lot colluded in passing it off as a forgery."

They entered the room.

"Ooh, certainly looks right. His early work had those brilliant colours; Venetian in style. Later he was influenced by Van Dyke and that morbid Dutch lot." She produced a magnifying glass and a jeweller's-style eyepiece. At length she said, "Well, certainly looks authentic. We will need x-rays, chromatography, scrapings of the borders."

Alf chipped in, "You could do dendrochronology of the panelling." He continued with involved explanations that they largely ignored.

Eventually, Judith said, "I suppose the shot hole and gunpowder burns will reduce its value?"

"Not necessarily," reassured Stella. "There is no actual hole, and I bet most of the 'burns' are powder residue. It can be restored. The rest of the face, from the eyes down, is OK."

They went on to discuss details in the portrait – costumes, the hair, and even the gun on the table – until the subject was exhausted and plans made to get the works removed for authentication.

Stella examined the other three hanging pictures with interest, but not much excitement.

"This tinted pen and ink's unusual," she said. "Done by Penelope Peverell, the lady in the portrait, mistress of the house, and presumably your ancestor?"

"Hardly. The Peverells were misguided Royalists," said Judith emphatically. "We Ransoms displaced them when King Charles lost. They disappeared into history and never even tried to reclaim the estate back after the restoration of Charles II."

Stella set up her camera on a tripod and took photographs of the pictures as a group and then individually.

"If any more secrets come up it would be best if I were here at first unveiling – helps prove they're genuine. You said there's another hidden space. Has that been opened?" Stella asked.

"No," stated Alf emphatically. "John and me oiled the hinges and eased the lock – there's no key. We'll need to prise the door open."

"Prise away, then!"

Standing squarely in front of the door to obscure their view, Alf went through a theatrical performance of crowbarring the door open. *For all his heaving and grunting of the words 'open you bugger', there was very little damage*, thought John.

It was dark and dusty inside.

"Can you switch the light on?" joked Stella.

"We've brought a couple of battery-powered work lights," replied John.

"And I've got gloves, as you suggested, Stella," added Judith.

Stella pulled on a white overall coat to protect herself against the dust, before venturing into the room.

"Crime scene, or what," muttered Alf.

"What's up, Alf?" said John. "Bad night? You're a bit gritty this morning."

Alf just grunted.

The room was more of a wide passageway, a second entrance into the suite of rooms that had once been Penny and Edward's bedrooms. There was no door at the other end, just more blanking off panels.

"All the years I slept through there," said Judith, "and I had no idea this was here. A real treasure trove. There's a fitted wardrobe across that end now."

Half the width of the passage was filled by two tall chests of drawers, the other half by racks of pictures, and a hanging rail of fine clothes. Both women took photos for the record before John and Alf carried the racks out into the daylight of the main room.

"It'll take days to go through this lot," remarked Stella. "If you agree to give us a mention and a credit in any announcements, I'm sure The Roman Baths Trust will allow me to spend time here. The Museum of Fashion might send Tamzin Studdings to look at these," she indicated the rack of dresses. "Rare to have a collection of clothes from this period."

John carried out two well wrapped swords. "OK if I have a look at these?" he asked.

Stella nodded. "Go ahead." She continued to thumb through the paintings. "These are just house decorations," Stella mused "Even some embroidery, and more watercolours by Peverell."

"I feel that woman's looking at me, John," whispered Judith.

"That smile – it's as if she's smirking at me."

"It was a wedding picture," John tried to reassure her. "The last time we spoke, she told me to love you and—" He faltered a bit. "Well, to value you and what we have."

"The understanding mistress," Judith hissed spitefully. "No, John, sorry. I am sure she was genuine."

"John, Miss Ransom!" Alf called. "Come and see this." He continued to talk as they walked to where he was holding up the brilliant work light to the armoire. "This is as fine a bit of craft as you'll see anywhere. The quality of the marquetry – like it was new."

"Were there any famous furniture makers working then?" Judith asked him. "Like Chippendale?"

"Far too early for him. I dunno. Need to Google it, but anyone can see it's good." He turned slightly. "Shame it's not a matching pair. The other one's more of a utility piece."

They carried each drawer from the chest out into the main room, noting and photographing contents in a methodical fashion. There was little of real interest – underclothes, costume jewellery, an ornate clock. Eventually, they reached a small top drawer of the utility cabinet.

"Item fifty-six," said Alf, who now seemed to have cheered up and fully entered into the spirit of discovery.

"Fifty-six?" repeated Judith, starting to type into her tablet, feeling excited about an ornate heavy bracelet she had clipped around her wrist.

"One large oiled cloth packet," said Alf. The string crumbled away as it was handled. "Enclosing a sheep's fleece wrapping?" he continued. "It's still flexible. Inside is a fine wooden box or case."

"Take a pic," said Stella sharply, glancing up from the rack of pictures.

"OK, OK. Box is heavy at one end. Measures twenty by fifteen by six inches."

"Can I have that in mils, Alf?"

"No, this was made two hundred years before metric – it's in feet and inches!"

The box was in fact a case for pistols, only one of which remained.

"Strange shape," said Alf. "No hammer?"

"It's a wheel lock," explained John, "like the one on the table in the big Dobson picture."

"Bloody hell!" replied Alf. "It's the same gun, I bet. You did well to spot that so quick."

"First-hand knowledge," suggested Judith sadly. "John knows all about Mistress Peverell."

"Marvellous condition," joined in Stella. "Must have been well preserved. Even got a little wood plug down the barrel. Called them tampons! Only ones they knew about."

Curiously, Judith picked up the pistol with a gloved hand. "Feels odd with a straight handle rather than a 'pistol grip'. You'd have to point this like pointing a finger. You try, John."

"No thanks. I don't like guns."

"Oh? You surprise me. I thought one of your lovers was a crack shot." Judith couldn't stop herself, but immediately regretted it.

John looked shocked at the remark and could only mumble, "Not fair."

"Oh, John, I'm sorry." She moved to give him a hug but he

backed away. "I'm really sorry, John." She whispered, coming close, "It's that Dobson painting. I still feel she's mocking me."

"It's like a posed wedding photo. Look at his smug expression."

"I know, I know. Look, John. I'm just bloody jealous. Being ridiculous." Judith looked around desperately to see if the others were listening – Alf was back at the cabinets, Stella at the picture rack.

"There seems to be a bit of prickliness in the air today," remarked John quietly. "Alf's like the proverbial bear with a sore head, Stella's like a school mistress and—"

"And I'm being a total bitchington," Judith finished. "Will try to do better, Mr Reasonable, and offer to buy us all lunch." She turned back to the passageway. "Alf's trying to twist that cabinet away from the wall. If you give him a hand, I'll unpack the last small drawer."

Behind the ornate cabinet was a long shallow recess that contained two unmistakable packages. Carefully wrapped and perfectly preserved were two hunting rifles.

By this time they were almost suffering from 'surprise fatigue' – little excitement left to offer.

"Was there anything in the last drawer?" John asked Judith as she handed him the 'finds' log on her tablet.

"Not really." She pointed to the notes. "One smallish heavy book – ledger or accounts, I think. Last pages are blank."

"Shame. We need a diary, or something like a journal." He didn't notice Judith's reaction to that.

"I'll need the camera," she said abruptly to Stella, still trying to stifle her jealous streak. "Better record all the details of the find."

It took two whole hours to record and pictograph all of the items that had been discovered, and decide storage for the most valuable things. By then, a sort of mental exhaustion had set in, and there was little enthusiasm even when Judith did offer to buy lunch. They decided on The Shoe, a friendly well-appointed pub on the road back to Bath.

At first, conversation was difficult as each person sat, obsessed by their own favourite treasure. As food was ordered and drinks arrived, Judith decided it was up to her to break the mood of reflection.

Lifting her glass she called out, "Let's have a toast to Penny and Edward Peverell, and hope their shades will be pleased we have found their treasure. To Penny and Edward!"

The others responded, much to the surprise of a few other diners seeking a quiet lunch. It was Stella who spoke up next.

"This has been one of the most exciting days of my career. Thanks, Judy."

"Me too, in a way," added Alf gruffly. "What the hell are you going to do with all the stuff? What's our next step?"

"A very cautious one," suggested John.

"Exactly," Judith agreed. "Please, no leaks to the press. We can do a joint statement later. First, we decide who looks after what. Stella, if you could take on cataloguing the artwork?"

"And I'll get Tamzin to look at the clothes." suggested Stella.

"I'll do the chests and woodwork, if you like," ventured Alf, sipping his Bath Ale. "Valuation, ages and dates." His face lit up as the waiter set an enormous plate of pie, mash and gravy in front of him.

"Thanks," said Judith. "Thanks, everyone. A great day!" As the others were distracted by the arrival of their food, she surreptitiously grasped John's hand under the table, and murmured softly, "Thanks, John."

CHAPTER 29

A bored and dispirited Edward Peverell was viewing the activity in one of Bristol's gun foundries. He was no metalworker, but from his cloth maker's perspective the processes were far from efficient and he longed to suggest simple improvements. However, it was not his workshop and he dared not antagonise the foreman and owner who were only working for the promise of payment by a king they hated and despised.

He turned as someone touched his arm, difficult as it was to talk above the din of hammering and gauging – Prince Maurice. Edward bowed slightly, as much for politeness as in deference to rank. The prince was dressed in full finery, from fashionable wig to stylish shoes. His waistcoat alone had probably cost more than the contents of Edward's wardrobe. That said, Edward had grown to quite like Maurice and found him much more approachable than his arrogant and rash brother, Rupert.

They moved out into the foundry yard where it was relatively quiet and conversation was possible.

"I see, Sir Edward, that you avoid my regal brother. You are always about the town, urging the workers on."

"Aye. They have no sympathy for our cause, but a little appreciation and paying a few crowns here and there helps keep the work going."

"You do not think my brother's threats have much effect?"

"None. Much as they dislike King Charles, they know he would not allow your brother to hang men or seize wives and children as hostages."

"In our Germany it was different," mused Maurice.

"Did intimidation work?"

"No. We had cannon that exploded on first firing, muskets that blocked up, and pike piles that bent. They sold us carefully crafted junk!" Maurice walked over to a rack of completed muskets and examined one closely, shrugged, and asked Edward, "Is it functional?"

"Indeed it is. Each weapon is proof-fired by one of the men who worked on it."

"As were our bloody cannon." Maurice forgot rank and slipped into English vernacular.

Edward smiled as he noted the change.

"I saw the head man test-fire a particular gun – all correct. In our first skirmish I was nearly killed when it exploded. How could that be, Edward? How could it be made to fail on the second firing?"

"Who provisioned the powder and shot for the test?"

"I don't know. Possibly the gun maker?" Maurice suggested.

"So, your man mixes a weak charge; too much charcoal in the powder. He uses a light ball. The barrel survives. Later in action, your gunner loads correctly and the stress on the flawed barrel..."

The prince swore in German. Well, Edward assumed he was swearing.

"How do you know these men do not play the same game?"

"I supply the powder. The quantity used is one quarter more than standard – a proof test, it is called. I provide good, close-fitting ball. I pick by chance which man fires each piece. Would you hazard sabotaging a gun you may have to test?"

The prince smiled and shrugged. "You are a cunning man, Edward."

"One has to be in business. You earn respect for being awake to your trade and then few men try to practise fraud on you. How many times did you try your pistols before you parted with money?"

"Agreed, agreed. We should have a trusted captain in every workshop, as Rupert says," suggested Maurice.

"Impossible to have a man there all the time; just often enough to see all is well. It would also be useful if they were sober and vigilant."

"I wager that villain, Cromwell, has one of his psalm-singing, bible-reading zealots in every place he has ordnance made." Maurice glanced around to check if anyone was within hearing distance. "It is because you are awake to fraud and are respected that I would like to place a commission on you."

"I am not in the army," Edward started to say in apology, "or a military man at all, sire—"

"I agree, but we have so few captains who are respected and trusted." Maurice waved his hand to brush Edward's protestations aside.

"Lord Hopton?" Edward ventured.

"Cannot be spared from his command. All the sensible Cornish gentlemen have been killed. Others would be too... well, too aggressive."

"So, it is a diplomatic task?"

"I fear so."

Edward looked away into the distance for a moment, thinking about Penny and how she would greet the news. She would, he knew, be firmly against him getting mixed up into the dangers of yet more fighting.

He asked, matter-of-factly, "I understand the king is at last resolved to move to London? It's the source of parliament's power and finance."

"Yes. We believe there are subjects loyal to the king even there," commented Maurice. "Protesters and riots against parliament have been harshly suppressed. His Majesty," he continued, "believes that when he rides into the city, the loyal people will rise up and shake off the rebel yoke."

Edward did not believe royal support in London would be that strong, but he nodded. "It is our only hope, I suppose. Each month sees our enemy grow stronger, and we cannot recruit or raise funds. But I have no influence in London." *Evidently, Maurice is no fool, and realises the war is going badly*, thought Edward.

Maurice continued, "No. We know that. Let me continue. As the king advances on London, the Parliamentarians will attempt to bar the road. There will have to be a pitched battle and the king will need every available man – horse and foot – if he is to prevail. To this end, we will abandon the siege in Taunton."

"The town is of little importance and—"

"Silence, pray to God," snapped the prince. "If we act rapidly, Lord Goring can bring another ten thousand to the king's army. He has been given written orders from Rupert, but has not moved; has not replied." There was a silence between them until Maurice said, "Your opinion?"

"I may speak?" Edward said sarcastically, but then tried to collect his thoughts and phrase his words so as not to offend Prince Maurice. He pulled on his top coat, discarded due to the foundry's heat, and said, "Lord Goring cannot move his army away from around Taunton, even if he wanted to, which I doubt."

Maurice looked unconvinced. "Continue."

"Goring's men have not been paid or properly fed for months. He has promised them total freedom to plunder the town when it falls."

Another German curse from Maurice. "Looting is expressly against His Majesty's orders!"

"The promise of plunder is all that has stopped mass desertion. The men will not move away from their prize, even if ordered."

Prince Maurice shifted his feet, took off his wig and ran fingers through his short, cropped hair in frustration. "The town may fall?"

"I have heard it is stronger now, stronger than last month. Parliamentary supplies and men have passed through Goring's ineffectual blockade; earthworks have been built to replace the shattered walls, and much of the city's outskirts have been reclaimed."

"How do you know all this?" said Maurice in disbelief. "You

who are not a military man."

"No, thank God! But as well as a landowner I am in part a merchant and cloth maker; I talk to others in trade. It is common knowledge that during lulls in the attacks, some West Country merchants are trading into Taunton. As early as September '43 my wife and I saw a Parliamentary supply train heading for Taunton unopposed. For Blake's puritans, gold in the cathedral and churches is anathema, so they have no scruples to strip it out and use it for buying food and powder. To them, it is funding God's work!"

Maurice stood aghast. "Sacrilege! How do you know so much while the king's commanders know nothing?"

"Because, sir, I am working, trading and listening while others ride out to hunt or hold soirees."

"Mind your insolence, sir!"

Edward just shrugged. "Exactly: mind my tongue. The truth, it's too painful. What happened to the supplies sent to Goring? They were detoured to his agent at Bridgewater. I lay they were sold off in the market at a discount." Penny had often told Edward he could be brutal and forthright when roused – a different side of his character to the one he showed her.

"I will not hear such slander against an honourable man!"

"Then I will get back to the gun makers," Edward answered in a flat, resolute tone.

The prince stooped down to flick some stray soil off his finely made leather shoe, trying to compose himself. "Stay, Edward. This is madness for us to argue. I wanted your advice; I considered you may be able to explain the gravity of the situation to Goring. You are one of the few who understands what is at stake."

"And your brother, Prince Rupert?"

"In part, but he still believes a glorious charge will overcome all odds."

"As it failed at Lincoln and Lansdown. In the next fight he may face Fairfax and Cromwell."

"I know, I know. Cromwell's horse and footmen are—" he sought for words, "Formidable. But as yet he has only two regiments, and builds his numbers slowly. That is why we must act." Prince Maurice was looking worried at the sheer enormity of the problems in rallying their army for the battle ahead. He sighed. "We must strike swiftly."

"The only action I can see working," said Edward, "is to collect all the coin we can muster. Pay Goring's men something on account, and provision them for the march north; food enough for them to reach Bristol and promise of more on the way."

"So much risk. It is a gamble to deplete our resources."

"As is an attack on London. If it fails, Bristol will soon fall anyway, so I would also strip Bristol of men for the main action." Edward continued, hoping to convince the prince that a military officer was essential for the task. "There is more, sir – I could not enforce this order. I have no authority. It needs a prince or general to despatch the money and stores, then one of your senior commanders to force Goring under pain of treason to move his army where it will be needed."

They parted company in low spirits, realising how badly the Civil War was going against them. As he walked away, Edward remembered the sacrifices that he and Penny had made in selling their family heirlooms in France. Surely the effort of persuading

Lord Goring to join the attack on London was worthwhile? He hoped Penny would agree.

CHAPTER 30

On a cold winter morning with light mist scattering the moonlight, John walked across Bath to Judith's flat. Stella had recommended an eminent gun expert, and they had decided to drive to London rather than lug items on and off trains and the underground. John rather hoped he might find Judith still in bed and be invited in for an hour or so. They hadn't been together for several days and John began to feel aroused with anticipation when he pressed the intercom. Instead, she acted rather coldly to him and was anxious to be off before traffic began to build up.

Judith had provided lockable storage cases for the guns but they decided that someone should stay in the Range Rover at all times as a safeguard. Judith also brought a large briefcase and several folders of details and pictures. She asked him to drive as there were a few things she wanted to read to him during the journey. By six thirty, they had made good progress through Bath up the A46 hill, past The Crown Inn.

They talked about the progress of John's stone carving and Judith's trip to a technical conference in Plymouth, but there still seemed a bit of a frosty edge to her manner. She passed him a croissant and settled back in her seat, nibbling half-heartedly at her own.

"It's strange," Judith said. "Most of us thought of Plymouth as a heritage site – naval ships and declining dockyards."

"Some high-tech companies are based around the city," suggested John.

"Exactly, and my old Dyson's lot have opened an innovation centre there in conjunction with the university."

John found the Range Rover a dream to drive – high with good visibility like his van but with speed and comfort. Terms like 'Chelsea Tractors' and 'dreadful reliability' did not apply.

It was not until they were speeding along the M4 that John said, "I have been meaning to ask: why were you so secretive about Penny's diary? I'm sure Stella would have helped."

"Exactly. It would have been like a wolf with a lamb. She's used to reading old documents."

"So?"

"Suppose there is an entry saying 'the ghost of Cousin John appeared, snogged me rotten and tried to have it off with me'? It would stink of forgery and reflect on the authenticity of the paintings."

"I did not try it on," he protested.

"Not that time! But you get my point."

"I do. Have you read much of it?" he added with a growing sense of unease.

"It's very difficult – small blocky italic-style writing, rushed in places – but I've made some transcripts to read to you. *This day was sewing and looking forward to Edward's return...* I couldn't read some bits here. *Cousin John Townsend appeared dressed in work clothes... him dead these twelve months and more. Bethought me it was his ghost and he did not know he was dead. Rushed to him to explain... did grasp me to him and kissed me most lustily.* In the next bit I think she confesses to responding to you, but then thinks of Edward and repulses you. Did she repulse you, John?" Judith asked quietly.

"Quite forcibly. We tried to explain ourselves and both got totally confused as to who was the ghost," mumbled John.

"You felt real to each other?"

"Very real."

"I bet."

John realised he had let the speed drop and was drifting across two lanes. "I've told you all this, there is nothing new. Is there?"

"Not really, it's just strange reading about you and her. What are *we*, John? Partners, lovers, friends? It's all very..." Judith's voiced trailed off.

"Does it matter?" he said. Then, with a grin, "As I recollect, we are currently lovers; officially, we're partners and," he sought for words, "you're the best friend I ever had."

"Knock it off, John." Another of those long silences until she said, "It's passion for Penny and jig-jig for Judith."

"Jig-jig? That's something I've not heard in a long time," he said with a laugh. "Where were you brought up?"

"Imperial College," she replied. "Bit of a throwback in culture there, even if the engineering was up-to-date. Some girls had 'jig lists' of their conquests, you know, firsts – a bloke beginning with A, like Adam. Then B, like Ben."

"Bit of a problem with Q and U!" John was relieved that the tension between them seemed to be lifting. Judith was good company; a best friend as well as the other thing.

"I doubt it. All very multicultural."

"How far did you get?" asked John.

"I didn't. I just filled in M and left it at that. More fool me." Judith relaxed and closed her eyes for a while as the Range Rover sped along.

John was lost in thoughts of his passion for Penny and how futile it all seemed. Would they ever have a chance to meet again?

Judith interrupted his reverie. "John, it could be so useful for me to have details of what happened back in the 1640s to help validate the pictures and other objects. A normal diary would be ideal but not if it was full of ghostly happenings relating to present-day people." As they turned into Reading Services for a brief break, Judith added, "It's such a shame, really. If we published her diary, Penny Peverell could be a female Samuel Pepys."

"How much have you been able to read?" he asked again.

"Not a lot," Judith replied. "As I said, I find it difficult. I found her diary date for meeting you by working back from the Battle of Lansdown."

"Clever," he said as he parked.

"I thought so, almost wish I hadn't. I know you've told me everything that's happened between you, John, but I'm still trying to get my head around it." She linked her arm through his as they walked to the café.

As John carried their tray to a vacant table he said nonchalantly, "I wonder if you could see what you can find in my left trouser pocket."

"What, here? I do know what's down there."

"Just look, please," said John.

"You're mad! I feel a long thin box." Judith struggled to pull it free as he was still walking. "Gift-wrapped. Is this a present?"

"Yep."

"And you're too embarrassed to hand it over?"

"Yep."

They sat down at a table and she asked, "Can I open it now?" He just nodded.

Judith opened the gift to find an exquisitely made necklace of dull silver metal, each heavy, flattened link in the chain slightly engraved. "John! Oh my God, it's lovely."

"Small token, you know. Didn't want the cliché of handing it over at a candlelit—"

"Small token?" She let the smooth heavy links slide through her fingers. "This is platinum. It must have cost—"

"I know you don't normally do jewellery," he said, "so I wanted to find something an engineer would like. It's short so it won't get tangled up."

"Shut up and let me kiss you."

After coffee a much more relaxed atmosphere developed, but as they returned, hand in hand to the Range Rover, Judith exclaimed, "Christ, John! We've just left a few thousand quid's-worth of antiques unattended in a car park."

"I did lock the doors."

A couple of hours later, John and Judith were carrying several large locked boxes from an NCP car park to the workshop and office of Campbell and Duran for a meeting with the antique gun expert recommended by Stella. They were hoping to get an opinion and possible valuation for the guns and swords that had been concealed in the blocked off passageway in Peverell House. They hadn't spoken to their intended contact, Peter Bisson, but his secretary had been able to make an appointment at very short notice.

Mr Bisson was quite surprised to see them as they staggered awkwardly through the narrow door with their cargo of boxes. He was a tall thin man of about thirty-five, dressed in a rumpled work suit.

"Oh," he said. "I understood from Mrs Lacey that you were just dropping in for a quick chat. You've brought the actual hardware!"

"That's right," said Judith, setting down the case of rifles and extending her hand. "Mrs Lacey said to bring in anything we had – photos, documentation. I've got original receipts for purchase of the guns."

Bisson looked confused, his eyes flicking to his computer screen. "One rifled wheel lock pistol circa 1635, and two hunting rifles of similar age?" he asked.

"That's right, and two swords. Since then, we've found some other items – a bullet mould, and what we think is a heavy fighting knife," explained Judith.

"You've brought them?"

John and Judith both nodded.

Bisson belatedly shook hands with John, and suggested coffee. They declined, anxious to get his opinion.

"We'd better go down to the workroom, then – not much space in here." Bisson took off his jacket and put on a white overall coat.

"You look surprised," queried John.

"I had expected a quick visit, a few papers and photos – not the Ransom family arsenal."

"This is from the Peverells," said Judith. "The Ransom guns are much more modern – shotguns and air rifles." As the gun dealer led them down a set of dingy steps to a large basement room, she continued, "I think the pair of Purdy shotguns are quite old – 1900 black powder jobs. My dad did say they shot modern cartridges very well."

"Surprised it didn't burst the barrel," muttered Bisson with a shudder. "Then they'd only be worth a few thousand or so."

The basement room was brilliantly lit and equipped with hand and power tools that immediately excited Judith's interest.

"Can you make guns down here?" she asked.

"We often make replicas," Bisson explained. "Some are made using only traditional materials and tools. Used for historical research and testing." He indicated some dis-assembled weapons. "Most of our work is in refurbishment, both the mechanisms and ornamentation. Some of my colleagues engrave modern sporting guns for select customers."

They started by examining the edged weapons, the two swords and several daggers.

"These are not my speciality, but I'll take a quick look for you and suggest an expert in the field." Peter Bisson drew one of the swords from its scabbard and said dismissively, "Quite utilitarian, this sabre has been used in combat or practice, at least. There are nicks in the blade, and other damage has been stoned out." He made notes. "Not worth a great deal but I can get you a valuation from our expert in a day or so."

Penny Peverell's two hunting rifles raised visible and growing excitement as he examined them in detail.

"Tschinke-style but German manufacture, about 1620; used and worn in places, some repair but perfect working condition; long thirty-six-inch barrel, small 0.35 bore." He was giving a muttered commentary as he examined the workmanship. "I know collectors who would be extremely interested in these. Best sold at auction, though. Reserve price about £8000. Ha! Down here on the trigger guard, almost worn away: *Stettin*, a German city, *1623*, and the maker's name. We can check all this."

"We have a sort of receipt for its purchase," said Judith, passing over a document in a plastic see-through folder. "It's quite fragile – cheap paper."

"Always good to have the provenance," said Bisson enthusiastically. He laid a large magnifying plate over the document and began to read. "This is the wrong one," he said. "It seems to refer to the sale of a horse – a mare called Connie."

"The last two lines," suggested Judith.

"Oh, I see. The rifles, these pair of splendid firearms, were just 'thrown in' with the sale of the horse, from Lady Constance Cavendish to Penny Peverell. Amazing! Did they choose their husbands to gain alliteration? Incredible to give the rifles away. These were exceptionally rare and valuable items, even then."

"Lord Cavendish died fighting for the king at the storming of Bristol in 1643," said John.

"A real bloodbath; a Pyrrhic victory," agreed Bisson.

"And Lady Cavendish decided to sell up and move to France," continued John. "She didn't want to be reminded of her husband's obsession with shooting."

Peter Bisson looked up at John, and then at Judith. "You

know a great deal about your ancestors, if I may say so," he enquired.

"As I said, not my ancestors, just previous owners of the house," replied Judith. "We have recently found some of their artefacts: paintings, jewellery, and the weapons all concealed in Peverell House. Also, there are some papers," she pointed to the receipts, "and Lady Peverell's diary, that runs from her arrival at Peverell until the death of her husband, Edward. That's when the house was given to my family. We have the deeds for that, of course."

"Remarkable. Has the diary been read? Is there a transcript?"

"It was only found last week," said Judith reluctantly, "and it's difficult to decipher."

"We have contact with experts on this period," said Bisson. "For a fee and a copy of the transcript—"

"No," cut in Judith emphatically. "It may contain things embarrassing to my family's interests."

"After all this time?"

"Possibly," said John.

"Mr John Townsend is an expert on Lady Peverell," said Judith bitterly. "We need to see what the diary says before it's made public."

Bisson only shrugged. "Let's take a look at this last box." He opened it gently, noting but ignoring the tension between his two customers.

Judith had moved around to Bisson's side of the workbench, more than anything to get away from John, trying to overcome the jealousy that kept crushing her like a heavy weight.

"It was handmade by a Mr Thomas Formby of London as an

engagement gift for Penelope, soon to be the wife of Edward Peverell," explained John. "Strangely called 'a gift of love'. The bill of sale and a dedication card are still in the lid of the box."

"It's unique," said Bisson excitedly. "Totally original features. I didn't know any work of this standard was done outside Germany. I need to check records." He held the pistol expertly. "Amazing. Precision mechanism, no decoration, perfectly functional." As Bisson began to cock the mechanism, a small quantity of black powder trickled out. "My God!" he exclaimed in alarm. "You've brought a loaded weapon in here."

"How were we to know?" retorted John. "It won't fire, will it?"

"Probably not. The sulphur in the powder will have corroded the steel on the inside." He ran his fingers through thin straggly hair, concentrating on the beautiful antique.

It took the gunsmith nearly half an hour to extract the pistol ball from the barrel and then the gunpowder. Judith was fascinated by the tools he used. John left them to arrange coffee. When he returned, Bisson was weighing the powder on precision digital scales.

"The gunpowder was in a waxed paper cartridge," Bisson explained. "There is no corrosion. This thing would shoot. Frightening!" Then he looked enquiringly across at Judith. "I don't suppose you know if the owner was left-handed?"

"She sewed with her left hand," John butted in without thinking. "Why do you ask?"

"The firing mechanism is on the left side of the pistol. I've never seen that before. It must have been custom-made." He began to give meaningless technical reasons why this would be an advantage to a left-handed shooter.

Judith remarked, "There is a portrait of Penny in Peverell House. She is wearing a bracelet that we also found, and the pistol is shown on a table."

Bisson was doing a calculation. "A woman's pistol? Unlikely. With this load in such a small gun it would have kicked like hell when you shot it. No, a woman—"

"She was a big girl," said Judith, looking pointedly at John with a hint of resentment, "and according to her diary practised her shooting most days, before going out riding." She passed him a photo of the portrait. "You can see the gun."

"Must have had wrists like steel!"

"Some men like that sort of thing."

John shuddered involuntarily at Judith's remark, remembering Penny's powerful embrace.

After a few minutes, Judith asked, "So, what do you think?"

"Have you got a criminal record?" asked Bisson jokily while oiling the gun with a fine artist's brush.

"No. Why?"

"With luck, I would say you could get off with a hefty fine."

"What! Why?"

Suddenly serious, Peter Bisson looked at them both. "Walking through London with a collection of edged and pointed weapons; carrying an illegal and loaded firearm in a public place – it goes on!" Carefully he worked the cocking dog and pulled the trigger. The wheel spun, and a few sparks escaped from the side of the gun and the faintest trace of smoke. "Bloody hell," he exclaimed. "I could 'ave shot meself!" His cultured accent slipped into South London.

"So, what do we do? Are you calling the police?" Judith asked, concerned.

"Sorry, a bit shaken." Peter Bisson hastily took a gulp of his cold coffee. "No, of course not. I'll give you a detailed itemised receipt and you leave it all here. I'll get a registered courier to return things to your Peverell House. You've got a safe or a secure gun cabinet?"

"Yes, for my dad's guns," said Judith.

John came over and touched her arm, feeling she had been through a tough morning.

She looked up at him and smiled wanly. "I've still got my shotgun certificate. Dad wanted me to get into shooting but I never did. Simon, my brother, and I have still to decide what to do with the shotguns."

"Please give me first refusal on the Purdy shotguns. As for this lot, you get the guns securely stowed away and then notify the county firearms officer. You'll have my full report by then and can say I have been down and advised you."

"I don't like leaving them behind," said Judith.

Peter Bisson said coldly, "If you're stopped on the street or even when you are driving, there'll be hell to pay. I'll do photos for you to take away; we'll get the receipt witnessed. Once your weapons are under lock and key, you can destroy the receipt and no one knows they've been out of Peverell."

For different reasons Judith and John felt quite stressed by the day and were relieved that the discussions with the gun expert were coming to a close. All they could think about was getting on their way.

Just as they were leaving the workroom, Bisson asked, "I

wonder if it's ever killed anyone. Lady Peverell's pistol, I mean."

"At least three people," said John.

"That we know of so far," added Judith.

"It would be very messy if she was using that pistol at close range," mused Bisson. "Still, a history like that could double its value at auction."

"Well, that was exciting," said Judith as they stood outside the Campbell and Duran offices as a fine rain began to fall. "I'm starving. I could treat you to a late lunch?" Absentmindedly she fingered her new necklace and felt a warm affection for John, despite her previous surges of jealousy.

"Ah, well, actually at two thirty there's an afternoon concert at St Martins in the Fields... playing Bach."

"Church near Trafalgar Square?"

"Yes. Do you want to come?"

"Bach? No, I don't. But if we walk through Trafalgar Square, I could push you in the bloody fountain."

"OK, what would madam like to do?" John was beginning to feel more composed now. Touching and discussing the guns that Penny had used all those years ago had given him a terrible jolt, stirring up his thoughts and emotions. Worse still was trying to conceal those feelings from Judith. He looked away along the busy road for a minute or two and then said, with a hint of a smile, "The Science Museum?"

"Ha-ha! I could have written the bloody guidebook for that place when I was a student." She looked at him unsteadily. "I've been a bit of—"

"A bitchington, I think you said?" suggested John.

"Whatever. And after your present, too." Her gaze was locked onto his face, quite serious. "I suggest we grab the Range Rover and get back to Bath; pick up a snack at Reading Services. I'll upgrade my offer of a late fry-up to a full dinner at The Bath Ivy. Perhaps I can stop sniping at you, and after dinner, we could try and remember why we are—" She faltered. "Well, partners, and best friends."

CHAPTER 31

"Penny, I have a small adventure for us!" proclaimed Edward as he returned to their lodging in Bristol.

"Let me guess," she called back from the small parlour at the top of the inn staircase.

Edward caught his breath when he saw her in the sunlight that filtered through the slanted window. The sight of her still excited him. How could he worry about war at that moment?

She shouted eagerly, "We take a ship to France again, or Spain?"

"Nothing so grand. We take a carriage to Taunton and visit George Goring." All Edward's procrastinations and objections had been swept aside by Prince Maurice and Hopton. Rupert would be pleased to have Edward out of the town and had not objected. Edward could no longer avoid the order and had to tell Penny.

"That odious drunkard?" she snorted. "Why? Has he captured Taunton at last?"

She ran down the stairs to him and he caught her in an embrace, kissing her full on the lips.

"I have to deliver messages and money. You could stay in Bristol, darling, but I thought a change of scenery..." He hugged her more tightly and stroked her hair, saying, "I am heartily tired of overseeing the manufacture of guns and clothes for the army. But, if you think it too arduous or dangerous, you could abide here until I return?"

Penny was horrified at the prospect of Edward spending several nights away. Especially so because their love had just been rekindled after those terrible scenes in Bath. Once again, she felt desperately fortunate that John had resisted her advances. She had so nearly succumbed, but her guilt had been melted away by Edward's loving. Of course she should accompany him, and enjoy a break from the boredom of Bristol. There was no reason why not. She did, however, refuse to be bumped and tossed around in a carriage as it struggled over rutted roads, waterlogged from recent rains. She much preferred to ride horseback.

"The money we take will need to be in the carriage and we must travel slowly to escort it," Edward was saying. "The weather could be bad."

Penny laughed softly. "Edward, dear, it is but a day's hard ride – two days if we proceed more slowly and stay at an inn overnight."

"But the coin we are taking to pay the men?" Edward spoke doubtfully.

"Will be safer if it is distributed in the saddle bags of our escort. If we are ambushed by rebels there will be no single point for their attack. We can fight or flee as circumstances dictate."

Edward and Penny rode out of Bristol on a cold, damp spring morning heading for Bridgewater, where Lord Goring had his headquarters. Well-muffled against the chill, Penny sat astride her grey hunter, Connie. She had wanted a mount that could keep up with Edward at full gallop, and Connie had immediately proved to have that speed, even if she initially lacked stamina.

Edward was proud that Penny was such a fine horsewoman but he had been equally fearful that Connie might be too much of a handful for her. His fears had been groundless and he smiled as he vividly remembered Penny's first trial ride on Connie.

"She just needs exercise," she had yelled as she raced off, seemingly oblivious to the hazards of the road.

Edward had followed with equal speed but more care. Ten minutes later, Penny had allowed Connie to slow to a walk.

"She's blowing hard," said Edward.

"Out of condition," replied Penny. "Hardly out of the paddock for months. A week or two's training and she will soon pick up. She's willing enough, aren't you?" Penny stroked the horse's long groomed mane.

"But do not push her too hard," Edward had cautioned.

Those days had long passed and now Connie had speed and stamina to match any horse in Bristol, including those owned by the princes. Not that either speed or stamina would be challenged on this journey. The troop of twenty dragoons and two pack animals under the direct command of a newly commissioned captain would travel at a more sedate pace. It was a long journey and their mounts were not of the best.

Penny and Edward took an inland route away from the coast for concern over Parliamentary foragers who could possibly sally out from Taunton or the small anchorages they used at Burnham and the River Parrett estuary. They passed through a gap in the

Mendip Hills at Rowberrow and stopped for food at an inn called The Swan. A fine name, but its village pond was only home to some scruffy wild ducks.

"That is a fine range of hills out to the west," observed Edward. "I haven't ridden this way before."

"There are three hills joined by low cols," replied the captain, who sat with them in the sun outside the gloomy inn. "There is a path you can ride out to Crooked Hill – that's the tor-like rocks at the end. It gives a good view out to the sea on a day like today."

"It would be interesting, but about six extra miles there and back."

"A narrow path down from Crooked Hill joins up with our road. It's steep but passable for a good, well-mounted horseman. The lady can come on with me and the escort and you could meet up with us without losing any time."

Penny stiffened with annoyance and shook out her red hair which caught the sun's rays, lightening its brilliance. "Are you suggesting 'the lady' is not capable?" snapped Penny. "I ride better than most men, and have the advantage of carrying less weight!"

"My pardon, no offence intended, but that high-stepping mare of yours is not bred for such work. A hill pony would fare better."

"The same could be said of my stallion," said Edward easily, "but at seventeen stone I would break the back of any hill pony on those inclines."

"Then we will go together!" laughed Penny. "The weak woman and the massive man."

"You can spy out the land for us," suggested the captain.

"There are good vantage points on the way. You can see right across the Levels".

The slow ascent through King's Wood through the trees had to be taken carefully as their path was crisscrossed with exposed tree roots that could easily trip a horse. Once above the tree belt it was clear, open grazing land up to the first hilltop. Then there was a slight descent before the rise to the next summit and on to the rocky, one-sided slump of Crooked Hill. As they approached, they were confronted by a sheer rock face – not high but too steep for any horse. Riding around to the south side, they found a gentle slope.

"He was right, our brave captain. The view from up here across the Bristol channel is fabulous," said Penny as she gazed around. "Is he always so keen to avoid the enemy?"

"Only when carrying the king's gold and protecting the gunpowder. Ned did teach him to be careful."

"What's his name, by the way? You all call him 'captain'."

"Jeremiah Bottomly."

"Oh!"

"Behind his back often referred to as Jolly Arse, but now he's promoted, Captain suits better."

Suddenly, Penny brought Connie up sharp, noticing a slight movement far off on the level fields below. "Is that a file of men out there?" she asked, pointing uncertainly.

"Yes, my sharp-eyed wife, a line of horsemen, and several carts." Edward vaulted to the ground and reached into one of his saddle-bags. "I had meant to show you this later; now I have an excuse to use it."

"What?"

"A field spyglass."

"A telescope?" she asked fascinated, as he remounted to gain height.

"Aye, twenty times magnification. Let me see..."

"Let me see, said the blind woman, and lo she could see," Penny quipped. "She can see that her husband has been buying expensive toys without approval!"

Edward focused the optics and observed, "Ten Parliamentarian dragoons, four carts with barrels—"

"Let me see!" Penny demanded impatiently.

He handed over the instrument. "Twist the eyepiece to—"

"I know, I have studied the natural sciences as well as you. How do you know they are rebels? They could be Lord Goring's men."

"The helmets – lobster-tailed helmets – none of our men wear them. They must be Cromwell's soldiers."

"I thought him in Norfolk?"

"He probably is, but his trained squadrons are being deployed far and wide to give grit and discipline to the general rabble," said Edward, taking the spyglass back. "See, they have two scouts ahead and men either side of the wagons. There would be no taking them by surprise."

"You see that copse, just past the stream they must ford?" said Penny, as Edward continued to watch the convoy below.

"It could hide several men on foot," replied Edward turning to study the treeline. "It is probably too dense for horsemen. But we must see that our own supplies of gold and food reach Taunton before we risk any attack."

"One long-range shot at the powder barrels?" suggested

Penny, becoming excited. "We send Captain on his way and can easily get ahead of the wagons. They will surely stop to water the horses at the stream – it's near midday."

"The fording place is about two hundred yards from the edge of the trees. Is it too far?"

"Not with one of my long-barrelled sporting rifles."

"Even if you score a hit, there is no certainty that the light ball would penetrate an oak barrel at that range."

Despite the words of caution, Penny could tell Edward was enthusiastic to try the idea. "They are too confident, trusting on the lax nature of Goring's so-called siege!"

∞

It was late afternoon before the Parliamentary supply wagons came into sight. Edward and Penny crouched, concealed at the southern edge of the copse. They had left their horses tethered on the northern edge of the narrow belt of woodland and clambered through undergrowth between trees and around bramble clumps to find a good sheltered position. For certain, no horseman would be able to ride through the congested undergrowth to follow them if they were discovered. Better still, a bulk of earth and fragments of drystone wall protected the coppiced wood boundary from browsing animals.

"By God's will, if I had Ned and my dozen dragoons we could account for all these rebel naves."

Penny threw off her light cloak so that she could move more easily. "It's too far for musket shot," said Penny as she checked the

287

priming of the rifle. "They will not expect to be fired on from this distance."

The progress of the wagons and escort was slow and they had probably stopped for a midday meal. Edward was stationed ten yards to the right of Penny to avoid being obscured by the smoke from her shot. Scanning the wagons with his spyglass, he waited for what seemed an age. The two lead escorts passed, then a captain with a red sash, several troopers and the first wagon. The second wagon with its powder barrels was as close to them as it would come.

Edward could see Penny motionless, the rifle supported by a prod rest as she squinted through the strange sight. Suddenly there was a flash of flame, a sharp crack, and far less smoke than from a musket. The ball flew true and Edward saw a puff of black spurting from a hole near the central cask. Powder trickled down the side onto the barrel below, but it didn't ignite.

There was a shout of warning from the rebel captain. Startled into action, the escort levelled pistols and carbines in their direction.

A ragged fusillade rang out even as Edward yelled, "Get down!"

A few carbine shots whistled through the trees but most had been aimed flat at the gun smoke and fell well short.

"To the horses," called Edward urgently.

"I have the second gun," shouted Penny determinedly, as she shoved the twin of the first rifle into the rest.

A shattering explosion drowned out her words, then a deafening roar as a succession of powder barrels exploded. The shock made Edward drop the spyglass but he could see the central wagon completely obliterated. The air was full of flying debris, bits of barrels, charred cart and dismembered bodies.

The Parliamentary captain was attempting to rally his men, urging them to save the other carts. Penny's second shot thudded into his breastplate. The bullet, too light to penetrate, skidded down and outwards, gouging his thigh as he rose in the stirrups to shout orders.

"Come on," yelled Edward, snatching up Penny's first gun and urging her through the trees to their waiting horses.

A figure stood just inside the treeline, sword in hand. Edward raised his pistol.

"Hold, sir, it is me, Jeremiah, the captain."

"What in God's name are you doing here?"

"The men are safe – off towards Bridgwater. I came back to help, or to guide you." A second series of explosions shook the trees. "What?"

"No time!" yelled Edward. "To horse! We can talk later."

"No need for haste," retorted the captain. "The rebels be in no state to chase after us."

As they rode away, Captain Jeremiah was chuckling and cackling to himself.

"None will believe it: a fine lady, riding as a man, shooting the bung out of a powder barrel at three hundred yards, shooting the cods off that rebel as he rises in the stirrups. 'Tis like witchcraft!"

"Hold your tongue, man! There's no witchcraft. Lady Penelope has ridden astride since she was a girl and practices her shooting daily." Then Edward added bitterly, "Would that the king's men did the same."

"We aye would," said the captain, "if there was powder and

ball to spare for practice."

"My pardon."

"Edward, what did happen? My shot just broached the cask. There was a delay..."

"A delay before the rebels returned fire," laughed Edward. "They fired their pieces across the broken powder barrel. Some sparks from the discharge must have ignited the spilled powder." He did not tell of gruesome bodies blown to pieces; horse's hair and clothing fired by the heat and blast.

For all the captain's assurance of safety, they rode rapidly for the first mile before settling down to a fast trot.

"How many men did I kill?" Penny asked Edward quietly.

Before he could reply, the captain shouted, "A round dozen, at least." He laughed. "A dozen will die any road, die of burns and smashed bodies. There not be enough sound men and horses to carry the dying from the field." He swept his hat off to Penny. "Madam, you have killed more men and destroyed more warlike stores than our regiment has done in the last month!" Turning to Edward, "And you, sir, if you had command, I'd wager we would have had the rebels hanging from Taunton Castle's walls months ago!"

∞

Kenneth Sumerton esquire, justice of the peace and owner of Waterside House outside Bridgewater, was a reluctant host to Lord Goring and several of the senior officers. Sumerton detested Goring: the drinking and the women and the boorish ways did not suit a man who claimed to be a nobleman and leader of a king's army. He also believed his lordship and generals should be billeted much closer to the Taunton siege lines. Anything to get him to leave the house so that Lady Sumerton could return from her sanctuary in Bath.

Squire Sumerton had felt obliged to offer Sir Edward Peverell and his wife, Penelope, a bed for the night prior to their return to Bristol. He had also politely invited them to dinner but discreetly suggested that Lady Peverell might take supper in her room, because the party at dinner were all male and their manners hardly refined. Personally, he considered that there was nothing refined in a lady who rode astride and galloped all over the country, even if it was with her husband. He had provided them with separate bedrooms as was the fashion for gentry, but the bed in Penny's room would serve for two! In return for the hospitality, Edward felt it necessary to attend dinner, although after a hard day's riding he would have much rather been in a soft bed with Penny.

Edward did manage a brief interview with Lord Goring after dinner, but it did not go well.

"You have the insolence of a country yokel, Peverell," Goring thundered when Edward asked about payment to the army and marching it north. "To question me – me? A peer of the realm? What do you know of my expenses, my needs?" He gulped half a glass of wine. "At the king's request, I marched this army east to take Portsmouth, at my own expense. I fought two battles to reach Fareham. There I was to be reinforced, re-supplied from Oxford and—" He looked down at the empty glass. "You want some wine?"

"No, m'lord."

"I do! We were to rendezvous with Prince Rupert and then

smash south into Portsmouth. Overwhelming force. With luck, capture the rebel fleet before it could sail." He poured more wine for himself. "And where were those bloody German princelings, nephews of the king and experts in war? My bollocks. They were still dancing in Oxford. My men in a hostile county, too few in numbers, most of my powder spent. A Parliamentary army under Lord Essex advancing, Portsmouth town had time to prepare." He ranted on, "Cannon from the ships brought ashore to oppose me, town militia armed." Another gulp of wine. "And where is Prince Bloody Rupert of the Rhine? He's dancing in Oxford. Lady someone is giving a ball, don't you know!"

Edward was so taken aback by this vehement tirade and explanation of Goring's conduct that he did not respond to the insult heaped on him. Instead he said coldly, "I have reason to believe, my lord, some of our patrols are being bribed to allow supplies into Taunton." He intended to tell of what he and Penny had seen the previous year and how the commander of the nearby patrol base had refused to act. It was obvious that Goring was quite drunk and still muttering.

"Your pittance, Peverell, does not repay a fraction of my expense. Not a fraction." He stopped as if hearing Edward's latest accusation. "Taking bribes, you say? Can you blame them? I can't pay the men, I can't feed them. I've no fresh powder." He rose unsteadily to his feet. "Get out, Peverell. Get out!"

Edward stood in silence, totally stunned by the drunken outburst, looking on in dismay as Lord Goring reeled from his chair staggering from the room.

"Mildred!" he called. "Where are you, woman? It's bedtime. I want you in bed!"

CHAPTER 32

It was early when Penny awoke alone in the bed she shared with Edward back at Peverell House. Dim morning light filtered between the heavy ornate bed hangings, hardly brighter when they were drawn back. Out of bed, she wrapped a thin gown over her nightdress and crept into the adjoining bedroom, sometimes used by Edward if she were too restless for him to sleep.

The spare bed was untouched; he had not slept there. Thudding sounds reached her and she moved back into their room, crossing it to look down from the latticed window. Below in that part of the garden they called the exercise yard, Edward was hacking at a thick pole with his heavy sabre, practising his sword cuts like a man possessed by fury. Dressed in simple breeches and a white shirt, he looked such a vigorous, manly figure. She liked to see him with his fashionable shoulder length hair tied back when he practiced fencing. He stopped, changed his sword over, and renewed his attack with the left hand.

Penny dragged on the soft leather breeches she used for riding, threw a simple dress over the top, and hastily bundled her long hair into a mop cap. Stopping only to grab coats and her box of pistols, she started off down the stairs to join Edward.

"Ah! Best of wives!" he called jovially as he saw her approach. "I hope I did not wake you?"

"Not at all. I noticed you were up early and came to join you." He grabbed Penny in a bearlike embrace and she felt a surge of passion. "Will you shout the hit points for me?" he asked, releasing her from his grasp.

She agreed and began to shout, "Cut heart, cut throat, left leg, lunge quarte."

At each order Edward used the point or edge of his sword to strike at the post in the relevant body position.

"Change hands! Lunge tierce, head..." she continued, until he was sweating and blowing with exhaustion.

"Enough," Edward called out, wiping his brow with the back of his hand. "My arm is numb with the shock. I would have killed twenty men!"

"Number twenty-one kills you, then," Penny said with a laugh, picking up one of the lighter practice foiled rapiers from the stand he had brought out from the house. "Now you are warmed up, I think you need to practice some finesse." Holding up her skirt she lunged towards him viciously.

He darted back, whipping up his sabre in an attempted parry. He had been half expecting something like that, but was still too slow, and the buttoned point of the rapier struck high up on the chest. Off balance, he almost fell as she tripped on her long skirt.

"All right, madam," he roared in mock fury, "to the death!"

"No, sir, best of three hits. I need you as a husband, even if your fencing is poor."

She was using a belt to hitch up her skirt to a more convenient knee length when Edward prodded her behind with his own foiled sword.

"Now we are equal – one hit each!"

It was fast and furious, and for all Penny's guile and skill, he won as usual.

"Some men would let their wives win," Penny yelled as Edward's deadly lunge sent her staggering backwards at the end of their final bout.

"Most condescending if they did. But then I know of no other wife who would make their husband sweat to get the last hit."

Penny handed him the jacket and long top coat she had brought from upstairs. "Wrap up or you will take a chill."

"I thought breakfast?" he replied, but struggled into the enveloping clothes. Then he pulled her to him for a kiss.

"In good time, at our normal time, sir. First, I will practise my shooting. As a treat, I will let you load for me."

"Grand lady, how can I thank you? Can I stand up the targets, too?" Edward joked.

Some time, and much burned gun powder later, they were seated at breakfast when Richard York, the butler and house manager, entered the dining room.

"I beg your pardon for interrupting, sir, madam, but there is a visitor and his servant in the yard outside. A Mr Marcus Bragg. I believe you know him?"

"Most well. Why did you not invite him in as a friend? See his servant has food and drink."

"I did invite him in, sir. Mr Bragg said he needs to speak to you before entering your house."

"Some jest on his part?" asked Penny.

"I think not, ma'am. He seemed most serious – almost fearful."

Edward stood up hastily, scraping his chair on the wooden floor.

"Then I will go down at once, even if my eggs grow cold!" To Penny he said, "I'll bring him up directly, do not wait to finish."

Edward swiftly descended the stairs, leaving Penny to her breakfast.

"What-ho, Marcus," he bellowed. "What's this nonsense to stand on my threshold like a stranger?" He was about to ask if Marcus had come with a challenge but the joke died in his throat when he saw his friend's face. "What is it? Bad news?"

"The worst, in some ways," Marcus replied, and blurted out, "I have deserted the king's cause."

"What? Declared for parliament?" said Edward in total disbelief. "You were so staunch."

"I have not joined the rebels; I have petitioned parliament's pardon for fighting against its authority. I declared I will support neither side and have agreed to pay a fine for my liberty and safe return to my estates." He waited for Edward's reaction. None came and Marcus added, "I would not enter your house under pretence of still being a friend until you knew what I had done."

Edward stared at Marcus with incredulity, finally saying, "You do not fight for parliament?"

"No."

"Then come in and join Penny and me at our breakfast table." To the butler he said, "See that Mr Bragg's man is taken care of, and have their horses led to the stable."

"Thank you, Edward. Thank you. I felt—"

"Not another word until we are upstairs. Penny will want to know all. And, most importantly, how are Jacinda and the children?"

Edward and Marcus made their way through the imposing hall and back upstairs to the breakfast table where Penny waited for them.

"We are still friends? You do not exclude me from—"

Edward held up his hand. "No, not unless you actively aid parliament, like that traitor Strode who led the commoners to rebel."

It took Marcus some time to explain what he had done and why he had abandoned King Charles. Without being asked, Richard York brought in a mug of small beer and a plate for their visitor. A parlourmaid followed with more food.

"After the battle of Naseby, I knew that all was lost," Marcus continued. "Cut off from my estate in Hampshire, I had no money left to support me in the king's fight." He looked imploringly at Edward. "You know that although I rode with the cavalry, I am no warrior. There is nothing else I could add." His voice trailed off dejectedly.

Edward looked at the slight man in what had been overly flamboyant clothes, now soiled and worn from hard campaigning. "No one can doubt you, Marcus," he said kindly. "You have fought in every battle from Edgehill to the defeat at Naseby. No man could have done more."

"I have no gift for command," said Marcus. "I just followed along to do my—" He broke off, too emotional to continue. "You cannot believe how it was at Naseby, Edward. We charged Cromwell's men; they halted us with pistol shot. We rallied, moved forward, and they fired their second pistols. Then that villain shouted 'in God's name we will prevail', and they charged our broken ranks. And where was Rupert? Plundering the baggage. Christ, Edward, it was carnage. All my companions – Ephron, Thomas, Percy – all friends from Peterhouse at Cambridge." Marcus took a gulp from his mug, trying desperately to shake off those haunting, terrible images of injured and dying men.

"I knew them all," said Edward sadly.

"Good men, all killed while I, the philandering rogue—"

"I have seen war, I know how it is," said Edward sympathetically. "A normal man can only endure so much."

Penny moved over to the more comfortable armchairs placed before the window, indicating one to Marcus who was pleased to stretch his legs out in the warming sunlight.

"Are Jacinda and the children well?" she asked, trying to break the mood of despair.

"Aye, well and thriving," muttered Marcus. "I had not seen little Benedict. He was born while I was with the army. God, I have been a poor husband and father. After the battle I thought, *why have I lived when so many good fellows died?* And then, *I must make amends; get home, be a good man, get the estate in order...* all that."

"I am surprised how little the Parliamentarian assessor fined you," said Penny. "I thought it would be much more punishing."

"Their aim is not to punish; not at this time. They want to take gentlemen like us out of the war. I had to swear an oath on the bible not to support the king."

"You swore an oath on the bible?" chortled Penny. "You are

more of a heathen than Edward. How many times have you sworn to Jacinda that your latest adventure would be the last? No more philandering, no wenches ruined?"

"Stop, Penny, please." Marcus looked mournful. "You know my past faults, but now I am reformed."

"Until the next comely wench appears," grinned Edward, walking over to join them. "But will you change sides back to ours if fortune swings to the king?"

"No. If parliament finds I have aided the king I would be hanged!"

"As may we all be," added Edward bitterly. He removed his light brown jacket and placed it over the back of his chair, thinking sadly of all the wasted effort. "My role at Bristol and financing the king this last half year will not be easily forgotten."

"Enough of this self-pity, the two of you!" said Penny. "Marcus, you have the fair Jacinda and the children, now."

"The love of my life!"

"Nonsense, Marcus," interjected Edward vehemently. "You use her like a—" He faltered for a word.

"A good wife," suggested Penny. She beckoned the maid to clear away their cups and then offered some early apples to Edward and their guest. "But come, Marcus, you got her with child and then abandoned her for that Flemish widow."

"But I did return to marry Jacinda," pleaded Marcus.

"Only when her father and brothers tracked you to Dover and challenged you!"

"There were three of them," grinned Marcus, totally unabashed as he sliced some apple. "And her father did offer a generous settlement, payable after the baby was born and if it lived for one year."

"How many times have you vowed to be true to Jacinda and then broken that vow?" asked Edward. He took up his pipe and began to light it carefully, enjoying the banter between them.

"Shush, Edward," said Penny. "We live in evil times. All of us have broken vows of fidelity," she said, staring into his eyes, "and have been completely forgiven."

Edward lowered his gaze away from her directness. "It is my deepest wish—" he started to say.

"To be forgiven," repeated Penny. "Looking into the eye of death or being driven to despair can cut one off from normal virtue."

"As if you could know," said Marcus. "You are safe here in Peverell." He lapsed into a reverie. "At Naseby when we charged at their line, a musket was levelled at my face. I could see down the barrel. From twenty yards away I saw the match fall onto the pan; saw the sparks. It did not fire. The change from elation to terror in the man's face as I rode him down... It was him or me; my sword or his gun. That night, despite our defeat, I feasted and drank. I celebrated being alive and paid to lie with a tavern whore."

"Stop it, Marcus," interrupted Penny. "We all know you are a philanderer, we need not have the details."

"The experience changed me, Penny, it truly has."

"Like when you had to fight a duel with Sir Rodney Palister? Was it his wife or his sister you seduced?" said Edward with a laugh. "I remember then you vowed you would reform."

"He forgave me," stated Marcus, "and up to a point I kept my word. This was different."

Penny stretched out her hand to Marcus, hoping to show some understanding and acceptance of his wandering behaviour. "I too have come close to violence and death," said Penny softly. "It changed my view of many things."

Edward nodded. "I too. We have all lost good friends."

"Next morning I deserted and rode home," continued Marcus. "The two youngest boys don't know me; the estate is in ruins; my bailiff is a lazy rogue. I cannot help the king anymore, and I have no money."

"Hard times indeed," commented Edward.

"You have no assets to sell?" asked Penny.

"Some jewellery of Jacinda's, if we could find a buyer."

"I could help there," suggested Edward. "We have contacts in France."

Marcus shook his head wearily and Edward noticed how lined and grey his friend's face had become lately.

"Also, and most immediately, there is un-threshed corn in ricks, and last year's wool clip."

"The wheat and barley should be fine," commented Edward, and poured out a second measure of beer for Marcus from a jug on the sideboard.

"I have tried to put all in hand," said Marcus, drinking his beer greedily. "The corn is threshing well, but some fleeces are rotting – the ones on the lowest racks in the barn. I have set the labourers to work sorting out those still good." He looked directly at Edward. "That is why I came to you – I will have near on a thousand fleeces to sell—"

"There is little market," cut in Penny. She turned to Edward noticing his strong features, admiring his steadfastness. She loved him dearly, and a warmth stole over her. She patted his arm and he looked towards her, realising her longing. It was difficult to pull those thoughts away, to change their focus on Marcus and his troubles. "If we meet Oliver Ransom's order for cloth, we will have little left. Marcus's fleeces, if they be good, could be washed, spun and woven to refill our stock."

"Oliver Ransom?" asked Marcus suspiciously. "He is for parliament?"

"To the hilt," agreed Edward. "That is why we hold back on the trade. Our cloth would go to Painswick, near Gloucester. There it would be dyed, and sewn into uniforms for Cromwell's New Model Army."

"God's teeth!" exclaimed Marcus. "I have surrendered the cause but will not help our enemies."

"Not with warlike stores," said Penny. "I would not countenance that. Providing breeches and coats will not help them fight. With all the disruption of war, cloth is in short supply. We turn a profit at Cromwell's expense."

"Little chance it will hurt his finances," said Edward with a groan. "London pays for all!" Explaining the arrangements, he continued, "Oliver Ransom is a man to be trusted. He agreed half payment in advance of delivery. I will pay full price for your wool as soon as I receive money from Ransom, possibly a little more."

"Thank you. Thank you with all my heart," exclaimed Marcus, extending his hand to shake Edward's gratefully. "I could pay my fine and start setting the estate in order."

"Grain prices are high," said Penny. "Once your corn is threshed it will sell well."

"You have saved me from ruin." Marcus smiled wanly,

finishing off his beer.

"Not quite," said Penny. "There is a condition."

Edward and Marcus looked confused.

"Your wife makes your deals, does she, Ed?"

"It is why I am solvent and others are destitute," laughed Edward. "My French trade depends on her."

"You must undertake to be true to your wife, my friend, Jacinda," said Penny with a smile, but her voice was serious.

"I have sworn so already," said Marcus with feigned solemnity. "Do you want me to swear on the book?"

"That would mean nothing, you heathen," commented Edward.

"What, then?"

"Your hand to your friend, and your promise," demanded Penny.

Shaking his head and sighing slightly, Marcus stood up and looked out of the elegantly draped windows, taking in the rich countryside of the Peverell estate. "Mistress Peverell – Penny," said Marcus, "I think you make too much of this. The demure Jacinda, the fine lady who sings exquisitely and dances with grace, has had more lovers than I've ever had."

"Never. This is slander, sir. Your wife—"

"My wife is at home surrounded by admirers while I sleep under hedges or in cow barns with the army."

"And you accept her infidelity?" asked Edward, shocked. "You could be cuckolded, raising another man's children as your own."

"Never!" laughed Marcus. "We both take precautions in our separate adventures. Protection from disease and unwanted children."

"These protection things – are they the sheaths of—" Penny started to say.

Edward interrupted quickly. "Please, Penny! Is this seemly talk for a respectable married woman?"

"Come, come, Edward, do not be so coy. We played with these things before our marriage and on honeymoon," she said with a laugh. "Marcus will think you a prude."

"I know otherwise," cut in Marcus, "from the stews of Cheapside to the 'backs' of Oxford."

"Before I was married," snarled Edward dangerously. "Before I met my wife."

"The old 'Wild Ed' lurks underneath," grinned Marcus. "I apologise, and will watch my talk, madam."

"My wife knows all my past, Marcus. It is left well behind me."

Penny gave him a meaningful stare, thinking of The Crown Inn and the violence Edward had shown to their attackers in France. Strangely the idea of the 'Wild Ed' did not engender revulsion, more a sense of excitement. It was a pity that she had no wild past to look back on. Thoughts of Jacinda's adventures and of John holding her in a passionate embrace came unbidden. She blushed and turned her face slightly, hiding her disquiet.

"This last turn of the conversation has not been to my liking, Marcus," Edward was saying. "It will not be repeated in my house."

"No, sir, I apologise." Mocking words from Marcus.

"I do not like this sale, Edward," said Penny rising from her chair, ignoring Marcus's talk of Edward's past. "I see it will aid Marcus and Jacinda, or I would not agree to a transaction with parliament. I will leave you to arrange price and details."

She picked up her warm shawl and wrapped it around her shoulders. It was not cold but she was trembling with strange, disturbing feelings. The men stood as she went out.

CHAPTER 33

John was fully engrossed with the final carving of a stone arch piece for a restoration phase of Bath Abbey. Traditionally, this would have been done in situ, but at his workshop he could proceed at the same time as other craftsmen completed the foundations and walls. As Judith had already pointed out, behind closed doors, no one could question his use of power tools to rough out the basic shape before finishing off with chisel and mallet. He smiled as he remembered Judith suggesting a computer-controlled grinding machine for the whole work. Given half a chance, she would probably have the arch 3D printed in some stone-textured plastic.

A small movement caught his eye. He looked up. Judith stood staring at him, hostile and white-faced, eyes red from crying. With the noise of the grinder and Bach playing in his headphones John hadn't heard her come in. Switching off the power tool, he turned easily toward her with a welcoming smile. Judith's whole body was taut like a rod – something awful had happened. Feeling very wary, he tentatively put out his arm to comfort her. She flinched, avoiding his touch.

"Judith, what's up? What's happened?"

"Nothing." She was fighting for control. Then shakily, "I'm going away." A gulp. "I've accepted that secondment in France – Airbus in Toulouse."

John was incredulous; couldn't believe it. Confused and annoyed, he said, "What are you talking about? We discussed that only the other day. With us together and the Peverell project you didn't want to go away for six months."

Judith curled her lip and said icily, "It's not six months, it's permanent. I'm not coming back!" She turned from him abruptly. "Nothing to say. Just came to give you this."

He glanced down at the documents Judith was holding.

"A transcript of Penny Peverell's diary, August 1645." She chucked a transparent folder of typed pages at him and started for the door.

"Stop, don't go. Can't we talk?" He staggered away from the bench and strode after her. "What's happened?" Raising his voice he said, "Please, don't just walk out like this."

"Sod off, John!"

He grabbed at her shoulder.

Judith spun around furiously. "Take your filthy cheating hands off me. I'm trying to be civilised here."

"You owe me some explanation." Shouting, he slammed down the folder on the worktable amongst stone dust and chippings.

"I owe you nothing. I'll see you get your investment in Peverell House back."

Even though Judith was wound up badly and very upset, John couldn't help but notice she had taken time to dress with a certain style. A semi-flared black and silvery grey skirt with a contrasting top emphasised her slim, attractive figure. God, he realised how much he loved her.

"It was all going so well," he muttered lamely. "What have I done?"

"Don't be all innocent with me." Judith stabbed at the folder. "It's all there in her diary, in black and white!"

"Black and yellow, I would—" *Hell, why did I say that?*

"Ha-ha, bloody funny! Oh, and you can keep this!"

She tugged viciously at the chain around her neck, the one John had bought her soon after their return from Dartmoor. She always wore it, seemed part of her. It was thick enough not to break easily. The clasp parted on the second tug, leaving a red wheal on her neck.

"You can reuse that for your next conquest!" She flung it into his face.

Instinctively, he ducked away. John stood open-mouthed and shaken, watching her strut out the door and across the yard to her Range Rover.

"Judith, please! Be reasonable."

The engine roared and she raced out of the open gates. Thank God there was little traffic around the industrial estate mid-morning. Without consciously thinking, John picked up the see-through folder. The title page said it all:

Transcription of Mistress P. Peverell's diary
August to September 1645
(Being an account of her lusty romps with Cousin John)

The title must have been Stella Rigby's idea of a joke.

John went to the small office, absentmindedly making tea as he began to read. It was shocking stuff. With Edward off to Gloucester city for trade, Penny had found John wandering the house and towed him back into her time, into her bed. A lust-driven week... Then the diary stopped abruptly, mid-sentence. John sat in a daze. He went back and re-read in disbelief, scanning through the text avidly. No description had been spared. There were notes of all the places they had made love, even 'three times in one day: what a lover'!

The trouble with the diary entries was that they were just pure fantasy – Penny's daydreaming, wild imagination. How could he ever convince Judith that this passion-fest never happened? John had strongly resisted Penny's advances in Bath when she had been in despair at Edward's confession of adultery. Judith knew all about it. After that, John hadn't even seen her at Peverell House. As far as he knew, she was reconciled with Edward in Bristol.

Despite his embarrassment, John read on carefully. Penny had put down intimate details; details she could not know about him otherwise. Judith would believe it all.

John walked despondently around the work area, not seeing the half completed arch and discarded tools. He felt sick in the pit of his stomach and his chest was tight. He had thought he and Judith were 'on a roll': her job, the refurbishment of Peverell House and, most importantly, their life together. His mind wandered. There was more masonry business than he could handle; Judith's career had picked up, and they were beginning to get some income from rents on rooms let out for company office spaces. More importantly, he and Judith had really settled down together, even if they still had separate homes.

"Play together, sleep apart," she had joked one night as she reluctantly left John's bed after a wild sex session. Judith generally drove home afterwards to her nearby flat.

John had planned to discuss when they would start their family; felt so confident as the close, loving relationship developed between them; confident enough to broach the delicate subject of babies. With a groan of despair and frustration he flung his cup in the sink, breaking the handle, shattering plates underneath. Oh God, how had this gone so wrong?

Morosely, John tried to phone her, but knew she wouldn't pick up. Would she read a text message or email? Answer a FaceTime call? Judith had to let him explain. He rubbed his eyes, trying to calm his nerves. Then the truth hit him: he had not had sex with Penny – *yet*. It was still in his future. Even so, Penny had written it up. His head swam. Whatever had taken place in the past hadn't happened to him. He could avoid it – take steps – go to France with Judith; avoid any seventeenth-century buildings. Bugger his firm. He could schedule the guys to work on... but without him in charge, would it all grind to a halt? No, John could sell out to Simon. Simon would organise stuff, keep the blokes employed.

He knew he was in a total fucking mess; couldn't straighten out his own thoughts. He must speak to Judith, somehow.

∞

Judith did not drive far, barely around the corner and out of sight of John's workshop. Sick at heart, she pulled over into a side road and slumped on the steering wheel. Shivering with suppressed emotions, she dissolved into tears. She couldn't believe it was over with John, her last chance of happiness. All the hopes she'd had of a family life with him had gone. John had betrayed her with that bloody ghost woman.

Her mobile rang. It was 'hands free' for driving, and she could see it was John. She wouldn't pick up, didn't want to discuss anything. She felt too upset and knew she would break down completely. She should drive to Peverell House and burn it to the ground, deprive that Peverell harlot of any place to meet John.

That's it! thought Judith hysterically. *The only reason for John's interest in me is to get into the house where he can meet that woman secretly.* She felt very, very alone. Even her only remaining friend, Simon's wife, Nancy, had been unsympathetic. Nancy just didn't get it, thought it all a wild tale of jealousy, or Judith's crazy mind with imagination working overtime.

∞

For Judith, the nightmare had all started a week ago, when John had driven up to Suffolk to visit his sister, Ann. It would have been nice to meet John's only remaining family, but Judith had an urgent report to write up for work so didn't go with him.

By Saturday evening she had completed the last chapter and decided to leave it until Sunday for a final edit. To fill in time she began looking through Penny Peverell's diary. Intriguingly it ended abruptly, mid-page, August 1645. Judith remembered Penny had left Peverell House spring 1646 before Oliver and Margaret Ransom had moved in later the same year.

From time to time, Judith had researched old family records and journals that were kept in Simon's office, intrigued with stories from the past. Glancing back at Penny's diary she noticed the date at the top of each page was usually written quite clearly. Judith decided to start reading in late July 1645 to get some idea of what had happened and why the diary entries had stopped.

At first it was all basic Peverell stuff, running the house, and sex, sex, sex with her husband, Edward. Christ, where did they get their energy from? It seemed he had the libido of a sex-mad rabbit, and she loved it! Then Edward off to Gloucester to deliver cloth, and barely a week later Penny's 'at it' with some other guy, initials CJ. The diary was quite messy, untidy and difficult to read, lots of scrawls and abbreviations. Judith was surprised the lusty wench found time to write at all after her daily and nightly sexploits. Bit of a laugh really, until the bombshell exploded.

CJ was Cousin John. Not cousin John Jackson, but *her* John, John Townsend; the one who had made such a thing of resisting Penny's advances when Edward had been seduced by Judith's ancestor, Margaret Ransom.

Judith sat in shock, hit by waves of nausea, numbness creeping over her. There must be some mistake, some other John. It was a common enough name, always had been. Besides, the text was a total jumble; she must have missed a point somewhere. Even so, it was no surprise the diary ended suddenly. Penny's husband, Edward, was evidently a man capable of violence – he'd fought battles, killed men. If he'd found Penny and CJ 'at it'– end of story. Except it wasn't. There were family records of Penny leaving Peverell House and being paid a pension as compensation by Oliver Ransom. At some time, Edward had died a violent death.

Consoling herself with the 'some other John' theory, Judith had initially put her fears to one side. The next day she had let herself into her work's offices and made a very high quality scan of the pages she had read. She would then ask her friend Stella Rigby, the art historian, for her version of the text, without indicating who CJ might be. She delivered a paper copy and a raw data file of the scan to the reception at The Roman Baths the following morning.

Back in her flat, Judith spent time enhancing the basic image on her computer. There was no doubt now: CJ was Penny's code for Judith's John, the bastard who had lied to her, and lied and lied again. Her world was upside down, crumbling. All her hopes and plans had vanished. What a bloody fool she felt now, trusting John, and being so hopelessly deceived. She sobbed uncontrollably, tears soaking the neck of her top, mascara running down her cheeks – she didn't care a monkeys. She hated John and Penny.

Judith smashed her framed photo of John; deleted picture files off the computer and her Facebook page. Nothing helped. She tried to steady her shaking hands, shuddering with pent-up feelings, struggling to compose herself. Mark, and now John. Were all men such double-crossing rats and scumbags? Was there something wrong with *her*?

Her only hope was to get away right now; get a new job, and start a new life.

CHAPTER 34

It had taken Edward Peverell over a week to arrange carts and an escort to transport his cloth from Bath to Gloucester. Finding transport was difficult, but the roads between Royalist Bath and Parliamentarian Gloucester were surprisingly open. All attention was on towns further south where Fairfax and Cromwell were carving their way through the remaining Royalist strongholds.

"It will be perfectly safe, darling," Edward had assured Penny. "Parliament's army is concentrated in Dorset, and Goring is holding the River Yeo against them. There is no armed threat this far north."

"We both know how inept Goring is. If he had moved his men up to Naseby..."

"I know, I know, but it's too late now," said Edward with a sigh. "I fear all is lost."

"It is not soldiers of either army I fear," argued Penny. "The country is totally lawless these days: robbers, deserters and foragers rob and murder at will."

Penny and Edward were talking as they strolled towards the stables where Edward's horse was being saddled and made ready for him.

"As do our army," replied Edward bitterly. "I've no time for that villain, Cromwell, but he is a man of principle. He hangs or shoots any looters, even his own men."

"With suitable bible reading, psalms and prayers," agreed Penny with a sad smile as she put her arm around Edward to comfort him. He seemed so forlorn this morning. She turned to look over the home pasture where the cows and their calves were grazing peacefully. "Edward, I am concerned for your safety," she said presently in a worried tone. "If there is any danger, leave the carts and ride for home – the goods aren't important."

He did not argue, but knew the cloth and money would be vital to them and to Marcus. Edward and Penny had embraced passionately in the privacy of their dressing room before his departure, dreading the separation, and risks involved. Now it was a brief leave-taking before he rode off, Edward promising firmly to go directly to Gloucester and straight back.

For all Penny's concern, it was an uneventful journey with dry, clear roads allowing the carters to make good progress. Oliver Ransom and Master Boscombe met them as arranged and the sale proceeded without a hitch.

"A word in private, if I may, Sir Edward?" asked Oliver as he walked with Edward back to his inn.

"At your service, sir. I was about to ask after your family."

"All well, by God's grace. Very well. You know my wife was delivered of a healthy boy?"

Edward nodded, feeling guilty again.

"A strong, growing boy. Margaret says he is the image of me but I think he favours her dark hair and blue eyes. I thank you for

315

your interest." He paused as if unsure how to continue and then blurted out, "You know the war goes well for us. Fairfax has taken Yeovil and will now cross the river."

"I had not heard," replied Edward.

"Only last evening news reached the town by courier to Colonel Massey, the garrison commander. Goring will be no match for Fairfax and Cromwell."

If he fights at all, thought Edward. "Your point, Oliver?"

"I know this is bitter to you, Edward, but after Naseby, your war's lost. Fairfax will roll up the minor towns, batter Bridgewater to submission and then march on Bristol."

This agreed with Edward's own assessment but he said nothing.

"I beg you, Edward, before parliament's final victory, petition parliament for pardon, pay the fine and swear neutrality."

"I cannot do that, Oliver. I will not desert my king; seek pardon from a group of self-serving rebels?"

Edward shook his head in despair.

Oliver Ransom moved as if to take Edward's arm. "I beg your pardon, truly. Margaret and I owe you a great debt, we think only of your welfare. What good will it do to lose all your possessions, possibly your life? You would leave a penniless widow. I am sorry if I give offence. My advice is given in friendship."

"And taken as such, Oliver. I do not take offence. I have no quarrel with you personally, only with parliament's cause. And, to thank you for your help in this sale, may I buy you a pie and jug of ale at my inn?"

"You may indeed."

They smiled at each other in mutual understanding.

A while later, the two men sat outside the inn with their food, overlooking a green space and a road where musketeers drilled and baggage carts passed.

"The garrison is very active," commented Edward, sipping his beer.

Oliver gave up the struggle with a piece of gristle in his mutton pie and replied. "Aye. Word is they will march down to relieve Taunton and then join up with Fairfax to attack Bristol. Their commander here in Gloucester is Colonel Massey. He may have been a London apprentice boy but he is a sound and able soldier now."

Edward feigned a lack of interest and busied himself with his food. His mind reeled. If Taunton was relieved from its siege, the Royalist army would be outnumbered and trapped between Fairfax and Cromwell in the south and Massey and Blake to the north. Any of those Parliamentarian commanders were better generals than that hopeless drunkard, Goring. Disaster would be inevitable, and as Oliver Ransom suggested, Bristol would fall in weeks. Bath of course would just change sides again.

As soon as Oliver Ransom finished his meal, Edward paid off his carters with a small bonus and left them to return to Bath. Edward himself hired a fresh horse and set off for Bristol. He desperately hoped he could give Prince Rupert advanced warning of Massey's plans. Penny would be furious with him for breaking his promise to return immediately but Edward could not ignore the chance of giving the prince this advantage. His last act before leaving Gloucester was to hire a messenger who would deliver a short note to Penny. Wary of its interception, he wrote it in Ancient Greek.

All Edward's good intentions came to nothing. Nearly forty miles of poor roads, with a change of horse at Dursley, brought him into Bristol but Prince Rupert refused to see him.

"His Highness Prince Rupert says he knows not this common fellow," a servant reported to Edward.

The insolence in his voice was insufferable and left Edward barely able to control his temper. General Hopton was not in Bristol, but Edward did find Prince Maurice. The prince was sitting disconsolately in the garden of a house commandeered to act as the Royalist garrison headquarters. A decanter of fine brandy and a plate of cracked nuts were close to hand.

He looked up, and Edward wondered if Maurice had been dozing from the effect of the heat and brandy. Despite the hot sun he was in his full finery, from wig to ornately tooled boots.

"Welcome, Sir Edward Peverell!" He indicated a chair. "Brandy, wine?"

Edward shook his head.

"Sit then and tell me the bad news. The fool, my brother, commands a deluded—" He sought for words then muttered an explosive phrase in German.

"Fucking idiotic cretins? As best as I can translate," asked Edward as he slumped in the cushioned chair, thrusting his long legs straight, pleased to be free of saddle and stirrups.

"You were always well informed, as I remember," said Maurice. "You knew more of what was happening around Taunton than all our 'intelligence' gatherers. Where are you journeyed from?"

"Gloucester, on trade," said Edward, and Maurice nodded.

"And to spy out the garrisons, I hope. What did you find? No wait, I need more brandy to hear this!" He refilled his glass.

"Yes, you will. The troops there are well trained and supplied. They are in good heart and have had successes in capturing some small towns we sought to hold."

"My brother says they are of no importance. I disagree. Success, however minor, builds success," Maurice said wearily. "Do they plan to attack us here?"

A servant brought out more brandy and water. A little friendly dog followed him and lay down in the shadow of Edwards's chair.

"Nothing so rash," replied Edward. "Massey has gathered forces to form a Western Association army and plans, I think, to march south to join Fairfax." Edward unthinkingly stretched down to stroke the soft fur of the dozing animal, so different from Rupert's coarse-haired hound. "And Fairfax already has that Puritan fanatic, Cromwell, with him," said Maurice shaking his head morosely. "Together, they will outnumber our army, and they are better led; better in all respects. I have met *Commander* Goring and seen his men." Maurice pondered a moment. "We must inform my brother, Rupert, and the council. Our cavalry is left in idleness. We could attack Massey on his line of march, or raid Gloucester itself and force him to return to defend it."

"I have tried to put this to your princely brother but he will not give audience to a 'common fellow' like me," said Edward bitterly.

"He will speak with me," said Maurice rising from his chair with a slight stagger. "In the king's name he will!"

Edward sighed. "Better we wait until tomorrow, sir; consider how best to phrase the words." *And clear your brain of the brandy*, he thought.

It was two wasted days before Prince Maurice was able to explain his plan to Rupert and the senior commanders. Rupert listened with a mocking contemptuous smile – if he listened at all.

"I think my little brother wants another gallant victory like Roundway Down, or some such minor place. Colonel Massey and his dour Presbyterian footmen will not leave the safety of Gloucester. 'Tis near a hundred of these English miles to Yeovil."

"They will bypass Bristol in five days' time—" Maurice started to say.

"If their boots do not wear through!" Rupert chortled loudly. Then, more seriously, "My uncle, His Highness King Charles, has charged me to defend Bristol and that I will do. Little brother, do as you are bid and refrain from any reckless skirmishes. This fight is not for your amusement. Go and leave the war to the adults!"

Guffaws accompanied Rupert as he sauntered away, ignoring Maurice.

Edward languished in Bristol as the guest of Prince Maurice. He felt he could not just leave, but his information and ideas had, as before, been totally ineffective.

∞

At the same time, inside Peverell House Penny was in a fury at Edward's note. He had promised he was finished with the war. He said he would ride straight back from Gloucester after the cloth sales and return to her at Peverell. Instead, he had sent her the briefest of notes with some money from the wool sale and sallied forth to Bristol to warn the princes. They would not listen;

they never listened. These foreign princes were as arrogant and hidebound as any feeble-minded English lord for all their claimed experience in war.

She ranted around the house with an anger and bitter disappointment that she rarely showed. The servants avoided her but she hardly noticed. Her greatest concern was over Edward being in Bristol without her. Could she trust him? There were widows and wanton wives enough to tempt the best of men. For all Edward's gentlemanly behaviour and courteous manners, he exuded an almost animal attraction for women. Hadn't Penny herself succumbed to it? She fumed with jealousy, but at the same time knew she was exaggerating and being unreasonable. In four years and with countless opportunities he had only strayed once – and that after a murderous, mind-shaking battle and slaying of a child.

∞

In Prince Maurice's house, Edward rose early as usual, dressed hurriedly and made his way down to the stable yard with a borrowed practice sword and his two heavy horse pistols. A thick line for drying horse blankets ran from the stable barn to a stout post. Edward had chosen this post for the sword practice and was soon hacking away with all his usual vigour. He completed his full routine as closely as he could without Penny to call out where to hit. Unbidden, he stopped his practice, vividly remembering her with her skirt belted up to show bare legs as she lunged and cut at him during their training bouts. There should be a fencing school for ladies like her. It roused him to remember her courage, uncaring and unflinching as they hacked and thrust at each other, taking the knocks like the best of men.

"Ho there, Sir Edward," called out an accented voice. "It's devilish early for this exercise!" Prince Maurice wore only white pantaloons and shirt, covered by a blue robe. Without the grand wig, his close-cropped hair made him look even more boyish than his twenty-four years.

"My morning ritual, whenever possible," replied Edward, transferring the practise sword to his left hand. "At home my wife often joins me, rapier against my sabre. It helps to keep my speed up."

"Does she fence?" the prince asked incredulously.

"Tolerably well," Edward replied dismissively. "She has a quick arm and eye."

"Shoots and rides 'tolerably well', as I have heard. Venus in the bedroom and Hippolyta on the battlefield!"

Edward grimaced with distaste.

"I meant no offence," said Maurice. "It is jealousy, no doubt! My swordsmanship is poor; my shooting worse, as my illustrious brother often tells me." About to go back into the mansion, Prince Maurice said, "When not on campaign I breakfast at half after nine. I would take pleasure in your company."

"It will be an honour, sir."

Edward completed three more sessions until both arms were trembling with fatigue. Taking advantage of a bench against a south-facing wall, he gulped down some small beer and began to devour a slice of chicken pie raided from the kitchen. It was a lovely summer morning but he took no joy in it. He missed Penny and felt very, very alone. Possibly he had done all he could and should return home.

Rested, he carried two large logs from the wood store and set them up twenty paces from his bench. Two smaller logs placed on top made improvised targets. He set his loaded and primed pistols down beside him on the seat, and sat as if on horseback. These powerful wheel lock pistols with their rifled barrels had cost him a small fortune ten years ago, almost as much as Penny's smaller ones. Now each of Cromwell's horse troopers – common soldiers – had one or two of them. They would be the more modern flintlocks, and smooth bored for ease of loading, but were still expensive to provide in the hundreds needed.

Calming himself, he waited to clear his mind and control his breathing. He took up a pistol and snapped a shot that just clipped the top of the log, setting it rolling across the yard. Penny would have laughed. He took more careful aim the second time and the half-ounce lead ball smashed dead centre, splitting the wood. *Tolerable?*

"Mein Gott, Peverell!" shouted Prince Maurice, running out into the yard, sword in hand. "Are we attacked?"

"Good morning again, sir. My practice continues." Edward could hear a horse cry out and saw it rear up as a groom led the frightened animal into the yard.

"You fool. You scare the horses!" the groom shouted, trying to calm the terrified animal.

"And you show due respect, if you would keep your position," said Maurice icily. And to Edward, " Our bloody horses should not shy at gunfire, but I don't want you to alarm the household." He pointed as scared half-dressed men rushed out with hastily grabbed weapons as they issued from doorways. "Best you limit yourself to sword practice. Join me for breakfast."

CHAPTER 35

Judith refused to see John before she left for France. Her phone, e-mail and WhatsApp links were all blocked. Neither Simon nor Nancy would let him have her new number or address.

In desperation and despair, he drafted and redrafted a long letter to Judith, changed it to a shorter one, and then started again.

A week or so later Nancy promised to pass it on but said, "Look, John, I think the stupid woman is absolutely bonkers the way she's acting. I can send it to her but doubt she'll read it. So what if you did have a fling with someone else."

"I did not have any sort of fling. Not with anyone."

"She seemed convinced."

"On the evidence of someone's wishful thinking."

"Not my call, John," Nancy shrugged. "If it was Simon, I'd get him to swear on his bank card and take his word for it."

"It's not a joke," John said bitterly.

"No, it's a sodding shame. Throwing away all you had going for you. I'd lock you two up in a dark room and not let you out until she was pregnant!"

John ignored that, hurt by her flippant manner. Overcoming

his anger with Nancy's attitude he pressed on. "Can you tell me if she's OK?"

"Yes, OK. Arrived in France; started work, enjoying it; best thing she's ever done. And she's a rotten liar even on a keyboard! You'll have to wait and hope she sees sense."

There was little else Nancy would say, leaving John in a limbo of uncertainty. Things he had enjoyed doing now seemed flat and pointless. Before meeting Judith he had loved being a solitary walker in open countryside. Now he missed having her there to discuss the scenery; just to mention random thoughts. Even at the gym, in the middle of a tough workout, he would sometimes falter and be overcome with sadness. He didn't want to go to Vespa's where they had often been together; he didn't want to look for someone else.

The first month drifted by, and John sank deeper into despair and self-pity. He knew it was ridiculous but couldn't muster enough energy to lift himself out of the rut. Penny Peverell often crossed his mind, adding to his feeling of isolation and loneliness. As far as John knew she was in Bristol with Edward. It was difficult to piece together the jigsaw of their separate, but intertwined, lives. Sometimes two days in John's time had appeared to be a month in Penny's world, or a week for John was only a day for Penny. He had resolved to avoid Peverell House; give no chance for the diary prediction to come true. He also avoided Sally Lunn's and any of the old buildings that had been standing in Penny's time four hundred years ago. He turned down more work in Bath Abbey for that reason. Inside, he was just raw and hurt.

∞

It was Tuesday on a brilliant August morning. John had made a visit to one site and was on his way to a second when his mobile rang. He looked down – Nancy Ransom.

His heart leapt, but resisting the urge to answer he pulled over and called back, trying to keep his voice calm. "Hi, Nancy, any news of—"

"No, John, nothing on Judith," she blurted out. "Can you do me a big favour?" Her voice wobbled and she sounded close to tears.

"If I can. What's up?"

"It's Charlie. I don't know where he is; can't contact him. I'm in London at Hatton Garden, Simon's in Amsterdam—"

"Nancy, wait. Who's looking after Charlie?"

"Sorry, John. He's with Ron, that's Charlie's great uncle – Greg's brother. They've been building a massive model train layout at Peverell House, in the old anteroom. I can't contact either of them. Phones ring, no answer."

"Oh, I thought Ron was very sick?"

"He is; not even allowed to drive. Taxi to Peverell. Charlie promised to ring. I'm so worried."

Nancy was gulping back tears but John thought she was over-reacting. Charlie wouldn't be the first boy to forget to phone his mum.

Nancy was still gabbling, "What if Charlie panicked? Something's happened to Ron?"

"Stop, stop, Nancy. I doubt Charlie would grasp the concept of panic let alone have a panic attack. Why not send Simon round to Peverell?"

"I said he's in Amsterdam! I'm in London, Hatton Garden."

"Diamond deal?"

Nancy ignored that and hurried on. "Could you go to Peverell, check they're all right? You got a key?"

John could hear Nancy was almost hysterical. "I have but it'll be open. Where is Bonnie?"

"She's with my mum. She's fine. It's Charlie..."

"Look, it will take me half an hour, maybe more to get there so don't worry – no need to call the police, or anything."

"Police – I never thought. No OK, I'll await your call. John, I owe you for this. Anything—" She caught her breath in relief.

"Judith's address," John asked.

"Email?"

Typical Ransom, always negotiating, John thought wryly. "No, Nancy. I won't take advantage. I'll talk to her when she wants to see me."

When John drove into the yard at Peverell House it was good to see so many cars parked there. In addition to the initial training area they had rented out space to three tenant businesses. There were two software development offices in what had been a dilapidated barn and another in the main house. No need for a key, he could walk straight through and find his way to the central section. With a pang he remembered the excitement when he and Judith had discovered the artwork, and again when Alf had installed his replica staircase. From the empty hall below Penny's dayroom, he heard the unmistakeable sound of small wheels running on metal rails.

Climbing the stairs John walked into the anteroom. He gazed

in amazement. The layout was worthy of an exhibition. At least four pieces of braced two-by-one metres of plywood had been formed into a rectangular table, with a hole in the middle for an operator. Three engines, two with passenger coaches and one goods train, travelled around complex scenery in crossing circuits. Impressive; even more so as no one was in charge. Uncle Ron dozed in a chair, head bald from chemotherapy, his train driver-style cap fallen off into his lap. Charlie sat engrossed with his gaming console. He looked up surprised as John entered, put a finger to his lips, and crept out of the room.

"Hi, Uncle John. Uncle Ron's asleep. What are you doing here?"

"Your mum's worried. You didn't call her."

"Sorryyyy, completely forgot."

"She called you."

"It's on mute, didn't want to wake Uncle Ron. He's very, very sick, John." There was a sign of tears as Charlie looked back into the room. "He's going to die soon like Grandpa and Grandma." His lip trembled but then he pulled himself together. "It's very sad, John. And Aunty Judith's gone away. And you don't come around anymore."

John desperately wanted to give Charlie a hug but was not sure how the boy would take it.

"Everyone's going away," continued Charlie.

"I could come and see you on Saturday."

"Could we go on a bike ride?" Charlie brightened.

"If your mum agrees. I didn't know you liked trains?" John said, trying to find a happier subject.

"I don't really," replied Charlie in a conspiratorial tone. "I did like building it though. Mr Hidson made the table for me, and Uncle Ron did the track and things." He pointed back through the doorway. "That green Battle of Britain loco was one that Daddy had – he sold the others. Aunty Judith was going to build a model plane with me," Charlie added mournfully. "Remote control, proper engine. That would have been more exciting."

There was a sudden yell of alarm.

"Charlie, where are you?" Ron was struggling out of his chair. "Oh, it's you, John. Must have drifted off. Thought Charlie had wandered away somewhere."

"We were just talking. I didn't want to wake you up, Uncle Ron."

John phoned Nancy and persuaded Charlie to talk to her. John himself, who had little interest in models or trains, then listened to a long, long description of how Uncle Ron had made the layout and how the controls worked. Despite Charlie's earlier comment, he did seem very knowledgeable, particularly with the remote control and programmes.

At last it was time to go and John called a taxi for them. Ron was dropping Charlie off with Nancy's mother where the boy would stay overnight. John could have driven them, but didn't for a number of reasons: he didn't want to undermine Ron's position, and he couldn't bear the thought of explaining his involvement to Nancy's mother. Moreover, now he was at Peverell House, he didn't want to leave. He was sure Penny would be in Bristol with Edward, but the house had also become important to him and Judith.

∞

Penny Peverell was angry and disconsolate. Why hadn't Edward returned directly from Gloucester as he had promised? One cryptic note and some money had arrived by courier, but little in explanation of when he would return or what he planned to do after he had delivered his information. There were no words of affection or love.

It was true more money had arrived by different messengers, which was prudent, but nothing more. She imagined Edward at balls and fashionable soirees in Bristol, cutting a dashing figure, provoking swoons of passion and love in women, wives of older men, widows, and girls of easy virtue. How many Margaret Ransoms would there be? Her jealousy and bitterness were making her imagine Edward in all manner of wild sexual encounters.

It was early afternoon on a sunny August day. Penny had exercised as if Edward were at home, ridden out for a few hours on Connie and, after a hard gallop, returned for a brief lonely luncheon eaten in the small dining room. Now she sat in the window seat, light behind her, attempting to read one of their many books. In her restless state she could muster little interest and even less concentration.

Instead, Penny's thoughts drifted to the past to her one and only romance before Edward. She was overcome with lost opportunities; lost chances with Cousin John. She remembered her great unhappiness at his banishment from the family's house, even their friendship forbidden. The excitement her friend Jacinda must have from all her chance encounters or amours with other men, some of whom were complete strangers! Imagine a stranger's arms, his touch, strength and passion.

With her heightened senses, Penny became aware of another person close by in the same room. She caught a glimpse of John – John Townsend – sitting dejected, and unhappily staring at nothing. The unexpected thrill of seeing him aroused her instantly. Perhaps this was her chance at last. She smiled and suddenly felt a surge of lustful feeling. Seduction would be exciting, and she felt a shiver of anticipation.

Quickly and quietly Penny crept away, summoning her maid to find fresh sheets and pillows for her bed. With a sense of delight, Penny selected a pale blue nightgown – silky and alluring – from the wardrobe. With her hair brushed and shining, John would find her irresistible.

∞

Alf Hidson had fitted the replica staircase, but John hadn't even bothered to go and see the result. Now he sat listlessly on a work trestle and wondered what he should do. Start going out and meeting people? Give up Bath altogether and begin afresh in another town? He was too apathetic to think properly.

Suddenly John's mind reeled. He sensed someone in the room and then felt two female breasts pressed against his shoulders. Large firm hands held his head to stop it from moving. An adrenaline rush of surprise turned to excitement.

"Guess who? No! Do not look around."

"Penny? How are you here?" The room had not changed; he was still in his own time.

"It does not matter, does it, Cousin John? We are both here, that is all that matters, on our own, deserted by our lovers." Penny stepped away from him and whispered, "Eyes front, do not look."

John tried to reply but he only gasped, inarticulate as his heart raced and his chest constricted.

"God, Penny, what's happening?" he finally managed.

"Nothing yet."

Her hands were now at the waist of his t-shirt, lifting it slowly up over his head. He heard the rustling cloth and spun round. She had unfastened her blue silky gown and let it fall to the ground.

"I wanted you to wait until—"

But John grabbed her to him, her bare breasts against his chest as he blocked off her words, crushing her breath with a kiss. She responded, desperately kissing him back and hugging in an equally strong grip.

After a time Penny gently pushed him away. She felt in complete control as, dressed only in her waist petticoat, she turned slowly around to display her body's profile and back.

"I have dreamed of doing this," she murmured, "so often; dreamed of being with you; seeing you respond to me. You are not shocked?"

"No," in barely a whisper from John. "I have wanted so long. Wanted... to be with you. You're so beautiful." His voice sounded his mixture of passion and confusion. "I can't—"

"It is past time to talk," she said with a hungry smile. "Come into my world, my time, and be my lover." She reached out to take him by the hand, leading him past the head of the staircase that changed imperceptibly from reproduction to original, through the resplendent luxury of the dayroom, down the short passageway that would soon be panelled over, and into the bed chamber where Judith's modern divan had been replaced by an ornate curtained bed.

Their last clothes slid to the carpeted floor and they closed for another embrace. Now Penny's voice was trembling as much as John's had been earlier.

"Please, Cousin John, do not disappoint me..."

CHAPTER 36

Edward thought over and over about the value of staying in Bristol. The commanders would not heed his warning, so why stay? His hope was that as events unfolded, he would be proved right and then they would listen.

He had details of the men and the guns that Massey was leading south: medium-sized cannon on new style gun carriages that could be moved rapidly around the battlefield. Master Boscombe, the Gloucester merchant who had taken Edward's cloth, had explained that Massey had spent weeks training his gunners to move and fire these artillery pieces.

"There is nothing to match these gunners," Boscombe had boasted, "either in the king's army or anywhere else in Europe."

To pass the time, Edward rode out with Prince Maurice and his gentlemen; exercised his weapon skills, and read some of the classical books in the mansion library. He wrote to Penny but after a few days there was little to say. Despite his boredom, he resolutely refused to attend any of the many social engagements, citing his lack of fine evening clothes and every other excuse he could muster. He wouldn't risk being led astray, even in a mild flirtation or dance that could be reported back to Penny.

Edward found that his morning exercise session attracted interest from the other gentlemen of the prince's household, and several began to join him for a bout with foiled swords before breakfast.

"I ask you, Peverell," said the prince one morning as they finished their food, "why should my swordsmanship be so poor when I excel at all equestrian sports?"

"Weak arms?" suggested one of the prince's men.

"Poor eyesight?" asked another.

Edward sat silent, savouring the toasted bread covered in scrambled eggs and chopped fried bacon.

"Come, Peverell," chided the prince peevishly. "Ignore their jesting and give me your opinion."

"I am no fencing master."

"I do not seek to fence, prancing back and forth with toy swords. I want to know how to fight. You have thrashed every man around this table."

"With rapier and sabre!" called out an attendant gentleman.

"Aye, I still have the bruises under my coat. Your secret, sir?"

Edward took a deep draught of small ale before selecting some fruit from a plentiful bowl. Presently, he said slowly, "I do not wish to give offence, sire. I think it is lack of true interest, lack of application, and practise." He wiped his beard fastidiously and continued, "You need to strengthen your arm and quicken your eyes."

"Twenty practise lunges every morning," someone called.

"Our new companion fairly hacks at a defenceless post," said another.

336

"Let Peverell speak," called out the prince.

"I am no fencing master, as I made clear," said Edward, "but best to work in pairs. One calls hit spots for cut or thrust, say twenty strikes, then you change over and repeat. That, with the heavy sword, to give strength and power. Then one lunges or thrusts at the other with foiled rapier while the other attempts to parry."

"That would be tedious – it would take hours."

"I agree," said Edward. "Better to play dice or cards to pass the time."

"Tomorrow, I will join you at your early hour," declared the prince. "But no contact from either cut or thrust – I bruise easily!"

Edward's 'school' continued for a few days and helped relieve the monotony forced on them by Rupert's stricture not to attack Massey. Then came news of disaster: while retreating back from his position on the River Yeo, Goring's Royal Army had been caught and virtually annihilated as a fighting force. Prince Maurice explained the situation to Edward and the others at an early dinner.

"For once Goring seemed to have done the right thing," he commented. "He left a strong rear guard to block the road; men concealed in hedges and broken ground; light guns in support."

"And what went wrong?" asked someone.

"Massey! The Gloucestershire Clod, as my brother called him. His cannon bombarded their positions mercilessly before his foot methodically cleared the way with pike and musket. Cromwell's Ironsides charged through the gap in our defence. It was all swiftly done before our army could react."

"Massey... I tried to tell..." Edward muttered faintly.

"There's worse still. Cromwell broke through unchecked, regrouped after his first charge, and reloaded pistols. He then defeated our own horse in a head-on fight. The man is unstoppable. Next morning our remaining cavalry regiment was surprised by a dawn attack and cut to pieces. Goring reports his surviving men would not fight again and he falls back to Bridgewater."

Edward ate what he could and left the table. He rode up onto the Downs overlooking the city, its wall and long cannon shot away. Fairfax had heavy guns and gunners trained to use them. Bristol's defences had been improved somewhat since its capture two years ago but it was still impossible to defend. How many men would Rupert allow to die before Fairfax, with Massey's forty cannon, pounded them to surrender? To leave Bristol seemed cowardly; to stay, futile.

The next day Edward was conducting his training session rather later than usual when Prince Rupert and a small entourage rode into the stable yard to speak with Maurice. Royally dressed despite the growing heat of the day, Rupert leaped down from his horse and called to his brother.

"What I like to see – gentlemen at exercise! Who is your sword master?"

Edward, who had his back to Rupert, turned and bowed formally.

"Sir Edward Peverell," called Prince Maurice disengaging from his own practice set. "You have met before."

Rupert moved away from Edward dismissively. "I have some recollection of seeing the fellow about. Country farmer, I believe?"

"A sad day, sir," said one of Maurice's gentlemen to Rupert. "Who would have believed that country clods from Gloucester, led by Massey, an apprentice boy, could change the course of a battle?"

"He was told," Edward interrupted curtly. "Their number, their quality and their intent."

"If I could have surprised them on the march," Maurice added. "They had few cavalry. I could have—"

"Enough," roared Prince Rupert. "I will not be lectured by a tradesman and a boy. I will not listen to this, hear me—"

"You should," Edward shouted back. "Listen to sense and to reason, not the drivelling of sycophants with feeble brains!" Edward could not control his angry words even though it was unwise to shout at a prince in that tone. Thank God Penny was not there to witness his loss of control.

"Silence, Peverell! How dare you insult your commander," growled Rupert. "I can have you hanged."

"You are not my commander," retorted Edward. "I am a gentleman, and Justice of the Peace appointed by the king. You have no authority over me." He was so enraged, any caution was lost.

"By God if we were not at war, I would demand satisfaction for that insult," shouted Rupert.

"It is no insult. You lose battles, throw men away, and have no stomach to fight man to man."

The equerry, Anderson, stepped forward, sensing a disaster.

"I would fight him for you, my prince," he said. "Teach him his place. Take no risks with your life, sire – the *King's Cause* needs you."

"Take risks?" retorted Rupert. "Take risks in fighting the likes of Peverell? If he could lay blade on me, I should surrender Bristol and resign from the king's service!"

"A blessing for our cause if you did leave the king," snarled Edward, all the anger and resentment at Rupert's stupidity welling up into total fury. "And typical of a coward who would allow a friend to fight for him."

Rupert roared out an oath in German, whipped out his light dress sword, and whirled on Edward. It was blocked by a sabre, the fighting dagger poised.

Edward bowed. "Your servant, sire. Is this to first blood or to the death? I care little either way."

With customary coolness, Prince Maurice stepped between them. "Gentlemen, gentlemen, this is most unseemly. Brawling in hot blood does not honour either side." He let a silence hang in the air for a few seconds and continued. "Could I suggest a 'training bout', with blunt—"

"Never! I will have blood for this," cut in Rupert snarling, his fine raiment and feathered hat incongruous against the dusty stable buildings and steaming midden.

"Then it should be done to code of honour," said Maurice formally. "My brother, Prince Rupert of Palatine, Duke of Cumberland, has issued a challenge?"

Rupert nodded, almost unperceptively, eyes unwavering, locked on Edward.

"Sir Edward, you accept?"

"I am eager to oblige the prince," replied Edward.

"Then, sir, you have choice of weapon," declared Maurice. He turned to Rupert. "You agree to this, Prince Rupert?"

"Aye, any weapon open to a gentleman, sword or pistol."

"I propose any war sword. My choice is a sabre and dagger."

"Rapier is my choice," spat Prince Rupert. And to the equerry, "Anderson, may I beg the loan of your weapon? I want no delay in settling this."

"Hold, sir," cut in Maurice. "I am your equal in birth and rank. This yard is my 'ground' so I command the field of honour. You will retire and return in two hours after noon. In that time we may appoint seconds—"

"Who will 'second' that oafish ploughboy?" scoffed Rupert.

"I will if necessary!" said Maurice vehemently. "I will not have it said that our family denied an opponent a fair fight."

Two hours passed and as expected there was no hint of a reconciliation or withdrawal by either party. Prince Maurice and one of Prince Rupert's attendants acted as marshals.

"You will fight until one of you yields. If a man is wounded and cannot stand en-guard, he is defeated. I will call rest after two minutes."

"That's realistic," called out Edward scornfully. "Please, Mr Cromwell, can we rest? My arm aches!"

"Silence. My ground, my rules!" shouted Maurice.

He and Anderson stood with drawn swords crossed between the combatants.

"Begin!"

The speed of Prince Rupert's first lunge caught Edward unaware. He was moving back and had his sabre locked on the

341

handguard of the prince's sword but still received a hit on the chest, drawing blood.

"My hit!" called Rupert triumphantly, retiring back to his start point.

"Do you yield, sir?" asked Maurice, again adopting the formal tone.

"Never," replied Edward. "A pinprick!"

The warning 'pinprick' taught Edward to treat Prince Rupert with more respect, parrying or blocking the lunges, beating the prince's sword down with his heavier sabre. His defence tactics frustrated the pure skill of the prince who began to tire under the repeated shock of Edward's blows.

"Time!" called Maurice.

They rested and resumed, Edward merely defending and battering, occasionally deflecting the point of thrust with the dagger and cracking his own blade down onto the prince's sword, numbing blows that were draining the strength from Rupert's arm. His hat, with its beautiful peacock feathers, had long since fallen and lay trampled in the dust.

"Fight, damn you!" called Rupert, and launched a last desperate thrust, all finesse gone due to his fatigue.

Edward turned the sword point away with his dagger, shoving Rupert to his right. A full swinging blow with the sabre struck into Rupert's unguarded right side. The onlookers gasped in dismay, but at the last instant Edward had turned his arm to strike with the flat of the blade. Instead of a killing stroke it only broke ribs and dropped Prince Rupert to his knees. The fight was again stopped.

"Do you yield, brother? Please," begged Maurice in his role as marshal.

"Never!" Rupert struggled to his feet, barely able to grip the rapier for the pain in his right side.

"Try your left hand," said Edward. "To be fair, I will do the same."

Rupert was hardly able to muster a credible defence, and Edward struck swiftly high up on the left shoulder, the blade penetrating through muscle and out of his back.

"Hold!" shouted Maurice, dropping his sword and leaping to his brother's aid. "Surgeon, here!"

The doctor looked stunned, unable to react. Maurice had fought in many battles; seen death many times without panic. He had his hand clamped down over the wound trying to slow the bleeding. Someone rifled in the doctor's bag for pads and bandage.

"Am I dying?" gasped Prince Rupert.

"No. No artery is severed. No vital organ punctured."

"Is it still bleeding?"

"Just seeping," replied Maurice, forcing calmness into his voice despite his concern for his brother. "I am sure it will heal in time."

Edward walked over to the injured prince. "Well fought, sire," he said reluctantly. "I am wrong in one thing: you have no shortage of courage."

"Just a lack of skill and practice," gasped Rupert, despair and pain twisting his face. "A sad day when King's men fight each other."

"A sad day in a sad year," replied Edward. "All is lost so make it no worse, sir. Remember your words: I will surrender Bristol and leave England—"

"Get out, Peverell," said Prince Maurice, looking up. He had cut away Rupert's waistcoat and shirt and was trying to bandage over the entry and exit wounds. "For God's sake, get out of my house and leave Bristol!"

"I seek to challenge Peverell," pronounced Anderson, "in the prince's name."

"No, enough of this," retorted Maurice. "A duel between men of honour is bad enough. We will have no vendettas."

"And no more futile loss of life," proclaimed Edward. "The prince has given his word on that."

Edward turned to leave, thinking only of returning to Penny.

CHAPTER 37

In Penny's bed John plunged into a maelstrom of lust and confusion. The passion of their first surrender to all his pent-up emotion and frustrations left him gasping for breath. Penny lay as if lifeless, motionless with her legs clasped around his back, her arms clamped around his neck.

"Oh, John, John," were the only words she uttered in a breathless voice.

He couldn't speak as shudders of excitement rippled through his body. His senses reeled and he drifted in time and space between his world and Penny's. He had no idea if he slept or hallucinated until Penny roused him to love her again, and again and again. Time passed – days. He must have eaten and drunk, slept and left the bed, but he had no sensation of that. Only the continual incessant sex with Penny. She did things to him that he had never imagined and demanded extreme treatment in return. Like a stag in the rut, his mind was filled with one idea only.

In between the action he saw, or imagined, scenes in Penny's world and his own: Edward fighting a form of duel, battering a prince into submission until he was totally demoralised; Judith sitting with a middle-aged man in a French restaurant, sipping wine, chatting and smiling a sad unconvincing smile. It was easy to see that the elegant man was not interested in Judith or even attempting to show sincerity, only impatient to take a younger woman upstairs to their hotel room. Before even a pang of jealousy or anger could start, Penny had shaken John awake, rousing him for yet another lust-driven encounter.

He collapsed back into semi-consciousness, exhausted by his endeavours. He saw Simon with Nancy, gently and affectionately making love after Simon returned from Amsterdam, far removed from the flippant 'doing it when we remember' that Nancy had commented to Judith.

He saw Charlie standing, fighting back tears until finally he broke down into heartrending sobs, then to be scooped up into Simon's arms – Nancy hugging them both. Someone had died? Oh, God, he hoped it wasn't Judith.

"Cousin John, you are not going to disappoint me, are you?"

John finally came back to full consciousness, utterly spent, confused and hungry. He was in a curtained, four-poster bed. Penny sat naked and cross-legged beside him, gently stroking his chest.

"You are back with me at last," she said softly. "I feared you would never wake, or just slip off to your world, your time."

He did not answer, trying desperately to re-orientate his senses. "How long?" he asked weakly. "How long have I been here with you?"

"A few days." She leaned over, brushing her nipples along his chest, moving to kiss his lips. "It has been so good; you have been so good to me. Now I have *une aventure amoureuse* to match Edward's!"

John looked at her anew: the broad almost man-like shoulders and strong face – handsome rather than pretty. He supposed powerful legs that could clamp around him so tightly came from horse riding, but how had she developed her strong arms? Even men did not do weight training in that era.

"I hope you like what you see. You look at me intently!"

John forced a smile. "I do. For the first time I see *you*, not a romantic dream."

"I am not romantic, just real." She chuckled, her hair all wild, but still beautiful. "Real, with real needs!" Penny continued caressing his chest and arms. "You are so smooth, no hair, not like Edward. More like a girl than a man." She moved her hand down his body. "But for all that," she continued, "you are truly a man, as you have proved. You must have made your Judith very happy."

"Not happy enough," he replied bitterly. "Not happy enough for her to trust me and stay with me."

"You still love her, don't you?" Penny asked.

For a while he didn't answer, though he knew that she was right. He truly loved Judith with deep affection. With Penny, it had been about nothing but sex and fascination – the forbidden fruit.

"As I still love Edward," Penny was whispering, her eyes full of tears.

CHAPTER 38

The only instinct in John's mind was to get back home to his flat and sleep. As he stumbled slowly through the modern, newly refurbished office area of Peverell House he was not sure if he was fit to drive. Looking into one of the computer workrooms, deserted and with all machines switched off, he realised it must be late. His watch had been scrambled into re-set mode but a wall clock, glimpsed from outside the office, showed seven thirty. It felt much later. He tottered out to his van, noticing it seemed dusty – contractors working nearby? The engine started reluctantly.

The mobile phone was still in its 'hands free' mode but dead, its battery now flat. It picked up, charging from the van, and beeped repeatedly from a stream of messages, texts and missed calls. The date showed Saturday August 17th, the time 19.57 p.m. John counted back.

"No, it's impossible! Five days... I could not be in her bedroom for five days..." He remembered the diary that had sent Judith away – all that sex and perversion. He shivered with a reaction. It could not be possible. His exhausted body told him it was. He felt delirious, unable to focus on the present.

Sometime later, he had recovered enough to ease the van out from Peverell House and drive back to Bath. Not to his workshop, where the van was normally kept, but direct to the flat in Henrietta Park where trade vehicles were discouraged and his little Fiesta was sneered at. Inside, he raided the freezer for burgers, sausages, oven chips and peas for a hurried meal – he had to eat and sleep. *Shave, shower, shit and sleep* slipped into his mind as some form of mantra.

∞

"Christ, John! What's happened to you? Where have you been?"

Judith stood over him as he slouched at the table in a deep slumber, head beside the greasy remains of his meal. John forced his eyes to open. Judith, in a dark grey skirt and jacket, stood glowering at him across the table.

"We've all been so worried."

"I bet." John, still dazed, tried to think of excuses, an explanation.

"Where have you been?" There was a pleading tone in her voice.

"Cotswold Way, walking. I wanted to get away."

"Bollocks, John. Your hike boots and walking poles were in the hall."

"OK, OK. Be satisfied: I was back in the past, fulfilling the prophesy of Penny Peverell's diary. That's what you wanted. It's happened!"

"No, John," Judith said shakily, "I couldn't accept anything like—"

"You just buggered off to France, no contact. You've got what you wanted and come back to gloat."

"You didn't have to do it."

"No? My hopes dashed, love scorned." *God, he sounded like a soap opera, even to himself!* "You know I fancied her, you've seen her portrait. Sod it, woman, you threw me to the wolves!" He slumped at the table again. "Sorry, out of order. I need sleep." Eventually, he staggered to his feet. "I'm off to bed, must sleep."

Judith moved to steady him and he realised the impact of the food and beer. He was almost too weak to move.

"You can't go to bed like that, John. You stink! When did you last shower? Let me get the worst off that beard, and at least have a shower for Christ's sake."

He nodded and slid back onto the chair. Judith's practical side took over as she sheared off the matted stubble with a hair trimmer and propelled him into the bathroom.

Half an hour later, John was characteristically snoring in bed while Judith sobbed, broken-hearted, at his kitchen table. She had half expected Ron's death, so it was no real shock, not like her dad's. An excuse to come home from France for Ron's funeral; support the family, show respect, and all that. She had hoped for hugs, kisses and reconciliation with John, pick up the pieces. But, like John had said, she had abandoned him, thrown him to the wolves – well, the she-wolf. Judith's despair grew as she remembered all his attempts at contacting her. She'd been hateful to him, unjust. Then stupid bloody Nancy had sent him to Peverell House and he'd been drawn back into the past and spat out like sucked fruit. Judith had seen grip marks and scratches on his back as she helped him into the shower; bites on his neck when he came out. What sort of woman was Penny Peverell? What sort of demented woman would have shot her husband's portrait in a jealous rage and yet every entry in her diary said she loved him? Then Edward's away less than a week and she's turned into some sort of sex fiend with another man and even writes the details in her diary?

As Judith churned everything over and over, there was still a hope, just a hope, that she might be able to salvage something with John. They'd had so much going for them; the companionship they had built, even planning a family together. She could not risk leaving the flat, could not risk John just shutting her out of his life the way she had left him when she'd 'buggered off to France'. Anger with John and her own guilt kept her awake for hours until eventually she fell into a fitful sleep on the living room settee, still praying they would be able to work something out in the morning.

CHAPTER 39

For the first few hours John slept deeply, then roused and checked his watch. Judith must have reset it for him. He realised she was still in the living room, but couldn't face going out to see her. He drifted back to interrupted sleep and a series of vivid dreams.

John was standing by the duelling ground. Two men in seventeenth-century finery were fighting with swords while others watched. One was Edward Peverell...

Suddenly it was over. Edward thrust; blood sprayed from his opponent's shoulder.

"Hold, it is enough!" shouted a young man incongruously dressed in decorated striped trousers and a ruffled white shirt. "Surgeon, here! Prince Rupert is wounded." Instantly he was on his knees, rendering emergency battlefield first aid to Prince Rupert.

As the prince's shirt was ripped off, they could see a grievous open wound high up on Rupert's left shoulder. It bled profusely despite the pressure applied with a field dressing. The doctor stood bemused while men accustomed to war took charge.

It had been a savage, merciless beating. Any one of the visible sword hits could have been pressed home to a death blow. The civilised Edward Peverell, who John thought he had half come to know, had beaten the prince into a humiliating wreck. Why?

"I took no pleasure in this, John Jackson," said Edward as he stood next to John. "Help me with this coat. He near did for me with his first thrust and my left arm is stiffening."

John gasped in surprise. He was back in the past again. He managed to utter, "Why? You could have finished this at any time."

"As I said, I took no pleasure in it, I assure you. A dishonourable affair." Edward shook his head, freeing his shoulder-length hair from the coat collar. "I was sorely tempted, I tell you, but killing Prince Rupert would change nothing. His idiot commanders would still try to hold out against Cromwell's trained army and forty cannon. I'd hang for nothing. I had to totally break his spirit; demoralise him into accepting all is lost; get him to surrender Bristol with no more senseless carnage."

Just then, Prince Maurice shouted at Edward. "Get out! Go! I never want to see you again."

The awful vision began to fade.

"Before my patience snaps!"

In Peverell House, John saw Penny sitting at her writing desk, contemplating her diary, tears of remorse and shame streaming down her face.

"Oh, Edward! It all went too far. How will you ever forgive me?"

As this picture faded, another coalesced. Judith was lying awake on the settee of his flat, staring vacantly into the darkness. He tried to speak to her, but couldn't get words to come. He knew he was still dreaming in some drowsy state, restlessly falling in and out of sleep, with thoughts and images jumbled inside his head, imagining the present and reaching across years and centuries of long ago.

Now John was riding beside Edward, who was on his way back from Bristol to Peverell House, and desperate to see Penny. Impossible. John had never ridden a horse, was terrified of the animal, more so than cows with calves, or savage dogs. Ahead of them came cries for mercy, gunshots and screams. A party of travellers were being robbed at gunpoint. Four Royalist soldiers with levelled muskets threatened pedlars while two others loaded their fallen packs into a small mule cart.

"Halt, in the king's name!" roared Edward, spurring his horse towards them, drawing both heavy pistols despite his wound.

The muskets turned to aim at Edward and John. Edward fired two shots: two hits, one fatal. In shock, John realised he was looking directly down the barrel of a matchlock musket only fifty metres away. He saw small puffs of smoke as the match descended, then a violent explosion of smoke from the muzzle. As the sound reached him, the ball shot smashed low into Edward's leg; another hit somewhere on his chest rocking him sideways in the saddle. Somehow Edward turned the maddened horse back down the road, seeking safety in distance and a steep slope. He was out of range and out of sight from the assailants, but as John watched helplessly, Edward slewed awkwardly in his saddle, attempted to recover, but toppled off into the drainage ditch beside the road. It was almost dry this late in the summer, and grasses and rushes grew up higher than a man. Edward disappeared without trace; the horse ran on. John was rooted to the spot, horrified. He was now standing on foot. Where was his own horse?

More shouts and screams, another shot. The pedlars had seized the advantage from Edward's charge and were using staves and knives to exact a pitiless revenge. Two musket men fled, abandoning the discarded weapons; another was clubbed to the ground and battered repeatedly. The man Edward had wounded was hauled up by his arms and his throat cut.

Sickened, John turned away, trudging back along the road, searching for Edward. The road had changed, becoming rocky and steep. There was no ditch, no Edward. Even in the dream, the killings were real. Very real.

John woke in a frenzy of sweat and despair at three thirty a.m. Not yet dawn. He could hear Judith snoring, comfortingly real and familiar. Thoughtfully, she had left a drink of water beside the bed for him. He sipped it gratefully, slowly recovering, trying to understand what was real and what was a nightmare.

There was no record of Prince Rupert fighting a duel in Bristol, or anywhere else. Certainly he had not been killed, and had left for France after only a token defence of Bristol. He had surrendered it without any real fight. Rupert was still alive when Charles II was restored to the throne.

"God, history at three o'clock in the morning!" John rubbed his eyes wearily.

He thought of Penny crying. *Was it over Edward's death or her passion with me?* He listened to Judith snoring until, gradually, he settled into a restful, dreamless sleep.

CHAPTER 40

John woke early as usual, but didn't leap directly up and into the shower. Instead he lay in bed, trying to understand what had happened to him. Why was he so exhausted? Were all those dreams just dreams, or visions of reality? Worst of all, why had he and Judith been so at each other last night? He had needed time to eat sensibly, freshen up and sleep, not a suspicious inquisition. After all, it was *she* who had left *him*.

John slowly slid from the bed, crept to the door and peeped out like some furtive teenager spying on a girl. Judith was still noisily asleep on the settee, head on a cushion, legs draped over the arm rest at the other end. Her knee joints would feel wrecked when she did wake up.

He showered again and sprayed himself liberally with a deodorant that Judith had left in the flat. Then he shaved carefully, more spray, and dressed quickly in t-shirt and shorts. Time to act nonchalant and hearty: no problems, thanks for last night, see you sometime and get her to leave before either one of them lost their temper. There were so many questions he wanted to ask Judith about France: why was she back, and for how long?

Most of all, he needed to question himself.

With forced confidence, John strode out of the bedroom. The cheery hello died on his lips as he saw her forlorn state and smudged, tear-streaked face. She had taken off the tight skirt and the jacket and lay in her blouse and pants like a crumpled, half-dressed doll, with one arm dangling off the seat cushions. It was not cold and already sun streamed in at the wide balcony windows. Last night neither of them had bothered to draw the curtains. Absurdly, his first thought was to fetch a duvet to cover her over. He had started toward the bedroom.

"Morning, John," Judith said crisply. "Where are you creeping off to?"

"I was going to get you a cover."

"Bit late for that." She wobbled from the settee.

He hesitated to steady her. "You OK?"

"Yeah, cramp. Knees are still asleep."

They stared at each other uneasily.

"Tea or coffee?" he asked lamely.

"Tea, I think." Then, "Sorry, John. Desperate for the loo, didn't want to disturb you earlier." She was off through the bedroom to the *en suite* facility before he could say anything.

"So much for my plan..." John mumbled.

He made tea for them both and sat at the kitchen table. A flush, a pause and then the shower running. The tea had cooled by the time Judith emerged clean-faced, damp haired, and in running kit.

"Thanks for keeping my stuff – same drawer."

He nodded. She had kept a small stack of clothes and essentials in one of his spare cupboards in case of emergency.

After an embarrassed silence he said, "Sorry, Judith, but I'm in a bit of a mess from the last few days. I need some time to get my head back together. Do you think we should leave it a—"

"No!" she said emphatically, watching him warily while towelling off her short dark hair. "I don't want to let you go off on some sort of guilt trip. Or get even angrier with me. I must have been bonkers to run out on you."

"Your sister-in-law's words exactly."

"Simon said worse. Look, John, I'm sorry about last night. I had no right to bawl you out. We were all so worried."

"Did I really stink that much?"

"No," she tried to smile. "We've both been worse after a day's hiking."

"Fox Tor Mire?"

"Was far worse. Even after the rain you still stank of peat and sheep shit."

"I didn't need to be put to bed, but thank you." *Keep it light*, John thought.

"Are you still angry about me running off to France?"

"Not angry. Bitterly disappointed. I really thought we could, you know, make it work for us."

Judith felt a wrench at her heart and caught her breath. She put her towel unsteadily over the back of the chair and moved to touch him on the arm.

"We still could."

"I doubt it, not after I've been with..." He tailed off.

"Do you think we could have changed it?" Judith asked. "Changed the past?"

"We could have tried." John felt very dispirited as he sipped at the cold tea, a sense of hopelessness crowding in. "Anyway, it's too late now, isn't it? I've ballsed it all up. It is as it is."

"It is as it is, as you say, so let's take it from here. I ran out on you, remember? No need to make a Greek tragedy of it. We weren't married or engaged or anything, so you were a free agent, as was I." Hesitantly, she added, "And in Toulouse I wasn't exactly celibate either. There were two—"

"I don't need to know this."

"Yes you do, we've got to be equal. I know all about you from—" She stumbled a bit. "From the written account. I've had two brief affairs in two months. They made me more lonely and miserable than when I left. Made me miss you even more. I came back to try and make up, move on."

"I don't need to know details, Judith, but was one of these guys a middle-aged man, say fifty, refined, short to medium height?"

"Could be anyone..." She moved towards the kettle, nervously thinking to make more tea for them both. "Shall I make toast?"

He nodded, remembering her need for nervous activity when she was stressed.

"Let's try some tea again, this is cold," she said in desperation.

"This French guy, thin face with a pencil moustache?" The mental picture he had of Judith with the man was burned in his mind's eye in painful detail.

"OK, but—"

"There's more. He's left-handed and wears a gold watch on that wrist. White jacket, green shirt and hankie in top pocket."

"John, have you been having me spied on?"

"No." He told her of the vision-like dream he'd had. "It was like floating into a scene of a play."

"Not the bedroom!" she gasped.

"No, thank God, and I had no idea there was someone else, a second... lover?"

"Young lad at the running club I joined. Only a few weeks, a few times." She turned away, studying the toaster. "Can you ever forgive me?" she asked in a very quiet voice. "It didn't mean anything."

"Why did you do it then? Were you trying to take your revenge on me?"

"No. I was miserable and lonely and knew I had been bloody stupid."

They sat in silence until the toast popped up.

"Is there any butter?" she asked.

"Bloody hell, Judith! I've had enough of this."

John stood up, grabbed her out of her chair, sat down with her on his lap and folded her up in his arms. She nestled into him, feeling contented for the first time in months, and tried desperately not to cry.

They cuddled for some time until John said, "If only Nancy hadn't sent me around to Peverell House," he murmured against her neck, half ashamed to face her.

"It was a good job she did. Perhaps you have burned Penny out of your system," she replied.

"There was no need for me to go there; Charlie was quite safe."

"I think there was. Your taxi dropped him off with Nancy's mother and then took Uncle Ron home. He had a heart attack in the hall. Never even made it to his chair. All such a shock. Think of the effect on Charlie if—"

"If they'd still been at Peverell." John shuddered. "Poor little chap." And then, "Wasn't it similar with your dad?"

Judith nodded. "With Ron we think it was the strain of the treatments. Frightening, really – Mum, Dad and Uncle Ron all having cancers. Nancy has booked Simon up for every private cancer test or screening there is."

"You mentioned Simon last night. Why was he checking up on my van?"

"We were all so worried when you disappeared. He had chalked you in as one of the family." Judith relaxed back in John's arms, comfortable and beginning to feel happier. With a shy smile she added, "Charlie asked me point blank how many cousins he was going to have."

"Bloody hell!"

"I thought you wanted children?" she asked seriously.

"I do, but not to please Charlie Ransom's plans!" John kissed her affectionately, hoping that forgiveness was not far away on either side. Light-heartedly, he said, "By the way, what have Simon and Nancy been up to? Something illegal with diamonds?"

"Not illegal, not with Simon. He's very risk averse. A bit shady, but they are like a couple of cats purring over each other."

"So what was it?"

"My honest answer is I don't know. But Charlie has it all worked out."

"I'm sure!"

Judith started to pontificate in Charlie's slow manner. "Nancy went to London, Hatton Garden."

"Fact," said John.

"But did you know the quarrymen went with her and tunnelled into the vault?"

"Rocks and concrete no object for them, of course."

"They stole the diamonds. Nancy put them in a remote-controlled drone and sent it to Holland."

"What drone is this?" asked John with a laugh, stroking Judith's back.

"The one I built at Airbus in France of course. That's why I went there. John, Charlie's fairy tale goes on and on. I think these stories help him deal with Uncle Ron's death." She glanced across through the open windows and into the treetops of Henrietta Park. It was always so comforting. At ground level birds were frantically picking up the crumbs of last night's picnics on the grass. It was a peaceful scene, with a slight breeze fluttering the poppy flowers and maples. "John, what time is it?"

"Seven thirty. Why?"

"Silly time to be up on a Saturday morning. Would you take me back to bed? If you're up to it."

"I will need a bit of time."

"Oh, sorry. How long?"

"About two minutes."

$$\infty$$

In the event, John did not go to Uncle Ron's funeral with Judith. They had been dozing in bed late on Saturday morning when John's house phone rang. Sluggishly, he untangled himself from Judith and reached over for the bedside extension.

"Hello, John Townsend."

"Hi, John. It's Nancy Ransom. Hope I didn't wake you."

"You did actually."

"Pleased you're back. Is Judith with you?

"Yes."

"Good. Good, you're both being sensible. Thought she must be with you, not taking calls."

Nancy rambled on and John's concentration lapsed.

"It's Nancy," he whispered to Judith.

"Tell her to call back, after lunch."

"John, I've got a big favour to ask. Probably affects Judith."

A wave of apprehension surged through John. The last 'big favour' had led him into the clutches of Penny. Nancy was still talking, about the funeral and how badly Charlie had taken Ron's death.

With some impatience John said, "Nancy, please slow down, come to the point. What is it you want?"

"Can Judith hear?"

"I suppose so, she's quite close by."

Judith was in fact trying to nuzzle into him, whispering, "Get rid of her, John. It's too early."

"It's ten thirty," snapped Nancy. "This is important."

John put the phone on speaker and Nancy explained her problem. Although Charlie was now eleven, they didn't think he would cope well with the Christian funeral that Ron had wanted. She hoped John would take Charlie off somewhere for the day; leave him with happy memories of his fun times with Ron, not all sorts of questions from the church service. Bonnie would be happy at Nancy's mother's as usual, provided there would be party food.

Judith was not pleased. "You've already invited John," she protested. "I'd rather hoped he'd be there to support me."

"No point now," replied Nancy. "You're back together anyway. In bed till eleven – that'll stop when you have kids!"

"I won't take Charlie to Peverell House," called John shakily. "The train set thing..." He was determined to avoid another meeting with Penny. He couldn't take any risks of destroying his future happiness with Judith.

"No, not that place. Forecast is fine for Wednesday so go somewhere neutral, outside."

∞

Judith had dropped John and Charlie off at the start of the canal in Bath, with plans for a leisurely ride along the towpath to the Dundas basin and aqueduct at the bottom of Brassknocker Hill, then a snack at The Angel Fish café. John's plan had not allowed for Charlie's furious peddling and it was still relatively early when they arrived at the café, so John had hired a canoe for a gentle paddle up the canal towards Avoncliff. It was pleasantly warm on the canal, and Charlie was excited to spot the flash of a kingfisher shoot through the willows, hanging over the water far too quickly for him to take a photograph. People were friendly and waved from their canal boats as they passed them.

By the time they had eaten an early packed lunch from the café and returned the canoe to the mooring, Judith was waiting for them outside The Angel Fish. She had left the small-sherry-and-sandwich reception after the funeral and gone back to her flat to change. Judith had smiled and waved as Charlie clambered out of the boat and ran towards her. Fondly, she reached for him to give him a hug, but he squirmed away. John noticed that, although Judith looked rather pale and drawn from the funeral, she had already changed out of her black, sombre clothes. The peachy-coloured shirt and tapered jeans set a much happier mood.

"If Charlie's too embarrassed for a cuddle from Aunty, I'm next in line." He put his arms around her and whispered, "You OK?"

"Not too bad; a bit sad."

He kissed her cheek, but they were both soon drawn into Charlie's earnest conversation on the choice of ice creams.

∞

Later, as Judith drove them back from returning Charlie home, she asked John, "Was it all OK?

"I think so."

"Lots of awkward questions?"

"He did ask a few but I think I coped. It's awkward with Ron being a practising Christian and his parents the opposite. Tried to keep... well, neutral I suppose."

"What did he ask?"

"Don't think I can remember. Not sure I should say, anyway."

"Man to man stuff?" she said with a smile.

"Some of it was very man to man."

Judith drove on. "There's no pressure, is there? Almost every day since I've been back Nancy has told me that if I'm going to have kids, I should get on with it."

"Oh, God!"

"And then there's Charlie on about having a baby cousin. Is that what he spoke to you about?"

"More or less – rather more, really," said John, laughing. "Even Simon has started to give me advice on upgrading my pension plan and insurance if I am going to settle down. And well, you know the rest!"

"Makes me think we should fly off to Easter Island. Somewhere remote, anyway."

"OK, you're on. I could make imitation statues for the tourists, but what would you do?"

"Look after your ten children!"

CHAPTER 41

It was three months since Penny's shameful orgy with John. Three months since she had heard the terrible news of Edward's death; brought to her by one of the pedlars whose life he had saved on the Bristol to Bath road.

Stricken with remorse and grief, Penny had immediately planned to leave Peverell and return to her father's house in Suffolk. She could not believe how much there was to arrange, and by the end of autumn it was obvious that she was pregnant. Her midwife believed she was carrying twins. The joy of this did little to dispel the waves of grief that swept over her.

During this melancholy time, Penny received an unannounced visit from Margaret Ransom. Margaret had driven to Peverell in her own covered cart with a maid and two-year-old Oliver in the back; an armed manservant riding alongside on horseback. Penny suggested the maid and manservant take little Oliver to Richard York's pantry and then show the boy some farm animals. Suspecting some serious conversation, Penny invited Margaret Ransom into her dayroom for refreshment.

Margaret was dressed in severe puritan black with the large

white linen collar of purity, but Penny immediately noted the quality of the lace and cloth used for the simple styling. *No sack cloth shift for the wife of a prosperous merchant.* Penny herself was wearing a pale green maternity dress that draped demurely over her bump.

The first formal platitudes over, Margaret leaned forward and said earnestly, "Mistress Peverell, I have wronged you greatly and—"

"Please, Mrs Ransom, stop. My husband has told me all that happened between you. I forgave him and I must forgive you also." She paused, unsure of how much to say. "At least your lying with Edward had a purpose – it was not just lust, as it was with him." She could not help adding bitterly, almost in a whisper to herself, "As it was with me."

"I sinned."

"We all sin! It is how we make recompense, how we—" she tailed off. "I don't have the words for this, I am no preacher."

"I pray for forgiveness but feel sure I will have no peace of mind until I confess to my husband." She looked up forlornly. "But it would destroy him."

Penny moved a little closer and put her hand over Margaret's in a comforting gesture, "That is it. You would ease your mind at the sake of his. Perhaps not to do so will be your penance. My wise midwife bade me to concentrate on the baby I am carrying. I assume that applies doubly once the child is born and needs both parents. Are you sure Edward is your little boy's father?"

"No. Edward and my husband are alike in colouring and stature. To my shame, I lay with both in the same week."

It is the eyes, thought Penny. *The boy's eyes are Edward's, I could see it at once.* She did not think sharing her opinion with Margaret would help either of them in any way, so she kept her own secrets and repeated, "You must seek God's understanding by being a loving wife and mother, not by loading your guilt on your husband. God will look at your actions – not hollow pious words of a confessional."

Margaret looked pained and gave a weak smile.

In her own thoughts, Penny was seared with her own guilt and grief – she had no choice in her actions. At least Margaret still had a husband, and a choice.

The two women were lost in thought for some while. At last the maid brought in some refreshments: small beer, and bread and cheese to Margaret's puritanical taste. As if freed from the trauma of the confession she had made to Penny, Margaret Ransom began in a crisp, business-like way to explain her situation.

The Ransoms had been rendered virtually destitute by the war. Their farm had been burned and pillaged, livestock slaughtered, the tenants dispersed. Only bare roofless walls remained. In Bristol the single salvo of Fairfax's cannon shot had started a fire that destroyed Mr Ransom's warehouses and stock; goods travelling to Taunton had been looted by foragers. Margaret's voice trembled with emotion as she described their perilous financial state.

"We have only a small townhouse in Bath and no income," she concluded.

Penny sat in silence. She knew Edward's own weaving shed and smithy in Bath had been seized by the mayor and alderman of the city, opportunists who had now reverted to being formally in support of the winning Parliamentary side. Peverell was still a prosperous well-run estate but she feared what might be said next.

"In recompense for our support and losses, the assessor appointed by parliament has ruled that my husband should be granted full title to all Edward Peverell's property." She raced on as Penny gasped in horror. "He did plead with Edward to seek a pardon from parliament before their final victory."

"Difficult for him, being dead!" Penny felt distraught, her heart heavy and sad.

There was another long, embarrassed pause before Margaret continued. She explained that given their own situation they had no option but to take up the grant. Margaret and her husband did, however, want Penny to stay on at Peverell; have her own suite of rooms, retain a part income from the estate. On and on her voice droned. Apart from the basic fact that she would lose the house and estate, the words passed by Penny. She was fighting against total panic; she had intended to leave Peverell in charge of her bailiff, Roger Howells, but assumed she and her children would continue to benefit from the estate's income.

Unable to take in the details, at last she cried, "Stop, Margaret, please! I could not stay on here, a dependent in my own home. It is a very generous offer, and I thank you profoundly, but I cannot stay here." *There is no need to heap more guilt on this woman*, Penny thought, and continued, "Since my husband's death, I have already decided to leave Peverell and return to Suffolk where my father still resides. Preserve my memories of a happy home."

"Please, you must at least accept the monies from the estate income?"

"I will, as a pension for Edward. I will have a child, maybe even twins, to support." She tried to force a smile. "Margaret, do nothing rash. I will be gone by Michaelmas and have another home with my loving family. Your husband is a good and generous man, do not sour his joy."

"God bless you for your understanding," Margaret said. "Shall we pray together?"

Penny bit back a scathing comment on the lack of God's grace and instead replied, "You must say the prayer. I will fetch my bible and afterwards we can sing a psalm together after we have prayed." She rose and went to her room. *Ironic*, she thought bitterly. *If little Oliver is Edward's child, as I truly believe he is, he will inherit Peverell. The Peverell line will hold true, only the name would change.* That gave her more comfort than a joint prayer for forgiveness, or their singing.

∞

While Margaret and Penny joined in guilt and the need for forgiveness, Margaret's very, very distant descendant Judith had decided that it was time to plan her own future with John. She had tentatively raised the subject during one of their long walks across the Mendips from Black Down to Crook Peak. The couple were quite unaware that, in a previous century, Edward and Penny had looked down from Crook Peak to see the Parliamentarian supply wagons heading southward towards Taunton.

It had been a long pleasant walk, not too arduous, but by the time they reached Crook Peak even Judith was happy to sit and gaze out over the Bristol Channel while they ate lunch.

371

"There's something about prolonged exercise that rather gets my hormones racing," murmured Judith after a furtive scan that confirmed there were no other walkers within several miles.

"Oh, it's the warm sun that affects me," replied an unsuspecting John as he leaned against the limestone outcrop and bit into an apple.

"Pleased to hear it," said Judith, peeling off her sweaty bra top. "And luckily for you, the grass isn't damp."

"Why?" He looked back from the distant view. "Oh!"

"Because you, dear, slow-witted man, are going to be lying on it while I make love to you."

∞

Sometime later, they slipped back into discarded, crumpled clothes. John drew Judith to him again and impulsively kissed her. Being together so intimately and unexpectedly, he had experienced an intense sunburst of pleasure; he truly loved her. Holding her hand, they continued walking back down the hill and into the trees of King's Wood. John had suggested they should start seriously thinking of the future if they were to have children.

Judith said nothing until they crossed the road into more ancient trees and started the slow climb up the track of Callow Drove towards Shipham. She had initially settled back into her old job in Bath, but after France she missed the design side of the work. With plenty of cash rolling in from their Peverell House Innovation Centre, Judith had taken a chance at starting her own design consultancy. So far, a modest start, but with plenty of projects commissioned. Was it a good time to have a baby? Would there ever be a good time?

She looked up at John as they walked. It had to be soon, strike while the iron's hot, and all that. Somewhat tongue in cheek, she suggested a serious meeting the following Thursday.

"I do mean serious, John," she added. "You know, clothes on; no booze or trying to carry me off to bed."

He chuckled at that. "Do I need to take notes?"

"I've a few ideas. I'll send you my presentation."

$$\infty$$

Judith arrived at John's flat promptly at six thirty p.m., a bottle of expensive red wine in one hand, briefcase in the other. To John's dismay, she wore a formal-looking black skirt and jacket with an office-style white blouse. Her greeting to him was not great.

"John, I did say dressed."

"I am!"

"I don't think so. Gym shorts and a gaping vest?" She poked at the holey garment, trying to look stern. "How do you expect me to concentrate with your bits bulging out and pecks showing through?"

"Sorry, ma'am, I had been meaning to change." He started for the bedroom. "It's been at least two days since I saw you. How about we clear the air, so to speak?"

"Sod off! Get dressed and I'll open the wine. It needs time to breathe and settle down, and so do you!"

Her plan was simple: baby Peverell in two years and a joint home for co-parenting.

"Baby Peverell," laughed John.

"Working title until we know the gender I've come off the pill now. Give it a year to clear my system. Conception next August, birth in May ready for the summer." Judith flashed him a happy smile. "How does that sound, *Dad*?"

John felt an upsurge of emotion at the thought of having a child at last; a child with Judith. Too overcome to speak, he stood up to glance across his balcony at Henrietta Park. The bright flowers glinting in the late afternoon sun brought a certain peace to his mind.

He shook his head knowingly. "I don't think it always works quite as easily as that."

"It will. No one in either of our families has had issues in that department, and we are fit and healthy." She giggled. "We're both in training, so I'm sure we'll have no problem."

"How do you know about my family?"

"I phoned Ann."

"You phoned my sister without telling me?"

"Sure, it's called a due diligence check. You don't think I'm going to risk hitching my perfectly toned body to some creaky old cart, do you?"

He sat down again, stunned, not sure if he was angry or amused at her effrontery.

"Come on, John, let's have a drink to celebrate!"

John walked over to the kitchen and took down two large wine goblets, sniffing the red wine in appreciation. He put the glasses carefully between them.

Smiling up at him, Judith took a large sip. "Mm, delicious! Now, next topic," she said. "How do we live?"

"We did say different homes, didn't we?"

"With me doing all the feeding, nappy changes, and the like? Not a chance! I know I said separate homes but I've been doing a lot of reflecting since then and I've had a better idea." She pulled out some sheets of paper from the briefcase. "How about this?" Judith showed him some clinically precise drawings. "Big neutral space in the middle here, we each have a separate bedroom, toilet, study either end. Kitchen could be a common area."

John groaned inwardly at the thought of sharing a kitchen with Judith. He supposed she could have her own microwave oven. "What's this?"

"Along the side we have a nursery and the children's bedrooms."

"Two?"

"Just two."

He nodded in agreement, drinking his wine. "How do you find a house like this, all on one level?"

"Wake up, John!"

Realisation dawned. "This is the second floor of Peverell House!"

"My, you're sharp."

"This bedroom?" he pointed.

"Is my old room. Penny Peverell's old room."

"Are you serious? You said you'd never live there again, and after—"

"I know. I've changed my mind. I'm not being driven out of my house by a ghost. If she comes back again, she can just be jealous. We can compare notes!"

John swallowed hard. "It will cost a fortune."

"We've got a fortune. Stella Rigby, our art historian, estimates the Billy Dobson portrait of Edward and Penny is worth a million, at least!"

"There's a time factor as well. Can we do all this work before the baby arrives?"

"Two years? Easy!"

"It's a lot to take in." John gulped some more wine, his hand unsteady.

"There is one thing."

"Only one?" he muttered.

"I'm going to need a long-term contract."

"A contract?"

"You know," Judith said, enjoying herself, "marriage, civil partnership, or even a legal agreement to contribute."

"You couldn't enforce that!" he said, grinning in delight.

"Don't you believe it. My family can enforce any contract. Ask Mark!"

"Point taken. As long as it's not Charlie's idea of a contract." John got up from his chair, overcome with happiness, walked around the table, and dropped onto one knee. "Judith Ransom will you—"

"Don't you bloody dare!" She darted out of her seat and across the room. "You're not going soppy on me."

"OK," he stood up. "We need a legal agreement before children – guarantee of father's access, and all that. So why not do the full thing and get married? Is that business-like enough?"

"Oh, John," she said softly, her voice trembling. "I'm honoured, I really am. Just a bit nervous." And then, "Good idea. Six months' time?"

With that she brought her arms around him and they kissed passionately, finally content.

CHAPTER 42

John rarely got to do anything approaching original sculpture, and so was delighted to have a commission for a memorial in the form of a contemporary angel. After several attempts at producing his own design he had, with the sculptor's consent, taken inspiration from a bronze statue he admired. John's copy in stone would be outside and so could not have any water traps or very thin, fragile sections. Even with these changes, he believed he had been able to imitate the dynamic spirit of the bronze original.

He was quite proud of the finished version and hoped to attract more commissions. In this happy frame of mind, he had set aside a day to do the final smoothing and finishing. Now he was spraying on a coat of silicone sealant that would soak into the limestone for protection. It was the same stuff that was used on restored buildings. Engrossed in his work, John didn't respond to a flurry of calls on his mobile and workshop phone in the late afternoon. He stopped, spray gun in hand, and stood back admiring his work.

"Don't you ever pick up your bloody phone?" shouted Judith, rushing across the workshop toward him.

He hadn't heard her drive through the gates or come in, and his curt reply of, "I'm supposed to be working," was lost in the protective spray mask.

"What did you say, John?"

He turned in frustration, but that quickly drained away when he saw the anguished look on her face. "What on earth's happened?" He was gripped by sudden fear, remembering the last time she had burst in on him.

"It's Charlie," she gulped as if close to tears.

"An accident?" He ripped off his mucky rubber gloves so he could hold her.

"No, John. He's been kidnapped by bloody Mark Davis, coming out of school."

"What! Come and sit down. Tell me—"

"I don't need to sit down, I need you to come with me. Now!"

"OK, OK. At least tell me what—"

"Nancy was walking with Charlie – from school back to the car." Judith tried to order her thoughts. "Mark must have been hiding and watching. As Nancy unlocked, he leapt out from somewhere, grabbed the car key and punched her in the face. Had some sort of Velcro straps for Charlie, bundled him into the car and drove off."

"Didn't Mark say anything?"

"'Don't call the law or I'll blow his head off'. Oh, John, he pointed a sawn-off shotgun at Nancy, then hit her with it and drove away. Nancy's shocked and concussed. A teacher wanted her to go to A&E but she refused until Simon arrived."

John couldn't believe it; it was all too sudden. Mark was history, and he'd never been violent.

"What have the police done? Can they trace the—"

"No, no!" Judith was becoming frantic, and tears were leaking down her cheek as she said, "They haven't told the police, or anyone. Simon's had a message: half a million in cash, or else."

"Mark must be mad! He'll never pull this off."

"Mark's been sleeping rough, we think. Simon stitched him up big time – job, money, everything. I grassed him up to the new girlfriend." Her voice tailed off. "Mark must be deranged. Now he's got Charlie. He could do anything."

"What do you want me to do?" asked John helplessly, unable to think clearly. Instinctively, he tried to put his arm around Judith, hoping to calm her, but she shrugged him off.

"Come to Peverell House with me. Mark's destitute, he couldn't buy a shooter on the street, and if he did it would be an East European army gun or something – not an old-fashioned sawn-off."

"So, where would he—"

"Peverell House. Dad's shotguns are still there in one of the secure cabinets."

John remembered the three robust steel cabinets with their double padlocks and security bars over the doors. As well as the antique weapons they had found from Penny's era, there were guns belonging to her father, Simon and Judith.

"I ought to have got rid of them when Dad died," Judith was saying quietly. "Neither Simon nor Nancy are keen on shooting."

"Would Mark have known all this?"

"Dad did try to get him interested at one time."

"Bloody dangerous leaving things like that in an unoccupied house," snapped John.

"Well, the storages are in that locked cellar. It's all been approved by the county firearms officer."

"Where are the bullets?"

"Cartridges – in a separate locked container. I think the only way Mark could get a gun is from Peverell – break into the cellar, force open the cabinets."

"Does this help us find Charlie?" asked John.

Judith wanted action; to do something. John was more wary.

"Mark must be at Peverell. Where else could he hold Charlie? He's got to get Nancy's car off the street and he has no home of his own."

"I'll ring the police," said John.

"No, John. I've given Simon my word."

"I haven't." He started moving towards the office.

Judith barred his way. "No, John. Please. Let's at least drive out to Peverell and see if Nancy's car is there."

"He's a maniac with a gun, Judith, we can't tackle that." He went to restrain her, but she shook him off impatiently.

"I'm driving out to the house – *my* house. Either come with me or stay out of this altogether."

"OK, but I'm not happy—"

"None of us are bloody happy, John, especially Charlie."

John started to rip off his painting overalls.

"Could be useful to have some of your safety visors," said Judith.

"Against gunfire?"

"Anything over twenty yards and the shot would probably be stopped."

John also picked up a long-handled hammer and crowbar

before following Judith quickly out to her Range Rover. Then almost as an afterthought, he stopped. "No, Judith, let's take my van – he'll recognise yours. Hard hat, overalls and high-vis jackets could make us look like contractors." John rapidly grabbed the gear for them both.

"Apprentice of the year, I don't think," she said, clambering up into the van's passenger seat enveloped in a pair of John's over large overalls. "I really appreciate this," Judith continued as he steered out of the yard.

"I just hope we don't regret it," John replied grimly.

Friday was a half day for the tenants of Peverell House, although some of the converted outbuildings were still occupied. First Judith and John toured the area in the van and spotted Nancy's car partially concealed under some dark foliaged trees. The registration plate number had been taped over and crude numbers drawn on with a broad felt-tip marker.

"As if that would fool anyone," said Judith bitterly.

"He's really lost it," warned John. "I suppose he thought the car would be hidden from the air."

"Right, let's check the cellar first," said Judith, a shake in her voice. She pulled the tinted safety visor down to check that it covered her eyes and neck.

"Stop it, Judith," John said seriously, "we're not Batman and Wonder Woman. The police are professionals; they've got the guns and body armour."

"No! That's just it: quick firing Heckler & Koch in a confined space. Charlie could easily be hit, like any innocent bystander. Come on, let's check the cellar."

John raced after Judith as she found a side door that had been levered open. Inside it was a short distance to the cellar door – wide open with the mortice lock gouged out. Down the cellar steps it was easy to see that one gun cabinet had been beaten open. Her father's pair of 12-bore guns and Judith's small weapon were still there, locked up by their trigger guards.

"Simon's 'up and over' is gone," whispered Judith in a scared voice, pointing to a hook at the back of the cabinet. "He never bothers to lock up properly."

John noticed a sledgehammer flung against the wall. "Not very subtle. Mark's smashed the padlocks to pieces. The din would have been terrific, someone would have heard."

"Must have been done last night." Judith was already studying the battered, smaller storage cupboard. "He couldn't get into the ammunition locker. He's got a gun but nothing to shoot out of it."

"Wait. Look here on this bench." John pointed. "Mark's sawn off half the gun's barrel."

"It'll be pistol size. There's not enough barrel left to work properly – it would spray shot all over the place. Pathetic gun and no ammo. I'm going to take the bastard apart!"

"Stop a moment! For God's sake, think!" John grabbed her shoulder. "If Mark's got no cartridges, why go to all this trouble with sawing?"

"For show?"

"Can you get your gun out, Judith?"

"No. Simon keeps the keys at his place," she replied. "And we'd need to open that other locker to get my cartridges." Judith jerked free of John, racing up the cellar steps and into Penny

Peverell's old living area. "Mark Davis, I'm going to kill you, you bastard!"

Unbelievably, at ground level, John could hear the sound of model train wheels running on Charlie's layout. Judith was still running ahead of John, up Alf's replacement staircase to the dayroom. In the side room Mark was sitting controlling the trains; Charlie cowed in a corner. The sordid detail stuck with John: packets of food, bread, bottles of water, even a sewage pail.

Lazily Mark picked up the sawn-off gun and ducked out from under the model table, advancing towards them. "My lucky day. I'm going to blow your face off. Leave you to bleed."

His voice was high-pitched and unnaturally eerie, sending a cold wave of adrenaline fuelled shock surging through John. Mark's wild eyes stared past them into the distance, unfocused.

"Shut it, Mark," Judith shouted. "We know it's not loaded."

Mark smirked. "It is, bitch." He levelled the gun at her head and pulled at the trigger. Nothing happened. "Safety catch." Still smiling, he used his left hand to click it.

John threw his hammer with all his force. Mark dodged and the gun fired.

A deafening bang in the closed room; smoke. Judith flew back, knocked over by the sheer impact of the shot. Blood appeared at her hands; several drops on her chest below the shattered visor. John swore. Behind Mark, Charlie screamed in terror.

Mark grabbed Charlie, dragging him along the floor. John was bending over Judith.

"It's not bad," she murmured. "Too bloody far away."

"It won't be next time." Mark threw Charlie down, flipped

open the smoking wreck of a gun and laughed as the spent cartridge ejected. He slipped in another and aimed threateningly at John and Judith. "I've got a pocket of these damn little beauties. Simon left them loose in the bottom. Any more stupid ideas and I'll blow Charlie's leg off." He was working himself up into a frenzy. "Once I get the money I'll finish all three of you. Fucking Ransoms should be extinct!"

Charlie was crying uncontrollably. John felt cold with horror and despair. The situation was so hopeless – they were all trapped with no way out.

Hell, the room was changing, slanting, deconstructing as before. Time melted, going back, shifting to Penny's time. Then the minutes accelerated, like leaves of a book turning, unfolding. John was completely disorientated. At first, he thought he was back in Penny's time, then realised it was Penny appearing through time and space to be with them. She was standing imperiously to the right of Mark, her wheel lock pistol pointed level and steady at Mark's right temple. John distinctly heard the whirl of the lock; a small puff as flame burst from the side in an instantaneous thunderclap of the full charge going off.

A gust of smoke and flame enveloped Mark. Blood, brains and bone were pumped out by the ball passing through his head. Almost gracefully he folded up, slumped slightly to the left as he fell. He twitched and then lay quite still. A pool of blood and other bits were spreading across the floor. Charlie was already up and darting towards Penny.

"Aunty Penny, I knew you would save me," he shouted.

Still holding the pistol, Penny picked Charlie up easily despite her obvious baby bump. She kissed him, set him down and squeezed his shoulder.

"Let's see to Aunty Judith," said Penny in a totally composed voice.

How the hell did Charlie meet Penny? thought John. *What the heck just happened?*

"I'm OK," said Judith. She could hardly speak; her emotions were in turmoil, trying to comprehend. Incredulous, she asked, "Where did you come from?"

"Peverell House, year of our Lord 1645. Your ancestors are about to put me out!"

"We did pay you, though," muttered Judith, thinking it was a stupid fact to remember at such a time.

"Mistress Ransom, I have done great wrong with your intended. I hope this—" Penny was saying in a level voice.

John wasn't listening. He was turning Mark's inert body over to see the whole left side of his head and face gone. He retched, somehow holding back the vomit, swallowing hard. Dazed, he remembered Peter Bisson, the gunsmith, saying how messy it would be if she used the pistol at close range.

"Mark's dead," John croaked unnecessarily.

"It's usually the case when I shoot someone," Penny remarked serenely, hardly looking at the gory scene.

God, thought John as he stood in a daze. Judith was asking Penny when the baby was due. A man had literally had his brains blown out and they were discussing babies!

"Due to my sinful behaviour, I do not know if my husband Edward or your John is the father."

"John and I are not married," Judith started to say. "I had abandoned him, so—"

"I was married," said Penny, "married to Edward Peverell, and—" Unbelievably, she began to cry, her first sign of emotion; the first sign of remorse John had ever seen. "He will never know he had a child."

Embarrassed, Charlie came over and stood closer to John and said in a level, controlled voice, "Not wrong to kill Mark – he deserved to be killed. I knew Aunty Penny would save me – she's shown me her guns before. I played with that gun, and she did the train when Uncle Ron was asleep."

How is he so composed after what happened? John thought, amazed. As he himself had said to Nancy, Charlie did not 'do' panic, but this calmness was absurd. Was he in shock? Was no one else worried about killing Mark?

"Uncle John," Charlie asked in the same matter-of-fact tone, "will Aunty Penny get into trouble for shooting Mark? They can't arrest a ghost, can they?"

"I'm not a ghost." Penny's tear-stained face smiled as she gripped Charlie's shoulder firmly in a reassuringly strong hand. "I'm alive. I'm going to have a baby, probably two."

"Two cousins?" cried Charlie with excitement, ignoring all the horror. "I will have two baby cousins!"

"Well, not exactly," said Penny.

They stood in silence for a moment as the smell of fresh blood began to fill the sparse empty room, mingling with the fading gun smoke.

"I will be going away," explained Penny sadly. "I will not see any of you again."

"That's not fair," cried Charlie. "You mustn't all go away."

"Not us," replied Judith. "I'm going to marry John and live

here with him."

"Be happy," pleaded Penny softly. "As Edward and I were."

"Do you live in a parallel universe?" cut in Charlie. "A different world?"

"Something like that." She smiled at him again. "Ask John, perhaps he understands. I was lucky to come and visit you." Penny looked directly at John. "So, so lucky. Now I do have to—"

"Wait," said John, at last finding his voice. "One last favour: can you leave the pistol? We are going to have a hell of a problem explaining this to, to—"

"The magistrate," Judith helped out.

"It's one Edward gave me."

"I know it's a big thing to ask, but you do have the other one. You will be gone, back to your own time. We can say Mark shot himself with it – out of remorse at shooting Judith and threatening Charlie."

"It will be our last secret, Aunty Penny," grinned Charlie, cunningly. "We won't tell anybody it was you."

Penny leaned down to whisper in Charlie's ear, "It will be our special secret, and one day, I will come back and teach you how to load and shoot my pistol!"

Even as Penny kissed Charlie goodbye, she faded away.

Her pistol clattered to the floor.

ABOUT THE AUTHOR

Brian Rayfield was born on a farm in Kent, and escaped to become an engineer as soon as he was old enough to leave home. After working as an electrical apprentice, he ultimately progressed to become a professional marine engineer. In addition to having a very technical job, Brian has an encompassing interest in history and the arts, which ultimately inspired him to write *Exchange of Love*.